# THE SAPPHIRE WIDOW

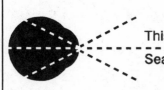

This Large Print Book carries the
Seal of Approval of N.A.V.H.

# THE SAPPHIRE WIDOW

## DINAH JEFFERIES

**THORNDIKE PRESS**
A part of Gale, a Cengage Company

**GALE**
A Cengage Company

Farmington Hills, Mich • San Francisco • New York • Waterville, Maine
Meriden, Conn • Mason, Ohio • Chicago

LIBRARY OF CONGRESS CIP DATA ON FILE.
CATALOGUING IN PUBLICATION FOR THIS BOOK
IS AVAILABLE FROM THE LIBRARY OF CONGRESS

ISBN-13: 978-1-4328-5860-5 (hardcover)

Published in 2018 by arrangement with Crown, an imprint of Penguin Publishing Group, a division of Penguin Random House LLC

Printed in the United States of America
1 2 3 4 5 6 7 22 21 20 19 18

# THE SAPPHIRE WIDOW

# 1

*Ceylon 1935*
*A Cinnamon Plantation*

His slight build makes it difficult to tell his age, but sitting under the hanging branches of the banyan tree he looks lonely and, as sunlight filters through the glossy leaves, it dances on his thin limbs. This boy, more wood sprite than child of flesh and blood, is the kind of child a mother longs to wrap her arms around. He selects a pebble and, with a furrowed brow, concentrates, then throws it to see how far it will go. Satisfied it's flown farther than the one before, he clambers to his feet and walks around the little rhododendron-enclosed clearing, scuffing his sandals in the twigs and leaves that crackle and splinter beneath him.

He listens to owls ruffling their feathers and shifting in the tree, watches a striped squirrel race up a tree trunk, and then he sniffs the air — citronella, burned earth, the aroma of cinnamon, and a tang of salty ocean he can almost taste. He picks a pale apricot blossom and buries his nose in its soft, fruity fragrance. This one is for his mother.

He watches a scarlet basker flitting from one leaf to another and wishes he had brought his book of insects with him. He's never seen this one before except in the book, along with other dragonflies, damselflies and butterflies. He knows there are thousands of them in Ceylon — this place his mother calls a pearl.

As a fresh breeze blows he feels it on his arms and his skin tingles. It's the best place in the world, this glittering sun-sparkled forest, and he eagerly awaits a walk with his mother, in the evening when it's cooler. She finds the heat of the day tiresome, but he knows all the shady places and there's always somewhere cool to hide. But then a change, comes over him and a trace of sadness darkens his face. Although he's content playing alone, something in him longs for more, and he shivers from an uncomfortable feeling of guilt.

The moment passes.

When he walks with his mother, her scent wraps around him, and he enjoys calling out the names of birds for her to laugh in pretend amazement that he knows so many of them. His mother doesn't laugh enough, though it's hardly surprising, he thinks, given their circumstances. That's the phrase he hears all the time: "given our circumstances," it's probably not a good idea. Or, "given our circumstances," perhaps we'd better not.

He has climbed almost to the top of the hill now, his favorite wide-open place. Here he can see for miles and if he half closes his eyes he can almost feel the ocean. He imagines the cool waves breaking over his burning skin; sees himself running on the beach as fast as he can with the wind blowing in his too-long hair; pictures the fishermen in the early evening before the sky turns pink and the sea turns lilac.

He's startled by a rustle coming from the trees and stands still to listen. It's probably a toque monkey, he thinks, or one of the langurs with the very long tails. You mustn't try to befriend or feed toque macaques, his mother says. If you feed them they think you are subordinate. It means they think you are lower than they are. Sub-or-din-ate. Subordinate would be bad. Nobody wants to be less important, do they?

# 2

*Ceylon, December 23, 1935*
*The 300-year-old walled Town of Galle*

It had been sweltering in the mid-eighties during the day and even now, at seven in the evening, it was still at least seventy-five degrees. Louisa Reeve's bias-cut gown in silver satin-silk had been made up in Colombo and copied from a dress she'd spotted in American *Vogue.* By the time the magazine reached her it was months out of date, but still, you did what you could. Galle tailors, though solidly reliable, were not modern, and everything they ran up turned a bit too Sinhalese in the execution, but in Colombo some of the tailors could copy anything. As she stood at five foot nine, the elegant flowing femininity of the style suited her and certainly made a change from the linen shirt and comfortable trousers she usually wore to ride her bicycle.

Elliot came up behind her and wrapped

her in a hug.

"Happy?" he whispered in her ear, before running his fingers through her hair.

"Hey, I've just spent ages on that." She had softened her wayward blond curls into finger waves, with an imitation-sapphire clip on one side.

"Are you feeling okay?" Elliot said, his eyes serious and concerned.

She reached for his hand. "I'm feeling fine, though I was thinking of Julia earlier."

"Really?"

She nodded. "I'm fine."

"Good. It's going to be a wonderful Christmas and you look ravishing." He turned to leave. "If you really are all right . . . I'll just check on the wine."

"Are you still planning to sail on Boxing Day?"

"I think so. Just for a few hours. You don't mind? Jeremy has a spanking-new dinghy and we're trying out a new-fangled trapez-ing harness too. He's had it made up by a local on plans sent over from England. Perfect for racing, I'm told."

He brushed past her on his way to the door and, as she caught the trace of cedar cologne from his skin, she smiled and watched his retreating back in the mirror. Even after twelve years of marriage she thought him still a truly handsome man, with short curly brown hair, lively green eyes and a charm that drew the world to him. He never had to try too hard. Friendship came quickly and easily to him and there was always a buzz when he was around. She had friends too, though it took her longer to get to know people and she didn't have Elliot's direct way. She loved working people out though, trying to understand what made them tick and, for her, once she made a friend, it was usually a friend for life.

She leaned out of the top-floor window and gazed at the blue sky and the shimmering turquoise seas surrounding Galle. The present tilted and the moment she had named her daughter, Julia, rushed back. Standing in this very spot, she'd held her for one precious hour until tears had blinded her vision. When had she died? Before or during the birth itself? To be born without life. What did it mean? These were the questions still haunting her. Just one more day and Julia would have been christened at the Anglican All Saints' Church — the very place she and Elliot had been married and she herself had been christened.

Even now, over two years later, the past claimed her and, guilt-ridden, she felt there should have been something she could have done, or not done. She closed her eyes and pictured a heady sun-drenched day. Julia playing on the beach with the dogs, Tommy, Bouncer and Zip, the runt of the litter, all of them coated in glittering sand, damp from the sea and smelling of salt, and her little girl shrieking with laughter. She pictured her collecting shells and running, running and tripping over her feet in haste, desperate to show off her precious bounty, only to forget about it moments later. And then, oh so real, she imagined gathering her daughter in her arms after her bath, smelling the trace of baby shampoo in her hair, all apple and mint.

She sucked in her breath and, allowing the dream to retreat, returned to the present.

All that remained for her to do was to ensure the staff were in place and none of the flowers were wilting. She walked out onto the veranda, took a match and a taper, and then lit the external oil lamps and the citronella candles to repel mosquitoes. On the tips of her toes, she checked a lampshade where a red-vented bulbul had made its nest, and made sure the lightbulb had been removed. She heard the *tchreek tchreek* of the parent bird as it kept watch. "It's all right, little one," she whispered. "The bulb won't be replaced until your chicks have flown away." The garden surrounded the veranda, where the pink hibiscus blooms scattered in the breeze, and she loved to sit and listen to the dawn chorus while everything glowed in the early sunshine.

She went back indoors to the living room, glancing up at the eighteenth-century wooden beams of the grand colonial house, where concealed lamps spread a golden sheen. She'd painted the room herself in orange and the door frames in turquoise: a look that startled some, addicted as they were to the regulation cream colonial walls, but she adored the brightness. Two dark-wood ceiling fans rotated the air and in one corner an indoor palm patterned the high wall with shadows. "I Only Have Eyes for You" was playing on the gramophone.

Their home at ground level housed the kitchen, the part-time housekeeper's room, the main living areas and the offices. The guest bedrooms and two bathrooms were located on the next floor, along with Louisa's sewing room. Then on the top floor there was her and Elliot's bedroom, their bathroom, plus an airy private living room, a sun-filled peaceful space opening out on to a roof terrace. At the back of the garden

14

another building housed the servants' quarters, though some lived locally in Galle itself.

A little later and, as the last of the guests arrived, Louisa and Elliot were standing together in the main entrance hall to greet them. She glanced up at the skylight, through which acres of sun streamed during the day. The plantation shutters at the bank of windows fronting the house had been left open, though the windows themselves remained closed against insects. She hoped that from outside the glittering lights cast a welcoming warmth. She wanted all their guests to be happy on this glorious shining evening, and a bubble of excitement ran through her.

One of Elliot's friends arrived. Jeremy Pike was the son of a well-to-do rubber planter and had known Elliot back in Colombo. A well-dressed, neatly mustached man, he often spent a few days at the family's summer residence in Galle and he and Elliot were frequent sailing partners, though Louisa had never gotten to know him well. He was what they called a man's man. After him an elderly couple, friends of her father, started commiserating about the oppressive heat when, behind them, she spotted a tea-planter couple getting out of a Daimler.

"Ah," Elliot said. "That's good. The Hoopers have come."

Louisa watched the slight figure of a dark-haired woman in a violet dress walk slowly to the door with her tall husband. The woman was very pretty with hair that seemed to fall naturally in ringlets, and eyes a perfect match to the color of her dress. She carried a baby wrapped in a lacy shawl and when she stumbled slightly the elderly ayah following behind reached out a steadying hand. The man placed his arm around the young woman's shoulders and Louisa thought how protective he seemed.

Elliot stepped forward to welcome them, a broad smile on his face. "Laurence and Gwendolyn, how lovely that you made it."

Louisa stretched out her hand to the man and then his wife passed the baby to the ayah before coming to Louisa for a kiss on the cheek. "I'm so happy to see you again," she said.

Louisa smiled. "It's been months since we met up in Colombo."

"Tea at the Galle Face Hotel, wasn't it? I loved looking out across the ocean and imagining Galle itself in the distance. And now here we are."

"You hadn't had the baby yet, then."

Gwen shook her head. "Gosh, no. It really

16

has been too long."

"Well, I'm more than happy you're here now. What do you think of Galle?"

"I love it. I was here once before, when I first moved to Ceylon, but it's been ages. The town is so sleepy, I can't wait to explore tomorrow morning."

"Would you let me show you around?"

Gwen nodded. "If you have time?"

"Lots of time, and I know the place like the back of my hand."

"You've lived here all your life, haven't you?"

"Except when I was at boarding school in England. I spend an awful lot of time cycling around. As you've probably noticed, we're on a promontory and totally enclosed by the sea wall on three sides, so it's very safe."

"I'd love to see it properly."

"Then that's settled. You must be staying at the New Oriental Hotel here in town?"

Gwen nodded.

"Then I shall call for you. Shall we say eight? Early is best before it gets too hot and sticky."

"Terrific. This is a little break for us. My mother is over from England and she's looking after our son, Hugh, but we'll be back in time for Christmas Eve dinner." She

17

smiled up at her husband, who began to speak, but Elliot interrupted.

"What say you, Laurence . . . to a shot of a rather good malt?"

As Laurence nodded his agreement Elliot clapped him on the back. "We'll leave you two women to it," he said with a wink at Laurence and then quickly touched Louisa on the hand. "That okay with you?"

She gave him a look that the others couldn't see, and hoped he wouldn't drink too much. But no, surely the gambling, and heavy drinking, were firmly in the past. Then she turned and smiled at Gwen. "What's your baby called?" she asked.

"Alice. She's six weeks old today, so too young to leave behind." She glanced around.

"Let me point you in the direction of a room where you can leave Alice to sleep."

While Gwen and the ayah settled the baby, Louisa wandered through the house. As she mingled with her guests, she sniffed air laced with a trace of lemon polish and the fresh scent of blossom from the pongam tree in the garden. She'd displayed swathes of its branches dotted around the house in large floor-standing ceramic vases. Early to bloom this year, the small flowers were pale purple and a favorite of hers.

She had invited some of her father's

friends, as well as her own, and had included many of the merchants from around the citadel that was Galle. A few were now on the veranda, wearing their best clothes, and gathering close to the citronella candles. The sound of their laughter trickled through to the hall. The nice thing about Galle was the way at least some of the British mingled with the Muslims, the Buddhists, the Burghers and the Hindus. It was a genuinely multinational, multi-faith place. There were lots of other lovely things too, like the enchanting maze of straight and narrow backstreets where she knew everybody by name, the smell of fresh ginger or mint tea on a sparkling morning, and the many goats, cows and lizards she encountered on her walks. She'd enjoy showing it all to Gwen.

Tea country was a fair distance from Galle, so the fact the Hoopers had come all that way to the party was a terrific surprise. As Louisa already knew everyone in Galle, seeing Gwen offered a fresh promise of enjoyment. It would be fun. She'd met her a few times before and had taken to her from the start.

As she turned away she saw her father, a widower, tall, thin, bespectacled, bushy-browed, and a little fierce if you didn't know him. And that proved her point, because a more open-hearted man than Jonathan Hardcastle it would be hard to find. Always on the lookout for unfairness, he treated his staff impeccably, though his pioneering spirit hadn't always gone down well with the powers that be.

He came across to her, arms wide open. "Darling. You've made it beautiful as usual."

They hugged and she smiled. "You always say that."

"And I always say your mother would have been proud."

They exchanged looks. His wife had died when Louisa was only seven and though she could barely remember her mother, she knew her father would never forget her. She had the same gold-flecked hazel eyes as her mother, and he'd often remarked how alike they looked. He had never remarried, which meant Louisa had grown up with an ayah who allowed her more freedom than a mother might have done. So, from an early age, she'd ridden her bike and done the rounds, as she was fond of saying, enjoying the simple continuity of her life. It didn't take long to cycle the whole of the ancient walled town and she'd grown accustomed to doing it every day, and people seemed to like that she stopped to chat.

"Shall we go through together?" her father was saying.

"You go ahead. I just want to give Ashan the nod. I think it's time the food came out."

"I can do that."

"Don't worry." She squeezed his hand. "Have a lovely evening, Pa."

As she crossed the small back hall leading to the kitchen she passed the open door of Elliot's study and, pausing, saw he was in there with a man she vaguely recognized. A dark-haired Burgher, that much was clear, with untrimmed eyebrows and an impassive face, one of the descendants of the Portuguese who had first discovered Galle. She was surprised Elliot hadn't mentioned inviting him to the party, and took a step forward to introduce herself. Elliot spotted her and frowned. Something about his irritable look troubled her, but before she'd had a chance to speak, a sudden movement caught her eye and she glimpsed a purple-faced monkey slipping into the kitchen. She'd have to have a firm word with the staff right away; certain windows and doors should not be left unlocked. The monkeys were clever and if you gave them an inch they'd take a mile. She hardly dared recall that her father had once said something similar about Elliot.

# 3

Early on Christmas Eve morning Louisa left her home in Church Street, carried on down the road, crossed Middle Street, and went to call for Gwen as arranged. They were to meet in the hall of the Regency-style New Oriental Hotel, imposing with its three-foot-thick sandstone walls. Louisa glanced up at the high wooden ceiling. The hotel had been built in 1684 by the Dutch as a barracks to house army officers, and now it was where visiting planters and traders stayed, as well as a steady trickle of tourists in more recent times. The impressive entrance hall, stuffed with ebony easy chairs and sofas, with just a few woven-rattan recliners dotted among them, was already busy.

Beeswax and cigar smoke impregnated the walls, along with just the faintest tang of yesterday's whisky, and a huge pine tree took up star position, hung with baubles and small candles in holders. Though pretty, it was such a fire hazard that the candles, once lit, needed watching constantly by one of the houseboys. Last year the boy had been caught napping and narrowly escaped being responsible for the entire place catching alight.

She loved the hotel with its dramatic towering front, facing the harbor, and had sketched it and most of Galle's buildings at one time or another. She always enjoyed drawing and had longed to become an architect, but there had been nowhere in Ceylon for a woman to study. She might have gone to Europe or America, but hadn't wanted to leave her father alone and so, enchanted by architecture and buildings, interiors had become her passion. She'd often be found sitting at the beautiful mahogany cabinet of her Singer sewing machine, running up curtains or making cushion covers until late at night. Or if not that, she'd be creating intricate line drawings and watercolor washes of Galle's buildings to hang on her walls. Ruining her eyes, as Elliot's mother, Irene, would say.

Irene's brand of suburban snobbery and pretentiousness was typical of certain Europeans, and Louisa hardly dared admit how relieved she felt that *she* wasn't coming for

Christmas this year. The Reeves, Irene and Harold, a civil servant, had been invited to Christmas with friends in Colombo and so it would just be Elliot, Louisa and her father.

A moment later, Gwen appeared wearing a cotton dress with a fluted shin-length skirt and a large sunhat. "Morning," she said and kissed Louisa's cheek before twisting the brim of her hat. "Not very Christmassy, is it? I need to wear it all the time. With skin like mine I burn quickly."

Louisa glanced at her own tanned skin. "Luckily I don't have that problem. I'm on my bike so much I always look as if I've been left out in the sun."

"At least it's fashionable these days."

"So," Louisa said as they walked through the cobbled streets, passing low-built bungalows with gorgeous ornamental lintels over the main doorways and terracotta roofs held up by rows of columns providing shade to the verandas. "Tell me what you get up to on that tea plantation of yours."

"Well, we're quite remote so don't tend to socialize a lot. Just the odd trip to Colombo or Nuwara Eliya for a ball. Although we did once go to New York for a month."

"That must have been fun."

"It was quite a time. We were in the

process of turning Hooper's Tea into a proper brand."

"Has it been a success?"

"Pretty much, though I'm not really involved in the business. Mainly I make cheese."

"Really?"

"If you ever come to visit you must try some. It's delicious, if I say so myself." She smiled and her sparkling eyes reflected the sun.

All the houses they passed had shutters, either open or closed; twisted frangipani trees grew in the passageways and monkeys grunted as they swung in their gleaming branches.

Louisa thought back to when she and Elliot had first moved into their home, soon after Elliot had been placed in charge of her father's gem cutting and polishing house. Her father had taken some persuading to employ Elliot at all, but in the end, despite Jonathan's lingering reservations, Elliot had proved himself. It was an important post with full responsibility for all the records of all the gems that went through their hands.

The two women chatted as they sauntered past Buddhist monks, as well as Muslim men in white with woven caps on their heads, and Louisa nodded at them all.

"I haven't got long," Gwen said. "We need to leave earlier than I expected."

"We'll just slip down here, shall we? Then let me take you to the ramparts. Elliot and I often walk around them just before the sky turns indigo at dusk and then darkness falls."

"How romantic. You are lucky. You have everything you could ever want here."

Louisa smiled but didn't reply.

"I think it's very pretty, magical in fact."

They smelled the fish before they came upon it, flapping in the breeze where it had been hung from a beam outside a shop to dry in the sun. The same shop also sold tuna sauce which was kept in large, highly pungent barrels. It was still early enough to see the fish seller, who waved as he passed by, balancing large panniers of fresh fish on either side of his bicycle, and with a trail of cats following behind. Everyone greeted Louisa.

"The fish man delivers anywhere you want in the Fort and tosses the heads and tails to the cats," she said. "As you can see, they are all rather fat."

They passed an enormous, softly scented frangipani tree and soon reached the old walls built from corals, lime and mud, where they looked out across the glittering ocean stretching as far as the eye could see.

"This is so beautiful," Gwen said. "And I love the smell."

Louisa laughed. "Of fish?"

"Yes, fish, but it's the gorgeous salty smell of the ocean too. We live by a lake, but I've often wondered what it might be like to live close to the sea."

"It's always changing. I love that. Sometimes it's silvery and serene, soothing to just sit and stare, sometimes, as now, it's speckled with gold."

As they sat on the wall Louisa felt more relaxed than she had for a while. She had longed to confide in someone, but hadn't found the right time or the right confidante either. Gwen was the first person she felt she might be able to trust not to gossip.

"You asked if I was happy," she said.

"Yes."

"Well, the truth is, I'm getting there. Two months ago, I had a miscarriage."

"Oh goodness. How awful for you."

"But that was not my first." She swallowed hard before speaking. Her stillborn and her miscarried babies were people to her, little people she still grieved for. Children who should have filled her arms and her heart. It wasn't an easy thing to say and she didn't want to talk about it, but found she couldn't remain silent either. "I had a stillborn child a little over two years ago, and a previous miscarriage too, eight years ago."

Gwen's face darkened. "I am so sorry . . . it must have been terrible."

Louisa murmured her thanks.

Gwen nodded slowly as if deciding what to say. "I lost a child too," she eventually said. "I still find it hard to talk about. Probably why I didn't tell you when we met for tea in Colombo. I just couldn't speak of it."

Louisa bit her lip to try to stop the stinging in her eyes.

"It's a long story. We kept it very much to ourselves. Her name was Liyoni," Gwen carried on. "Her loss broke my heart."

Louisa understood. "But at least you have your lovely little Alice now." And even as she said it she knew it had sounded all wrong. "Oh, gosh, that was clumsy. I'm sorry, I didn't mean . . ."

Gwen glanced at her. "Don't worry. But nothing can replace what you have lost, as I'm sure you know."

Louisa nodded. With these shared confidences, something had shifted between them and Louisa felt a strong affinity with Gwen. "Thank you for telling me," she said.

As tears filled her eyes, Gwen reached out and the two women sat together in the silence that eased around them.

The next evening, both still replete from a prolonged and very late Christmas lunch with her father, Louisa and Elliot walked out to the ramparts together to sit near where she had been with Gwen the previous day. People were eating snacks as they sat on the walls, and Louisa glanced at the crows lying in wait, eagle-eyed, watching for scraps of food to fall.

"I think I have drunk rather too much brandy with your old man," Elliot said and closed his eyes.

"The fresh air will help," she said, feeling a touch disappointed.

As the temperature dropped the locals began streaming out for their evening constitutional.

Regaining her equilibrium, she smiled at him. "The party was great, wasn't it? I'm so glad you invited Gwen and Laurence. But why didn't you invite the man I saw you with in your study to stay on? The Burgher."

"I did, but De Vos had other commitments."

"You seemed annoyed when I almost interrupted you."

"Not at all."

"So, what did he come for?"

"A bit of business."

"Oh Elliot! You promised no business over Christmas."

"Sorry." He linked his arm through hers. "Let's not talk about that. Let's just enjoy the evening. We're happy, aren't we? You're managing?"

She leaned against him again. "I am."

As the sun began to set, the sky flared into an astonishing display of fiery scarlet and pink, and then they heard the melodious call to prayer coming from the mosque. Suddenly, all the men in white turned on their heels and hurried off in its direction.

Louisa loved the dusty peacefulness, though at times the atmosphere was almost tinged with sadness. Because Galle was certainly quieter these days. Her father remembered when five hundred passengers a day had arrived by steamer, spice vessels had crowded the docks, and fighting flotillas had come to replenish their supplies. Now some of the cosmopolitan Europeans still made it their home, at least for part of the year, and though it remained a trading center for jewels, cinnamon and rubber, much of the tea trade had moved to Colombo.

Meanwhile, Louisa enjoyed meeting the merchants who still came from Malaya,

India and China. Galle just about held its own, and she loved to hear the repetitive melancholic Islamic call to prayer at dawn, at midday, in the middle of the afternoon, just after sunset, and two hours later. The sound had been around throughout her life and though there were fewer Muslims now — most of the Sinhalese were Buddhists — they lived in harmony with each other. She knew about the occasional outbursts against the British, everyone did, but they happened far less frequently now everyone had the vote, and there were far fewer than in Colombo. Yes, things had changed in Serendip, as Ceylon was once called — the island of jewels — and for the better.

# 4

A week after Christmas, on New Year's Day, Elliot had gone to dive off Flag Rock, which stood at the southernmost point of Galle Fort. Louisa thought it a risky pastime, but danger was Elliot's addiction. Along with driving too fast and racing a dinghy, he took life at a ferocious speed. Although she tried, Louisa found it hard to keep up, but then Elliot didn't internalize things in the way she did. Hating the tension he sometimes saw in her face, he called it unnecessary dwelling. She had asked him to bring her back a surprise from the market where he'd found the sapphire hair clip he'd given her. Imitation, of course, and he could easily afford the real thing, but they liked to find each other gifts from the various markets and bazaars. It had been their custom throughout the years, though he had been too busy lately.

Last week he had been away at Cinnamon

Hills, a cinnamon estate in the countryside a little over twenty miles from Galle, where he owned shares in the business. The estate had been neglected by previous owners, Elliot said, and as it needed extensive work to get it back on its feet, he had been helping out. Last month he'd also been in Colombo, checking up on his spice trading business there, and that was as well as having a full-time job in her father's firm.

She tried not to dwell on her latest miscarriage and keep positive but it wasn't always easy. She thought about her meeting with Gwen Hooper. There was something fragile about the woman but, though she had also lost a child, she carried on with optimism. What women go through, she thought. What they go through and still manage to smile.

After a breakfast of fruit, buffalo-milk curd and hoppers — lacy, biscuity baskets, sometimes with eggs inside — Louisa gathered her three springer spaniels together and set off to walk them through the main gate of the Fort and across a channel to the park. As she passed the flower seller on his ancient bicycle, she remembered how when she and Elliot were first married they'd go to the park before breakfast and then walk back to Lighthouse Beach. She remembered how once, they'd dared each other to wade out as far as the reef while the tide was out and the water was shallow. Feeling like children exploring an unknown world and laughing so much they slipped and, clutching each other, fell, they'd then been forced to return wet and sandy, creeping upstairs so the servants didn't spot them. Life had always been fun with Elliot.

Her father was a much more serious and thoughtful man than her husband. There tended to be four types of British men in Ceylon: army officers, planters, civil servants and businessmen. Her father was in the latter category. Perhaps losing his wife had made him graver than he might otherwise have been. It saddened her that she couldn't remember how he had been before her mother died.

After her walk she lay on her bed under the fan and put a palm on her belly. If only, she thought, but then checked herself. Elliot never showed his sadness over the loss of Julia, but she knew it hurt him. He was a man made for fatherhood, especially as he had lost a younger brother years ago to cholera. The child had only been five and Elliot seven, while their younger sister, Margo, had just been a toddler. That was why, despite everything, Louisa felt sympathy for Irene Reeve, though it was obvious that was not the only reason Elliot's mother seemed perpetually dissatisfied. Louisa sighed, catching the smoky coconut fragrance of food being cooked. Irene would be arriving from Colombo in time for supper, so it was time for Louisa to calm her curls and tidy herself up a bit.

Over a typical Sinhalese dish of rice and curry they managed to get by with small talk. Elliot's father had not been able to join his wife on this extended visit, because of work.

"It's a pity Harold couldn't make it," Louisa said. "We had hoped he might, didn't we, Elliot."

Elliot nodded. "Never mind. It's lovely that you're here, Mother."

"Yes, it is, Irene," Louisa said dutifully.

Irene sniffed tetchily — even after all these years, she still seemed displeased at her daughter-in-law using her first name. "One does what one can, but you know what he's like. If he had a more senior position he might have more choice over what he does, but you know your father. He isn't even a member of the Colombo Club."

"I'm sure Father does what he can."

She smiled. "You, dear Elliot, always see the best in people, but I know your father could have been so much more. But we are where we are, and that's the long and short of it. You're very lucky to have married a man like my son, Louisa."

Louisa nodded but intended to steer clear of this conversation. It had been repeated so many times she could foretell what would be coming next and while the spotlight wasn't on her, so much the better.

Elliot muttered something soothing, as she'd known he would, and then a servant came in to clear the table and the family fell silent. Another servant, a young dark-eyed, dark-haired woman called Camille, brought in a pineapple milk pudding but Louisa shook her head when offered a portion.

Camille served the others and then left the room.

"I know it's none of my business," Irene said. "But don't you think a milky pudding might put some meat on your bones? Why not get yourself an English cook or maybe even French? I'm sure all this Sinhalese cuisine isn't good for you. Apart from the puddings, I mean."

"Actually, we have a French girl called Camille working as a kitchen maid. She just served the pudding. Didn't you notice her? Although she's French she usually wears a sari. Perhaps that's why you didn't spot her."

"How very unusual. A European working as a lowly kitchen maid."

"It's rather a curious story. Apparently, she fell in love with a sailor who got her a job in the galley of the liner he was working on. But then he abandoned her here in Galle with no funds."

"So, you just stepped in and took her on. How like you to be so kind."

Louisa could see from Irene's disapproving look that she did not think it kind at all. "She's all alone with no family. I felt I had to, and anyway, our previous kitchen boy had moved on."

Irene inclined her head. "I see. Well, with your permission, naturally, I think it might be opportune if I stay on a little longer than originally planned. Somebody needs to ensure you eat properly."

Louisa groaned inwardly.

# 5

Louisa lay beside Elliot turning things over in her head while he read. He had always been incredibly solicitous whenever she wasn't well, and it crossed her mind that he might prefer her not to be strong, that maybe something about her incapacity made him feel needed. She curled up closer to him and stroked his stomach. Funny how easily doubt crept in, even in the strongest marriage. But when he closed his book and reached for her, she quickly dismissed the fleeting thoughts and then they made gentle love for the first time since her miscarriage.

Afterward he fell asleep.

She couldn't rest, however, as her skin felt prickly and her legs too heavy. No matter how she lay she couldn't get comfortable, and within moments she would be shifting around again. She waited for a while, but after an hour of fidgeting, she climbed out of bed and lit a candle to keep the light low and not wake Elliot. He hated to be woken suddenly and, if he was, it would send him into a mood for the entire following day.

In the bathroom, she turned on the light. They'd had electricity in Galle for the last seven years, and though it had transformed their lives, Louisa missed the romance of indoor oil lamps and the soft glow of candles. Sometimes the nights were hard to get through and she often found herself sitting on the edge of the bath for a while. She gazed around her, then went to open the window and lean out, closing her eyes and breathing in the scented night air. Damp. Sweet. Salty. Being on her own at night gave her such an intense feeling of timelessness, it instantly calmed her restless mind. She opened her eyes on a full moon, the garden glittering and shining in its blue light. Wouldn't it be wonderful if, after tonight, she was pregnant again?

She splashed her face and after another half an hour went back to bed and thought of her children. In her mind, they played and scampered and shrieked as children did, but her thoughts misled her and it hurt too much that they were not really there.

At one point Elliot woke up and wrapped his arms around her.

"I do love you," she whispered.

"As I do you," he muttered, half asleep.

Then she managed to nod off.

Over the following weeks Louisa's life went on normally. She took Tommy, Bouncer and Zip for long walks, concentrated on her sewing, and went outside to trim her shrubs. The evenings brought her added solace — when the sky turned red and purple, suddenly in the way it did, and she heard the call to prayer coming from the mosque. The huge dramatic sky hanging above a lilac ocean stretching all the way to the South Pole always struck her with a feeling of awe. But just as soon as everything was completely back on an even keel, and she felt genuinely happy, Elliot went away again, this time spending even longer than usual on business up at the cinnamon plantation.

She continued walking her dogs and taking care of her household but then, one morning in early February, after Elliot had arrived back home, her father came to sit with her on the veranda. It was a warm dusty day with flies buzzing in the heavy air, so Louisa was constantly brushing them from her eyes. They had tea brought out and before her father picked up the *Ceylon Times,* he grunted and held out a hand to her. She took it and he squeezed gently.

"There's my girl," he said.

She nodded and then let go of his hand. He buried himself in his paper but she always felt comforted by having him near. As she sat gazing at the garden and listening to the birds, watching them dip in and out of the branches, she felt a stirring of pleasure. It was still early but the morning was alive and the smell of the jasmine lifted her heart. Life had to go on. The third failed pregnancy had been a blow but she had a beautiful home, a good husband and a father she loved. Many could not say the same and soon she'd start fundraising again for the children's orphanage in Colombo. Maybe a French-themed meal would be something different, with Camille's help, of course. She had held coffee mornings, bring-and-buy sales and extravagant lunches, all in aid of the orphanage. Elliot would joke that every time she went there, he half expected her to come home with a couple of brown babies tucked under her arms.

A little later Elliot turned up and his mother joined them on the veranda too. Louisa had to face the fact that she was going to have to insist Irene went back to Colombo soon. She'd long outstayed her welcome, if you could even call it that, and had been with them a month. She dreaded her mother-in-law still being there when she and Elliot hosted their traditional anniversary party toward the end of the month.

"Shall we have more tea?" Louisa said and rang the bell, ordering the tea when Ashan, their small, trim-looking butler wearing the traditional men's sarong knotted at the front, sprang quickly to her side. His long hair was coiled up on his head and fastened with a silver-edged tortoiseshell comb.

"Thank you, Ashan," she said. "I can always rely on you."

He gave her a broad smile. "I should certainly hope so, Madam."

She glanced across at her husband. It seemed from his shining face that Elliot had something to announce. For a moment or two he didn't speak but just sat smiling with an unfathomable look in his eyes.

"Well, what is it?" her father said, picking up on it too. "Spit it out."

Frowning, Louisa gave her husband an inquisitive look. "Elliot?"

He took out a packet of Camel cigarettes, struck a match and lit one. Then he paused before speaking. "I have bought the old Print House." He leaned back in his chair, pursed his lips with satisfaction and nodded emphatically.

"Oh darling! How marvelous," Irene gushed, beaming with maternal pride.

Jonathan Hardcastle looked up from his paper, looking less than happy. "You've *what*?"

"I've had a marvelous idea." Despite his father-in-law's reaction, Elliot was still looking pleased with himself.

"What's your idea, darling?" Louisa gently said.

"It just came to me out of the blue a few weeks before Christmas. The place has been empty for ages but I thought we could turn it into the biggest jewelry and spice emporium in Ceylon. Put it right at the heart of the whole business. I just need to make the final payment."

"What were you thinking? We are not jewelers," Jonathan protested. "We're gem merchants."

Elliot's expression did not change and, Louisa knew, from the light in his eyes, nothing was likely to deflate him. "Isn't it time to expand, Jonathan? Take a risk?"

Her father shook his head. "While we're so stretched? Of course not."

"Why not hear Elliot out, Dad?"

"No. The gem trade is faltering because of the improved imitation-stone technology and you're well aware these are flooding the bottom end of the market."

"Even more reason to expand the business in another direction," Elliot said.

"No. It's madness. I've had to focus on high-end, high-carat jewels, and that ties up a huge amount of capital in stock."

Ashan brought out more tea and they stopped speaking until he had gone. He had been with the family for years and was the soul of discretion but, all the same, Louisa liked to keep sensitive issues private.

"Pa, surely you can find the cash," Louisa said. "It's a good idea, isn't it?"

"No. Absolutely not. The timing is all wrong."

"But . . ."

Jonathan held up a hand. "I'm not for this at all, and that's the truth. Now I have work to do. I hope not to hear any more about this idiotic idea." He folded his paper and marched off with it under his arm.

Now, suddenly deflated, Elliot puffed out his cheeks.

Louisa felt torn. She wanted to support Elliot, but she loved her father too.

"Well." Elliot shook his head. "That went swimmingly!"

"I'm going to go for a lie-down," Irene said as she sniffed, and then took a few steps. "I feel one of my headaches coming on. Disagreement does not sit well with my delicate constitution."

"I'll bring you some mint tea, Mother."

After Irene had gone Louisa gazed at Elliot. Wanting to find a way to support him, she sighed. "I'm sure he'll come around."

"He's wrong, but you know he won't change his mind." Elliot drained the last of his tea. "He has never really liked me."

"Don't be so peevish. Of course he likes you. But maybe you should have told me first rather than announcing it so suddenly," Louisa said.

He shrugged. "Maybe. I wanted to make a splash. I thought you'd be on my side."

"Come on, Elliot, I am, but you know my father. He needs to be persuaded."

"You think you can still do that?"

"I can try. Just promise me this isn't another of your madcap schemes."

"Are you my keeper now?"

She sighed again. "Of course not, but if you need my help . . ."

"Do you ever consider how it feels for me having to come cap in hand?"

"Elliot, I didn't mean —"

"You're referring to the racehorse, I assume?"

She smiled. "Well, he *was* lame."

He got to his feet and glared at her. "Honestly, Louisa, will you never let me forget it? I know I'm a disappointment to you, but this is quite different."

"Calm down. This is silly. You aren't a disappointment." She held out a hand to him.

He took it and came to sit beside her.

"As it happens, I do think the emporium might well be a good idea. Tell me how you financed it."

"The spice business has been very much in profit. That took care of the down payment. And it was going for a good price."

"Have you considered the actual costs of refurbishment?"

"Of course. It shouldn't be too expensive. The place is in good condition. We need to clean it up and then redecorate and do some fitting out — but it's all doable."

"Would it take long?"

"Not if we get the right people on board."

"I'm wondering if we could fund it ourselves, prove to Dad it's a good idea?"

He seemed to hesitate before speaking. "Lou, the thing is, I'm a little strapped for cash just now."

"I don't understand," she said. "You just said everything's going well."

"Yes. Yes. Of course. It is. This is just a

temporary cash-flow issue while I wait for payment on a large shipment in transit."

"And that's all?"

"Absolutely."

"Not a return to your old trouble?"

He looked horrified and hurt. "Of course not. Be right as rain once the payment is in. You know how these things go."

She trusted Elliot, of course she did, but still she paused to think before carrying on. Some things were hard to forget, let alone forgive, and yet, she wanted to believe him. His smile, disarmingly gentle, convinced her.

"It might be a risk," she said, "but on the other hand, my father might be wrong."

"I think he is."

"Well, let's look into it and, if it's solid, I'm sure I can figure out a way to make the final payment on the Print House myself. I could do with a new project."

"I don't want you to fall out with Jonathan."

She shook her head. "They're my shares and we're a team, remember. Once I've seen the place, I'll put some shares on the market as quickly as I can, so we can at least complete the deal."

"Good girl! I knew I could count on you."

"And, while I'm at it, I'll see that there's

enough in your account to cover the refurbishment. Just until you've balanced your books."

"Magnificent."

"Then we can get the plans ready together. I'll love designing it." It was true. A project might be just the thing. "How about sparkling white walls to contrast with ebony counters? Dark against light works so well, and Ceylon ebony is such an even dark color. It'll be fabulous."

"I hoped you might want to take charge."

"You did this for me?"

"Well, not exactly. But I do think a new start might help."

"And once Dad sees how brilliant the place looks and how many jewelers are interested in displaying their wares, he'll come around, I'm sure."

"I'm lucky to have you."

She smiled and reached for his hand. "We're both lucky."

"Now look," he said. "If you're feeling happier, I'm needed back at the cinnamon plantation."

Inhaling deeply, she attempted to ward off how crushed she felt. "Again? Aren't we going to get on with the plans for the emporium?"

"That can wait. There's such a lot to do

at the plantation right now."

"Like what?"

"You've never shown an interest before."

"Well, I'm asking now."

He didn't appear pleased to be questioned so closely, and seemed to be considering his answer. "Well, if you must know, I'm looking at ways to make the place more productive. Clearing more of the jungle. That sort of thing."

"Maybe next time I'll come with you. A trip away; just the two of us."

He didn't reply.

In the silence pooling around them, everything felt on hold.

# 6

When Elliot returned from the plantation
two days later, he had seemed in a very positive frame of mind. Glowing, in fact. Louisa
had again proposed her idea of accompanying him on his next visit, but at first he
hadn't been keen, claiming the plantation
was somewhat primitive and she wouldn't
enjoy it. She had persisted, however, and
now just a few days later they were on their
way. He had insisted it had to be on this
particular day, without explaining why, but
at least they were going together. A flying
visit only, there and back in one day, as
Hardcastle Gems had new stones in and he
was needed to oversee the records.

The road toward Cinnamon Hills took
them out of Galle Fort, bypassing the docks
and wharves where rubber and other goods
were stored before being loaded onto the
ships, and where Louisa held her nose:
when there was a rubber shipment the stink

was awful. They skirted the calm waters of Galle Bay, where the larger vessels were moored, and the southern end of Rumassala Hill, commonly known as the Watering Point, the place ships once took on fresh water from a reservoir. And from there you could see two rocky reefs, where so many ships had met their dreadful fates during the southwest monsoon.

"It's such a brilliant view from the top of Rumassala, isn't it?" she said. "We should walk up there again soon."

They passed the small cemetery, the last resting place of British civil servants and sailors, and after that Louisa rolled down the window, enjoying the fresh air.

"I love the legend of Rumassala."

The ancient Sanskrit epic of the Ramayana told of a time when Hanuman, the Indian monkey warrior-god, needed herbs to treat the wounded in his army during his battle against the demonic King Ravana of Ceylon. But there were no medicinal herbs to be found here, so Hanuman went back to India and brought back a piece of the Himalayas, where the plants he needed grew, but he accidentally dropped it at Rumassala. Louisa knew local folk believed this accounted for the rare medicinal plants found in the area.

"I'm thinking of trying medicinal herbs," she said. "See if they'd help me."

"Doctor Russell would be horrified."

"He doesn't have to know and it might be worth a try. The locals swear by them and it's up to me, isn't it?"

When they arrived, an hour and a half later, the tough loneliness of the plantation appealed to her. Halfway up the hill was an old estate house, or *walauwa,* a bungalow set amidst a small overgrown lawn and surrounded by trees where orchids thick with butterflies decorated the garden. Beyond the track to the house, the low penetration of light meant the forest looked deep and dark. A place to lose yourself, she thought. Where nobody would see your movements in the shadows and anything might happen.

As they made their way up the main drive, she glimpsed another building at the very top, a more contemporary house dramatically set above the plantation. When they finally reached it and left the car, she gazed down at the most extraordinary view to the sea, then turned back to look inland where misty purple hills merged with the sky.

"The light changes constantly from sunrise to sunset here. Do you like it?"

"It's absolutely breathtaking."

"I'll see if Leo McNairn is in. He runs the place."

He walked up to the main door and a servant opened it and told Elliot that Leo was away in Colombo.

He came back to where Louisa was still staring out toward the sea. "He's away, but there's nothing to stop us pottering about a bit. Let me show you some of the cinnamon trees."

"I love the smell," she said. "Is it just cinnamon?"

"Citronella too, I think."

"No wonder you like coming here so much! I'd be happy to stay here for a few days next time."

"Well, as I said, Leo's place is rather primitive. When I stay it doesn't matter to me."

"I don't mind primitive either. Surely you know that."

"Shall we have a look around?"

Louisa followed Elliot down a meandering path between sparse shrubs and ground orchids, beyond which tall dark trees enticed the unsuspecting into the gloom. She could feel their pull, though heaven knew what they might hide.

"Just watch out for snakes," he said, interrupting her thoughts.

"Poisonous?"

"The black and white krait."

"But they're only a problem at night, aren't they?" She glanced around. "I'd love to know about how the cinnamon is produced."

"It's all a bit tedious."

"Still."

"Well, the trees are usually first harvested after about three years. Then regular coppicing increases the yield but also keeps the bushlike appearance, and makes harvesting easier."

"How do they do the harvesting?"

"It's a bit laborious, but the bark is stripped, and then processed carefully."

After a few minutes of walking, she heard a shuffling sound behind her. She peered in that direction but saw nothing at first. As she moved off again she could have sworn she heard footsteps and twisted around to have another look. This time she thought she caught a flash of coppery red. She stood still and for a moment it seemed as if a red-haired woman was watching her from a distance. She turned and called to Elliot but when she glanced back, the woman was gone.

"What is it?" Elliot said. "Something wrong?"

"I thought I saw a woman watching me."

"Probably one of the natives."

"Yes. I couldn't see clearly. But the thing is, I thought she had red hair."

"Unlikely around here. Probably a scarf. One of the cinnamon peelers' wives, I'd say."

"Yes. You may be right. Let's go to the top and look at the view again."

As they climbed back up she spotted a pair of black-headed orioles, glamorous black and yellow birds singing a beautiful liquid song. She was about to point them out to Elliot but he seemed distracted, clearly surprised to see a Royal Enfield motorbike next to their car. "I really should be getting back to the office now," he said, and she noticed unexpected tension wrinkling his brow.

But then a tall lean-looking man strode out of the house. The fierce sunlight slanting through the trees cast shadows on his cheeks. He wore shorts and an open-necked shirt and was very tanned. Louisa stared at his handsome craggy face, the stubble on his jawline and his auburn-red hair, and wondered if it was him she'd seen earlier. How strange to see red hair so soon again, she thought, but no, I don't think it was him I saw among the trees. As Elliot wasn't saying anything she held out a hand.

"Hello, I'm Louisa Reeve. Elliot is just showing me around."

The man frowned slightly and scratched his head. "I see."

"So . . ." she said.

"Forgive me . . . Leo McNairn," he said. Louisa noticed he was looking hot and a bit sweaty.

There was a moment of silence as she stared at him. Something about the intense darkness of his eyes unsettled her. She expected him to smile but he held her gaze without speaking. The feeling of being under scrutiny and unable to look away embarrassed her. The moment seemed to stretch out too long, but then a sudden shaft of sunlight almost blinded her. She blinked rapidly before finally glancing away. Then he spoke again.

"Just been chopping down some old trees," he said. "Over on the other side."

"Well," Elliot said. "We'll be off now. Come along, Louisa." He twisted back to Leo. "Nice seeing you again. My wife just wanted to visit the place. Your man said you were in Colombo."

Leo narrowed his eyes. "Right."

"But you're back early."

"Trouble with the bike." With another

frown, Leo looked away, and Louisa felt he had spoken in a slightly offhand manner.

Elliot put an arm around her and began to walk away. "Well, cheerio," he said over his shoulder.

When the man just nodded and Elliot pulled her toward the car, Louisa was gripped by a weird feeling of unease.

"Well," she said as they reached a lower level of the hill. "Not the most talkative man. I felt quite uncomfortable. Is he always like that?"

"Probably has something on his mind."

"Why didn't he invite us in? It seemed very odd to me."

"He's a man of few words."

"Evidently, though it is a shame he was so unfriendly."

After a while she shook off the dark thoughts. "Anyway, I do like this gorgeous, bittersweet place."

"Bittersweet?"

"Yes. Don't you think?"

He frowned.

"There's just something about it. Special, you know? But at the same time a little unnerving. Still, I'd have preferred not to have to rush off. I got the feeling I'd met Leo before, or seen him somewhere, at least."

"You may have seen him in Colombo. With hair like that he does stand out."

# 7

The next morning Louisa was preparing to go to the grocery store just as Irene came into the hall. Louisa nodded at her, then picked up her shopping bag and headed for the door.

"Where are you off to?" Irene asked.

"Just to buy something."

She frowned. "You surely don't do your own shopping."

Louisa smiled. "Just odds and ends. I like to get out."

"In which case, I'd be happy to accompany you."

"Really? There's no need."

"Nevertheless. A little outing? Just the two of us. What do you say?"

As Irene pinned on her hat she continued to maintain they shouldn't have to buy groceries themselves — after all wasn't that what servants were for — and she couldn't help adopting the superior attitude that so irritated Louisa. Jonathan had brought her up to respect all people, no matter what their color or religion. But Irene truly found it difficult to understand Louisa's love of mixing with the locals and fervently believed the British should be sticking to their own kind, with the civil servants being the pick of the crop, of course, and never associating with the hoi polloi.

"I like getting out on my own and seeing people," Louisa said. "I only want a few candles so it won't take long. We can take a rickshaw, if you like."

Irene shrugged. "I'd rather walk."

"Won't Margo be arriving soon?" Louisa added. "You'll be wanting to get home, I imagine."

Margo, Irene's daughter, had been working as a nurse in England and had now decided to return to Ceylon, though nobody knew why.

"Yes. Very soon. Though, for heaven's sake, can you imagine her working at the hospital here? She had a perfectly good job at the London Hospital. Just throwing it in seems very unlike Margo. She's usually so sensible."

Louisa secretly wondered if Margo had become disenchanted with being the sensible one, and couldn't help thinking that perhaps she'd only grown up that way in re-action to Elliot's daredevil personality.

Out in the street Louisa glanced up toward the north where lowland forests rose to a ridge of lilac hills as far as the eye could see. She never tired of the view, nor of the familiar background sounds of waves crash-ing against the rocks, the seabirds squawk-ing overhead, and the horns of ships sound-ing as they entered or exited the harbor. She listened out for church bells and noticed the twittering of birds in the trees. Such simple daily things intensified the feeling of belonging. Outside the houses a profusion of zinnia and canna graced a variety of tubs, and purple bougainvillea tumbled down the walls.

They could smell the cinnamon, cloves and coffee before they even reached the store. Luckily there was no dried fish hang-ing at the entrance today. If you so much as lightly brushed your hair against it you'd stink of fish all day.

In the dark interior Janesha, a local Sinha-lese woman dressed in a green and blue sari, stood behind the counter. Her raven hair was swept back in a bun and the scent of coconut oil and sandalwood drifted from it. And just as she kept herself immaculate she kept everything in the shop in equally

61

perfect order. Jars of syrup and pineapple, sacks of rice and bags of spices on one side, with ripe bananas, papayas and mangoes on the other, though Louisa had no idea who might buy preserved fruit when there was such an abundance of fresh.

Although Louisa could speak adequate Sinhalese, she knew Janesha spoke English, so after a brief chat about candles, she asked the woman how her son was.

"He is causing me many problems. I think I told you before about his school report."

"You did."

"He was a promising student but since he turned thirteen he isn't interested."

"I'm sorry to hear it. What does your husband say?"

"My husband is too busy fishing to take much notice. It is always up to me. But how are you now?"

Louisa smiled. "I'm doing well, thank you."

The woman looked concerned. "These things do take time."

"I think I'm as well as can be expected. Probably better."

"At least you have color on your cheeks. I —"

"What are you two nattering about?" interrupted Irene, instantly reducing Janesha to silence. "Her accent is so strong, I can barely understand a word."

"Irene, please, she can understand you." She turned to the woman. "I'm sorry, Janesha, I think I have to go."

The woman nodded.

They walked home the long way around, just as a fine drift of sand was carried on the breeze. This happened regularly and you'd frequently have to shut your eyes if the wind picked up. Shading their eyes, they walked on, with Irene tight-lipped all the while.

When they arrived home, they entered the garden by the back gate and as they walked through, a family of geckos fled for the rockery at the sight of them. In the kitchen, Louisa smiled to hear the cook cursing at the boiler, but she put down her shopping and left him to it, before making her way into the small back hall.

As they passed Elliot's study, Irene looked in cautiously and then, drawing back, beckoned to Louisa. "Do you know who that is, in there?"

Louisa took a few steps forward to glance into the room and saw it was the same man she'd spotted Elliot talking to during their Christmas party. "Just someone Elliot is doing business with. Let's go back into the garden."

They carried on through the main hall and then out again via the French windows of the sitting room which opened on to the shady part of the garden. Louisa called Ashan for two fresh mango juices and then reached for her secateurs.

Irene picked up a magazine, an old American *Vogue,* and was idly flicking through it when, after a few minutes, Elliot came out. "Christ, this heat," he said and ran a finger under his collar.

"So how are things going, son?" Irene asked, looking up at him.

Elliot shrugged. "I'm very busy with work, mainly."

"Bringing work into the house, are you?"

He frowned. "I take it you spotted De Vos?"

"I always think work and home should be kept apart. A man needs to relax. I say the same to your father."

Elliot looked annoyed. "What I choose to do really isn't any business of yours, is it, Mother?"

Irene looked taken aback. "I'm just looking out for you."

"I don't need your concern," he snapped and unfastened another button on his shirt.

"Really, Elliot," Louisa said. "Your mother

was just —"

Elliot cut her short. "For goodness sake, don't you start too! You're as bad as each other."

Her heart sank. "Elliot! There's no need to be so tetchy."

There was a short prickly silence.

"I have to go to Colombo to meet a new spice client. I assume I have your permission."

Louisa bristled at his tone. "In that case, perhaps you might like to take Irene with you. Margo will be arriving any day now and Irene needs to be at home."

"Actually, Louisa," Irene said, "Margo won't be there yet and I'd prefer to stay on to help you out."

"No. I can't keep you any longer. Harold will be missing you."

Elliot looked annoyed but nodded his acquiescence anyway. Louisa knew something was bothering him — perhaps just pressure of work — but she also knew if he had decided to keep it to himself, then that was that. Elliot in a mood could not be pushed.

While he was away, Louisa passed her time flicking through seed catalogues and beginning a new bedspread. This was to be patchwork, something she hadn't tried before, and she was using a combination of silk offcuts along with some sari fabric she had cut up herself. As soon as she began to sew she entered another world, a place where her mind could drift unfettered as she focused on the job at hand. She didn't often allow herself the luxury of hope, knowing it could crumble as swiftly as it arrived, but with space in her head, she thought about the future. What did she want? A child, of course, that went without saying. But what else? A less risky hope than that, perhaps?

Elliot had been in Colombo for two whole days and, when he came home on the third evening, he seemed in a far better frame of mind. While Louisa was at her sewing machine, the three spaniels at her feet, he ran up the stairs and entered her sewing room carrying an armload of flowers.

"What a lovely picture of domesticity," he said and came to kiss her on the forehead. "Sorry I was such a grump the other day, darling. The heat gets to me sometimes. Anyway, these are for you."

"Guilty conscience," she said with a smile and he laughed.

She finished off the seam she was sewing

and rose to her feet to take the flowers. He may want to blame the heat, she thought, but I know different. However, if whatever had riled him had blown over, so much the better. Elliot could be difficult at times, but she'd long concluded it was just his way.

"You were right about Margo, by the way," he said. "She arrived yesterday, but she'll be coming to visit us very soon."

"That will be lovely." Louisa smiled. She was fond of Margo and was always surprised how soothing her sister-in-law's calm demeanor was, so different from Irene's simmering hostility. "How was she?"

"A bit quiet."

"Why has she come back now?"

He raised his brows and scratched his head. "Beats me. My guess is a failed love affair might be something to do with it. She wouldn't trust me with the details and I'm pretty sure she doesn't want Mother to know, but I'm certain you'll be able to winkle it out of her."

"Really?"

"People do confide in you, don't they? Now, how about I run you a bath with some drops of lavender and rose water. It will help you sleep, and then maybe tomorrow we can start work on the plans for the old Print House?"

"I'd love that. I've finished here anyway."

"Early night for you, my love."

She carefully placed the flowers on a side table.

"I'll get one of the houseboys to put those in water," he said.

"Are you coming to bed now too?"

"No, I think I need a couple of drinks after that drive. The coast road seems to get worse every day."

"Don't stay up too late, will you?"

"Just a couple of drinks."

After her bath, Louisa unpinned her hair and, closing her mosquito net, made herself comfortable in bed, hoping to drift off with the scent of jasmine wafting through the open window. She always slept with the windows open, which was fine as they also had a mosquito screen to protect them. Although she was so much better in many ways, sleep was still the one thing eluding her. In the complete blackness of night her lost children nudged at her mind. They almost seemed to speak to her and she found herself talking back, imagining them alive, thinking about how different her life would have been. She saw them racing around the garden together and playing tag with the dogs. Saw them in their school uniforms on the first day of term, looking shy and proud at the same time. Saw them running past the tall coconut palms near the ramparts and whooping for joy. Saw them asleep in their beds, eyelashes fluttering in a dream.

During daylight hours she was happy enough, of course she was, but the dark of night brought back what she had been able to forget when the sun was shining. I must steer my mind toward the good things, she frequently told herself, because when she focused on the positive she always felt better. And at least Irene had, at long last, gone home. Perhaps half the problem with Irene was that she was lonely and didn't have enough to do? Louisa found it strange. There was always something to do in Galle Fort, but Irene would insist on standing on her dignity so.

Louisa was half asleep when she heard the murmur of voices. Wondering what was going on, she fumbled for the light switch and then glanced at her clock. Half past one in the morning, and Elliot still hadn't come to bed. She got up and unhooked her robe from the back of the door, then slipping it on, padded out of the room, and stood on the landing at the top of the stairs to listen. The voices from downstairs trickled up to her. Strange that Elliot hadn't said anything about having friends around tonight.

# 8

The very next evening Elliot went, he said, to see Jeremy Pike — but was still not home by midnight. He'd promised to be away only for an hour or so, and that had been at eight. He also hadn't kept his promise that they'd start making plans for the Print House, but instead had been out sailing all day, also with Jeremy, dashing in just to grab something to eat in the early evening.

Louisa decided to wait up, and at about half past twelve heard an almighty crash in the hall. She rose to her feet and went to look. She was horrified to see the hat stand lying on the floor and Elliot leaning against the wall looking disheveled: his hair a mess, his tie undone.

"You're late," she said, though she could smell the whisky and realized she'd get little sense out of him.

"So? Why didn't you just go to bed?" He wasn't exactly slurring his words, but she

71

could see something in his eyes that disturbed her. Their green irises had darkened,
and there was a dangerous edge to his voice.

"I was waiting for you," she said.

"Stating the bleeding obvious!"

She walked across to pick up the hat stand
but left the fallen hats on the floor. "You
did say you wouldn't be long. I wanted to
spend some time with you, that's all."

He closed his eyes and didn't reply.

"You were out all day, too."

He shrugged.

"So," she said, losing patience. "Where
the hell have you been all this time?"

"Ah, the wifely concern . . ."

"Elliot, don't be like that. I have a right to
know."

"A right?"

"Yes. So, tell me?"

He sighed deeply. "If you must know, I
had a little game of poker with the boys."

She took a sharp breath in. "How little?"

He laughed. "Well, not so little, actually."

"For Christ's sake!"

He pushed past her and stumbled into the
living room and, as she followed, she
watched him pour himself a whisky, then
throw himself onto the sofa.

"Don't you think you've had enough?"

He pulled off his tie, letting it drop to the

floor and then, after awkwardly balancing the glass on the edge of the sofa, threw open his arms. "Well, aren't you going to give your adoring husband a kiss?"

She narrowed her eyes. "Not while you're stinking of booze."

"Have one yourself. Then you won't notice it." He waved his arm about and knocked the whisky glass to the floor, where it shattered.

"For heaven's sake, Elliot, this is too much!" She went to the kitchen and came back with a cloth, dustpan and brush.

"Always the good little wifey," he said.

She'd had more than enough — putting the things down, she took a deep breath and stood tall. "You come home late, stinking of booze, and tell me you've been gambling. You said that was all behind us."

He shrugged as he let out his breath in a loud puff.

"You promised me. I *believed* you. And I can't keep on saving you."

"I don't need you to rescue me."

"So how much have you lost this time?"

"Enough. But you've got the means, so what does it matter, and Daddy will always come to the rescue."

"You just said you didn't need rescuing. Tell me it was a one-off, that you won't do this again."

He staggered to his feet and came right up to her, waving a finger in her face. "Proper little schoolmarm. You don't get to tell me what I can or can't do."

She took a step back. "Was it a one-off?"

He inclined his head and grinned. "Not exactly. And now I am going to bed." He turned away but then twisted back. "Don't worry, I'll sleep in the spare room."

She watched him walk to the door and enter the hall, listened to his footsteps on the stairs, and then she sat on the sofa with her head in her hands. Not again. Please, *not again.* They'd had enough trouble — Elliot had caused so much pain a few years back, and she couldn't bear to think of it starting all over again.

She hardly slept and woke early to hear the Fort cockerels crowing and the waves crashing on the rocks. She slipped on a dressing gown and went to see if Elliot was still asleep, but found he was already up. He seemed to need so little sleep and yet could still function, whereas lack of sleep made her heavy and slow, at least until she'd had some coffee. She felt hung over, even though she'd had nothing to drink, but forced herself to wash, and dress in trousers and a loose white shirt. After that she went in search of coffee and Elliot.

Camille was just bringing a fresh pot to the living room where Louisa found Elliot with a large pad of paper and several pencils.

He looked up and grinned at her.

"I thought we'd start planning," he said. "Once you've had your coffee, of course. What do you say?"

She didn't smile back. "You can't just brush what happened under the carpet."

"What if I say I'm truly sorry?"

She glanced at his face. "You more or less admitted it wasn't a one-off. Was that true?"

"No. Of course not. I was drunk and being an idiot. Darling, I am sorry, you know how I get when I've had too much to drink. Believe me, as God is my witness, it was just the once and really won't happen again."

She exhaled slowly — perhaps it really was just an aberration.

"Louisa, it was just one night. Don't turn it into something it's not."

"You really were unpleasant. It hurt, Elliot — I don't want to go back to that awful time."

He rose to his feet. "I'm so, so sorry. Come here."

She took a few steps toward him and he

75

wrapped her in his arms. Then he whispered in her ear, "On my life, I promise it will never happen again. I am really sorry. Truly. Let's look to the future. Don't we have this wonderful new project to focus on?"

He was right about that. They did have an exciting new project. It wasn't that she minded the drinking so very much, it was the gambling, especially as he'd taken on the old Print House and it was her who'd be stumping up the cash to complete the purchase.

She drank two cups of strong black coffee with two sugars and despite feeling upset, decided to see what Elliot had done so far. She would have to trust him and let the past be the past.

"Look," he said. "My idea is to have a central arena with a gallery all around at first-floor level. Can you see? I know my drawing is hopeless but do you get the gist?"

She nodded.

"And there will be open archways through to all the rooms on the ground floor. If we can persuade enough jewelers to trade there, it will get us off to a good start while we set up our own jewelry-making business."

"Do you have anyone in mind?"

"Yes. I'll be going over there later today to

have a chat. So, what do you think?"

She still felt unsure of him but if they were to go ahead with this, what was the point of continuing to dwell on what had already happened? She would just have to hope that he was sincere in his apologies. She'd also have to keep her eyes firmly open.

"Well," she said. "I think we should do it in an art deco style, something really chic and streamlined. And maybe we could have a section selling paintings. There are so many terrific artists in Colombo."

"You could display and sell some of your own line drawings too."

"And it could be just the place for the rubber planters to bring their wives when they come to town. We could even serve tea."

"Yes, instead of just parties and socializing at the New Oriental, give them a taste of real culture here."

She nodded. "I'm sure the wives would be tempted to buy, but I don't think we should only sell jewelry and art, I think ceramics too, and maybe other handmade items."

"So where do we start with the drawings?"

"Leave them to me. I'm sure I can come up with something."

Elliot got to his feet. "So, do you feel happier now?"

She nodded again, though a shiver ran

through her and a small part of her still couldn't quite believe, despite his protestations, that it would not happen again. She recalled how it had been last time — the rows and recriminations — and felt a little sick.

"I wanted to ask you something," she said, and he sat down again abruptly. "The night before last, I heard noises from the living room sometime after I'd gone to bed. That wasn't a game of poker, was it?"

He frowned. "Must you always do this?"

"Do what?"

"Treat me as if I were a child."

"Elliot, I'm not. Surely you can see I'm just worried."

He stared at the floor for a moment, his jaw working, then stood up and came across to her, looking repentant. "Of course. You have every right to ask. And no, it wasn't poker, I promise." He squatted down beside her and held out a hand for hers. She gave him her hand and he squeezed it.

After he had gone out, Louisa spent the day in the garden, having changed into an old shirt and a pair of frayed shorts. Working in the garden always soothed her, so first, she painted one of the two benches a deep shade of green. It was an old cast-iron one her mother had loved, and she hoped the paint would preserve its life a little longer. Then she planted nasturtium seeds in terracotta pots on either side of the bench and thought of her mother again as she patted down the red earth. She trimmed back a clump of feathery bamboo, grown too tall, and pruned the roses, raising her head at the sound of barking but quickly ascertaining it was not one of her spaniels. Probably a hungry pariah dog, she thought, and glanced across at a large russet-winged hedge crow searching for snails. Afterward she sat on the other bench, stretching out her legs and enjoying the feel of the sun on her skin while doing her best to steer her mind away from the horrible row they'd had.

The next day they walked the short distance to the Print House. The old building on the corner of Pedlar Street had been a warehouse before it was a printer's premises and did look relatively worn from the outside, though it had lovely fanlight windows. Nothing that a lick of paint and some patching up won't rectify, she thought. Inside it was dark, so Elliot threw open the old plantation shutters.

"Some of these need repairing but they're

all essentially intact," he said.

"We could paint them cream like ours. I don't like the dark brown. The whole place should be brighter."

"Maybe we'll have chandeliers."

"Yes." She glanced up. "Look, there's a wonderful glass cupola. It's covered in leaves and goodness knows what else, but if we get it cleaned up, light will just flood in, and you can put the chandeliers in the side rooms."

They looked around at the mess. When the Print House had closed, the owners had left sheets of paper littering the floor and had also abandoned one or two of the older machines.

Elliot scratched his head. "We could polish up one of the presses and use it as a centerpiece. But the first thing to do is to see what lies behind these doors."

He went over and threw open four large doors, one after another, and they walked into the spacious airy rooms. Only the central area had a second floor, where the gallery would be. These other rooms were single-story and would be perfect for displaying goods. In one of them there was another door. Louisa tried the handle but it didn't budge.

"Let me," Elliot said. "It's probably just

stiff." He turned the handle and put his shoulder to the door. Nothing. "Well, it doesn't matter. There's probably a key knocking around somewhere."

"But don't you think it's odd? None of the other doors are locked, so why that one?"

"Probably got a dead body stuffed in there," he said and laughed.

They walked back into the central area and he lit a cigarette. "So," he said. "What do you think? Painted white with gorgeous ebony counters, as you suggested, wouldn't this make a terrific emporium? There are also several smaller rooms at the back which we could let out as workshops until we need them ourselves."

Feeling happier, she smiled at him.

"You like it? Shall we go ahead?"

"I think it's perfect. I'll instruct the bank to sell my shares, so the money will be in your account soon. Thank goodness things have improved since the financial crash."

They left the building and walked the long way around to the jeweler's, past the light-house, where they were splashed by sea spray.

"I love to think the lighthouse flashes its light as far as the Antarctic," she said. "It's such a wonderful thing."

81

"I doubt they'd see it that far — it's a huge expanse of water." He shivered.

"What's wrong?"

"I don't know. Sometimes so much water seems like too much water."

She nodded. "And we are so small."

"Exactly."

"It's blowy," she said. "Listen, Elliot, couldn't we walk out on Lighthouse Beach? Remember how we used to?"

"The tide's in. Maybe another time."

"I love to feel the sand between my toes. Let's just see how much beach there is."

They went back past the lighthouse and onto the tiny strip of sand covered in shells. She removed her shoes and whooped as she felt the water come up to her ankles.

"Come on, Elliot. You too. Bet you can't catch me." And she began to run.

She felt the wind in her hair and the wet sand between her toes. This is what she needed, what she loved. Yes, they'd had a row, and yes, he'd spent one night gambling, but they were good together, weren't they? She glanced back to see he was now carrying his shoes and coming after her.

He caught up with her and threw his shoes out of reach of the water, then he picked her up and made as if to throw her in.

"Put me down this instant!" she shrieked,

but ended up laughing. He joined in, and she knew laughter would be the thing to make everything right.

When they had wiped the damp sand from their feet and put their shoes back on, they walked on while gazing out at the waves and the surf.

"Actually," she said when they were back on Hospital Street, "while you're at the jeweler's, I'll go to the Court Square market. I have an idea about something we might sell in the emporium. I'll see you back at home."

"Very well. See you in a while."

Louisa loved the dusty market and its fantastic variety of brightly colored goods — a clashing kaleidoscope of smells and sounds, with beautifully embroidered goods on sale, jewelry and ornaments made by the town's silversmiths, and intricately carved ebony elephants too. Today it was bustling, with random goats gnawing on red palm plants, sleeping mongrel dogs, women hoping to buy, and street sellers shouting their wares. A group of people stood nearby, absorbed by the lilting sound of a flute, and she tossed the musician some coins as she listened for a moment. Then she examined a stall selling tablecloths and lace, in case any of it would be fine enough for their emporium.

The woman who ran the stall had a heavily lined nut-brown face and looked far too old to still be so occupied. Her entire family were lacemakers and often could be seen sitting outside their houses, busily working, but now the old lady just sold the goods. Louisa fingered the delicate pieces for several minutes, but then told the woman she'd come back another time — it was a different kind of stall she had in mind today: one selling beautiful boxes decorated with carved flowers and animals. The young man in charge of it was Sinhalese and welcomed her warmly. He showed her a box, and then she picked another up and felt for the panel that would slide back to reveal a secret compartment. She pressed other panels revealing ever smaller openings. These mahogany boxes were very popular and would sell well. Traditionally used for hiding gemstones, you could keep anything small and precious inside. A key, a folded letter, maybe a lock of your baby's hair. She sighed. No, not that.

She questioned the stallholder about the quantities his family might be able to produce and then, much to his pleasure, bought a box. She'd give it to Elliot as a present. Perhaps when he found the key to the locked room he could keep it in the box. It would be a nice memento of their first visit to the Print House together.

# 9

Two days later Margo arrived by bus from Colombo, a long and rickety journey taking all day with all the inevitable stops and delays. The following day, in Elliot's absence, the two women went for a cycle ride around the Fort.

Margo was a down-to-earth, sporty woman, who had the same dark curling hair as Elliot, the same green eyes and a warm, encompassing smile. You could picture her married with a brood of children who she would manage expertly and calmly. In fact, she was neither married nor a mother. It's strange the way people so often don't match one's expectations, Louisa thought. When the opportunity to be a nurse in London had arisen, Margo had jumped at it; now she was back, but wasn't giving much away about her plans and, of course, that made everyone curious.

"So," Louisa said as they cycled two

abreast away from the Sun Bastion, following the line of the ramparts flanking the harbor. They turned into the interior, avoiding the occasional lizard running across the street and the semi-feral dogs that dozed in doorways or hung about the entrances to shops. "Are you going to tell us what's brought you home? Or is it a secret?"

"It was time."

Louisa nodded as they passed a mother toque macaque cradling her baby in an alleyway. "And are you staying?"

"I haven't decided."

"Right. And that's all you're going to say."

"It's not a big secret. I just got involved with the wrong person and I needed a break to clear my head."

"What kind of wrong person?"

"Louisa!"

"Sorry."

There were a few moments of silence before Margo came to a halt and spoke up. "Well, if you must know . . . he's married. But keep it under your hat. I'm not proud of it."

Louisa felt a flash of worry for her sister-in-law and reached across. "Do you love him?"

"I thought I did."

"And now?"

Margo shook her head. "Well, he isn't going to be leaving his wife any day soon, if that's what you mean. Though in a way I'm glad. The guilt was awful."

"I'm so sorry. Did you know he was married at the start?"

"I pretended that I didn't . . ."

"Oh Margo."

"But I'm ashamed to say I really did know. He didn't mislead me."

"I didn't mean to pry."

Margo's lower lip quivered. "I only have myself to blame."

"And now you have no choice but to put it all behind you."

"Exactly. I wish things could be different but they are not. I'm the scarlet woman and I've had to face facts."

"But their marriage . . ."

"Well, it's not happy, he says . . . Anyway, enough about me. Let's cycle on."

Louisa reached across again to touch her hand. "If you ever want to talk, you know I'm here."

They carried on past one of the open drains where a monitor lizard seemed to be sleeping.

"I don't much like them," Margo said, pointing at it.

"You've been in London too long! You

know they won't hurt you, although . . ." She paused for effect. "I did hear a story, probably apocryphal, that a baby was snatched by one . . ."

Margo smiled and raised her brow.

When they arrived at the steps of the library, Louisa brought her bike to a halt and Margo followed suit.

"Shall we take a break?" Louisa asked. "Read the papers?"

They went inside a darkish building with a polished concrete floor, the main room of which housed the library. High glass-fronted cabinets clung to the walls, with rows and rows of leather-bound books lining their shelves. Small table lamps helped the reader to see clearly once a book had been chosen.

The place smelled a little musty and the librarian, a white-haired old Muslim man, sat in a corner surrounded by tottering piles of books. He had once been a teacher but had jumped at the opportunity to spend his later years among the words he loved so much.

"How are you, my dear?" he asked, rising from his corner and walking over to her with a distinct stoop.

"I'm fine. Thanks for asking, Mr. Bashar."

"Do you want anything in particular?"

"I think we'll just flick through some of

the papers."

"Well, recent newspapers are over there on the table, local and from Colombo. If you want to go any further back, older ones are filed in drawers according to date."

Louisa made herself comfortable and began to search the papers.

"Are you looking for something special?" Margo asked.

Louisa shook her head. "Not really. But I was fascinated by the cinnamon plantation we went to see the other day, and I'd like to understand more about cinnamon production in the area. You should have seen it, Margo. The views are amazing and the air is drenched with this gorgeous smell."

"No wonder Elliot has invested in it and likes working there."

"And yet there was something not quite right."

Margo didn't pick up on her sister-in-law's misgivings. "I'm sure there will be lots to read up on cinnamon here."

They passed a pleasant hour in the cool of the old building flicking through the papers and magazines. Suddenly Louisa paused. "Gosh! I didn't expect this. It's an article about Cinnamon Hills. That's the very one we went to see. Elliot's there now, in fact, but should be back later today. He's been away a lot lately," she added a little sadly.

"Maybe you give him too much rope."

Louisa shrugged and looked down at the year-old article in a local newspaper.

"It says here, Leo McNairn took over Cinnamon Hills when his grandfather died some years back. The place had become quite run down and Leo is breathing new life into it. It also mentions he lives there with his cousin. I met Leo when we were there — but not her and I'm not sure why, but my hunch is she might be a bit of a recluse. There's a picture of Leo but none of her. Look." She held up the paper.

"Oooh, he's quite a catch, wouldn't you say."

Louisa grinned. "I wouldn't know."

"Oh, come off it. I know you are devoted to Elliot but you can look at other men."

"Well, if you like the disheveled sweaty look."

"Just how I do like them."

Louisa laughed. "Really?"

"Why not? More manly."

"Was your man in London . . ."

"Manly?"

"Yes."

Margo winked. "Very. William was a landscape gardener working mainly in Kent.

Anyway, if you've found what you want let's call it a day. I've had enough of being cooped up inside."

Elliot had returned in time for supper and the three of them were having a coffee at the end of a meal which had consisted of roast goat masquerading as lamb, followed by mango mousse. The lamps were lit and the evening was calm.

"Honestly, Elliot," Margo was saying. "Do you think you should leave Louisa alone so much? You're so often away or out sailing."

"Louisa is fine."

"Yes but —"

"Margo, come on, you know I have matters to attend to. I can't just sit at home playing nursemaid."

"She's not herself yet. Women who have . . . you know."

He held up a hand to silence her. "No one is more aware of the situation than I am. Louisa is fine. She's strong and independent. Sometimes too independent."

Louisa raised an eyebrow.

"You still need to be here more," Margo continued.

He shook his head. "Louisa has her father, and our mother was here until recently, and now you're here."

"Fat lot of use Mother is where Louisa is concerned. Maybe she doesn't mean to be unkind, but I'm surprised you encouraged her to stay so long. Anyway, it's you Louisa needs."

He frowned. "Has she complained?"

"You know she never would."

Louisa spoke up. "For heaven's sake, I *am* in the room. Please, both of you stop this bickering. I can take care of myself, Margo. I don't need nannying."

"But I still think . . ." Margo carried on.

Louisa scraped back her chair and smiled as she stood. She'd seen these spats between Elliot and Margo before. "Well, I'll leave you two to slug it out. I'm having an early night. Don't forget that tomorrow we'll need to take care of the last-minute planning for our anniversary party."

# 10

On the morning of their wedding anniversary on February 26, Elliot brought her breakfast in bed, with the most perfect red rose in a tiny glass vase. He had been away for a couple of days again but now he was back and seemed pleased with himself.

"You spoil me," she said.

"Shove up a bit and I'll put the tray on your lap."

She shuffled up to a sitting position.

"You're very beautiful in the mornings," he said and ran his fingers through her blond curls. "I'm a lucky man."

"Because my hair's all over the place?"

He smiled. "No. Because you are so good for me. I hope I am for you."

She poured them both a coffee and, after they had drunk it, he took the tray from her and placed it on the floor. "I have something better than breakfast for you."

As he removed his dressing gown she saw

he was naked underneath. He slid into bed with her and kissed her firmly on the lips. She loved to feel his body close to hers like this and hugged him tightly.

"I love you," she softly said.

"As I do you. Are you ready for this?" he whispered in her ear.

She nodded. "Of course. But it isn't the first time since . . ."

"I know, but I like to be sure." He ran comforting fingers through her curls.

She had missed this intimacy and now, being this way with him, she felt the bond between them growing stronger again. They had always enjoyed a healthy sex life, although over the years it was their friendship she had grown to value most. She loved how he would tease her and then laugh, until she finally joined in, realizing he was joking. And if, at times, he was less than perfect, well, that was normal in any relationship, wasn't it? She had her own faults. Maybe at times she was a little detached — perhaps a little too absorbed in her own inner space. She'd always enjoyed her own company and liked nothing better than allowing her thoughts to wander in the peace and quiet of her home. Perhaps she wasn't as easy to live with as she hoped she was?

He was gentle now, stroking her where she

wanted him to, and feeling the thrill of surrender, she found herself responding with more passion than she could have imagined. Afterward they lay side by side, their legs tangled in the sheets.

"Are you okay?" he said as he lifted her hand and kissed her fingertips.

She smiled. "Do you think we might have made another baby?"

"My darling girl. Maybe. In any case we will try again until we do. Hopefully it won't be too long."

"What if it happens again?"

"Let's not tempt fate. We'll face whatever happens together."

"I know." She paused, thinking of the day ahead. "Anyway, I have to be up. Time and tide and all that. There's a great deal to do before the party this evening."

"You have remembered I'm sailing with Jeremy Pike today? We're racing the latest dinghy he's had sent over from Britain. I'll be skipper to him as mate. We're trying out the technique of trapezing again. It didn't go so well last time."

"Well, stay safe. It is a little bit windy."

"I'm sure it'll be fine," he said. "The wind won't last."

"Don't worry about today, you'd only get in the way, and Margo is going to lend a hand. Everything is under control."

Louisa spent the day checking everything was all set for the evening. She and Margo fixed some bunting at the front of the house and placed lotus flowers, swathes of jasmine and water lilies in every room. The house-keeper had offered to see to the flowers but it was something Louisa enjoyed doing herself. She also ensured incense fragranced with cinnamon and sandalwood sweetened the air in the garden, and hoped the wind wouldn't blow out the citronella candles.

The kitchen was a hive of activity all day, with Cook losing his temper at one of the houseboys, while Camille, the French girl, stayed well clear. Ashan, with his placid, sensible nature, was the only one who knew how to calm the cook, but today even he kept his distance.

When it was time, Louisa had a good long soak in the bath and then dressed in a silver floor-length gown, with a rope of pearls around her neck and matching earrings. She heard the melodious call to prayer and by six o'clock when Elliot wasn't back she began to fret. He was cutting it fine if he was to get spruced up in time for the start of the party at seven.

There was a knock at the door and Margo

came in. She wore a red, shin-length dress, in a shiny satin fabric that set off her green eyes and dark hair beautifully.

"I thought I might pin up your hair," she said.

"Thank you. Whenever I try to get it under control the pins just slide out."

"I think if we give you a couple of waves at the front and pin up the back it'll look lovely."

As Margo worked, Louisa continued to worry. "I'm just a bit annoyed Elliot is still not back."

"He'll turn up at the eleventh hour. He always does. And he'll roll in with five minutes to spare, change in a rush and then emerge looking like a Hollywood star."

Louisa sighed. Margo was right but it didn't pacify her. He wasn't always reliable, but at least he could have tried to be on time for this.

The two women went through to the kitchen, where Cook poured them a glass of champagne and by seven o'clock they were both feeling a little merrier.

"I'd better stay in the main entrance hall now," Louisa muttered, "but I wish Elliot would hurry up. It really is too bad."

The first to arrive were two rubber planters and their wives. Louisa passed the time chatting about the price of rubber and then a few more couples turned up. So it went on for another half-hour. But there was still no sign of Elliot. Louisa had hired a string quartet to play and now they began tuning up as people mingled. Gwen and her husband hadn't appeared, though Louisa hadn't expected them to; it was such a long journey from their tea plantation.

A few of the locals had graced them with their presence. The Burgher lawyer, Mr. Derek Muller, and his wife; the old librarian, Mr. Bashar; plus Edward Russell, their family doctor. Her father had already arrived, of course, and a few other friends too.

A little later, and the house was full. Margo found Louisa staring at her watch. "We need to serve the food, don't you think?" Margo said.

Louisa nodded. "Fine wedding anniversary this has turned out to be. But yes, could you tell Ashan, please. I'll just make a short announcement."

She asked the quartet to stop playing and then she rang a little hand bell. The room hushed and those who had been outside came in to see what was going on.

"I'd like to thank you all for coming. Unfortunately, my husband has been unavoidably delayed, but please, eat, drink and enjoy yourselves." She indicated the music was to start up again and soon the sound of it and gentle chatter filled the room.

At nine o'clock there was a rap at the front door. Ashan answered it and a now worried Louisa watched from the doorway of the living room as Police Inspector Roberts, with his usual thatch of wiry hair and red complexion, entered the hall. But the grim expression on his face suggested he had come from the Southern Provincial Head Office with some bad news. Her mouth went dry and she held on to the door frame.

Margo stepped forward. "What has happened?" she said.

The officer glanced at Margo but then focused on Louisa. "Mrs. Reeve."

Louisa took a few steps toward him.

"Is there somewhere quieter we can go?" he asked.

"Just tell me. Is Elliot all right?"

Margo held out an arm. "Let's go into your sewing room, Louisa."

The three went upstairs into the sewing room, Louisa rushing ahead with any number of possible scenarios chasing through her mind, and anxiety hammering at her heart. She could barely wait for the man to speak.

"Now," Louisa said, feeling increasingly

worried. "Please."

He cleared his throat. "I'm very sorry to have to tell you that your husband, Mr. Elliot Reeve, met with a fatal accident this afternoon."

Margo and Louisa just stared at each other in disbelief. A chasm opened in front of Louisa.

"What do you mean?" Margo said.

"He died, Miss. I am so sorry. My sincerest condolences."

Louisa felt a rush of anger. What on earth was he saying? She could hear the man's voice but none of his words were making sense. "Could you say that again?"

"I'm afraid your husband died this afternoon."

No. This wasn't possible. Though it was warm, she felt herself shiver. "Died? How? How could he have died?"

"A sailing accident?" Margo asked in a tight voice. "Is that what you mean?"

Roberts shook his head.

"But he went sailing today with his friend, Jeremy Pike, didn't he, Louisa?"

As Louisa nodded the officer spoke again. "I'm afraid he died in a car crash on his way to Colombo."

Louisa shook her head. "No. That's impossible. He wasn't going to Colombo today."

"I'm so sorry, Madam. The car, a 1928 Vauxhall, was a complete write-off."

"But that's not even our car! We have a newish Triumph Dolomite. Are you sure it was my husband?"

"There was identification on the body."

"I . . ." Louisa began, but the words died in her mouth.

"If there's anything I can do," the policeman was saying.

"I must know if it's really him," Louisa finally said, now feeling icily cold.

This was a nightmare. Surely she'd wake up any minute now and find out it wasn't real. Because it could not be real. Elliot wasn't someone who could die young. He was too full of life. No, it was quite impossible. She and Margo stared at each other as if begging for a different outcome. *Not this. Please. Not this.*

"When can I see him?" Louisa demanded, trying to maintain control. "You must have made a mistake."

"I wouldn't advise it tonight. I would be grateful if you could formally identify the body, though tomorrow will do. Or maybe Mr. Hardcastle could. The body . . . He's . . . well, he's a bit of a mess. Let them tidy him up."

"I don't want him tidied up!" Her voice

rose sharply. "I want to see my husband *now*! Where is he?"

"In the mortuary, Madam."

"Right." She turned to Margo and her face contorted. "Please. Tell me this isn't real, Margo."

As Margo took a deep breath, Louisa turned at the sound of her father entering the room. He frowned and glanced at the policeman.

"I'm afraid there's been a fatality, Sir," the inspector said.

"It's Elliot, Dad. They're saying . . ."

Jonathan went straight to her and attempted to hold her close, but she took a step back and shook her head. She couldn't allow him to hold her. Not now. She needed to find the strength to take this in. She tried to explain, stuttering her reasons, but the scrambled words choked her. All she could do was shake her head again. Part of her wanted to sink into her father's arms, but the other part knew she must do this without him. If she did not she might never stand on her own two feet.

Although she appeared calm on the outside, inside she could hear herself screaming. Elliot dead. *Elliot dead.* Suddenly she began to tremble. She clutched at Margo, who was looking white and pinched. "You'll come with me, Margo, won't you? I have to see for myself."

Margo swallowed, visibly shaken. "Are you sure? I don't know if I can. We could wait till tomorrow, like the Inspector says."

Tears sprang from Louisa's eyes. She brushed them away angrily. She would not believe this until she saw him with her own eyes. "No. We have to go now."

"I'll get Ashan to take care of the guests," her father said. "He'll know what to say. But, darling, I'm coming with you too."

"No. Please stay here. Tell Ashan not to say what has happened unless he has to."

Her father gazed at her. "Louisa . . ."

"Really, Dad, I'd rather you stayed here."

The inspector drove them to the mortuary. There, they waited in an anteroom while the body was being laid out in a small chapel of rest. A feeling of terrible anticipation flooded through Louisa, and then horror at the awful randomness of sudden events that could change your life forever. She felt frightened, though surely the most frightening thing had already happened. Surely nothing could ever frighten her again. There would be no fear, just an endless straight line through life with no bumps and thumps, no twists and turns. Nothing. A life without Elliot.

Just before they were asked to go in, Louisa's heart pumped so hard she felt as if it was about to burst from her chest. Then, as she went in, she saw Elliot laid out on a trolley with a sheet covering his body but not his face. She heard Margo gasp and she froze as the shock hit her in the stomach, lodging like a rock behind her ribs. How could she bear to look at her husband's lifeless face?

After a few moments, she gathered her courage and took a few steps toward him. She glanced at his face. It looked all wrong, doughy and gray. Her breath caught but she forced herself to touch his forehead. It was unmarked, but when she pulled down the sheet a little she saw his neck had been lacerated and blood was congealed all around the wound. She felt a rush of heat and an intense burst of nausea. She closed her eyes, willing herself to hold on. When it passed, she looked at him again but she didn't have the means to process the pain. To see him destroyed like this when he had been so whole, so handsome, so alive. How did people cope?

"Tell me, Elliot," she whispered. "For Christ's sake, tell me this is a dream." She twisted back to look at the inspector. "How? How is this even possible?"

105

"He hit a tree at the side of the road. We can only assume he was driving too fast."

"Elliot was an expert driver."

The officer shifted from one foot to the other.

"I . . . I need to sit down," Louisa said.

The man pulled up a chair and placed it beside the body. She sat down and bent forward, resting her head on the edge of the trolley. Margo was standing beside her and Louisa could feel her sister-in-law stiffen.

"I'll have to leave you," Margo said with a catch in her voice. "I'm sorry, I can't . . . I think I need some air."

Louisa nodded then heard Margo run to the door.

As the inspector and Margo left the room, Louisa closed her eyes. How could this be happening? One moment Elliot was Elliot — and now he was this. In the unnatural silence of the room she gulped back a sob and covered the awful sight of his neck with the sheet again. Now she understood why the inspector had wanted her to wait.

She gazed at Elliot's face once more. She'd never forget the image for as long as she lived. And the way, despite his curling dark hair looking just as it usually did, he seemed like an imposter and the entire room felt as if it were a film set. There was nothing real about it. Nothing. She longed for him to open his eyes so she might see him alive one last time, so she could say a proper goodbye. But of course, he could not. He never would again. It was an impossible thought. Then she stood and wiped a smear of grease from his forehead and stroked back his hair.

"Oh, my darling," she said. "How am I to go on living without you?"

And as she stared at him something pulled at her, something she'd never felt before. She saw herself standing right at the edge of a well, knowing she would be dragged inexorably into its depths. Struggle was pointless.

Louisa didn't sleep though Margo stayed with her. All night, images of Elliot tormented her. The contrast between his living self, so full of energy, and his lifeless body was too much to absorb. She kept expecting him to suddenly sit up and say it had just been a joke. *There you are, Lou, fooled you. Ha ha ha!* She felt locked up inside herself and even though she wanted to cry, it was as if a perpetual lump had stopped up her throat. The tears wouldn't come, nor would anything else; just a horrible feeling of blank disbelief and a loveless life opening out before her.

The inspector had promised to return at ten o'clock in the morning to give them the full details of what had happened. Until then Louisa had to go through the motions. Wash. Get dressed. Brush hair. Drink coffee. Margo, meanwhile, was in floods of tears and apologizing constantly for them. Apart from Margo's sobs, the house was strangely silent, as if the bricks and mortar had somehow absorbed the shock and were only just about holding the place together. The servants, always lightfooted, were soundless, gently padding about, and even the cook, who was prone to raising his voice, kept his words to a minimum. The news had spread around the party after all, the evening before — bad news traveled fast — but Ashan and her father had managed to swiftly send the guests on their way.

When Margo telephoned Irene in Colombo just after dawn, her mother had been utterly hysterical. Neither of the younger women could explain why they had waited until morning, but it was as if they had both needed to assimilate the death a little bit more before having to deal with Irene. They didn't know when she would come, or even if she would come, she was in such a shocked state.

Jonathan had stayed the night and now was full of comfort and practical assistance. Quite early on, the doorbell began to ring with people wanting to inquire after them and to offer their condolences. Although Jonathan suggested seeing them in her place, Louisa needed to take care of this herself, but she did ask him to sit with her. Then she went through the motions, serving tea, nodding politely at her visitors' kind words while staring past them at the windows, where she watched the clouds slip over the sun. Mr. Bashar, the librarian, came, as did Janesha from the grocery store, plus less welcome visitors, such as the chief flower arranger at the church, Elspeth Markham, who was something of a snob and a gossip. Louisa managed to find words to answer their questions. *How are you coping, my dear?* Fine, thanks. *If there's anything I can do.* I'll let you know, of course. *If you need any help, anything at all.* She just thanked them and asked them how they and their families were, listening to their voices but not hearing the words. And all the time it was as if she wasn't even there. In her mind she was with Elliot, wherever he had gone. That pale, bloodied body was not him. She wanted the real Elliot, and could not comprehend she would never feel his touch again.

The constant stream of visitors was beginning to wear her out so eventually she let her father take over and, detached from the reality of Elliot's death, she went into the garden with a large gin, bothering with the tonic but not with the ice. Who cared if it was lukewarm? It was the alcohol she craved. Only alcohol would allow this almost catatonic state to continue. Only alcohol could stem whatever might be edging closer. She thought vaguely about a funeral. But it seemed a shadowy, unlikely sort of thing, quite unlike the parties she was fond of throwing. Unable to cry, she judged herself for her lack of feeling. Wasn't she supposed to weep and wail, fall into a faint, rail at God, collapse into a sobbing heap? Wasn't she supposed to do something? Anything? She felt hungry but at the same time it was as if she and her body had parted company; it was a hunger that could never be assuaged by food. All her attention was focused on one single question: how could the world go on as normal? How could people go about their daily lives, complaining about this or that, when all that mattered was life itself?

Just after ten, when the inspector arrived

with the local doctor, Louisa felt herself growing inexplicably hot, her palms sweating as she struggled to suppress a rising sense of panic.

Margo showed the two men into the dining room while Jonathan continued to receive their well-wishers' condolences in the living room. Margo had just come off the phone to her mother again. Elliot had been the apple of Irene's eye, her darling boy, the one positive in what had turned into a somewhat disappointing life. Louisa shot Margo a commiserating look and her sister-in-law gave her a wan smile.

The two women sat together on the sofa opposite the officials.

"I suppose you'd better tell us," Margo said.

"Well, as you know, there are bends on the road to Colombo. Mr. Reeve crossed the bridge over the inlet to Rathgama Lake, and soon after a fisherman spotted the car coming around at speed, then it veered off the road and crashed into the tree. He may have swerved to avoid an elephant or a bullock cart. The witness wasn't sure about that, but he raised the alarm. Unfortunately, by the time help arrived it was too late. I'm so sorry. We haven't yet been able to establish whose car he was driving, but there was no passenger in the car with him."

Louisa bent her head for a moment and then looked up again. "But why was he driving somebody else's car? Can you tell me that?"

## 11

A couple of days later the funeral had already taken place. You couldn't hang about in the heat of the tropics; the bodies went off too quickly. In a kind of trance Louisa had managed to organize everything, from the order of service to the floral tributes of scarlet hibiscus, while Margo had been the one to inform Elliot's friends on the plantations and in Colombo. Irene had wept copiously, while Harold had remained stoic, intent on supporting his wife. Louisa had watched him putting an arm around Irene, murmuring in her ear, trying to make something that could never be all right, all right. He wore a constant look of resignation, and kept polishing his glasses with his handkerchief, as if that might wipe away the pain he was so hopelessly attempting to disguise. Both Margo and Louisa had remained dry-eyed. At the end of the service, as they stood with Jonathan in the church doorway, they shook hands with friends and accepted their sympathy.

The turnout was on a grand scale. Sudden, premature death would do that, Louisa thought, whoever had died. But the truth was that Elliot had been popular; with such a winning smile and easy manner, people were drawn to him. Louisa recalled the times when Elliot's eternal optimism had been a bit tiring and then immediately felt guilty to have thought it, especially today.

The only notable absence was Elliot's sailing partner, Jeremy Pike. She had always thought he had valued Elliot's friendship, and they had spent so much time together. At least Leo McNairn from the cinnamon plantation had come. He held her hands in both his large ones and looked into her eyes. The compassion in them shook her.

"I am so terribly sorry for your loss," was all he said and, though she struggled to maintain the mask of calm dignity, she felt her tears welling up. Not here, she said to herself. Not in front of everyone. He moved away and by the time Louisa had thanked everyone, she felt exhausted.

Back home, when the truth of what had happened finally punched her in the chest, she phoned Gwen at the tea plantation. She needed to confide in someone, and yet she didn't want to speak to anyone here in Galle. In a halting voice, she told Gwen in more detail what had happened to Elliot and, though it was hard to say the words, it did make them feel more real.

"If it would help," Gwen said, "you'd be welcome to spend a bit of time here. We're in a very peaceful spot, and it might save you from having to face people while you're feeling so raw."

"That's very kind. Can I think about it and let you know?"

"Of course. I am so very sorry."

Louisa gulped back a sob and got off the phone. The raw pain of losing Julia had never gone away. Never would. And now this too. And that was when she began to cry. Everyone had been so kind, but she'd been so determined not to believe the evidence of her own eyes that it was only now, when she understood he wouldn't be coming home anymore, that she allowed herself to feel it. She went to her bedroom, drew the curtains and curled up on her bed, hugging her pillow and sobbing until her eyes felt swollen and her face was puffy. She cried for her own loss, but she also cried for Elliot himself. To be cut off so young, deprived now of ever having the chance to be a father. Nothing about this was fair. And when she was finally silent, all emotion spent, it was then she heard his voice. Saw him talking, laughing, making love. See. Not dead. Not dead at all.

The world she now inhabited shocked her, as did the fact she could somehow, inexplicably, still be alive while he was not, and so she tried to talk to him. But he was gone again and his absence was something so big, so terrifying, she could not comprehend it. How was it possible to be and then not to be? But strangely, the absence was not an empty space. It was full of images and memories and the feelings attached to those, as well as the feelings that sprang from knowing there would be no more memories. She spoke to him out loud. *Where are you, Elliot? Where have you gone?* But there was no answer. And when she asked him why he'd lied about going sailing when he was really going to Colombo, and driving somebody else's car too, the silence curdled inside her. And in that silence, she imagined awful things.

# 12

The transfer of the proceeds from the sale of Louisa's shares — a considerable sum — to Elliot's own account had been completed several days before he died. And now, just a fortnight after his death, Louisa had a meeting with her accountant and the solicitor who had drawn up Elliot's will. Of course, she knew the contents already, but the process had to be endured and it would be crucial to quickly pick up the financial reins of her new life.

The solicitor was a bright Sinhalese called Silva, the nephew of their old family solicitor, now retired. A slight and serious-looking man, he was young but seemed very keen. She had given him permission to visit the bank in Colombo on her behalf and bring back statements summarizing how much remained in her own account and in Elliot's, so she'd know where she stood. Usually she would have had to go to the bank herself but, under the circumstances, the bank manager, an old family friend, had agreed to release the statements.

Their accountant, Bob Withington, was someone they'd known for years, and now the three sat together in what had been Elliot's study. It had seemed a good idea at the time but, surrounded by Elliot's things, Louisa wished she'd taken up their first suggestion of convening the meeting in Colombo.

Once the will had been read, Margo had coffee brought in and the two men exchanged pleasantries. Basically, Elliot had left everything to Louisa, minus the balance of a separate deposit account, which was to go to Leo McNairn.

"It's just a trifling sum, but do you know why your husband might have wanted to leave money to this particular beneficiary?" the accountant asked.

"I have no idea. He runs a plantation called Cinnamon Hills. Elliot had shares in the business there, so maybe he intended buying more?"

"I didn't realize that," Silva said. "Do you know where the share certificates are?"

"Surely he lodged them with you?"

"I'm afraid not."

"Well, they're probably here somewhere."

She pointed at a mahogany filing cabinet. "I'll make time to go through that soon."

"Now, Mrs. Reeve — Louisa," the accountant was saying. "The bad news is your husband's main account was virtually empty."

She frowned. "It can't have been. I had only recently transferred a large sum to him."

"Yes, I see the transaction here."

"Half of that money was to pay off the outstanding sum for acquiring the Print House, so I'm not surprised that's gone. I'm expecting the deeds in the post any day. But the other half should still be in there."

He shook his head.

"So where did the money go?"

"It seems your husband withdrew it in cash."

"Then it must be somewhere here." She waved vaguely at the room. "Though I don't know why he would have taken it out so soon."

"There was also a legally binding contract for a loan he had taken out but not paid back," the solicitor said.

"I don't understand."

"He had borrowed money from the bank and the sum is still owing. It will have to come out of his estate."

Louisa was again surprised and fought the urge to simply leave the room. She'd had no idea Elliot owed more money. He'd only ever admitted to a few gambling debts.

"Are you all right, Mrs. Reeve?" Withington said.

No, she thought, I am not. Her mind raced and, as she imagined Elliot's hand caressing her hair, his lips moving over her skin, she felt a tremor.

Irene and Harold had returned to Colombo, but Margo was staying on to support Louisa, though Louisa secretly thought it was because her sister-in-law found it less painful dealing with her than her mother. Louisa thought about Harold, with his thinning hair and toothbrush mustache. His defeated expression didn't prevent him from somehow managing to remain kind. He must have been handsome once, like Elliot, but now he was a faded man, and Louisa felt a sense of pity whenever she met him. His constant attempts to soften his wife's sharp comments often fell on deaf ears, but it didn't stop him from trying. That he loved Irene, for all her faults, was never in doubt. Louisa felt sure he was the reason Margo and Elliot were as decent as they were. But poor Margo, who had cried a great deal at first, now seemed to have settled into a controlled kind of practicality. Louisa hoped she wasn't bottling up her feelings.

As it happened, Margo had waited in the garden while Louisa had been with the solicitor and accountant. Then, after they left, Louisa went straight outside to join her.

"Heavens!" Margo said. "You look pale."

"Could you get me a brandy?"

While Margo went indoors Louisa sat and blankly watched the wind rustling the leaves overhead, thinking over what she had been told. A strong scent of jasmine drifted across from the hedge and the canna lilies glowed bright yellow and red.

Margo came back and passed a glass to Louisa who sipped the liquid, grateful for its soothing amber warmth heating up her insides. She felt uncertain, wanting to talk to Margo, but at the same time feeling disloyal to Elliot. There had to be good reasons why he'd withdrawn the money, why he'd taken out a loan, and why he hadn't lodged the plantation shares with the solicitor, as you would normally do. But whatever the reasons were, he hadn't in-volved her. In the end, she decided to tell Margo what had happened.

"There's probably a simple answer, but I need your help."

121

"Anything."

"It seems Elliot emptied his entire account before he died. I need to search his study for the cash."

"Gosh. Very well. I'll help you look."

"Not only that, I also need to find his share certificates for Cinnamon Hills. I thought the solicitor would have them but he knew nothing about it, so they must be here too."

Once back in the study, Louisa opened the safe and found it empty but for the usual few notes and some of her jewelry. Then she glanced around. Elliot's study wasn't tidy. His desk was strewn with papers and letters, so while Margo examined those, Louisa began the laborious task of plowing through his filing cabinet. She found two of the drawers held duplicates of transactions at their gem polishing and cutting center and only the top drawer contained anything personal. She had expected to find a life insurance policy but, so far, there was none. She did find some old letters from Irene but no share certificates and no cash. There were several cardboard storage boxes on one of the shelves so they divided them between them and began trawling through the contents, but found nothing there either, except

122

more polishing and cutting records.

Margo tried all the drawers of the desk, but again there was nothing of note. "But where else might he have secreted the share certificates?" she said.

"I'm sorry to ask, but do you think you'd be able to check his chest of drawers in our bedroom? I haven't felt ready to touch his personal things yet."

While Margo was gone, Louisa attempted to tidy up the mess they'd made. If Margo found nothing the only place left was his office at Hardcastle Gems, though as far as she knew Elliot had never kept anything personal, or domestic, there. But where had the money gone? She was just on the point of coming to the conclusion that everything must be in the bedroom when Margo came back in shaking her head and looking drawn.

"Gosh, that felt awful," she said.

"I shouldn't have asked you to do it."

"It's okay."

Louisa slumped down in Elliot's desk chair.

"Come on, Lou. Don't despair. The money will be somewhere, don't worry. I'm sure we'll find it, and the certificates too."

Louisa glanced up. "I just wish he'd talked to me about what was going on and explained where everything was."

There was a short silence.

"What is it?" Louisa asked when she noticed Margo was frowning and looking a bit uncomfortable.

"I'm sorry about the timing of this, but I need to go back to Colombo tomorrow. My father called earlier. Mother isn't doing too well and he can't cope with her on his own. He thinks she needs me."

"I understand."

"I'm sorry. But I'll be back as soon as Mum settles down."

Louisa shook her head. "Take however long you need. I'll be fine. My most pressing concern right now is that I need to find either the money, or the share certificates. I inherit, of course, but first the repayment of the loan will have to come out of Elliot's estate: in other words, out of the cash, investments, property or possessions he left behind."

"A loan?"

"I'm afraid so. He has a significant debt at the bank. God only knows what my father will say."

"And you knew nothing about it?"

"God, no! Nothing."

Then Ashan, with a concerned look on his face, came in to whisper to Louisa that the police inspector wanted to speak with her. She sighed and followed him into the living room.

# 13

There was only one thing for it and so the next day — a beautiful sunny morning soon after Margo had left at the crack of dawn for Colombo — Louisa set off from Galle Fort in their Triumph Dolomite to drive to Cinnamon Hills. She hoped to be able to recall the route from the time Elliot had taken her there.

As she drove she went over the inspector's news. Apparently, the car Elliot had been driving had belonged to Elliot's sailing partner, Jeremy Pike, who he was supposed to have been out sailing with on the day he died. The inspector didn't know why Elliot had been driving that car, but it had definitely belonged to Pike. This had been confirmed by Pike's housekeeper — he himself was away on business. It didn't make sense to Louisa. If Elliot had wanted to go to Colombo, why hadn't he just said so? And why hadn't he taken their own car?

She carried on thinking as she followed the road.

Luckily there had been no shipment of rubber so there was just the heavy salty air to contend with, and as she drove around the crescent of Galle Bay, passing its small deserted islands, she glanced out at the larger boats anchored at the southern end of Rumassala Hill. After several miles of coastal road, she turned off to the left and began the climb up to the house at the top with the wonderful views. It was a potholed driveway, more of a track than a road, and she hoped not to get into difficulty.

She wound down her window and, enjoying the rich cinnamon-scented air and the sweet fragrance of orchids and rhododendrons, couldn't deny the seductive pull of the place. She heard voices, a shout, maybe that of a child, and then an adult replying, but she carried on past. It had nothing to do with her.

A little farther on, she gasped as searing emptiness pulled at her edges. How would she find a reason to get up, to live, to breathe? And still the living and breathing went on anyway, automatically, without her say-so. It should be me and Elliot, she thought, not just me on my own and now, instead of joy, loneliness and fear twisted inside her. If someone as young and healthy as Elliot could die, then how fragile was her world? How fragile was life itself?

For a moment she considered turning back, but she had to find out if Elliot's share certificates were kept here at the plantation. She felt sure they must be — after all they hadn't been at his work office either, so there was nowhere else to look. If she could settle that one question maybe the others wouldn't feel so bad. And yet the reason Elliot hadn't mentioned he was going to Colombo on the day he died still perplexed her. Surely, he'd have no cause to hide that?

At the top of the drive, she pulled up and noticed Leo McNairn's motorbike parked in the same place it had been before. She felt a momentary doubt, but as she stepped out of the car and he appeared in the doorway, she reminded herself he had come to Elliot's funeral and been kind.

"Mrs. Reeve," he said, and she noticed the flecks of lighter color in his red hair. "How are you?"

She shrugged. "Well, you know . . . but do please call me Louisa."

"I'm so sorry about your husband. It must be terribly hard for you. Is there anything I can do?"

She hesitated for a moment. "There is. I

need to ask you a question."

He smiled and there was genuine warmth in his eyes. "Of course. But come inside. It's too humid to talk out here."

They went up a staircase and into a living room, and then through a metal door to a veranda. It had a dark wooden-beamed roof, walls painted in ochre, a floor tiled in terracotta, and it overlooked a jungle of palm trees. Hanging from the roof were baskets of pale green ferns, and the view beyond them was startling.

"It's beautiful," she said, staring down the hill over treetops to the bay of clear blue water.

He indicated she should sit.

A faded chaise longue was pushed to one end of the veranda, along with several chairs and a low coffee table covered in books. After Leo called the houseboy to clear the table and bring some tea, they made themselves comfortable in two worn rattan armchairs.

"Too damn close when there is no breeze."

"But it can't always be this bad? Up here, I mean."

He nodded. "You're right. It's all down to the time of day. So much better for the workers just before nightfall and soon after sunrise. It's pleasantest then and perhaps more importantly, most productive."

She twisted her head for a moment to listen to the noise coming from the uncleared vegetation behind the house.

"Monkeys," he said, seeing her look. "North of here is still all jungle."

She plumped up a cushion and waved an arm across the view to the sea. "You must love it here."

"I do, though at first I was reluctant to take it on."

"Why was that?"

He puckered his chin and gave a slight shake of his head. "It's a huge commitment."

"But this view is very soothing, don't you think?"

She glanced at his handsome tanned face with dark eyes that still seemed to reflect something of the sky. Dressed casually in shorts and an old threadbare shirt, he wasn't a man who cared about his appearance, or who wasted words, and as they sat in silence for a few moments she became aware of conflicting feelings. He was someone who was impossible to ignore, and she was surprised by how much she wanted to soak up the unexpected comfort she felt in his presence. It had been the same at the funeral, when his condolences had almost made her cry.

The boy arrived and the noise of rattling teacups broke the silence.

Leo poured, then leaning back in his chair with his arms resting on the sides, he gazed at her. "So? Tell me. What can I do for you?"

She took a breath, wondering how much to say, and noticed his eyes, fixed intently on her, as he waited.

"The thing is," she said. "Well, it's a bit awkward, but I wondered if Elliot's share certificates are here. I can't seem to lay my hands on them."

"Share certificates?"

"Yes. I'm awfully sorry, but I think I'm going to have to sell."

He frowned.

"I'm talking about Elliot's share certificates in the plantation. He owns shares here, doesn't he?"

Leo shook his head and, surprised by the hesitancy in him, she watched as he glanced around the veranda and then stared at the ground before looking at her. "I don't understand, I —"

She interrupted. "Elliot told me about them. It's why he used to come here, isn't it? For planning meetings. To get the plantation back on its feet."

"I'm so sorry, Louisa, but Elliot has never

owned shares here."

Stunned by this wholly unexpected news, she couldn't take in his words. "What do you mean?"

He looked as confused as she felt and, scratching his chin, frowned.

Not knowing how to behave in these circumstances she hoped at least to hide her shock, but she felt so disoriented that everything seemed to be spinning. Elliot had told her about the shares. Had explained it all to her. When her hands began trembling in her lap she got herself to her feet and went to lean on the railings, pressing her palms down hard on the wood.

She swallowed and attempted to speak but the words failed to come out, only a strangled sound halfway between a moan and a cough. She felt as if all the parts of her had become separated from each other, and she had no idea how to put herself together again. Like Humpty Dumpty, she thought. At least he'd had all the king's horses and all the king's men. She turned to face Leo.

"That can't be right. Are you sure?"

"I'm afraid so. I own the plantation outright. There are no shares."

She remained where she was for a few moments. "He has left you some money in a deposit account. Why would he leave you money?"

He glanced away before replying, and she got the distinct impression he had wanted to say something but had then thought better of it. Now the atmosphere between them had changed — had somehow become more charged.

"I don't know," was all he said.

She frowned. "I don't understand any of this. Why would he come here so often then? Or was he even really here? Why would he tell me he had shares?"

Leo shook his head.

In the short silence that followed she stared at her feet. "Well, I should be going. The money's not much but I'll see you get it."

His replies hadn't helped Louisa understand where Elliot had really been when he'd said he was at Cinnamon Hills, and she longed to know why he had lied to her. Elliot's sudden death had marked her and now, to find out the man she had loved so much, who she would have trusted with her life, had been lying to her — and not just about going sailing. She felt a rush of heat and then a sense of rising panic. If she could not believe in what she thought they'd had, if she could not believe in the truth of the past, then what *could* she believe in?

She glanced at him. "Where is your cousin?"

"She lives in the old bungalow halfway down the hill. She's an artist." He got to his feet. "Louisa, I'm sorry."

She took a deep breath but didn't speak.

He moved a step away. "Come on, I'll show you out, but please" — and he turned to gaze at her — "do let me know if there's anything I can do."

She followed him and at the bottom of the stairs he held out his hand.

After shaking it, she took one last look at him then sat in her car and began the drive down. After a few minutes, she pulled up and left the car, wanting to take a closer look at the plantation. Treading carefully, she followed a path winding between the cinnamon trees, or bushes as they appeared to be, and soon found herself not quite halfway down the hill. A trail of ferocious-looking ants crossed her path and a striped squirrel raced up one of the trees. Startled by a loud crash she glanced around. She couldn't see what had made the noise but imagined it must be one of the elephants routinely used to clear land by uprooting trees and then moving the logs. She stood still for a moment. As a drift of butterflies passed overhead, the smell of the trees and the shady magic of the place lifted her mood a little. There was such a sense of timelessness here, otherworldliness even; if not exactly lessening her worries it made her feel strangely peaceful. But then, in a small clearing, she stumbled across a red-haired woman leaning against the trunk of a huge tree; her eyes were closed and from her blotchy complexion she looked as if she had been crying.

Louisa wished for invisibility and didn't know whether to tiptoe away or to speak. The woman was obviously distressed — she didn't look as if she'd even brushed what was very wild hair and her clothes seemed thrown together. Louisa wasn't sure she was even dressed in day clothes — she wore a kind of robe that might have been a dressing gown.

"Is there anything I can do?" Louisa said as she took a step forward.

The woman's eyes flew open. "Who are you?"

"Louisa Reeve."

The woman stared at her feet.

"You must be Leo's cousin. What a wonderful place to live. You are —"

But the woman turned on her heels and began threading her way through the trees and away from the clearing. As Louisa returned to her car a flock of at least twenty bright green parakeets with red beaks and rose-red collars fluttered from one tree to the next. Consumed by such a muddle of emotions, she watched them. And, although she wondered why the woman had been so distressed in such idyllic surroundings, she felt again that sensation of bittersweetness. Why? What was it about the place that had gotten under her skin? She dwelt on what Leo had said: Elliot had no shares. *No shares.* But was Leo telling the truth and, if not, how would she ever find out?

# 14

It was Elliot who had given structure to her life, Elliot who had given it meaning. She still imagined his sleeping body lying beside her, and when she opened her eyes in the morning and her gaze settled on his empty side of the bed, there was always a painful shiver of shock that he was gone. Since his death there had been times when Louisa simply forgot to breathe and she would find herself suddenly gasping for air. Breathe, she would command herself, breathe. But that didn't help and she'd double over after a few minutes clutching her tight chest and sucking at air, as if sucking at life itself. Even if he had lied about the shares, surely there must have been a sound reason.

As her thoughts spiralled, she longed to be with someone who had gone through a loss and come out the other side. While her father was comforting to be around, and she knew he understood, he rarely spoke of

Louisa's mother's death. What she needed was another woman who had felt the same rising panic, the same sleepless nights, the same painful disconnection. Louisa didn't know what she wanted to say exactly — just that she wanted the relief of being able to talk. Gwen had not lost her husband, but she had lost a child. One was neither worse nor better than the other. They were different, but Gwen seemed like the one person who might genuinely understand that she felt as if the large stone lodged in her chest would remain there and that her heart would never open again. At that point she called her friend to see if the invitation to visit the tea plantation still stood. Gwen assured her it did and so a few days later Louisa began the long drive to the hilly tea country.

She hadn't driven so far before on her own, and despite Gwen's detailed directions was still a touch unsure of the route, but right now anything was better than staying at home. After leaving Galle she drove through the rainforest and noticed how heavily the area was being logged. Then she passed alongside the Gin Ganga River where gaggles of barely dressed children played at rolling stones in front of a large police station, but when she reached the crossing point, she hesitated. The narrow bridge over the river was supported by concrete pillars, but at its sides had only some flimsy-looking steel railings.

When her hands began to tremble she stopped the car and got out. She gazed down into the rushing river and then looked up at air shimmering with flying creatures and, hearing the noises of animals in the undergrowth, she took deep breaths. Birds were screeching overhead and apart from several pariah dogs which lay dozily at the edges of the road, the whole place was teeming with life. Yet when she thought of driving again, fear whipped through her, and she prayed for the courage to continue the journey.

As she negotiated the bridge she gripped the steering wheel, but all went well and she drove on, bypassing several rubber estates, to the point where she turned off on to a more minor road, just past a temple. Glancing out, she saw a group of yellow-robed monks sitting on a step, one of them smoking some kind of pipe. A little later, she turned off again and eventually, after crossing a second river, started climbing through a densely forested region. There the road wound up a mountain pass. Though Gwen had warned her the drive was grueling and would take the better part of a day, she had to admit to a feeling of excitement, despite the tiredness and hunger. It was all so new and she found, to her surprise, she was enjoying it. She pulled up just after another temple, which had to be about the halfway point, and decided to take a break and eat the sandwiches Camille had prepared for her.

While she ate, a group of purple-faced monkeys eyed her silently, and as the enormity of what she was doing fizzed through her, she laughed. If only Elliot could see her now.

When she had finished she drove on, climbing the many hills on the way to Hatton. Once she had taken another turning, she eventually arrived at the top of the hill overlooking the Hooper tea plantation, and the view took her breath away. A row of tulip trees lined the driveway below her, and she could see the plantation house was built in an L shape. She stopped the car to get out and gaze down at the shimmering lake. The place was truly gorgeous and she felt a slight stirring of hope. Perhaps this really was the right place to be?

At the bottom of the drive she parked and as she got out of the car Gwen came running out of the house in an instant, ringlets flying in every direction.

"Louisa, I am so happy you made it. Was the drive absolutely awful? You must be exhausted."

Louisa shook her head. "I was surprised. I didn't get lost at all."

"Well, leave your case. One of the house-boys will bring it in. Let me take you through to the veranda at the back. We'll have a long cool drink brought out."

They walked into the house and out again through some elegant French windows. And, blinking in the brightness, Louisa remarked at the buzzing and chirping filling the air.

"It really feels wildly alive out here."

"It always does, especially in the morning, or late in the day like now."

Their drinks arrived and Louisa was grateful for the cool feel of the glass beneath her hands.

"You'll want a rest and maybe to freshen up, but I thought we could have a quiet chat for a few minutes."

Louisa gazed down at flower-filled gardens sloping down to the lake in three terraces, with paths, steps and benches placed between them, and the lake itself was the most gorgeous turquoise color.

"So," Gwen was saying. "How are you

coping? I am so terribly sorry for what has happened. You must be devastated."

"It's not easy. And, although my father is good to have around, my sister-in-law has gone back to her parents' in Colombo. And nobody else really knows what to say to me."

"It was similar after Liyoni died. Everyone tiptoed around me until I felt like screaming."

"How did you cope?"

"In some ways, it's hard to remember the early days. I felt as if my world had come to an end, but then it became a case of putting one foot in front of the other and doing whatever there was to do next. It wasn't long ago but it has become easier."

"I'm scared I'll never feel normal again."

"Well, you won't feel the way you did before. It will have changed you. It's more a case of working out who you are now and getting used to that."

"I find myself crying at impossible moments."

"I know. Me too."

"Do you still?"

Gwen nodded. "And I still feel such anger."

Louisa nodded. "It ambushes me when I least expect it and is so strong I can literally shake."

"I felt my world had ended, and it had. I didn't feel alive: I felt broken. Truly. Broken."

"Thank you for being so honest," Louisa said. "I'm so glad I came."

"I hope it will help. At the very least it will pass a few days. If you can just keep going, keep living, keep caring, you will find your heart does ease."

They sat in silence for a few moments.

"I'm afraid we have a visitor for supper tonight. I had hoped it would just be the three of us, but Savi Ravasinghe has arrived to see Laurence on a plantation matter on behalf of his wife, my cousin Fran. She is a shareholder, you see, but you'll like Savi. He's an artist and very kind. Can you tolerate that?"

"Yes, of course."

"Because you could have a tray in your room, if you prefer?"

"No. It will do me good. I've been so little in company since Elliot died."

"Well, Savi is a lovely man. You can talk to him about anything. Come on, let me show you your room."

They went indoors and up a sweeping staircase, and then along a corridor to the very end. Gwen flung open the door to a room with windows in both exterior walls.

"I love this room because it's so airy. Will it do? The bathroom is next door. Dinner is at eight."

Louisa looked around her. "Thank you. It's absolutely lovely."

After Gwen had left, Louisa went to the window overlooking the gardens and part of the lake and leaned out to breathe the air. Rising up around the lake luminous tea bushes grew in symmetrical rows, and the women tea-pickers wore brightly colored saris. A riot of pink, green, purple and blue. There was such a feeling of calm about it all, Louisa relaxed. It was a magical place, and she already felt as if the weight in her chest had lightened — for a few minutes she had actually forgotten Elliot.

It didn't last. As she lay on the bed to rest she felt torn between grief at his loss and being burdened by his lies. The worst thing was the fear that after twelve years she didn't know who Elliot had really been. What if the love at the heart of her marriage had not been the love she had imagined?

She listened to the sounds of the birds and saw the sky darken. It was time to dress for dinner and put on a mask of cheerfulness. Gwen wouldn't expect it, but something within Louisa meant she knew it was what she would, nevertheless, do. She decided on a navy dress, nipped in at the waist and with a wide belt, and after she had brushed her blond curls she felt a little better.

As she entered the drawing room for drinks before supper she saw a bank of tall windows running across an entire wall. Their shutters had been left half open so she could glimpse the moon lighting the garden beyond. This room fronted the shining, silvery lake. The walls were painted in a soft blue-green and the whole place felt cool, with comfy-looking armchairs, and two pale sofas piled high with embroidered cushions depicting birds, elephants and exotic flowers. A leopard skin was draped across the back of one of the sofas.

"Come and sit down with Savi," Gwen said as she stood to greet Louisa.

An elegant Sinhalese man rose at the same time. He had longish hair, a slightly hooked nose and smiling caramel eyes with heavy brows. He held out his hand. "You must be Louisa. I'm Savi Ravasinghe."

"Lovely to meet you," she said as she shook his hand.

"Will you sit?" he said.

"Yes, sit with Savi," Gwen said. "I need to check that Ayah is with the baby. Laurence will be down in a minute. Are you happy with Sinhalese food, Louisa?"

"Oh, perfectly. Thank you."

"So," Savi said as they seated themselves. "Tell me about you."

She took a quick breath. It was awkward meeting new people. "I don't know what you already know."

"I know you have only recently lost your husband. I'm so sorry. Do you mind me mentioning it?"

"Actually, I prefer it."

He smiled. "That I understand. You know Gwen's little girl died?"

"I do. I think that's why she invited me here."

"And she is a very sympathetic woman. My wife thinks the world of her."

"Where is your wife?"

"She has business interests in England and we live most of the year there, but I like to come back home from time to time and spend a few months here. I have an apartment in Colombo in Cinnamon Gardens. My wife, Fran, often comes too, but this time she didn't."

It was unusual nowadays in Ceylon to come across a mixed marriage, but Louisa knew it had once been perfectly normal at a time when Englishmen had been in short supply.

"Have you faced many difficulties?" she asked. "You and your wife, I mean."

"More so in England, to be honest." He smiled. "But most people here tolerate us."

"I'm glad."

"You live in Galle, I hear."

"I was born there and wouldn't swap it for the world, though it's lovely here, of course. And recently I had cause to go to a cinnamon plantation. I couldn't help falling in love with it."

"I knew someone who went to live on a cinnamon plantation not too far from Galle, or at least that was the rumor. She was a well-known artist in Colombo and then she simply upped and disappeared. I'm just trying to recall her name."

"Oh?"

He frowned. "It was an unusual name but I just can't remember it."

Louisa felt surprised. "Did she have red hair?"

"Yes! You don't know her, do you?"

She shook her head. "I don't know her, but I think I may have met her just the once and then only very briefly."

"Small world."

"Do you know why she left Colombo?"

"I don't think anybody really knew. I've spotted some of her apparently new canvases for sale from time to time so she must still be painting."

"But nobody ever sees her?"

"No. Ah look, here is Laurence."

Louisa nodded, and watched Gwen's tall husband approach. He was broad-backed with short light-brown hair flecked with gray at the temples, and he wore a wide smile on his face. She thought of the last time she'd seen him, at their Christmas party, when everything had seemed all set to be wonderful. And suddenly it was as if a cold wind swept through her heart. How swiftly life could change. How drastically it could all be gone.

# 15

When Louisa woke the next morning, soon after dawn, she rose immediately and enjoyed gazing out of the window at the still lake. A pearly mist lay over the water and the air felt fresh and pure. It will be a good day, she told herself. It will be a good day. Gwen's son Hugh was due back from school in Nuwara Eliya and they were all set to have a picnic beside the lake, although Mr. Ravasinghe was leaving first thing. Before going down to breakfast, she washed and dressed in a pale green muslin dress with short sleeves, and then tied up her hair.

Laurence was wearing shorts and already standing at the breakfast table with a plate in his hand when Louisa entered the dining room.

"Morning. Would you like to join me on the veranda?" he said.

She glanced across to where he was pointing at the wide-open French windows.

"Breakfast always tastes better outdoors," he added. "Don't you think?"

She smiled and looked down at the table where a serving dish had been topped with a rounded silver cover.

"Kedgeree," he said. "If you want anything else cooked, just ring the bell. Cook makes a pretty good fist of poached eggs. Tea and coffee will be brought out along with the toast. I'll see you out there."

She spotted a bowl of buffalo-milk curd protected by a square of netting, and baskets of fruit: mangoes, passion fruit, apples and bananas. She helped herself to a bowl of the curd and then drizzled honey over it.

By the time she sat down at the wrought-iron table outside, the mist had burned away. It was turning into a brilliant day, with the sun glittering on the lake and a light breeze to cool the skin. She watched a cloud of brightly colored butterflies floating just above the white lilies growing in earthen pots all along the edge of the veranda.

"I hope you slept well," Laurence said with a smile.

"Very well."

"It's our hill country air."

She nodded and met his eyes. "I suppose it must be. I'm glad to be here. It was kind of Gwen to invite me."

"My condolences about Elliot. We didn't have a chance to speak alone last night."

"No."

He paused before speaking again and she noticed a muscle in his jaw twitch. "You may know that my first wife died," he eventually said.

"Savi Ravasinghe told me. I was sorry to hear it."

"It was a long time ago."

She wondered what had happened and deliberated about asking him. Would it be insensitive? But with Elliot's death still uppermost in her mind she felt she had to ask.

"Do you mind telling me what happened?"

He sighed. "She took her own life."

Louisa gasped. "Oh gosh. I am sorry. I shouldn't have asked."

"As I said, it was a long time ago." He paused again. "Anyway, enough of dwelling on the past. The present is what matters today. And this picnic will be delightful. I'm sure it will do you good."

"I already feel better just being away from home."

"Being in a different environment can take one out of oneself. Even if it is only temporary."

A couple of hours later, when Hugh was

due to arrive home, Gwen and Louisa were in the large sitting room with baby Alice. Gwen asked Louisa if she was happy to hold the baby while she went to settle a few final details of the picnic. At first Louisa felt nervous at the thought but then, as Alice fell asleep in her arms, she watched the fluttering eyelashes and softly stroked the child's rosy cheeks with her fingertips. She bent over to smell the baby's hair and when a feeling of peace washed through her, she felt a sense of gratitude toward Gwen. Holding Alice had silenced the noise in her head. Coming here had been the right thing to do.

A few moments later a tousled-haired boy tore into the room followed by Gwen.

"Say hello to Mrs. Reeve, Hugh."

"Hello Hugh," Louisa said. "Do call me Louisa. Just back from school?"

He nodded.

"And how old are you now?"

He beamed at her and spoke proudly. "I'm ten."

"That is quite an age. And are you looking forward to the picnic?"

"You bet! Can I see Alice?"

"Of course."

He came across and knelt at her feet. "She's very little, isn't she?"

"Do you want to hold her?"

He got to his feet. "No. Mummy says I've got to change now." He grinned at her. "Will you come swimming with me?"

"Oh, I didn't bring a costume."

"I've got a spare one," Gwen said.

Gwen and Louisa remained in the sitting room for another half-hour and then, when Hugh came racing back in, Gwen settled Alice in her Moses basket and called the butler to ask him to carry her down to the lake. After that she collected Laurence from his study and they all made their way down. A couple of houseboys carried the hamper and several bags, along with the rugs. They also extracted three chairs from the boathouse at the edge of the lake. As Laurence, Gwen and Louisa made themselves comfortable on the chairs, they were watched by a pair of long-tailed toque monkeys sitting at the base of a nearby tree.

Gwen was wearing a blue gingham cotton dress with loose sleeves covering her arms down to her wrists, and she now opened a large white sun parasol attached to her chair, designed to protect her delicate complexion.

Hugh ran up to Gwen, who gave him a towel and his bathing suit. Then he went across to the boathouse to change. Louisa watched all this with a feeling of anticipation. It was such a stupendously lovely place and the sky was so blue you couldn't really be sad. She gazed across at where the bright green tea bushes grew and could see the women tea-pickers, or "pluckers" as she now knew they were called. It seemed too hot to be working so hard, though of course it was cooler here than in Galle. A gust of wind whipped a loose strand of hair into her eyes and they watered. As she wiped her eyes and then tucked the curl behind her ear, Gwen leaned over to her.

"Are you all right?"

"It's just the wind."

"Good. When Hugh has changed would you like to use the boathouse? Here are my spare bathing suit and a towel. The bathers were always too big for me but as you're taller they should fit." She passed a bag to Louisa.

"Thank you."

As the wind got up a little more, Louisa stood, letting the warm air blow through her hair. Above the shimmering lake, a cobalt sky stretched across the horizon. She closed her eyes against the intense glare of a yellow sun reflecting off the rippling water, and acknowledged how good it felt to be momentarily released.

By the time she had changed and was approaching the water's edge Hugh and Laurence were already in the lake, splashing each other and shouting.

Gwen came down to the bank. "I need to give Alice her feed now but do join the others. Just watch out for leeches at the edge."

Louisa glanced down and ventured slowly into the water. "It's cool," she said. "How lovely."

"I always find it refreshing," Gwen said, then turned her back to walk across to the boathouse.

Louisa waded in, and despite going deeper was relieved to still be able to feel the rocky bottom. Laurence and Hugh were farther out now and swimming across to a small island. Not being familiar with the lake, she decided to remain in the shallows, and as she slid through the water she enjoyed a wonderful sense of exhilaration. Just feeling weightless with her body moving like this seemed to reconnect her to herself in some way; a simple but vital pleasure. That's what going on living meant. Not just struggling through one day and the next, but fully experiencing what it meant to be alive; she had been missing this more than she realized.

After a while she left the water and stood

in the sunshine, towel-drying her hair. She could see Laurence and Hugh were taking a breather over on the island and Gwen was back in her chair under the sunshade, holding the now sleeping baby in her arms.

Louisa settled down next to her. "That was absolutely marvelous."

"I often swim here with Laurence," Gwen said. "Our daughter loved the water."

"You must miss her terribly."

"I do, but it was complicated. She had a wasting disease."

"I'm so sorry."

"Anyway, it's you we should be talking about now. How are you feeling?"

Louisa pulled a face. "Pretty good today, and all this helps so much but . . . well, you see, I've found out certain things about my husband I didn't previously know."

"Things? Do you want to talk?"

Louisa sighed. "I just don't know what to think. Please don't tell anyone, but the thing is, he lied about owning some shares in a cinnamon plantation."

"Is that so bad?"

"Well, he seemed to spend an awful lot of time there. And now I don't know where he really was. Plus, he had debts I didn't know about. Although he denied it, I'm worried his gambling had gotten out of hand. It's just so awful having to face the fact that I didn't know what he was doing."

"Men do seem to have this ability to compartmentalize their lives."

"Surely not Laurence?"

Gwen shook her head. "It was a long time before I got to the truth about his first wife's death."

"He told me she took her own life."

"And that shows how far he has come. When we were first married, he refused to discuss it. He had bottled it up for so long he didn't know how to unburden himself." She paused. "I don't know, but maybe Elliot had gotten himself into trouble and kept it to himself to protect you."

"Maybe. But lying about having shares, how was that to protect me?"

"I don't know. It is odd."

"And it just leaves me feeling tainted by something I don't understand. I want to grieve over him, and what we have lost, but all this makes it so much harder. Home feels full of ghosts."

"I do understand . . . Look, I'm not sure how to say this, but was he still in love with you?"

"I thought so."

"And you with him?"

Louisa nodded. "Very much so, even after

157

twelve years. Don't get me wrong, he had his faults."

Gwen laughed. "Don't we all!"

They sat in silence for a while, gazing out across the water, Louisa thinking about what Gwen had said. After a while she let it go and allowed herself to simply be present at this beautiful lake, sitting in the sun with a woman who was proving to be a good confidante and friend.

"I'll hold Alice, if you'd like to swim," she eventually said.

"You don't mind?"

"Not at all. Give her to me and go and change."

Gwen stood and Louisa took her place under the sunshade, then adjusted the frilly bonnet Alice was wearing.

Louisa watched Gwen, Laurence and Hugh swim, the three of them bobbing about in the water, splashing each other and laughing. She glanced down at the sleeping baby and then back to the little family in the water. How happy they look, she thought. And though it seemed unlikely, she hoped, once she came through to the other side, she might find such happiness again. The past she couldn't alter, but she couldn't let what had happened shape her entire future, nor could she let Elliot's death be the only thing that defined her. The trick would be finding a way to prevent that. A few moments later, Alice woke up and gazed right into her eyes, with no hint of displeasure that she wasn't waking up on her mother's lap. Louisa helped the little girl sit up and they both watched the others playing in the water.

"Shall we go and see what Mummy and Daddy and Hugh are doing?" she said, then eased herself out of the chair and as she carried Alice down to the lake for a closer view, she hummed to herself.

# 16

Louisa stayed at the tea plantation for a few more days but then felt she needed to be at home after all. To forgive herself for living, when he did not, she decided she must make something of her life. After all, she was the sort of person who needed to be doing something to feel energized, and she still had the Print House to think about. She knew the only way to survive was to put one foot in front of the other until it became second nature. Live through one hour and then another until the day was done. And then do it all over again. Eventually the happiness she had rediscovered at the lake with Gwen would become normal.

She was resting with her feet up in the garden, her secateurs on the table, with Tommy and Bouncer vying for her attention. While she gently fondled Zip's soft ears as he lay on her lap, Camille informed her there was a man to see her.

"Who is it?" she asked.

"I do not know his name, Madame. But I have seen him here before."

She frowned. "Didn't you ask?"

"He just said he wanted to see you."

"Where's Ashan?"

"He is out. He asked me to see to the door."

"Well, I suppose you'd better show him through, but I'm not going inside. You can bring him out here and then would you please get us something cool to drink."

She got up to put away her secateurs, taking care to look out for one of the venomous Russell's vipers, sometimes found in garden sheds. But she was accustomed to being cautious and knew they were fine if left undisturbed. Today she saw no snake.

When she sat down again she straightened her back and then turned as the visitor approached.

The man was small and stocky with dark hair and a swarthy look. She recognized him instantly as the Burgher she'd seen with Elliot in his study during the Christmas party and then again, a few weeks later.

He came up to her and bowed slightly. "Pieter De Vos at your service, Madam."

"Will you sit?" she said and offered him her hand.

The dogs began to growl.

"Hush, boys," she said, and put a hand out to stroke one, but Tommy got to his feet and was backing away. Bouncer and Zip remained by her side. She reached out and stroked Bouncer's head but he gave a warning growl, his ears lowered against his head.

"I do apologize. They can be a little overprotective."

"Not a problem. I have dogs of my own," he said.

He was a serious, softly spoken man, and Louisa had to lean forward to hear properly.

He then sat on a chair a few feet away from her own. A breeze got up in the garden and Louisa watched as the leaves on the trees shivered and small birds shifted on the branches under the great blue sky, and the heat rose from the earth in waves.

"I'm sorry to intrude at such an unfortunate time," he said. "But I thought I should introduce myself."

"Yes, I've seen you with Elliot but we've never actually met, have we?"

He nodded. "I thought it was long overdue."

"It's very kind of you to come."

"Not at all. My pleasure entirely."

She didn't speak again until Camille came out.

"Mint and lime juice?"

He nodded and then gazed at her with a consoling look. "I do hope you are managing. It must be very hard."

She was quiet once more and held her hands together in her lap and glanced around the garden. Usually it was so well maintained but she had been neglecting it. The jasmine had grown wild.

"So," he said, inclining his head as he smiled. "You may already know your husband and I had shared business interests."

"He mentioned something."

"I just wanted you to know there are a few loose ends to be tied up."

"What kind of loose ends?"

"There's no need to go into detail now. Plenty of time for that in due course." He paused. "Your husband was a wonderful man. You must miss him terribly."

"I do."

Louisa wiped her moist hands on her shirt and stared at him as he sipped his drink.

"Well," he said. "It's been a pleasure to meet you properly. I just wanted to pay my respects. But if there's anything I can do to help, just let me know. Anything at all."

"Thank you."

They both rose.

"We'll talk again, Mrs. Reeve."

"Indeed."

Louisa longed to be able to sit Elliot down and ask him exactly what he'd been doing and why there might be no shares in Cinnamon Hills. More than anything, she longed to put her memories of him away somewhere safe where they could not be contaminated by doubt. Elliot was the only one who could make that possible. Surely, he'd tell her it was all a mix-up, nothing to worry about. A misunderstanding.

But, for now, she had to let it go. Her father was due to arrive back from a business trip and, though she wanted so much to confide in him, she couldn't bear for him to know about her fears.

She watched the sky turn pink then went indoors to prepare for supper. In the bathroom, she stared at herself in the mirror. For a moment just witnessing the lost look in her hazel eyes made her want to cry. She pulled herself together and, instead of crying, she washed and dressed, sprayed a little eau de toilette behind her ears and then sat at her dressing table to fasten a rope of pearls; an anniversary present from Elliot, they were real. At least Elliot had said they were. She put one to her lips and rubbed it against the edge of her front teeth. Yes, there was a gritty feel to it, and that meant they were real. She felt ashamed for doubting him.

When she heard the front door being opened, and then the sound of her father's voice, she steeled herself not to show her distress. She had already decided what they were to talk about. It was time to decide what to do with the Print House.

She went through and greeted her father in the hall.

"Sorry I'm late," he said, "but I got delayed at the cutting house."

"Have you put somebody in charge there?"

He shook his head. "Not yet. I'm seeing to things myself for the time being."

"Well, shall we go straight through?"

Once seated at one end of the dining table, he gazed at her. "So," he said, while she toyed with her food. "I hope you're feeling better after your trip away. I do think distraction helps."

She chewed the skin at the back of her lips while she wondered how to answer. "Is that what you did? Why you never talked about my mother?"

"Not exactly. I was kept very busy. I had a young child to look after and a business to run. It would not have helped if I'd sat about and moped."

"*Moped?* Do you think that's what I'm doing?"

"You and I are different. I'm a practical man, but you turn your thoughts inward. I just meant it must have helped to be able to spend time with Gwen Hooper. Talk about what's been eating you."

"It did help . . . I'm managing to find my way through."

"Is there something more?"

She nodded. "Just something I want to discuss."

"Oh?"

"The Print House."

"Ah. It's a bit of a white elephant now, isn't it?"

"How do you mean?"

"The emporium idea. Surely you're not going to go through with it?"

She shook her head at the conflicting thoughts crowding her mind, then took a breath before speaking. "I think I will go through with it. And that's exactly what I want to talk about."

"Is it money? You want me to back this?"

She smiled. "It would be wonderful if you could. But maybe I could cash in some of my remaining shares too, though it will be tight."

"I can't let you do that. What will you live on?"

"I'll survive."

"No. Whatever you decide to do with the place, your income comes from your investments and the life insurance Elliot left you with."

Louisa glanced down at the table.

"What is it, darling?"

She shook her head.

"Don't tell me there's no life insurance!"

She glanced up at him and could see the look of impatience on his face. "I haven't been able to find a policy. I . . ." Her voice trailed off.

"Well, of all the irresponsible things! Have you checked with the solicitor?"

She nodded sadly.

"Very well, if you are determined to hang on to the Print House, I will find the funds to provide the backing you need, though I can't help thinking that selling it might be best."

"I need something to do."

"I do understand."

"Do you?"

He nodded. "I certainly hope so. As I said, distraction, or at least keeping busy, helps."

"And I'll go crazy without a project."

"Well, we can't have that. So, it seems this is cause for celebration. The signs are we shall be in business together. Have you champagne in the house?"

"Of course."

As she smiled at her father, a new feeling of excitement seized her. It seemed the Print House would be the thing to save her. If she could keep steering her mind in the right direction, this might give her just the chance she needed.

# 17

Margo arrived back in Galle a day later. Now, the following morning, the two women were talking over a breakfast of tea, toast and fruit with buffalo-milk curd. It was still early and though the dawn chorus had ended, birds were still singing in the garden. Louisa had thrown open the French windows so they could enjoy the sound.

"Gosh, I'm starving," Margo said, and yawning, stretched her arms out wide. "I'm sorry I couldn't talk last night. I was just so exhausted from the bus journey and, I have to admit, from being with Mother."

"How is she now?" Louisa asked as she poured the tea.

Margo paused before she spoke and Louisa could see the tiredness etched on her sister-in-law's face, especially in the purple shadows under her eyes. She hated seeing the girl looking so worn down. Now Margo screwed up her forehead and pulled a face.

"Not good. The thing is, I can find no way to comfort her. Nothing I do or say is right, though I'm not sure anyone can help her just now. I've done my best and don't want to be disloyal, but if I wasn't to end up screaming, I had to get away."

Louisa, listening to the hum of insects in the garden, could well understand Margo needing a break from her mother.

"It must be terribly hard for her," she said and passed a cup to Margo. "I understand that."

"I'll go back when I think I can be of some use. I hated to leave her, but I think she's best left alone for now. Luckily, my father has work to think about, so that keeps him out of the house. Gosh, I hope I don't sound callous."

"Not at all. We all know Irene can be tiring."

"She can be awfully difficult, but I *am* worried about her! Think about it. She has now lost two sons, after all."

Louisa nodded. "Yes. Yes, of course. It's unthinkable."

There was a short silence.

"Anyway, tell me," Margo said. "How are you?"

"Honestly? I don't know. Some days I feel numb. As if everything is far away from me.

Or that I'm not even me. But it's become even more complicated, you see. I've found out Elliot doesn't appear to have any shares in Cinnamon Hills, after all."

"No!"

Louisa nodded. "Well, that was what Leo said."

"Can you trust him?"

"I thought so. I liked him and why would he lie?"

"It would benefit him to maintain full control of his business, wouldn't it?"

"I suppose so. Anyway, I have no idea where the money went and I have no idea where Elliot really was when he said he was at the plantation." She paused, unsure how to say it. "It hurts to feel I didn't really know my husband."

"You poor thing. But how very strange."

"Isn't it. Anyway, he bought the old Print House shortly before you came back from London. He never got a chance to show it to you. We planned to renovate it and turn it into an emporium selling jewelry and other crafts."

"Are you sure you're up to it? It'll take a lot of energy."

"I don't know." She sighed deeply. "Grief is terribly exhausting, but I must do some-thing!"

"It would be a focus, I suppose."

"That's my view."

She noticed Margo didn't speak and something flickered over her sister-in-law's face.

"What about you, Margo? I mean not only about Elliot, but also your man in London. William, wasn't it?"

Margo took a deep breath before she spoke. "If only he was my man. But I do miss him terribly. Not like me to be so sentimental, is it?"

"It's a loss all the same."

"Yes. Though of course the loss of Elliot is far worse. I still can't really believe it."

"I know. Every day I expect to see him coming through the door."

They drank their tea in silence, slapping at the flies attempting to land on their hair. Margo closed her eyes and seemed to be thinking. When she opened them she smiled. "So now, I think we need cheering up. The question is, what shall we do for the rest of the day?"

Louisa sighed. "Well, there's work to do on the Print House."

"Let it wait. Let's get away from Galle and go to one of the south coast beaches. I fancy a swim, away from prying eyes."

■ ■ ■ ■

They drove along the coast road past the wild hyacinths and mangrove trees, and then the coconut palms fronting the golden shore, eventually stopping at a turn-off for the beach at the base of the Cinnamon Hills plantation.

As she parked the car Louisa couldn't help thinking of Leo. Part of her wanted to storm back up there now to insist he tell her the truth about the shares. Surely he had been lying? After all, Margo was right, it would be to his advantage to conceal shares owned by Elliot. But she'd need to wait. Once she had withdrawn the money from Elliot's separate deposit account, it would give her an excuse to go.

She gazed around her at the palm-fringed shore and the sandy beach littered with seashells and then, out beyond the shallows, the coral reefs. Small brightly painted fishing boats bobbed on the deep blue water, but luckily the beach itself was empty, so they had the place to themselves.

"Beat you to the water," Margo said as she stripped off her clothes to reveal a swimming costume beneath.

"Unfair advantage. I've still got to

change."

"I win!" Margo shouted as she ran down across the silvery sand to the water's edge. Once she had plunged into the water and begun to swim, Louisa changed and followed her down, whooping as she felt the soft chill of water on her skin. It was wonderful to be in the water so soon after the lake. Perhaps that would be the answer — a daily swim to ease out the knots in her neck and shoulders.

She began swimming after Margo, but couldn't catch up. Margo was an ace swimmer and though Louisa could swim well, she was unable to match Margo's superior strength. After a while Louisa lay on her back and angled her head to look at the palm trees before gazing at the sea again.

The sun speckled gold all over the water and the sky shone a seamless pale blue. Everything was silent apart from the slooshing sound of the gentle waves and the squawk of the occasional seabird. If only life could always be like this, she thought and began to swim back to the water's edge. She sat in the shallows, letting the water wash over her legs, and then she stretched out her arms to the sky. Thank you for this, she whispered. *Thank you.* And when she remembered being so in love with Elliot as they had watched the turtles wading on to this very beach to lay their eggs, she didn't feel sad. She stayed like that for several minutes and only gradually became aware of a sound behind her. She shook her hair and twisted around.

"Oh," she said when she saw him in his bathing suit. "Hello."

"I swim here," Leo said, pushing the hair back from his eyes. "I hope you don't mind?"

Despite what she had been thinking earlier about storming up to him to demand the truth, she managed to smile up at him. "No. Of course not."

As he plunged into the water, she noticed how supple he was. Seeing such a well-defined body, you could tell he worked on the land and not in an office. She watched as he swam smoothly through the surf. When he had finished, he came out to dry himself.

"I'm here with my sister-in-law," she said. "You can just about see her out there."

He shaded his eyes with his hand while he looked. "Ah yes."

"Never seems to tire, but I hope she doesn't go out any farther."

"And how are you?" he said. "Are you coping?"

She nodded. "It's so gorgeous here, isn't it?"

Neither of them spoke during a too-long silence, and she felt a little self-conscious with him standing there so close and her sitting in just her wet swimming costume.

"Swimming is such a release," he eventually said, as he squatted down beside her. "Life gets fraught on the plantation. I get too bound up in it."

"Perhaps you need a social life."

"Maybe."

"What about your cousin? Do you see much of her?"

"Zinnia? Yes, I see her."

"I didn't know her name, but I think I saw her the last time I was there."

He glanced away and seemed to her a little uneasy. She couldn't say exactly why; it might just have been the pulse in his jaw and the way he didn't meet her eyes.

"She seemed upset," she added, hoping he'd say more.

He nodded and then got up too quickly, his arm brushing hers. She felt a distinct shiver and couldn't help thinking he had stopped himself from saying something.

She swallowed her indecision and looked up at him as she spoke. "About those shares. Are you certain Elliot had none? There will be records somewhere, if he did."

He gazed at her. "I realize this must be difficult for you but, Louisa, I promise you. He really had no shares."

She met his eyes and then nodded.

"I'm afraid I have to get back."

"Yes."

"Well . . . Hope to see you around?"

"Yes," she said again, because in spite of everything she couldn't help wishing he'd stay a little longer.

"Take care of yourself." Then he turned his back and began striding toward the road.

A moment later Louisa looked out to sea to check on Margo's progress and was taken aback to see she was in trouble. She was attempting to swim back to the shore but was waving frantically with one arm and seemed to be treading water.

"Leo! Help!" Louisa shouted as she got onto her feet then raced deeper into the water. She heard his feet pounding the sand as he ran to catch up with her.

"Swim out to Margo with me, please! I don't know what's wrong. It's not like her."

Louisa began swimming but with a faster front crawl Leo quickly reached Margo, who was now spluttering and gasping for air. He grabbed her under the arms and then swam on his back, holding her against him with one arm, until they reached the shallows. Then he put her down and she hopped awkwardly over to Louisa, who was now out of the water too.

"You went out too far," Louisa said.

Margo took a deep breath and rubbed her leg. "I'm fine now."

"Honestly, Margo! You need to be more careful."

"I've never had a cramp before." She turned to Leo. "Thank you for being my knight in shining armor."

He inclined his head. "I'm glad you're safe. I'm Leo, by the way, Leo McNairn. Owner of Cinnamon Hills."

"Well, thank you," Margo said with a smile, and then resumed rubbing her calf muscle. "We read about you, didn't we, Louisa?"

He grinned. "Really? And where was that?"

Margo glanced at Louisa. "At the library, wasn't it?"

Louisa nodded and felt embarrassed, as if she'd been caught out being nosy.

"Anyway, thank you again for your gallant rescue," Margo continued.

He helped Margo walk until they were all safely sitting on the sand. He glanced across at Louisa. Unable to fathom what he was thinking, she looked away and gazed behind her at dozens of lanky coconut palms, then farther back at the little shacks of the fishermen. After a moment, she twisted around to face the water again and while she watched the seabirds — egrets, herons, sandpipers and kingfishers — she thought about what he'd said. *No shares.*

After a while he spoke to Margo. "Does it feel better?"

Margo nodded.

On the journey home, Margo was full of Leo and how chivalrous he had been, until Louisa almost began to regret their trip to the beach. And yet she couldn't help feeling pleased at having seen him again. There was something about him that made her feel that things might not be so bad. That the darkness might not fall and she might not slip off the cliff edge, after all.

"I think you're smitten," she said, raising her brows at Margo.

"Well, do you blame me? He's gorgeous. I love the lean rugged type. So, what did you two talk about while I was busy drowning?"

"Nothing. I asked him about the shares once more, but he said again there were none."

# 18

Louisa had been to the print house with Margo and drawn up some initial plans. She still hadn't found the key to the locked room and decided she would have to ask a locksmith to force the lock at some point.

Margo had gone for a bicycle ride while Louisa pored over the plans, now laid out on a coffee table in the downstairs sitting room. She was hoping to construct four different rooms or departments. Added to these, there would be a circular central counter where some of the more expensive sapphire jewelry would be displayed and sold. Archways would open into the individual spaces, which would be destined for less costly jewelry in one, hand-carved woodwork in another, and silk products in the third. There might even be two rooms of jewelry if she could find enough jewelers to participate. She had decided to name the emporium *Sapphire,* as Ceylon was especially renowned for the quality of its beautiful sapphires. Soon she would need to organize extensive insurance and ensure all the locks and windows were secured with grilles too.

She was attempting to draw the building's exterior but decided she needed to check on it again, having spotted something in the drawing that didn't look right. Just when she was concentrating, Ashan entered the room and told her there was a gentleman to see her.

"Well, show him in," she said rather irritably, running a palm over her hair and feeling annoyed at the intrusion, though she was instantly sorry to have been short with Ashan. His loyalty had never been in doubt, and she had always tried to treat him with respect. Surprised when Leo walked into the room, she stood immediately and then held out a hand.

He held it briefly.

"I'm afraid I haven't been to Colombo yet to withdraw the money Elliot left you."

"It isn't that," he said, standing with his hands gripping a leather hat and twisting the rim round and round, looking so stiff and awkward she couldn't help thinking he'd prefer to be elsewhere.

"Would you like some tea?"

With a somber look, he shook his head. "No." He paused. "Maybe we could talk in the garden?"

"Of course. I'll just get my sunhat."

She slipped into the hall to retrieve her hat and then they went outside via the French windows. The peaceful garden glittered in the sunshine and a slight breeze rustled the leaves. The three dogs followed them out and lay down to pant in the shade, tongues lolling. She refilled their water bowl from an outdoor tap and placed it on the ground in front of them.

"So," she said as they walked on.

She saw him swallow nervously — he seemed to be gathering his courage. "It's about my cousin, Zinnia."

"Oh?"

"I'm afraid she's ill, and there's nobody looking after her son, Conor."

"I didn't know she had a son."

"He's seven. A sweet little thing who lives in his own little made-up world. Zinnia teaches him at home and so he rarely sees other children. I do what I can to help." He took a breath. "She has a divorced friend, you see, who brings her daughter from time to time, but that's all. I think she feels she and Zinnia are both a little outside 'normal' society. To be honest, things aren't really satisfactory. Conor runs wild at the best of times but now . . ."

She had never heard him say so much in one go before and felt surprised by it. "I'm sorry to hear it, but why are you telling me?"

"Well, that's the difficult part." He suddenly stopped and there was an odd little pause.

She didn't speak. Whatever it is, it should unfold at its own pace, she thought.

He began to talk again. "But, after seeing you at the beach, I felt I had to speak up."

"Shall we sit in the shade," Louisa said. "I'm getting hot."

They moved to the shady area and sat together on a bench. The garden felt unnervingly quiet and now she sensed there was something a bit strange about Leo coming to see her like this.

"So?"

"I believe the money your husband left me was actually meant for Zinnia."

She felt a slight chill despite the heat of the day and gave him a long, hard look. Rooted to the spot, she waited for him to speak again.

"There's no easy way to say this . . ."

"Go on."

"Conor is Elliot's son, Louisa."

She gasped and blinked rapidly. The

garden seemed to shiver and now she was aware of her heart knocking in her chest so loudly she was amazed he couldn't hear it.

He shook his head and stared at the ground. "I know this must be hard to hear."

A long uncomfortable silence deepened while Louisa reeled from this. Confused by the vision of Elliot's face, still clear in her mind, and the look in his eyes, the warmth, the love, it was impossible to take it in.

"That's why Elliot used to come to the plantation so often," Leo eventually said, glancing up at her.

"Conor is Elliot's son? That's what you're telling me?" She felt a dozen emotions collide within her and such a burst of heat she felt she might pass out.

"Yes."

It couldn't be true. Elliot would never have done such a thing. And hearing Elliot's voice in her head, she refused to believe it. "You can't mean this."

"I'm sorry."

"How can you lie to me like this?" she said. "Why are you doing this?"

He gazed at her. "I thought you had a right to know."

"*No!* First you say there are no shares, something I still find hard to believe, and now you tell me this."

There was another profound silence. The words she wanted to say thickened and refused to spill. She felt as if she'd never be able to breathe again.

"Louisa, I . . ."

"No." She held up a hand. "Don't say a thing."

She rose to her feet and moved away to stand with her back to him. "You expect me to believe Elliot went to the plantation to see her? He had no shares. It was all *her*?"

He didn't reply.

"You didn't think to tell me this before?" She twisted around to glance back at him, desperately trying to prevent the choking sensation in her tightening throat and silently entreating him to say it wasn't true.

He shook his head miserably. "I didn't want to hurt you, but it's true he came to see Conor, and Zinnia too, of course."

Louisa felt tears burning her lids, but carried on staring at him. Time seemed to accelerate backward, and she saw Elliot's smiling eyes as he gave her that last bunch of flowers. Now she felt they had only been to assuage his guilt. As if flowers could make up for this. She promised herself she would not cry in front of Leo and stood straighter, bracing herself. She bit her lip until she tasted blood, watching him all the while.

"Why tell me now?"

He took a deep breath before he spoke. "As I said, I felt I couldn't leave you in the dark. I couldn't go on pretending I knew nothing and felt you deserved to know the truth."

She frowned at his explanation and then took a step toward him. "You come here and tell me my husband has a child, an illegitimate child . . . a *bastard*!"

He stood up. "Look, I know this is a shock."

She backed away and squinted into the harsh light. "You're damn right!"

He hung his head for a moment and then looked up.

She laughed a hard, sharp laugh. "This is all nonsense. Are you insane? Completely mad?"

"I wish there —"

"Stop right there, Leo." Her voice had come out thin and rasping. She swallowed hard, horrified by her own display of raw emotion. She longed to curse at him, shout, scream that this was wrong. All wrong. Elliot would never have betrayed her.

"I can't think what possessed you to tell me this," she said in a tight voice. "Now please leave."

"I'm sorry," he said. "Truly. If there's

anything I can do?"

"Go. Just go!"

He turned on his heels and within moments he was gone.

She collapsed back onto the bench, staring after him, the dogs whimpering at her feet. She wrestled with what she had heard. Sucking in her breath, she fought the urge to weep. She picked up Zip and hugged him to her, breathing in his damp doggy smell and feeling hollowed out, as if she'd been kicked in the stomach. At first, she tried to deny what he had told her. It couldn't be true. And yet Leo would have no reason to lie, would he? Was this somehow tied up with the shares? She bent forward and cradled her head in her hands. Then she sat up straight again and clenched her hands into fists. The feeling of wanting to lash out intensified, the pain and anger too overpowering to bear. How could he possibly have lied to her all these years? They had been married for twelve years but he had a seven-year-old son. *No.* She let the words sink in until they echoed so loudly she clapped her hands over her ears. *A son. A son.* No. It couldn't be true. How was it possible she had never suspected a thing? Had she been fooling herself all this time? Had the love between them never been real? The questions crashed around in her head but there were no answers. There never would be.

By the time Margo returned, Louisa was sobbing. She hadn't moved from the bench and, though she was aware of feeling terribly hot, it was as if she'd lost the ability to stand and walk away. Tommy and Bouncer had wandered off in search of shade, though not before whining their own anxiety over her distress. Zip remained on her lap although he was now fidgeting.

Margo slid on to the bench beside her and put an arm around Louisa's shaking body, waiting for the sobs to subside before she spoke. When Louisa was a little calmer, Margo took hold of her hand and gently nudged Zip away.

"Darling, it's best if we go inside now. You're overheating. I'll take you to the upstairs sitting room and get some mango juice sent up, then you can tell me all about it."

For the following few days Louisa felt bereft, as if the news of the child had reached into the heart of her and knocked her soul out. Everything, her life, her marriage, her hopes for the future, had come crashing to the ground. Deeply shocked, she dug her fingernails into the fleshy part of her palm to ward off the sickness she felt. She wanted to think of something else, but Zinnia and her child took over every waking thought. She lay on the bed with a pillow over her head as if to shield herself from the truth. Margo came to sit with her but didn't ask questions. Louisa was grateful. She wasn't ready to say the dreadful words aloud. Sometimes she saw Margo's worried look but had no strength to lessen her sister-in-law's concern.

Then one afternoon, she squinted up at Margo and shared what Leo had said. She watched the shock of it register on the younger woman's face, saw the way her hand flew to her mouth, saw her lips begin to tremble and her eyes widen in disbelief. Louisa then started crying. She made a horrible gasping sound as the pain poured out. Margo wept too and the women held each other.

Eventually Margo pulled away. "Dear God. I can't believe it. You're sure it's true?"

Louisa took a shuddering breath. "Why would Leo lie about it?"

"I just can't believe it of Elliot."

"I know. I've been over and over it in my head."

Margo doubled over and Louisa wrapped an arm around her.

They stayed like that for several minutes, but after a while Margo straightened up and wiped her damp cheeks. "Sorry. It's the shock. I can't take it in. I just can't believe my brother would do such a thing."

"I feel the same."

"What are you going to do about the money Elliot left Leo? Presumably it was for this woman and her child?"

Louisa nodded. "I shall go to the bank, withdraw the money and send someone to Cinnamon Hills to give it to him. It isn't much, but he can give it to Zinnia. What else can I do?"

Margo shook her head. "I wish Elliot were here. He'd straighten all this out."

"You really believe that?"

Margo shrugged. "I don't know."

They sat in silence for a few minutes.

"So, what's next?" Margo eventually said. "You're very flushed. Do you feel able to take a bath and get dressed? You haven't eaten a thing for days and your father has called twice too. I haven't known what to say to him. Do you think you might eat some toast?"

Louisa nodded and felt a burst of energy. "If I'm not going to fade away I shall have to face the world sooner or later."

"There's no need for anyone to know."

"I'm sure there are people who do know. I don't see how he could have kept this completely secret for so long. Do you think people have been pitying me, when all along I was congratulating myself on having a wonderful marriage?"

"Nobody has ever breathed a word. I don't think anyone here knows."

"I feel like such an utter fool."

"I'd be bloody furious if I was you. In fact, I *am* bloody furious with my brother!"

"And all the time I was losing his babies he already had a child. It hurts, Margo. It really hurts."

# 19

Louisa tried to convince herself it had all been lies. She didn't know what Leo stood to gain by it but she simply could not accept Elliot had been unfaithful all that time. He had loved her as much as she had loved him, so how could this be true? Drenched in sweat, she cycled around the streets of Galle, knowing if she was less than her usually friendly self, people would put it down to delayed grief over Elliot's death. Everything else was a fabrication she could not allow to destroy her. And yet, while she still refused to completely believe Leo, the doubt growled and clawed at her, especially at night. When it did she slipped out of bed and read a book, or pored over her plans for the emporium, then stared into the loneliness of the nighttime silence pressing up against her window. Mainly she plowed on through by burying herself in examining samples of the kinds of goods the emporium would sell, and pushing everything else to the back of her mind. But how she wished for a return to ordinary normal life!

One morning, after a slightly better night, she made her way to the Print House with Margo. They were due to meet the locksmith she had finally hired. Margo tried talking to her about the child, but Louisa refused to engage. If she paid no attention to it, the whole business with Leo would go away. That was how she was dealing with it. Margo didn't press her.

On their way, they planned to call on a jeweler who might be keen to sell his goods in the emporium. Still too soon for the monsoon, it was another sweltering day, though the sea was looking a bit choppier than usual. Accustomed to the way the weather affected the sea, Louisa gazed out at it in silence. They hailed two wooden rickshaws for the ease of it and when they reached the jeweler's, Louisa waved at a peddler she knew who passed them balancing vast bunches of king coconuts on his bicycle. Apart from the bars at the windows and the tall wooden doors painted yellow, the jeweler's looked like a normal house. Inside it was anything but.

The women walked through the solidly beamed entrance hall and rang a large rope bell. A young man appeared through an imposing arched doorway and led them through to a second room with a tall, airy ceiling. In there, two old Dutch chests were kept locked, and several glass-fronted antique cabinets housed the other treasures. Louisa nodded at the assistant and asked to see the owner, a man distantly related to the famous Macan Markar family of jewelers. They waited for a few minutes while admiring the embellished mirrors on the wall, and then an elderly man with a slight stoop came down a wide staircase.

"Mrs. Reeve," he said. "This is a pleasure indeed. Will you take mint tea with me in the roof garden?"

Louisa glanced at Margo, who nodded, and they followed the man up the stairs to a roof garden shaded by vines growing over a wire pergola.

"How lovely," Louisa said as she gazed at the tops of coconut palms in the streets surrounding the garden and, beyond them, to the view of the deep blue sea.

He indicated chairs where they were to sit and the women made themselves comfortable. The garden was mainly lawn, unusually for a roof terrace, and bright red flowers peppered its borders. Decorated urns held yet more flowers, and the whole effect was astonishingly bright and airy. Below them they saw women hanging out washing on the red-tiled roof tops, and there was a good view of the Dutch Reformed church and the hill of Rumassala.

After the tea had been served, Louisa explained her idea for the emporium and asked if he'd be interested in being part of it.

He listened carefully and there was a momentary silence while he was clearly thinking over her proposition. In the end, he sighed deeply before speaking. "I do not think I have the means to open a second shop here. Things have been, well, shall we say, a little tricky. But I have a cousin, also a jeweler you understand, who works in Colombo. I know he is looking to expand his sapphire collection. Why not allow me to approach him on your behalf?"

"Thank you," she said, rising from her seat. "That would be a great help. But now, we'd better get on. I'm meeting a locksmith in ten minutes."

He led them downstairs.

As they reached the bottom, the assistant was in the middle of showing another man through to the back room. Louisa was surprised to see it was Mr. De Vos, who was now gazing at her with a broad smile on his face. The owner took a step to the side and while he exchanged a few hurried words with his assistant, De Vos spoke to Louisa.

"Mrs. Reeve. How lovely to see you. I was hoping to pay you a call later this morning. Maybe we could have a few words outside."

"Of course."

They stepped through the front door and she smiled at him. "So?"

"Well, it is a little bit tricky. As you know, your husband and I had joined forces in a business deal."

"Yes."

"Well, the awkward thing is, he gave me a post-dated check to cover his share of the transaction — but unfortunately, when I presented it at the bank, the check bounced."

"I see."

"I know your husband was an honorable man so I wondered if, or rather when, you might be able to make good on the debt."

She steadied herself before she replied. "You have a contract for the transaction?"

He smiled again. "Indeed."

"And how much did my husband owe you?"

He scribbled an amount on a piece of paper and handed it to her.

She tried to conceal her shock when she

saw how much it was. "Let me see the contract and we'll take it from there."

"Thank you," he said, and gave her a little bow before twisting around to walk back into the jeweler's.

As she turned to leave, she felt her heart beating against her ribs. More debts!

"Well," Margo said as they walked away. "What was that about?"

Louisa swallowed hard. "Apparently Elliot owed money for some business transaction. I don't know what to think."

"Owed it to that man?"

"Honestly, Margo, it's a small fortune, would certainly buy you a house or two . . . Oh God, you don't think he borrowed the money for the down payment on the Print House as well? He told me he'd used profits from his spice business."

Margo shook her head. "He wouldn't, would he? Have you spoken to your father?"

"Not yet. I think I can handle it."

"If I were you I'd tell him. You don't want to deal with everything alone."

As they walked on some low-lying clouds scudded across the horizon and for a moment it looked like rain. When they reached the Print House, Louisa drew out the bunch of keys and unlocked the large front doors. Inside it smelled a little musty and she sniffed the air. "I need to get the cupola cleaned so we can allow light to stream in, but let's open some of these windows for now. At least it will smell fresher."

"Who's your builder going to be?"

"Himal maybe, but I need to finish the plans first."

After they had opened the plantation shutters and then the windows she showed Margo around the ground floor of the building. Then they climbed a metal stairway that led to the gallery circling the hall, where they noticed a spotted house lizard scamper up the wall and then lie still.

"Now that one has come in, we can't leave until he has either gone back out, or at least hidden himself from us."

"You believe the old wives' tale?"

Louisa laughed. "I just enjoy the idea. Do you like it up here?"

"Very much," Margo said.

Louisa grinned. "I thought maybe we'd display paintings here. Once the light comes in, they'll look gorgeous, and people can walk around viewing them while also gazing down at the stands below."

"You've got it all worked out, haven't you?"

"I had — until I heard about this new debt Elliot has left me with." She shook her head. "The unpleasant surprises keep coming, don't they?"

"It'll be all right."

"Will it? I'm not sure how. Whenever I think about Zinnia and the child I just feel sick."

As they were talking someone entered below and Louisa, glancing over the rail of the gallery, saw a small, wiry man eyeing the place and carrying a satchel.

"Ah, it's the locksmith."

Louisa went down, leaving Margo on the gallery.

"Mr. Hassid," she said and held out her hand. "Thank you so much for coming. The door is just through here."

She led him through one of the side rooms to the locked door. "Shall I leave you to work on it?"

He nodded and she went back into the hall. "Margo," she called. "Come down and look at these old printing presses. I was thinking about having one cleaned up and keeping it as a centerpiece."

Margo came down the stairs and ran a palm over one of the presses, which was partly attached to the beam above by chains. "It will take up a bit of room. Maybe the smaller one?"

"You're right."

At that moment there was a loud thump. "I think he may have gotten in."

They both went through to the previously locked room.

The man glanced up. "I'm afraid I had to remove the entire locking mechanism. I can install a new lock if you like, though I don't have the right kind with me."

"No need. I don't know what I'll be doing with the room yet. Now, how much do I owe you?"

After Louisa had paid, and the man had left, the women entered the room. A desk and a swivel chair were the only furniture. "This must have been the office. Let's see what's in the drawers."

She pulled open the top drawer. Empty. Then the second drawer, which contained just a few sheets of yellowing paper. And when she opened the third drawer she found it empty too.

"There's nothing in here," Louisa said.

"I wonder why on earth the room was locked then?"

# 20

After cleaning up the print house a little, Louisa settled on having a bath and changing for supper, while Margo went to dive off Flag Rock and go for a swim.

Louisa's bathroom was tiled in blue and white with a window overlooking the garden which she now opened. She took out a clean white towel from the airing cupboard, ran a bath, lit a few scented candles and then, as the warm water slid over her, and she rinsed the dust and dirt away, she listened to the chorus of birds in the trees. She craned her neck to look out of the window and saw a burst of parakeets fly from one tree to another, but then she sank back into the bath. Apart from the birds, there was no other sound and the peace soothed Louisa.

But, after a moment, completely unbidden thoughts of Elliot invaded her mind. That's how it often happened now. She'd be busily doing some sewing, or some pruning outside, and would suddenly have to fight the rising panic when she heard his voice as clearly as if he had been standing beside her. She had not told her father of Leo's claims about Zinnia and Conor. Telling him would make it seem too real. But, while she did her best not to dwell on it, how could she avoid considering whether Leo had been telling the truth or not? And, if it was true, how had Elliot managed to keep the child secret for all this time? This thought made it hard to breathe and as she struggled for air, the heat made her eyelids prickle. She stuffed her knuckles into her eyes to stop the tears from surfacing.

Once she'd climbed out of the bath and had dried herself, she slipped into a dress with a nipped-in waist and a very nearly ankle-length skirt. It had light shoulder pads and a floral pattern, another of her dresses made up by the Colombo tailor. She kept her curls under control, pinning her hair up at the back and keeping the fashionable close-to-the-head look. Despite her tan, she still retained a natural-looking complexion which she highlighted with the use of a rouge in light pink. She usually didn't bother, but something told her tonight was important, even though it would just be

Margo and her father for supper.

A little later as she went down the stairs, she was surprised by a knock at the front door. It was too late for a casual visitor so she couldn't imagine who it might be but, opening the door herself, she was taken aback to see Jeremy Pike, the man Elliot used to sail with and whose car he had crashed, standing on the doorstep.

"I thought it was time. I owe you an explanation," he said.

"Come in."

They stood together in the hall and he gazed about, hands clasped behind his back. "Hard to believe Elliot's gone, isn't it?"

"Very. But what can I do for you?"

"I wanted to explain what happened the day he died."

Louisa took a quick breath. "Will you come through?"

"No, this won't take a moment. You see, we had been planning to sail that day, but when I saw the wind was getting up, I phoned to postpone. To be honest, Elliot seemed relieved, and then asked if he might borrow my car."

"Why?"

"I don't know. But I agreed, of course — he was a good friend. Though I did ask why he didn't use his own."

"He didn't say anything?"

"He just said he had a private meeting with somebody somewhere on the way to Colombo, some kind of deal he was involved in, I think."

"And that's all you know?"

"It is."

"Well, thank you for telling me."

"It's long overdue. I'm terribly sorry I couldn't make the funeral. I had to go to Bombay at short notice. Only recently returned."

"But have the police spoken to you?"

"I gave them a statement earlier today. It confirms what my housekeeper told them while I was away."

"What about the car? I should make up the loss."

"No need to worry. The insurance will cover everything." He paused. "But now I must be off. Please accept my deepest condolences."

After he'd gone she went across to the sitting room and saw her father was already there, listening to Margo playing some Liszt on the piano. She sat and leaned back in her chair to listen and think about Jeremy Pike.

Though Margo played moderately well and it was a pleasant way to spend the early part of the evening, Louisa's mind was on Elliot's accident and the reason behind his drive that day. Her father sipped his drink and closed his eyes, and Ashan came and stood quietly while Margo finished the piece. When she had, he asked both women what they'd like to drink and then, as he went to mix their cocktails, Jonathan spoke. "So," he said. "What are your plans, Margo?"

Margo sighed. "I haven't really decided. I suppose I'll eventually return to England, try to get my old job back."

"You wouldn't consider nursing over here? The country is crying out for well-trained medical staff."

"I'd consider it, of course, and I do love it here, but I've made a lot of good friends in England."

"You could make new ones here and keep your old friends too. Think about it."

"Maybe."

A smiling Ashan handed both women their gin rickeys: a fizzing mix of gin, lime and soda. "I hope they give satisfaction," he said. "I mixed them myself."

"Thank you," Louisa said.

Jonathan came up to Louisa and squeezed her hand affectionately. "I haven't told you how well you are looking this evening, Louisa. It's a pleasure to see."

"I know you've been worried about me, but I am coping. And Margo being here has helped so much."

Margo left the piano. "I'm glad to be here, though I'm sure Mother will be itching to have me back with her before long."

"In the meantime, if you can prevent my daughter from giving in to despair we shall go on enjoying your company, won't we, Louisa?"

"Actually Dad, I wanted to talk to you," Louisa said, once Ashan had gone. She leaned toward him, but then Camille came in to say dinner was served and they all stood up.

Throughout dinner Margo talked a lot about Irene and Harold and how they were struggling in the aftermath of their son's death, and the moment for telling Jonathan about Elliot seemed to have passed. I'll tell him tomorrow, Louisa thought, though she didn't relish the task. Her father hadn't trusted Elliot at the start of their marriage and it had been she who had persuaded him. Now it seemed he had been right all along.

# 21

"So, before we go to the cutting and polishing house have you any questions?" her father said as he pulled on his boots. "It would be good if you understood a little bit more about the business. I know it's never been of great interest to you, but now . . . well, now Elliot's gone, it might be time to learn."

"I do already know a bit."

He raised his brows. "Well, you say you do."

"I do! I know gemstone mining here is mostly from secondary deposits."

"Which yield sapphire, ruby, cat's-eye, garnet."

"Tourmaline, topaz, quartz," she added.

"So, you *have* been listening. I always thought the talk of gems bored you."

She laughed. "I do love a pretty sapphire ring, but you know I've always preferred buildings."

"We have the perfect geological conditions —"

"I know," she said, interrupting him. "Enough. Ready, Pa?"

They left the house and meandered along the lanes, passing the shops laden with fruit and vegetables and the fishmonger too. At the corner of a narrow passage a toothless elderly lady was sweeping her doorway with a stick broom while a little boy watered a large pot of red canna lilies. Jonathan nodded at the woman and they turned into the alley and veered toward the cutting house. As they walked, Louisa thought about their entire gem business. Once gems had been mined they had to be traded and only then were they cut and polished. That was the point at which Hardcastle Gems sold them on. Elliot had been proud of his work at the cutting house but, so far, they hadn't been involved in the actual design and manufacture of jewelry.

Once they entered the gloomy hallway of the building, Ravinath, the supervisor, came out to greet them. He was a wiry-looking middle-aged Sinhalese man with a slightly bent back from years sitting over a cutting bench.

"So, everything going smoothly today?" Jonathan asked. "I've just come to show

Louisa the ropes."

"Of course," the man said, and they followed him through to the office.

Jonathan made himself comfortable behind the desk while Louisa pulled up another chair.

After the man had bowed and shuffled out, Jonathan laid out the cutting house records.

"Elliot kept a close eye on all this, of course, but now I need to do it for myself."

Louisa allowed her gaze to travel around the room. Framed photographs of various stones decorated the walls, as well as a shot of Elliot with the cutters all grinning at the camera. As she felt a wave of grief pass through her, she could almost breathe in the scent of him.

"Actually Dad, could we do this another time. I need some air."

Louisa went ahead and her father followed a few minutes later. Once out on the street she stood motionless and took deep breaths of salty sea air to try to calm herself. Then she turned to her father and reached out. He took her hand as seagulls circled above them. "I'm so sorry, Louisa."

She looked straight at him and saw the pain in his sun-creased eyes.

Her mouth had gone dry but she knew

she had to tell her father everything. She swallowed hard before she began and held his gaze. "The thing is, Pa, there are some things about Elliot I haven't told you."

"Well, let's not talk in the street. Home for a good strong coffee and, I don't know about you, but I'm stopping off for some cake." Louisa agreed. She knew her father was fond of *bondahalua,* a sweet cake made from coconut and jaggery, though her stomach was so knotted she didn't feel much like eating.

Back home she unpinned her hat. Looking in the hall mirror, she noticed how pale she was. Then, hearing a noise coming from Elliot's office, she went toward it while Jonathan went straight for the sitting room to order their coffees. Those damn monkeys again, she thought, and felt annoyed that one of the houseboys must have left a window open.

She unlocked the office door and gasped. Papers were strewn everywhere, a chair had been upended, and the filing-cabinet drawers had been left hanging open. All their contents now littered the floor. The cardboard boxes on the shelves had also been emptied. She glanced at the window and saw a broken pane, which meant the intruder had been able to unlock the window and climb in. Jasmine flowers blown in by the wind covered the floor and desk. She'd often said they needed to put bars at the downstairs windows at the back, and yet they'd never gotten around to it. Any valuables were kept securely in the safe in the wall so they hadn't thought it a great risk. She applied the code to the safe's dials and it opened. Everything looked the way it should. All they kept in there was some cash for the running of the household and, usually, Louisa's better jewelry. She checked carefully. Nothing missing. So what had the intruder been looking for?

She called her father and he shook his head when he saw what had happened.

"Who could have done this?" she said. "It's been completely ransacked."

He shot her a look. "I think we'd better have a talk, don't you?"

They sat on the sofa together and in a halting voice Louisa told him about Elliot's new debt to De Vos, and that Leo had said there were no shares in Cinnamon Hills. She explained that Elliot had also had an outstanding debt with the bank, which she had now repaid, but that he had emptied his account of the money she had transferred to him.

"Mr. De Vos tells me there is a contract

showing Elliot owes him money."

"I'd get that scrutinized. You don't want to be paying out to every Tom, Dick or Harry who purports to have a claim."

And finally, not without a tear, and stumbling over her words, she told him what Leo had said about Zinnia and the child.

At the end of it, he rose to his feet and began to walk back and forth. "Of all the things. A child he kept hidden? I find that hard to understand, let alone forgive."

"I still don't know if I can bear to believe Leo," she said, looking up at him and feeling annoyed with herself as a tear slid down her cheek.

He glanced at her. "If I could get my hands on him now! He had everything with you. What more could any man want?"

"Children, Pa. That's what." She almost choked on her voice as she said the painful words.

"My dear," he said.

And when he sat back down next to her, and put an arm around her, she couldn't stop herself sobbing into his chest, her curtain of blond curly hair concealing her face.

# 22

Jonathan had stayed the night and over breakfast the next day he was ready to inform the police about the break-in.

"We have to let them know," he said. "I'll do it."

Louisa wondered if it was somehow connected to Elliot and felt an ache in her heart. She blinked rapidly to keep tears at bay. Despite her father being there, a feeling of vulnerability took hold in the way it often did at night, but now it was daytime and it was still as if she had no skin. "But what if it's something to do with Elliot?" she said in a small voice.

He sighed. "I'll ask the police to keep it a low-profile matter. But I do have to tell them."

"How did anyone know we weren't in and the house would be quiet?"

He shook his head. "My guess is we've been under observation."

"Do you think they were looking for money when they ransacked his study?"

"That, and valuables."

"What do you think Elliot did with the money?"

He shrugged. "Probably used it to support this woman and her child."

"I suppose."

"By the way, sorry to raise this now, but I've been meaning to say, you'll need to do something about his spice business in Colombo. I can take it over or sell it if it's too much for you."

"No, I'll take a trip to Colombo to the bank and go to his office while I'm at it. I think I'd like to oversee it."

The phone rang and they heard footsteps and then Margo's voice. A few minutes later she came into the room. "Well," she said. "I'm wanted at home. I knew it would happen sooner or later and it's best if I go. I only hope I can be of some use to Mum this time. Anyway, it's that darned bus for me again."

"I shall have to go to Colombo myself quite soon," Louisa said. "I could drive you. Though I don't think I'm up to it today."

Margo narrowed her eyes. "You do look pale. I wish I could stay."

"No. Your mother needs you. It's only

214

right you go. I'll be fine."

"I can't see how."

"I'm going to keep busy," she said, though secretly Louisa agreed with her sister-in-law.

A little later Louisa had taken a sketch pad and pencils to the Print House. The eighteenth-century mansion was typical of the colonial architecture of Galle. But she still needed to record what the front elevation looked like and then trace in how she wanted to change it. In truth, she didn't feel like drawing; what she really wanted was to curl up and forget everything with a large gin. But she withdrew a 2B pencil from the case and began sketching the huge arched windows with their wooden shutters, in front of which was a veranda. Then she drew the large windows of the gallery floor and, finally, the beautiful old red-tiled roof. While she worked all she could think of was the humiliation and embarrassment of telling her father about Zinnia and the boy. And now, even while she tried to focus on her drawing, she couldn't stop thinking about it.

What was she to do?

She couldn't spend the rest of her life wondering if it was true. Wondering if all the time Elliot had been in love with somebody else; somebody who had been able to give him a child while she herself had not. Although the very thought of it made her feel ill, perhaps her only option really was to speak to Leo again.

She went through the building and then, by way of the wide back doors, out into a courtyard garden. It struck her as a perfect place to serve tea and coffee. She sat down in one corner and drew the columns supporting an upstairs balcony, where she pictured the railings festooned with tumbling flowers. She hadn't given much thought to the outside space until now, but it was an idyllic place to sit and think, surrounded as it was by tall coconut palms, and, though the courtyard itself was overrun with bougainvillea and unchecked weeds, it wouldn't take long to fix.

Once she was done, she packed up her drawing equipment and walked back home. There she sat in the garden, gazing at her flowering shrubs and nursing a ginger tea. A green male garden lizard, with white stripes on its body and a crimson-crested head, stared at her from where it perched on a log. It made her smile, but when Zinnia and the child continued to prey on her mind she decided she simply had no choice: she would have to return to Cinnamon Hills.

■ ■ ■ ■

Two days later, once Margo had left for home by bus after all, Louisa gathered her courage. Now it was May, the weather had become a little wetter. It was still warm, at least in the low eighties, and it would remain that way throughout the summer, when the monsoon would bring heavy rains from June until September. Louisa didn't mind the rains and looked forward to the relief they could offer, when Galle's streets would be running with water and the sea would be wild. But, for now, a light drizzle meant humidity was high, and she wiped her hand across her brow as she climbed into the car. It would be a sticky journey today, though she didn't know if she was sweating because of the weather, or because of what she was preparing to do. She'd dressed carefully in lightweight trousers with a simple cotton blouse, and had tied her hair in a knot at the nape of her neck. It was too hot to wear it down. At the last minute, she threaded through her favorite sapphire earrings. They had once belonged to her mother and something about them always made her feel better.

# 23

Louisa soon arrived at the same beach where she had swum with Margo. She and Elliot had liked to collect large shells together but she hadn't searched for any since he died. Shoeless, she walked slowly along the fringes of the ocean, feeling the sun-baked sand between her toes, while staring at the silvery blue water and thinking all the time.

She picked up a few pretty shells and then made her way back to the car, where she sat to dust the sand from her feet before starting up the engine. After that she made a left turn off the main road and began the now familiar climb up Cinnamon Hills — but with her heart racing, she had no idea how she would approach Leo. All she knew was she had to hear the truth.

She soon reached the house at the top with the gorgeous views. She knocked, but when the houseboy answered the door, he told her the master had taken a doctor to see his cousin and would return in a little while. Louisa deliberated: was this an opportunity to turn around and go straight back home? She took a few steps toward her parked car but then paused. If she didn't do this, there would always be doubt. Never-ending doubt. She had to see Leo.

She went a little way into the plantation, but walked straight into a giant wood-spider's web strung across the track between the cinnamon bushes. She brushed its sticky strands from her hair and, nervous of losing her way, returned to the house, where she sat on a small bench in the shade of the upstairs veranda. Then, listening to the squeaks and chatter from the forest canopy, she waited in the sweltering heat. Relieved when the houseboy brought her a lemonade, she drank it quickly and flicked away the flies buzzing around the rim of her glass.

After about half an hour she spotted Leo walking up the track. He paused when he saw her and then came straight up to the bench. Their previous meeting hung between them and for a moment neither spoke.

Eventually he tilted his head. "Louisa?"

"Leo."

She gazed at him. He wore frayed shorts

and a turquoise short-sleeved shirt against which his deep tan shone, although there were also red scratches on his arms. Wanting him to say something first, she waited, but when he did not, she knew it had to be her. "I wanted to talk to you."

"We'll go indoors. I was bitten to death earlier on, cutting back the undergrowth."

"Oh."

"Hell of a job. That's how I got these scratches."

She got to her feet.

"After you," he said, and held open the door.

They went inside and then up the stairs. She stood still, glancing around her and feeling nervous. So far, they were being very polite and careful with each other and the atmosphere felt uneasy.

"I'll get Kamu to bring us a beer." He called the boy out and then turned back to her almost as an afterthought. "Sorry. Will beer do you?"

She nodded, and thought again about the wisdom of coming here. Then, waiting for her beer, she breathed in the scent of cinnamon that hung around Leo. He sat too, and puffed out his cheeks. "Kamu told you where I was?"

She swallowed the lump that had developed in her throat. "He said you'd taken a doctor to see your cousin."

He nodded. "She refused to even see him."

The boy brought out their beers.

Finally, she found the courage to speak. "I wanted to ask you . . ."

"Yes?"

". . . if everything you told me was true." He grimaced.

"I'm afraid it is. I'm so sorry."

She stared at him while he looked away and gazed across the treetops.

There was another long, uncomfortable silence. She didn't want to know or even to ask, and yet she sensed she had to.

"How old is the child again?"

"Seven."

"Where is he now?"

He glanced up at her and then away again. "About the place somewhere."

"Doing what?"

He shook his head. "She won't let him go to school because of the stigma of being il-legitimate. People around here know there's no husband."

"A boarding school?"

"Too expensive."

"Nanny?"

"He needs education at this stage, not a nursemaid."

"Oh. I see."

"Zinnia teaches him, but she's not well enough now and if she won't accept medical attention . . . well." He spread his hands out wide.

She looked down at the terracotta-tiled floor and then up at him and felt sick. "Did you see Elliot when he used to come?"

His eyes narrowed, as if he found the whole conversation difficult. "Kept themselves to themselves," he said, now gazing at her with such a look of compassion that she took a deep breath and then exhaled slowly.

"And Conor knew Elliot was his father?"

Leo nodded.

"You might not know, Elliot and I had a stillborn baby. A little girl. I called her Julia."

His eyes softened even further as he looked at her, but then she turned away as the memories assailed her.

"I didn't know, no," he gently said.

She didn't know the sex of her two miscarried babies but thought of them both as boys, with Julia sandwiched between; one older than his sister and one younger. The daughter who had not even breathed was dark-haired, like Elliot.

"She'd be getting on for three, had she lived," she said.

She didn't say that her hair would be curly; she'd have Elliot's lively green eyes too. And she'd always be demanding they push her higher and higher on the garden swing. Higher, Mummy. *Higher!* Shrieking and shrieking with unbridled excitement. The boys were harder to picture, but she thought they might have her own fairer coloring. She allowed the images to fade and turned back to look at Leo.

"I'm very sorry," he said.

"I had two miscarriages as well, so you can see that finding out about this child is particularly distressing."

"It really isn't something I would have lied about."

She shook her head. "I think I knew all along. I just didn't want to believe it."

"Forgive me. Maybe I shouldn't have told you."

She shook her head again. She couldn't tell him that she felt as if her heart had been ripped out and it was taking every shred of her strength not to fold. "I can't believe how Elliot was able to keep this secret for so long."

It went quiet between them and the silence persisted. In the end it was Leo who spoke.

"I'm worried about Conor. Zinnia is ill and can't look after him. Neither can I. At least not well enough. Because of the drought up north, my cinnamon is now in huge demand. I just have to keep going."

"Have you thought about having him fostered or looked after in a children's home? Temporarily, I mean, while Zinnia is ill."

"Dear God, no. I couldn't do that — do you know what those places are like? And Zinnia obviously wouldn't countenance it!"

"No, of course. It was a stupid idea."

"If I had the funds I'd send him to boarding school in Colombo, but I don't. As it is, I need to find a way of distributing my cinnamon more widely to properly shore up the business."

"I've been thinking . . ." She hesitated for a moment and inhaled sharply. "Would it be possible to see your cousin?"

"Are you sure?"

"I'm not sure of anything at the moment. What's wrong with her?"

"I think she's suffering with her nerves. I doubt she'll see you. Half the time she won't let me in, though I try to sort her place out when I do get in. She's living in a bit of a mess."

"Do you mean since Elliot died?"

He nodded.

She sucked in her breath. "She loved him?"

"I think so."

"Can we go there?"

He frowned as he scrutinized her face. She took another deep breath but didn't speak.

"Won't it distress you? There are portraits she painted in her house."

"Of Elliot?"

"Yes."

She gazed at him with an increasing sense of determination. "I think I need to see for myself."

"Very well."

He led her out of his house and then down the track, past undergrowth where a laughing thrush was singing. About halfway down the hill, there was a little turning toward a small building, an old bungalow, almost hidden among the trees. They passed a row of heavily overgrown scented plants in pots, then he went ahead of her and opened the front door. He twisted around to her and whispered, "We can still turn back."

"I want to see."

He took her into a living area, and she gasped when she saw the canvases hanging on the walls. There were paintings of a red-haired woman with golden skin, paintings of a small boy at different ages, and paint-

ings of Elliot. Many, many portraits of Elliot, either on his own or with the child.
Louisa felt her legs shaking and reached out
to Leo. He steadied her, then held her by
the arm.

"Who is there?" a voice called out.

"It's me, Leo," he answered.

"She sounds fragile," Louisa whispered.

"She is. In more ways than one."

It was suddenly all too much. Louisa
turned on her heels and ran outside, Leo
following behind her. She stood with her
arms wrapped around herself, shaking from
the devastation of this betrayal. I'll never
forgive him, she thought. *Never.*

"Come on," Leo said. "I'll take you back
to the car."

Just then a boy walked up to the house,
kicking the leaves as he did. He stood and
stared at her, and Louisa immediately saw
Elliot's dark curly hair, and his bright green
eyes. There was no mistaking this was Elliot's son. She saw Elliot's smile, his way of
looking out from under his lashes; she saw
his charm. And the image in her mind was
a photograph Irene had once shown her of
Elliot as a boy. All this time he had been the
father of this boy. She heard his voice,
pictured him playing with Conor, cuddling
him at night. It hurt more than she could

ever explain. She heard the noises of the plantation, the sound of the birds, the rustling of the many creatures scuttling about, and the breeze in the trees. In the background, she could even hear the sea. Everything seemed to distil into this one moment, and she felt as if she might never emerge from it.

She nodded numbly and blinked rapidly to suppress the tears. For a moment, nobody spoke. Then Leo broke the silence.

"Say hello, Conor."

The boy just stared at his feet.

She twisted away. "I can't . . . I can't do this."

He told the child to go inside and that the houseboy would bring him down some lunch, and then he took Louisa back up to her car. They stood together, the sun blazing down, but Louisa was unable to even speak.

"I think you'd better come in. You don't look as if you're in any state to drive."

"I need to get away . . ."

"Come on, Louisa. A drink and a sit-down is what you need."

She longed to be able to sob out the pain and the grief but her eyes were dry. The paintings flashed in her mind and she took a step away.

"No. I need to go home. I need to be at home."

She got into her car and drove down the track onto the main road. When she reached the turning for the beach she decided to take it. She parked, and pocketing the shells she had collected earlier, she walked down to the water's edge. Once there she threw the shells into the water with as much strength as she could muster; then she sat on the sand with her head in her hands.

# 24

Elliot's betrayal had scarred her deeply and Louisa's sense of self had taken a battering. Just the thought of putting her trust in somebody other than her father filled her with anxiety. She pondered Elliot's absences. There had been so many but she had simply accepted his excuses, tolerated his occasional ill-humor too. She felt a burning sense of shame that somewhere along the line she had settled for less and must have chosen not to see.

She felt her world rocking and it frightened her, so for the next week she worked all the hours she could to finish drawing up the plans for the emporium. When her father dropped by for coffee on a morning when the early haze had cleared to reveal a sunny day, she tried to say she was too busy to stop, but he took her by the hand and insisted she come to the sitting room with him.

"So," he said while Ashan poured their coffee. "You're definitely going ahead with the emporium?"

"Yes. I have a potential jeweler on board, and I'm going to Colombo next week to see him and some artists too. I'd like to have a gallery of artworks for sale as well. I met one of the artists I'm considering when I stayed at the Hoopers' tea plantation — Savi Ravasinghe. I'm also going to sell some of those little secret boxes and carved ebony elephants. There's a silk designer in Colombo I want to see too. I've already been looking at some samples. I'm not sure if we will stock fabrics or not but it's an idea. And —"

He interrupted. "Darling, take a breath."

She felt suddenly deflated and stared at the floor.

"What's the matter? Won't you tell me? There's no need for you to be working this hard."

"I have to."

"But there's something you haven't told me, isn't there?"

"I went to the cinnamon plantation," she said flatly and without looking up.

"Ah."

"It's all true." She gulped and couldn't look at her father. Saying it could only make it even more real. She pictured again the curly dark hair, the green eyes, the composed look. "I saw the child. There's no mistaking who his father was."

He reached out a hand to her. She took it, squeezed it once and then let go.

"It's not so bad if I keep busy." She had to go on pretending everything was normal — for how else was she to cope?

"Are you sleeping?"

The truth was, when she slept, it was to dream everything was ordinary again. Elliot was alive. There were no debts and definitely no child.

"Only if I have a strong gin first," she said. "Then I sleep. Fitfully."

He sighed. "That's not good."

"It's worse when I stop. I just don't know what to do with the anger. I go off and cycle like a lunatic. I swim. I've even been diving off Flag Rock. But it's cluttering my head all the time. Boring away at me. I want to know everything about Elliot and yet at the same time I don't."

"My love. You have to slow down. Let the pain out."

"How? I want to shout at Elliot, scream at him, but I can't. I want to hurt him. Really hurt him. That's what makes it so much worse."

But that didn't express the true violence of her feelings, or the awful things she imagined doing to him.

"He's gone and there's nothing I can do to show him what he has done to me. I feel he has taken me away from myself. Do you see?"

"I'm wondering if you should see the doctor."

She had considered it. Thought maybe she was going a little crazy, constantly fending off the echoes from the past, and feeling as if she could stretch out her hand to touch them, yet unable to find a way.

"I don't want any pills."

"Do you want me to come to Colombo with you?"

"No. I'm meeting Margo there. She'll accompany me to the meetings."

On the way to the capital Louisa passed the usual Buddhist shrines and temples. Groups of saffron- and ochre-robed monks sauntered along, while drumming and chanting could be heard from nearby villages where a wedding or some other ceremony was happening. She held her breath at the place where Elliot had veered off the road but couldn't stop herself feeling angry. Maybe I'll see a devil dancer, she thought, knowing

Ceylon's wild men of the jungle were famous for worshipping the demons believed to be living in the trees. Maybe that's what I need. A demon. Elliot had taken her to one of these rituals where she'd witnessed the horrible masks they used. It had scared her but the atmosphere had been electric too. And something about that matched her own ragged feelings.

In contrast, the packed streets of Colombo smelled of coconut, cinnamon and fried fish, plus the sweet scents from the various tea and cake stalls lining the pavement. Louisa parked close to the fancy red and cream brick-built building that was Cargills department store, closely avoiding a bright blue bullock cart, creaking and groaning as it swerved in front of her. Flies and mosquitoes swarmed everywhere as she walked through the Chinese bazaar on Chatham Street, passing small fabric outlets laden with silks, two or three herbalists, and several shops selling lacquered goods.

Everything shone in the fierce heat and dust.

Further on, in air now smelling of dung, fruit and spices, British civil servants and missionary ladies mingled with Sinhalese and Tamil workers. Crows soared above them, perching where they could as they spied out any scraps of food. She had to maneuver around several rickshaws blocking the way, until she eventually reached the tea shop she was looking for, and spotted Margo sitting in the window. The younger woman gave her a wave and a broad smile and Louisa steeled herself. This was to be a working day and she simply could not give in to her emotions. She pushed open the door, heard the tinkle of the bell, and approached Margo.

"I've ordered tea for both of us," Margo said.

"Lovely." Louisa seated herself and put her bag on a spare chair. "So how have you been?"

"I'm fine. Although Mother isn't. She wants to come and stay with you again, but I've been trying to put her off."

"Why does she want to come?"

"I think she wants to be where Elliot was."

Louisa shook her head. She didn't want to tell Margo how bad she had felt lately, but Irene would really be the last straw. "To be honest, it's a terrible idea. I could kill Elliot, the way I feel right now." She winced. "If he wasn't already dead."

"It is true, then? About the child?"

She inhaled deeply before replying. "I saw

him, Margo. He's the spitting image of Elliot."

"Oh, my love. I am sorry."

Louisa sighed and decided to change the
subject. There were times when talking did
not help. "Let's not talk about it. I'm more
interested in you."

"Me? I just feel such a fool for having gotten myself involved with a married man and
pretending everything was normal. He said
his marriage was over and I allowed myself
to believe it because I wanted to."

Louisa thought of Elliot and almost re-
treated into silence. She forced herself to
speak for Margo's sake. "We've both believed what we've wanted to believe. Maybe
you couldn't help falling in love with William."

"It's what I told myself, but really there's
a point where it became a choice. I could
have turned my back on him."

"Is that how Elliot felt, do you think?"

"That it was a choice, or that he could
have walked away from it?"

"Both, I guess."

"Who knows? All I'm sure of is William's
marriage wasn't over, and neither was yours.
I feel guilty as hell."

"But at least you ended it. Elliot didn't."

"Yes."

"Do you still miss William?"

"I miss having somebody in my life. The thing is, he made me feel so special. I've never felt special before."

Louisa patted her hand. "You're special to me."

Margo flashed her a quick smile. "In our house everything revolved around Elliot. He was the one who got all the attention. He could do no wrong. Even the slightest achievement was hailed with cakes and treats. At the school sports day, when he came third in the hundred-yard dash, you'd have thought he'd won all the races of the day. Whatever I did, my mother barely noticed me. Anyway, it's all done and dusted . . . Now how about a cream bun? You are looking too thin."

"You, my dear, are sounding like your mother!"

They both laughed and the mood lightened.

Louisa put on her business face as first they went to see the jeweler, the cousin of the dealer Louisa had spoken to in Galle. It turned out he was keen to expand and would be delighted to sell his sapphire range at the emporium and supply the stock for the main display. Louisa was satisfied. Next, they followed a narrow alley between tall buildings and found the silk designer's sign. The woman took them upstairs to her workshop, a huge room flooded with light from floor-to-ceiling windows.

She mainly made scarves and kaftans, but all the silk was hand dyed, hand painted or batiked into fabulous patterns in myriad colors. A row of the pieces hung like pretty flags from a line running the length of the room.

"They're still drying," she said, seeing them looking and gently touching one or two. "Then they'll be ironed and packed in tissue."

"Well, as I said in my letter, I'm looking for artists and craftspeople who would consider using my emporium as an outlet for their goods. We've floor space for a nominal rent, and I'd be happy to offer it free for the first three months. You sell and we take a percentage. For that we maintain the premises and take care of advertising. How does that sound?"

"Interesting."

"I can employ reliable sales staff, unless you have somebody in mind."

"I have a friend who lives in Galle. Her children have just started school so she might be interested."

"Well, either way we'd love to have your

beautiful silks."

The woman smiled and they discussed prices for a while and, when the deal was done, shook hands.

The next stop was Elliot's office for the spice business. As far as Louisa was aware of, the business ran itself so this was more of a courtesy call than anything else. Nihil, the middle-aged manager, was expecting her and when she arrived he commiserated over the loss of Elliot.

"We were all so shocked," he said, "when your father let us know what had happened. He told me to carry on as usual and that you would be coming at some point. And now, here you are."

"Thank you for your concern," she said and smiled, managing to keep the exchange light. "That's very kind."

"And may I ask if you have any plans?"

She nodded. At least here there were no memories assaulting her. "The only plan I have is to keep going."

Nihil looked relieved. "I did wonder if you might be selling up."

"Not in the foreseeable future, but I'd like to look at the accounts."

"Of course. I shall fetch them directly."

He went to a large cupboard and brought out two black ledgers.

"Your husband transferred a capital sum, to cover an acquisition, I understand."

"Can I see?"

"Yes. Look here."

She glanced at the figures and confirmed to herself that the amount Elliot had taken out from the business account could have covered the deposit on the Print House. It still didn't explain what had happened to the missing half of the money she had transferred to his personal account and that should have been left over after he'd paid the balance on the building.

"But we're not in the red, are we?"

"Absolutely not. In fact, I feel we are approaching the point where it would be sensible to expand."

Louisa could see it wasn't a huge enterprise but it ticked over nicely, and she promised to come up to Colombo once a month to ensure everything was running smoothly and do anything she could to increase supplies.

After that they drove to Cinnamon Gardens, so named after the former cinnamon plantation that had once existed in that area, where they were to meet Savi Ravasinghe. The streets were lined with trees and grand colonial mansions, and he lived on the top floor of a large house divided into two apartments. It was surrounded by an extensive garden, resplendent with tall trees and rhododendron bushes. Louisa was feeling the heat and ran a palm over her forehead.

"Aren't you hot?" she asked Margo.

"It's close today."

"I'm actually looking forward to the rains." Louisa didn't add that she felt something about the rains, the hot drumming intensity of them, might somehow wash away the sense of grief and doubt that constantly consumed her. When she was a child she had loved to sneak out into the garden at night in just her pajamas and hold her arms up to catch the rain. Her ayah had usually found her and dragged her back in, but she had loved the freeing wildness of being out in the downpour.

Savi met them at the door, looking as elegant and exotic as before.

"Lovely to see you again," he said and held out a hand to Louisa.

After she had shaken it she introduced Margo, and then they followed him up the stairs and into a large open space. Sunlight flooded in from huge windows running right across one wall, the floor was tiled and laid with gorgeous rugs — Persian, he told them — and the pristine white walls were hung with paintings.

"These aren't all yours?" Louisa asked.

"The portraits are mine, but the land-scapes are by a friend."

Louisa stared at them, admiring the subtle colors of the landscapes and the singing colors of the portraits. "I like that you paint ordinary people. I would love to show some of these in my gallery."

"I have a few more portraits through here. Not by me, though." He pointed the way to a long corridor and she followed him through. But when she saw the first portrait her mouth went dry. Staring out at her was an unmistakable image of Elliot, his arm around a red-headed woman.

"These are by an acquaintance," Savi was saying. "Zinnia. I think we spoke of her when we last met, though at the time I couldn't remember her name. I came across them just recently as a job lot in a warehouse sale and, as I acquired them for a good price, I thought I might sell them on. They are particularly fine, I think."

Louisa made some excuse and said she'd prefer to look at the paintings in the main room. They were more what she was after, she said, but Margo had followed her into the corridor and, when Louisa glanced back, she saw her sister-in-law standing and staring at the painting of her brother.

"They're good, aren't they," Louisa called out. "But look at these, Margo."

They caught each other's eye and Margo came back to the main room, visibly shocked. For a moment Louisa stood and gazed at the light from the huge windows. All the colors of the room began to swirl and meld together and she felt herself growing far too hot again. For one horrible instant she thought she was going to faint and reached out a hand as if to break her fall.

"Are you all right?" Margo said, and the sound of her voice brought Louisa back.

She took a few deep breaths and after she had regained her self-control, she told Savi she'd be delighted to display his own work and the landscapes too, though it would be some weeks before the conversion of the building from a printer's to a shop would be complete.

"I'd be happy to make some pictures especially for you. Maybe some smaller, more easily portable ones? Next time I'm back in Ceylon."

"Yes," she said, "that would be perfect."

As they walked away from his place Margo turned to her. "Are you really okay?"

"I think so. I saw similar paintings when I went to the plantation."

"But it must have been a shock. It was for me."

"I'd seen pictures of him with the child, but not with her. And I didn't think these paintings were for the open market. I don't know why, but I imagined she just kept them all. That they were somehow private."

"She must have needed the money."

"Yes. Though I suspect some of Elliot's debts were because of her. I don't imagine he would have wanted her selling any portraits of him. To be honest, I felt like buying them all and burning the lot."

"They're a bit too graphic."

"It brings it home." Louisa swallowed hard and then she spoke again in a low voice. "I thought they looked happy together, didn't you?"

"So, if they were so happy, why didn't he leave you?"

"Why didn't your married man leave his wife?"

Margo shrugged but looked sadder than before. "It was never in the cards."

"I suppose people must fall in love with the wrong person all the time."

"It happened to me, but that doesn't excuse Elliot."

"Why not?"

Margo sighed. "I can't justify what he did, but I can't justify what I did either."

"Did you try to stop it?"

"At first, but then it seemed to become a compulsion. I found myself thinking of William all the time and, in the end, I got in touch again."

"It's not really even the fact that Elliot fell for someone else. Well, it is, of course it is, but it's the deception that cuts me."

"I can't forgive myself, you know. Maybe Elliot was sorry for what he'd done too?"

"Well, he had every reason to stay with me, didn't he? Plenty of money, a nice big house, his job. My father would hardly have kept him on if he'd abandoned me. I've been such a fool to give my heart to someone who treated it so recklessly."

"He was always careless of other people's feelings, but he loved you. I'm sure of it."

"Are you?"

# 25

Louisa paced her bedroom, glancing from time to time at Elliot's chest of drawers. She chewed her fingernail and, wanting to finally be done with him, decided the only thing to do was to be rid of his things. *Out. I want all of it out,* she thought. *If everything was gone then he might be gone too.*

In an overbright and determined tone, she instructed one of the houseboys to help her build a bonfire in the garden, but not to light it yet. They both carried old newspapers out and dragged across branches that had been pruned and left to dry. When the stack was tall enough, she went back indoors to their bedroom, where she gazed inside the wardrobe for a minute, then took out all of Elliot's suits and shirts, leaving them piled up on the bed. After that she opened his chest drawer by drawer and heaped the contents up on the floor. She felt as if her heart might stop as she ran her hands over the familiar shirts. She held one to her nose to see if she could catch a trace of the familiar cedar scent of him, and then she tried another, but they had all been laundered and so there was nothing. She went through the pockets of his suits and jackets and then, from an old pair of corduroys, she fished out an envelope. It was sealed but not addressed, and so she ripped it open and removed a single sheet of paper. She read:

My darling,

I can't tell you how distressed I am that you feel you must end it. As you know, I haven't been able to see you as much as I've wanted since Louisa lost the baby and I have had to remain close by her side. It hasn't been my choice. You do see that, don't you? Please will you reconsider? I will try to come to you again soon and you must know I love you. You have to believe it and I promise the time will be right for us very soon indeed. I'm sorry it has taken so long, but I can't wait to be with you and am not far off from being able to look after you both permanently.

I need to make a little more money before I can offer you the life you should have and I'm best placed to do it if I stay here a little longer. I have bought a new business, an old print house, and after a little work, hope to sell it at a profit. I did tell you at the very beginning that I still loved my wife. Do you remember? But of course that changed once Conor came into the world. Please look after yourself and him too. I shall send money via Leo if I can't get to you soon and then I'll take your next batch of paintings to Colombo to sell.

But whatever else you may feel, please reconsider. Don't end it, my love. I just can't face that.

Always your
Elliot

Louisa read it through twice and felt sick. Then she ripped it into tiny fragments and hurled them at the wastepaper basket, feeling as if she was ripping up her whole life. Not only had Elliot never intended to make the emporium a reality, he had been planning to leave her too. It seemed like the final nail in the coffin of their marriage and she felt as if her heart was separating from her soul.

As silence wrapped around her, a burst of anger surged through her. She took an armful of his clothes with her as she went outside to light the bonfire. Once she had a proper blaze going, she began piling on Elliot's clothes, his suits followed his shirts, and his shirts followed his ties. She went back in to fetch more, watching as each item burned. Gone, she thought. All of it gone. That's what she wanted. The houseboy observed all of this with a look of bemusement. It must seem incredibly wasteful to him, Louisa suspected, but she couldn't bear for Elliot's clothes to exist. She had loved him so much and now, as she listened to the crackle and hiss, she began to laugh wildly. As the flames caught at the edges of each piece of clothing and then devoured it, the fire was not simply feeding her anger — the destructive energy had become energizing.

She felt exhilarated. Almost lightheaded with relief.

Suddenly she heard a voice, and twisting around, saw Irene standing there in the garden with a look of horror on her face. Harold stood beside her with an arm around her shoulders. And Ashan stood behind them holding their suitcases. "I'm sorry, Madam," he said. "I wanted to inform you of their arrival first, but they insisted on coming through."

"What are you doing?" Irene screamed. "What are you doing with my son's clothes?"

Louisa stood completely still. "I think, Irene, you may have worked out I am burning them, lock, stock and barrel."

Irene ran up to the fire and, grabbing a stick, attempted to rescue a partially burning shirt. It hung at the end of her stick as she held it aloft, charred and smoking. Louisa almost laughed again as she watched her mother-in-law's futile attempt at rescue and Harold pulling her away.

"Leave it!" she commanded.

Irene frowned. "But why? Why are you doing this?"

"What do you expect me to do?"

"Isn't it a bit too soon?" Harold said. "It's as if you're getting rid of him."

Louisa stared coldly. "Honestly? I wish I could. No, more than that, I wish I'd never even met him."

And with that she turned on her heels, went upstairs and locked the bedroom door behind her. Then she spent the remainder of the afternoon in her room nursing her anger whilst feeling she no longer lived in a world of her own devising. Ashan knocked several times with drinks for her, gently encouraging her to open the door, but she couldn't bring herself to see anyone.

That evening Louisa decided to dress for dinner. She was expecting her father and would make an effort for him.

Although she was furious Irene and Harold had arrived unannounced, she could hardly turn them away, and anyway the letter she had found overshadowed everything else. The euphoria from the effect of the fire hadn't lasted and now, every time she thought about the letter, she struggled against a desire to rush to the bathroom to vomit. As for Irene, Elliot had been her only surviving son, and it would require a great deal of self-control on Louisa's part not to spoil Irene's illusions. Louisa didn't know if she was up to the deception especially as, in Irene's eyes, Elliot would have become even more saintly than he had been in life.

Louisa sighed. Why did everything have to be so difficult? She took a bath and washed her hair to rid herself of the smell of smoke, then dressed soberly in a light gray silk dress, slipped on her pearls and made her way to the main sitting room downstairs, where Irene and Harold were already ensconced on one of the sofas. As she entered the room she glanced about. Irene had a habit of moving ornaments to where she considered them more appropriate and, though Louisa had argued with Elliot about it, he had convinced her it was such a trivial matter there was no point causing a scene. Louisa saw it now as yet another sign of the woman's interference.

Irene sat up a little straighter and sniffed, her gray eyes steely. "So, you have deigned to grace us with your presence."

Louisa gritted her teeth. "I'm pleased to see you, Irene. And you too, Harold."

He gave her a wan smile.

"Maybe you might like to explain why you were burning my son's clothes?" Irene continued.

"It was time."

"You didn't think to ask if we might want some of them to remember him by?"

"His clothes were nothing to do with you. You may have his pen, pipe or hairbrush. Take all of them, if you like. There are still plenty of items. Take your pick."

"But nothing he actually wore."

"I didn't think —"

Irene interrupted. "That's exactly the trouble. It always has been. You don't think of me, do you?"

"Come now, Irene, I'm sure you don't mean that," Harold said, attempting to take his wife's hand, though Irene was having none of it and shook him off.

Louisa turned her back and stiffly went to the decanter to pour three sherries. She took one across to Irene and offered it to her, then gave one to Harold. "Please let's not squabble. I'm really just too tired."

Irene didn't reply but took the glass.

At that moment, the doorbell rang. Louisa listened as Ashan answered it and a minute or two later he brought Louisa's father, Jonathan, into the room, followed by Margo.

"I found her struggling from the train station with her case."

Margo laughed. "And so he did the gentlemanly thing and carried it for me. I came on the train to try to catch up with Mum and Dad. Luckily it wasn't a stormy day, or the train would have been deluged with sea spray."

Irene stood and held out her hands to Margo.

Margo hugged her mother, who seemed to cling to her.

"I hope you don't mind me descending on you like this, Louisa."

"Not at all, Margo. The more the merrier!" she said, in fact intensely relieved to see her sister-in-law. "I'm sure Cook can be creative with supper."

After the new arrivals had seated themselves and had also been supplied with sherry, a strained silence descended. Perhaps sensing some awkwardness, Jonathan took it upon himself to get the conversation going.

"So, how do you think the government is getting along, Irene?"

"You'd have to ask my husband. I don't bother myself with such matters, though I believe Harold is in full support of it, aren't you, dear?"

Harold nodded. "Broadly speaking, yes."

Jonathan inclined his head. "You don't think the board of ministers should have control of the police and army too?"

"He believes that keeping them under the control of the British is the better option," Irene chipped in, while Harold gave a resigned sigh. "After all, who wants these people to be in charge of ensuring law and order. No, that's best kept in our own hands."

"These people, Irene?" Jonathan said, his brows raised questioningly.

"I think you know what my wife meant," Harold said.

Margo stepped in. "You don't always have to stick up for her, Dad. Now come on,

Mum, shift up so I can sit next to you for a bit."

Irene moved and Margo took up her place next to her mother and father.

"So," Louisa said, turning to her father and speaking softly while Margo and Irene seemed to be talking about the bus journey and how uncomfortable it was. "Did you go back to see the police? Do they know anything more about the break-in?"

He raised his brows. "I've done what I said I would do. Fat lot of good it will do, though."

"Won't the police take any action?"

Jonathan shrugged. "They weren't sure what they could do."

"Take action?" Irene piped up. "Must you speak in riddles."

Jonathan glanced at Louisa before speaking. She in turn gave a brief shake of her head. "Just a spot of bother."

"Well, I found your daughter burning all of Elliot's clothing today. What do you make of that?"

"I'm sure my daughter is only doing what has to be done," Jonathan said. "She can't hold on to everything, and nor should she."

"Anyway, it's up to Louisa, isn't it, Mum?" Margo added.

"Exactly. This has to be Louisa's decision.

My daughter is having a tough enough time without us interfering."

A look of fury crossed Irene's face. "Nobody thinks to consider my feelings," she said. "Nobody."

"Now, Irene, that's not fair," Harold interjected. "I know we're both upset but —"

"I'll tell you what's not fair. Marrying a woman who couldn't give him a living child. That's all I ever wanted. Was it too much to hope for? You know Elliot would have been a wonderful father. So caring. So dutiful."

*"Mother,"* Margo said in a warning tone at the same time as Harold shook his head.

"A grandson was all I ever wanted."

In a flash, Louisa got to her feet, her anger over the letter she had found uppermost in her mind. "Well, you've certainly got your wish, Irene!"

"What on earth are you talking about?"

Louisa glanced at Margo, who was gesturing wildly at her to stop, but Louisa had already gone too far to draw back, and now couldn't help herself. "You *do* have a grandson, Irene. A little illegitimate boy. I hope that satisfies you."

As Louisa got herself ready for bed, she went over what had happened. She felt

255

mortified that things had come to this and knew telling Irene had not been wise. She would either deny all possibility of an illegitimate child, or she would want to take over. Either way Louisa would have to let Leo know. She picked up Elliot's pen, the one he always kept on his bedside table, and began writing to the plantation owner. She'd give the pen to Irene in the morning and let her choose anything else she might want. As she rolled it between her fingers she pictured Elliot writing notes to himself just before he turned out the light.

She thought back to the moment they first met. She'd been out on her bicycle and, despite early signs of rain, had decided to head for the coastal road. But after only an hour the monsoon had begun in earnest. After seriously misjudging the weather she'd been swept off the road, grazing her leg in the process. She had crawled and found a rock to shelter against, but by then was completely soaked through. Half an hour passed and she'd felt immense relief when a car finally pulled up and the driver jumped out to help her. He bundled her into the car and her bike into the trunk and brought her back to Galle Fort. They each drank a mug of hot chocolate and her leg was bandaged before he prepared to resume his journey.

But with weather too wild 
tinue to Colombo he ha
and then the next day, a
that. She'd fallen for Elli
good looks right from the sta
full of hope for the future.

She put the pen down and de
send the letter to Leo. She woul
instead.

# 26

Louisa rose as dawn was painting the sky a subtle shade of lilac, reflecting in the sea as palest pink. It was her favorite time of day. She glanced through the window up toward the hills to the north, still shrouded in a mist, and even in her garden the leaves were dripping with dew. She might occasionally spot a civet cat tempted into her garden by the sweet palm seeds, but not today. Her durian and jackfruit trees attracted birds in large numbers, and she usually liked to watch them, though today just one solitary imperial pigeon with metallic-green wings strutted on the lawn.

She didn't have time to linger. With a house crammed full of people, she hoped not to have to mention where she was going. Even Jonathan had stayed the night, perhaps feeling his daughter might need moral support with Irene so likely to make trouble.

After Louisa's shock announcement, the questions had gone on and on. *Who is this child? Are you sure he is Elliot's son? How did you find out? Had you known all along? Why hadn't I, as his grandmother, been told?* And when Irene discovered Margo had already known about Conor, she turned puce with anger. She hadn't, however, seemed the slightest bit concerned that the existence of this child meant Elliot had betrayed his wife.

Louisa dressed quickly and then went down to the kitchen where the cook was still stoking the boiler, so no coffee on the go yet. As she got into the car she turned over a new idea she'd had for what was now her spice business. Her manager, Nihil, had said the business was ripe for expansion, so this might be just the thing to enable its growth. While driving along the coastal road, she considered what she might say when she got to Cinnamon Hills. First, she'd have to tell Leo that Irene now knew about Conor's existence. It might not come to anything but, knowing Irene, Louisa couldn't be sure; and, next, she would run her new idea past Leo.

As she turned off the main road and began to make her way up the hill, she passed the place where you could just make out Zinnia's bungalow nestled among the trees. Her jaw stiffened. What am I doing? she thought. Was it foolish to involve Leo in her new idea? Perhaps not, because something inside her, something in the place where the remnants of hope and faith still resided, was forcing her hand. Maybe in some convoluted way the very reason she was even considering this plan was an act of defiance, conceived despite Elliot's betrayal. In any case, she would not be cowed.

She stopped the car before she reached the top and climbed out to smell the air, enjoying the mix of cinnamon and the salty scents of the ocean. She glanced around her expectantly. Would she spot Leo at work, or maybe glimpse the child playing in the clearing? But then, seeing nobody, she continued on. While the child's very existence had shaken her to the core, she had to remind herself he had lost his father and, as someone who had grown up motherless, she accepted how devastating that was for a youngster.

She pulled up at the top, stilled the engine and then got out to stand and admire the panoramic view. The birds were still singing and she relished the feeling of being in the midst of a plantation bursting with wildlife. When it came, his voice startled her and she spun around. He was wearing his usual threadbare shorts, and a bright blue shirt that brought out the color of his eyes and the red of his hair.

"Leo."

"Hello. I didn't expect to see you again."

"I have something to tell you."

"Shall we walk?"

He led her along a narrow path between the cinnamon trees. Just then a drift of exotic butterflies flew past.

"So. What did you want to say?"

She swallowed nervously before she spoke. "I'm afraid Elliot's mother knows about Conor now."

"And?"

"Well, she isn't the easiest of women. She may interfere."

He scratched his head. "I don't know. If she is prepared to lend a helping hand while Zinnia is ill, that might not be so bad."

Louisa was aghast at the idea. "I don't recommend it. It would never be just lending a hand. She'd take over completely, and that would be awful."

"Does she know he's here?"

She shook her head. "I've given her no details other than that he exists. I wish I hadn't said anything."

"I wouldn't worry." He hesitated and appeared to be thinking. "Hopefully Zinnia will be better soon. In the meantime, I'm doing what I can for Conor. He's lonely, so I try to have lunch with him every day and take him with me when I can."

"His illegitimacy might prevent Irene from becoming involved."

He nodded, took a few steps and then twisted back to look at her.

"What?" she asked.

"I was wondering if you'd like a drink. Or, if you have time, maybe see more of the plantation?"

This was just what she wanted and, thinking of her new idea, she nodded. "Tell me about it — I'd love to know how the cinnamon is produced. Is it very labor intensive?"

"Well, the first thing to know is that the workers are paid a share of the profit, so the more productive and profitable the team, the more they get paid. So yes, a third of my revenue goes to labor costs."

He led her along a wide, leaf-strewn track. "The harvesting process is laborious. We can harvest twice a year, but it's better if the bark is peeled during the rainy season, when the sap flows freely."

"So you aren't harvesting quite yet?"

"We are, but we're mainly coppicing and gathering the dried leaves to produce oil."

"Hard work."

He smiled and she noticed how at ease he was in this environment.

"Once the branches are cut, the outer bark is scraped off and the inner bark is cut, then peeled so that it coils up into quills. The larger sections are rolled up together then filled with small quills and broken pieces to add strength. These are then cut into pieces of three or four feet in length."

"And Ceylon cinnamon is particularly good?"

"It has its own identity and is world renowned. Did you know it was first taken to the Middle East by sea in antiquity? And Nero is said to have used it at his wife's funeral. Our cinnamon has even triggered wars. I can show you how we produce the oil if you like."

"Please."

"The peelers collect the stems for the day's work in the morning when it's cool and take them to the peeling sheds on carts or tractors, although we can collect the leaves at any time."

While they had been walking, Louisa had seen he had been taking her down the hill toward a place where smoke and steam almost obliterated several straw-roofed sheds from sight. He led her around the corner where another fire had been lit in a simple boiler.

"We produce the oil from leaves and twigs. It's steamy work."

She watched as a man filled a tall cylindrical vat with leaves while another worker inside it was treading the contents down.

"Gosh, it must be hot."

"Yes, he'll tread down the leaves until the column is tightly packed. Watch, he's just about finished."

The man climbed out and then, using mud, sealed a lid onto the vat.

"See the pipe at the bottom?"

She nodded.

"The steam passes through that from the boiler, extracts the oil from the leaves and then passes out again. The steam condenses to a liquid as it travels through a pipe submerged in cold water."

"And then?"

"The oil is skimmed off from where the liquid is collected in tubs. Gravity takes care of the separation for us."

"It's fascinating — and seeing all this brings me to my second reason for coming to see you."

"Shall we go back up to the house for a coffee?"

"Thank you."

They walked in silence with just the sound of their feet crunching the dry leaves on the path. Once they reached his house, they took the stairs to the veranda and he ordered their drinks.

"You love this place, don't you?" she said.

His smile spread slowly and lit up his eyes as it widened. "I suppose I must do, though sometimes it has me tearing my hair out!"

"Like all the things we love."

"I guess."

She took a breath before beginning. "I don't know how you are placed to export your cinnamon, but Elliot had a spice company, exporting all over the world. It's mine now, and I think it's time to expand . . . I was wondering if I could tempt you to export through us. I'd ensure my manager offered you good terms."

"Well, I wasn't expecting that," he said, but looked genuinely interested. "I've been wondering about changing my middleman. I deal with a chap in Galle, but the quantity I'm now producing is becoming too large for him to handle."

"I could take you to meet Nihil, the manager in Colombo. How about the day after tomorrow?"

"Sounds good to me. Kamu will look after Conor just this once."

"Yes."

He grinned. "Deal. I can't offer you a lift in the van, it's conked out and the mechanic can't work out what's wrong. But . . . I'm not sure if this would appeal . . . We could go all the way on the motorbike, if you like, though it's an old bone shaker and it will mean coming back very late."

Why not, she thought. Wasn't it time to spread her wings? "I like the idea," she said, then hesitated for a moment, wanting to appear calmer than she really felt about what else was on her mind. "How is your cousin?"

He shrugged. "She has been a little better lately."

"How shall I put this?" she said. "If we are to do business together I'd prefer not to see her."

"She doesn't usually come up here. I go to her."

"What is she living on?"

He looked a little embarrassed and pulled a face. "Elliot helped her out. She might have a little of that money left." He glanced away and then back at her. "I'm sorry."

She shook her head. "She sells paintings too?"

"Elliot took them to Colombo for her."

"I saw some of them." Louisa took a deep breath and let it out slowly. "When we go to

Colombo I shall withdraw the money Elliot left to you. Will you see that she gets it?"

"That's very kind."

"No, it isn't. It's the law. And she has a child to support. Does she go to the shops in the village? For supplies, I mean."

"She used to, but since she's been ill, my houseboy has been getting things for her when he gets mine."

"So you've been supporting her."

He shrugged. "As best I can. It's Conor I worry about. He's a strange little boy but he touches my heart."

"Maybe he needs to go to school, as you said before? Children need other children, don't they?"

"Try telling Zinnia."

When she got home, Margo was waiting for her. "Mum's taking a nap and Dad has gone back to Colombo for work. We had lunch but there's plenty left. She won't stop talking about her grandson, I'm afraid."

"I was worried that might happen."

They walked into the dining room and Ashan agreed to bring in her lunch.

"It's just a salade niçoise made by the French girl, Camille. So nothing to keep hot. I didn't know how long you were going to be," Margo said.

"I went to see Leo."

Margo's eyes widened and her eyebrows shot up.

Louisa laughed. "He and I are going into business together, or at least we may be."

"Well, I'm all for you seeing more of him."

"He showed me around the plantation."

"It's obviously his world. But listen, the reason I came is because I have something to tell you. With everything else going on last night I didn't get a chance to say anything, and then you were gone so early this morning . . ."

"So?"

"Right after Mum and Dad left on the bus yesterday, a man came to their house. Said he was looking for Elliot's parents to talk to them about some of their son's debts. He didn't leave his name. I haven't mentioned it to Mum or Dad but I thought you should know."

"These awful debts . . . really, it breaks my heart. Did you recognize him at all? Was it that man, De Vos, the one we saw at the jeweler's the day we went to the Print House? Do you remember?"

"No, it definitely wasn't him. I think he had some sort of accent, but I'm not really sure. I was a bit taken aback. Do the police really still have no idea who broke into the house?"

"No evidence to point them in any direction, they say. I just don't see how the burglars knew we'd be out."

## 27

When De Vos finally turned up, apologizing for the slight delay and handing her the contract, she saw at once it was an agreement to broker a particular shipment of rubber. In his usual courteous manner, he told her it was a blue carbon copy, but he held the original in his safe and he hoped it would satisfy any uncertainty she might have about the debt.

"I'll tell you what we'll do," she said, feeling confused as she gazed at the contract. To her knowledge, Elliot had never had any dealings in rubber. "Leave this with me and I'll look it over."

After he had gone, she gathered the dogs and walked out to the ramparts. Now they were well into May the sea was wild and the air hummed with flying insects. The wind lifted her hair, blowing it into her eyes and making them stream. On the horizon, a streak of yellow separated the ocean from the graying sky, and shrieking gulls wheeled and dived above her. She listened to the breath of the ocean as the waves swelled and faded: a sign the monsoon was not far off. Although aware that traveling to Colombo on the back of a motorcycle was hardly wise, she longed to escape from living her life in the shadow of Elliot's death. Riding pillion on a motorbike would be perfect. Even if she might get drenched, the excitement and speed would get her blood pumping faster. She twisted the wedding ring she still wore. Was it time to take it off?

The next morning, she rose at six to wait for Leo. She opened the French windows to look out at the huge blue sky, but when Irene came down early too Louisa could see her eyes were red from crying. She felt a twinge of sympathy for the woman.

"How are you, Irene?" Louisa asked in a conciliatory tone. "Would you like some tea?"

Irene wrung her hands over and over but didn't speak.

"Irene?"

The words burst out fiercely. "To think he had a child all this time. How was it possible you never knew?"

"You never knew either," Louisa said softly.

"But you lived with him!"

"He was away a lot. I'd become accustomed to it."

Irene shook her head.

In the following pause, Margo came in.

"You're both up terribly early," Louisa said. "What's going on?"

"I've persuaded Mum to go back to Colombo today."

"If you think it's for the best," Irene said, a slight sob catching in her throat. "I hardly know what's right any more."

Louisa glanced at her mother-in-law. She looked folded in on herself, as if the glue that held her together had dissolved.

"Sit down, Irene," she said and pulled out a chair. Irene almost collapsed into it.

"But Mum, if anyone comes asking you to pay off Elliot's debts you are to inform the police straight away," Margo warned.

Irene frowned, then gazed at her daughter with a bemused expression. "Why? What debts?"

"The thing is, Mum, I didn't want to tell you — but it appears Elliot was in some difficulty."

Now Irene managed to control herself. "I'm sure it can't amount to much. Your father and I will happily pay off anything he owes."

"No, Mum. We are talking a small fortune."

"I don't understand."

"You'd better tell her everything," Louisa said.

While Margo explained all she knew, Louisa stared at the floor and felt her heart plummet. Hearing it all laid out like this was appalling. What kind of fool would not have suspected a thing? And now, as Elliot's uneasy spirit crept closer, she tried to listen to Margo but couldn't block out the whisperings in her head and the image of him laughing behind her back.

By the end, Irene was bent forward in her chair with her head in her hands.

Louisa and Margo exchanged looks, but then Irene straightened up and jabbed a finger at Margo. "I refuse to believe a word of this! How could you both stoop so low as to blacken his name like this? You've always been jealous of your brother, Margo."

"Mum, it's the truth. It's been shocking for all of us."

Irene's face was contorted by a spasm of anguish. "But it's too much. Too much."

Her protective shell torn from her, she looked raw, and Louisa, seeing the scared woman beneath the harsh exterior, attempted to reach out to her. "He was a good husband to me. I had no reason to suspect anything."

Irene gazed at her with damp eyes. "And this child. What of this child?"

"He's called Conor."

"Have you met him?"

"Not really, but I have seen him."

"And is he like Elliot?"

"He's the spitting image."

"Well, all I can say is I'm glad to be getting the bus back to Colombo today — unless you're willing to drive me?" She looked up at Louisa hopefully.

"Actually, I do have plans to go to Colombo today, but on the back of a motorbike."

"Isn't that rather risky? And with my dear Elliot so recently gone."

The *dear* was the thing that did it, and Louisa was unable to bite her tongue. "*Dear* Elliot, who had been having a secret affair for eight years? Do you mean *that* Elliot, Irene?"

And the words were left spinning in the air.

A little later, Louisa climbed onto the back of the motorbike and then cautiously wrapped her arms around Leo. Holding her nerve, and excited by the close proximity and warmth of his body, she inhaled deeply. She could smell the cinnamon on his clothes and the tang of some kind of aftershave lotion. As they got going she relaxed, leaning closer, and enjoying the feeling of intimacy. How she had missed this! The connection. The heat. The nearness. And although she hardly knew Leo, she clung to him with a growing sense of release. It felt so good to be this close. So good.

The journey to Colombo was hair-raising, but she didn't care. Despite the speed she felt she could trust him, and whenever he accelerated she experienced a sensation of being freed from normal constraints. The wind blew in her face and the thrill of it invigorated her. From time to time she glanced up at the darkening sky and across at the ominous-looking sea, but so far it remained dry. It was a bouncing, jolting journey and she constantly felt aware of her body so close to his. Eventually they arrived, a little shaken but in one piece. As she climbed down her legs felt wobbly but he reached out a hand to steady her. She grinned at him and he laughed.

"Feeling better?" he asked.

"Very much so."

He parked the bike and told her he needed to pick up some supplies, but he would meet her at the office. When he put a hand on her shoulder she felt a slight shiver at his touch. Then she watched him walk away. Today he wore twill trousers and a waxed cotton jacket over a shirt and tie. Still a casual look, but she had never seen him look so smart. Then she walked past Cargills and on down to the alley leading to the spice company office.

At the end of the alley a man stood waiting. As she drew closer, she saw his icy-blue eyes had not left her face. When his voice broke into her thoughts it was with an Australian accent.

"Mrs. Reeve?"

"Who wants to know?" She felt a twinge of apprehension and wished Leo hadn't left her, especially as this man towered over her and blocked the doorway.

He smiled. "Time we had a nice friendly chat."

"I'm rather pressed for time. I have business to attend to." Although nervous, she kept her voice firm.

He shook his head. "My condolences about your husband."

"You knew my husband?"

The man nodded. "And I think you may

have something of mine in your possession."

She felt her breath shortening but met his unwavering gaze. "Who are you?"

He smiled again. "You can call me Cooper."

"I'm sure I don't have anything of yours."

"I'm all for keeping this amicable. It's a certain financial debt I'm talking about. I believe my colleague, Mr. De Vos, has mentioned it."

"He's your colleague?"

He nodded.

"That is already in hand, then."

"Make sure it is." As he reached over and took her by the arm she glanced up the alley and then back at the man.

"I'd like you to let me go."

Hearing a sound, Louisa twisted her head again, and saw Leo was ambling up, pushing his motorcycle. He left it to lean against a wall and then, apparently noticing something was up, walked rapidly toward them. At Leo's approach, the man released Louisa's arm. Leo stiffened and took a step closer. Although the man was tall, Leo was clearly the stronger. In a swelling silence, they faced each other.

After a moment, the man chuckled softly to himself and gave a shrug.

Louisa had thought Leo was about to

throttle the Australian, but instead he stepped back.

"What's going on here?" he demanded.

The man didn't reply.

"I suggest you go about your business."

Cooper brushed himself down while smiling coldly at Leo. Then he walked off.

Leo turned to her. She took a step back and exhaled slowly, then put a palm over her thumping heart.

"Thank goodness you came when you did," she said, a little anxiously. "The man's a bully."

"What did he want?"

She took a deep breath and then explained about Elliot's debts. It hurt her to say it all out loud, just as it had hurt to hear Margo telling Irene, but she knew she could no longer protect Elliot's reputation.

"Should we go to the police about this man?" she said.

"And say what? I'm not sure it will do much good. He'll be long gone now, and what could he actually be charged with?"

"He said his name was Cooper."

"I doubt that's his real name. Shall we go up now? Are you still happy to do this?"

She nodded.

"I'll just get the bike."

He parked his bike right by the door to

the office, and pushed it open for her. "My worry is that he seemed to be expecting you — how on earth did he find out you'd be here today? Who knew?"

She felt a chill run through her. Who indeed?

Upstairs, Nihil greeted Louisa warmly and then he ordered coffee for them all.

Leo and Louisa seated themselves and Louisa explained why they were there.

"So," the manager said, looking at Leo. "You can guarantee a high quantity? Many of my cinnamon suppliers from farther north have been affected by drought so I am most interested in what you have to say."

"I'm working day and night, as are my staff. We produce the very best quality. I have a sample here."

He removed a quill from his satchel.

Nihil took it, rubbed it between his fingers and then smelled it. "Excellent. I'm sure we can offer you a worthwhile deal." He scribbled something on a sheet of paper and then handed it to Leo. "How does that sound to you?"

Leo nodded. "I think we may have a deal."

The two men shook hands and Louisa promised to have her solicitor put the agreement into writing, ready for Leo to sign.

"By the way," she said and looked at Nihil.

"Did you tell anyone I would be here to-day?"

"I may have mentioned it to my family but that's all."

By the time they had finished the meeting and were back on the street, the rain was coming down in sheets.

"What do you want to do?" he said and held out his hands to the rain.

She glanced at the sky and pulled a face.

"I have waterproof capes on my bike if that's any help?"

"Or we could have a bite to eat and see if it eases off."

"It might get worse."

She smiled and glanced at her watch. "Yes, but aren't you hungry?"

He nodded.

"Then let's go to the Galle Face Hotel. My treat."

"You don't have to."

"I'd like to. They do terrific seafood if we're not too late. We can eat on the veranda and watch the rain. I need to visit a solicitor afterward to check something out. Do you mind hanging about? It'll mean riding back in the dark."

"Not at all. Though I wonder if we made the right choice to come here and back in a day."

Leaving his bike in the alley, they began to run and when they were finally seated in comfy rattan chairs on the hotel veranda, lined with beautiful colonnaded arches, the rain had become even noisier, drowning out the clink of cutlery and glasses.

"Isn't this lovely," she said, speaking in a loud voice.

"Wonderful."

They ordered and as he gazed out at the rain she watched him. He'd pushed his wet hair back from his forehead and his skin glistened. She couldn't help wondering about this man. So attractive and yet alone. She glanced out at the rain splashing up a full yard in the air, and as she turned back she saw his eyes were fixed on her. He smiled a slow lazy smile and she longed to reach out and touch his face. Instead she stared down at the table and felt the heat rising in her cheeks.

In fact the temperature had dropped, and apart from her burning cheeks it was a release to feel cool after sweating in the numbing humidity.

"So, tell me about you," he said.

She looked up. "My life's been very ordinary."

"I doubt that."

She thought about it. "Well, until recently."

"Louisa, I . . ."

"Yes?"

"I'm enjoying today." He smiled again and the lines around his eyes fanned out.

"Me too. Apart from that awful man, Cooper."

After they had eaten, the rain seemed to ease off a little. She drew out the copy of the contract De Vos had given her, checked the address of the drafting solicitor on its first page and then rose. "Come with me, if you like."

They walked the short distance while the rain held off, and before long found themselves on the doorstep of the impressive offices of Jefferson and Chepstow.

They entered the reception area, asked to speak to one of the partners, and waited until a small balding man came out to greet them.

"Brian Chepstow," he said. "How can I help?"

He indicated they should follow him into his office, where she handed him the contract. "I believe your firm drew this up," she said. "Could you take a look at it and maybe check your records?"

He glanced at it and frowned. "Well, that's

our old redundant letterhead on here, not the one we've had for over a year. We're now 'R. A. Jefferson,' not 'G. Jefferson.' Richard, my current partner, is old Gerald Jefferson's son. This is apparently signed by Gerald — but it's dated six months after he died, and he retired six months before that. I don't need to check my records at all, I can tell you right now and categorically that this was not drawn up by us. Added to which, all our carbon copies are green. This is blue. I am of the strong opinion that this could be fraudulent." He wrote down some details. "Who gave you this?"

Louisa fudged her answer, not wanting to divulge too much. "I found it among my late husband's papers."

"Well, I might have to do some investigating. I'll contact you if I ever discover anything, but at this stage I can confirm that this so-called contract would have no validity in any court of law that I know of."

Louisa thanked him for his time and she and Leo left.

"What was all that about?" Leo asked as they stood on the pavement a few moments later.

"Somebody gave me that contract as proof of debts Elliot has incurred, but you heard what Mr. Chepstow just said."

"Strange."

"Very." She wondered whether to mention that Cooper had claimed to be an associate of De Vos, who was named on the contract, but decided to put it to the back of her mind for the time being. "But perhaps we'd better get going now that it isn't pouring."

"You don't mind a bit of damp weather?" he said.

She laughed. "I'm an outdoors kind of girl. Let's fetch the bike."

As he rode them out onto the coastal road she held on tightly, once again thrilled at being so close to him. She could feel the strength and power in his body as he tensed, guiding the bike through the screaming wind. The rain held off at first, but about an hour and a half later the sea became even wilder. He stopped while they slid the waterproof capes over their heads, but it was already dark and when the rain fell in a solid wall, they couldn't see much in front of them. When the bike began to skid, he slowed the pace, but it wasn't enough — a huge gust blew them off the road and toward the ocean. The bike was almost pushed right over but he managed to halt it before it hit the ground.

"We're near the Madu Ganga wetland, I think, near the fishing village of Balapitiya.

We're going to have to take shelter some-where," he said as he sat astride the stilled bike.

She squinted into the darkness. "But there isn't anything for miles."

"From memory, there are some fisher-men's huts somewhere near here. Let's head in their direction. I'll wheel the bike."

They made slow progress and just before they reached a hut, Louisa tripped and fell. He helped her up but her ankle hurt.

"I think I went over on it."

"Why not sit on the bike? I can just about see the shape of a hut. It's only about twenty yards now."

He shone a flashlight and they managed to find their way to a bamboo-framed hut, covered with woven coconut fronds. He pushed open the door, wheeling the bike inside and then helping Louisa. She sniffed. Though it still smelled of fish, the hut felt damp and abandoned. His flashlight lit up a few old ropes coiled on the ground and some sacking in one corner. He helped her to sit away from a leak in the roof and then took out a hurricane lamp from his saddle-bag and sat next to her. He lit the lamp and she watched as it threw shadows against the walls. Feeling a little apprehensive, she shivered. Even from inside the hut she could hear the wild waves crashing against the rocks.

"Are you cold?" he asked.

She smiled. "Proper Boy Scout, aren't you?"

"I'm always prepared when out on the bike."

"Well, I'm not really cold. I'm just wet."

He took off his cape and then his jacket and put it around her shoulders. "You sound as if you need a stiff drink."

"Yes."

In the dim light from the lamp he brought out a hipflask of whisky, unscrewed the cap, which acted as a tiny cup, poured some out and then offered it to her. She took a sip and the heat curled in her chest.

"So," she said, very aware of the fact that they were alone together in this small hut and trying to think of something normal to say. In fact, nothing about the situation was normal and nothing about him was ordinary. The truth was, she found him vitally alive and exciting to be near.

"It must be lonely up at the plantation," she eventually said.

"I'm not much of a social animal."

"You enjoy your own company?"

"Yes. But I'm busy all the time."

"Did you and Elliot ever talk?"

"Not much."

A flash of lightning lit up the hut, turning his face blue.

"Do you have electricity there?"

"Not yet. We're quite basic."

"Elliot said so too."

Leo nodded but didn't meet her eyes. He poured another whisky and drank it.

"Will the bike still go?"

"It's not damaged."

She attempted to get to her feet but her ankle hurt. She sat down again, not wanting to go back home anyway — and couldn't help dwelling on thoughts of Leo. There was something untouchable about him, as if he were a little out of reach, and she wanted to know more. Was he lonely up at the plantation? He appeared to live a lonely life. But how to ask him more without seeming to pry too much?

"So," she eventually said. "Have you always lived alone?"

"Pretty much. I've traveled around a bit, here and there. It was only when I inherited the plantation that, I suppose, you could say I started to settle down. Now I'm nearly forty, I guess it's about time I did it properly."

She hesitated for a moment, then smiled at him. "You never wanted to marry?"

287

Another flash of lightning lit up his face and she saw him hesitate.

He met her eyes and there was a still moment. "Never seemed to be in the right place at the right time, or with the right person," he finally said.

"But there must have been women?" she said.

She heard his sharp intake of breath. "Oh, yes."

"Any in particular?"

"Just the one."

"Do you want to tell me about her?"

He shrugged. "Not much to tell. She married someone else."

"What happened?" she asked, and though he had spoken resignedly she sensed some hurt in him still.

"It was about eight years ago. Her name was Alicia and she was a singer in a Singapore nightclub."

"And?"

"She was beautiful, long chestnut hair, bright blue eyes and the voice of an angel."

"Sounds like you loved her."

He sighed deeply. "We were going to be married."

"What happened?"

He bowed his head before looking up at

her. "Turned out it wasn't me that she loved."

"Were you actually engaged?"

"We were."

There was a short silence and she reached out to touch his arm. Something flowed between them and she felt it acutely.

"I'm sorry."

"That wasn't the worst of it. She walked out on me one night and I never set eyes on her again. Later I discovered she had married my best friend, and had been seeing him for months behind my back."

"Oh God! That must have hurt," she blurted out.

There was a prickly silence.

"So," he said at last. "I really do understand how you feel about Elliot and Zinnia."

"Yes. I see that. Did you ever hear from them again?"

He lowered his voice and she had to lean in closer to hear. "Eventually, yes. A couple of years later I received a letter from him saying Alicia had died in childbirth."

"Gosh, that's awful."

She glanced at the ground before looking up and meeting his gaze. A gaze that had not wavered and did not now. "You must wonder about what might have been."

"Maybe. I'm not really given to dwelling. The future is what matters to me."

"And the past?"

"I was searching for something when I was younger. I thought she might have been the answer."

"But she wasn't?"

"No."

"Did you ever find it? The thing you were looking for."

"Not entirely. I don't think I even knew what it was."

"We're all searching for something, aren't we?"

"I imagine we are."

Deeply conscious of him sitting so near to her, she inhaled slowly then let her breath out as she tried to weave through her complicated feelings.

"What is it you've been searching for, Louisa?" he continued.

She liked how he'd said her name. The way it felt new and special. "Perhaps it's more of an unfulfilled need than a search. I wanted children. I wanted them badly."

"I am sorry."

She glanced at him and even in the dim light of the lamp felt heartened by the compassion in his eyes.

"Motherhood. It's what we women are

programmed to do, isn't it? To be a mother. My childhood without my mother was lonely at times, and I suppose I wanted to make the family I'd never had."

"Hard for you."

"Very. But there it is."

He gave her a long searching look. "I admire how you've coped with everything."

She swallowed the lump in her throat. "Really?"

"Absolutely."

"Thank you."

They sat in companionable silence for a few minutes, Louisa thinking about her lost children and Leo thinking of she knew not what.

"But what an exciting life you must have had," she eventually said. "Tell me about some of the places you've been."

"You really want to know?"

"Yes." She felt her tension unraveling and understood that since being in this little hut and listening to the rain, she wanted to stay like that, secluded together, talking, hearing his voice.

"Well, I worked on a rubber plantation in Malaya for ten years, and I've spent time in Indonesia. Mainly I've been around the tropics one way or another."

"Sorry to pry," she said, wondering if

she'd asked too much.

"Not at all."

She heard a movement. "Are there bats in here?"

"I doubt it."

But she jumped when he shone his flashlight on a lizard creeping out from a corner and scuttling across the floor. As they slipped into silence again she could smell the spicy salty scent from his skin and the paraffin from the lamp. It was then he leaned toward her and gently stroked her cheek.

She closed her eyes and felt it throughout her entire body. And yet, after a few seconds, she pulled away. She heard the cry of some creature out in the rain, a lonely disturbing sound, followed by the hooting of an owl.

"Leo . . ."

"I'm sorry. I shouldn't have."

"It's just —"

"I understand."

"Let's just sit here until the rain eases off."

Neither of them moved and although troubled by what had almost happened, and what it might mean, she felt aware of a still center of peace within her.

# 28

Cooper, the Australian man, was still prey-
ing on her mind, as was the fake contract.
Louisa felt uneasy about both so, in the
morning, after Leo dropped her off and
before walking the dogs, she asked Ashan to
come to the main sitting room. Fortunately,
her ankle hadn't been twisted and was
hardly bothering her now, and she prowled
the room as she waited, watching the slanting sun layering the floor in stripes of light.
The whole room seemed to sparkle, but it
was one of those times when she wished Elliot was with her: times she still couldn't
prevent from arising, no matter how much
she struggled against them. And what had
happened with Leo, and the fact she had
wanted him to touch her so much, only
made her feel more unsettled. She felt
starved of physical contact, but in her mind
she was still a married woman and, despite

everything, it wasn't easy to just switch that off.

She didn't ask Ashan to sit, but gazed at him from where she stood. It upset her to think somebody in her household might be to blame but she had to ask the question.

"Look, Ashan, you've been with us as butler for years."

He nodded and gave her a broad smile. "Ten years, Madam, and houseboy to your father before that."

"And during your time as butler you have looked after us well, for which I thank you."

He made a slight bow. "It is my pleasure."

She sighed before broaching the subject. "I've got a little problem and I wonder if you can help me. You've always assisted me, and my father before me, in choosing new staff. Haven't you?"

"Yes, Madam. Glad to do so."

"So, I have a question for you."

"Madam."

"I wondered, is there anyone here you don't fully trust?"

He frowned as if to say the question bothered him. "Some I know better than others, but I trust them all."

"Well, I need you to keep your eyes open. I fear somebody may be passing on information about what I'm doing. Can you manage that?"

"Certainly, Madam. That would indeed be a worry."

"And I don't have to say we must keep this strictly between us."

She dismissed him and then sat for a while considering the members of her household and hoping there wasn't one she couldn't trust. The cook had been with her father long before moving with her after her marriage. He'd had a kitchen boy under his charge who was a bit slow but very cheerful, but now he had the French girl, Camille, who had proved indispensable. There were two further houseboys who took care of cleaning and serving, one was a nephew of the cook and the other had been with her for about six months. There was also a part-time housekeeper and a laundryman. Only Ashan, Camille and the cook lived in. There was a gardener too, but he was rarely privy to her whereabouts.

While the rain held off she collected the dogs and set off to visit Himal, a Sinhalese builder she had used before, to ask for a quote for the refurbishment of the Print House. As she walked she threw a ball for the dogs. Usually Bouncer jumped on it first and wouldn't return it, but today Tommy caught it and brought it to her to be thrown again. They played while the street was quiet, then she put them back on their leads.

When she reached the builder's yard, she quickly found Himal. Though not the cheapest, he was both trustworthy and reliable and he'd successfully added a whole new floor to her house. In his office, she unfolded her plans and laid them on his desk. While he bent his head and pored over them, she pictured the emporium in her mind's eye: a gleaming glittering palace of exquisite sapphire jewelry and fascinating objects, an Aladdin's cave of opportunity.

"As you see, I want to keep the upper galleried area to display artwork, and then turn each downstairs room into an area selling specific goods. But I do need to keep the costs down."

He glanced up at her with an intelligent expression. "Do you know if any of the walls are partition?"

"No. Will it matter?"

"It might. I'll need to see. But really, it seems a question of cleaning the glass and the floor, making sure everything is sound and giving the whole place a lick of paint. Is there electricity?"

"Yes. The building will need fitting out, of course. I thought jak-wood cabinets to keep costs down but beautiful Ceylon ebony counters."

"I have excellent carpenters," he said as he scratched his head. "I'm sure we can keep the costs down while maintaining the quality you want if the building is sound, but, as I said, I'll have to give it the once-over. Can you let me have the key?"

She gave him the key and asked when he might be free to make a start.

"In a month or so, I reckon."

He agreed to get the quote to her within the week and she left feeling happy things were getting organized and, at long last, her glittering dream was about to become a reality.

Two months passed by slowly. Louisa still thought about Elliot, but gradually she found herself waking with a lighter heart. Household tasks began to interest her as much as they had always done, and she enjoyed long walks on the beach. She had accepted Himal's quote and work was now well underway. She had also finally put the Australian man and De Vos to the back of her mind. No one had come back to her so far.

In less than a fortnight, they would be celebrating the annual Galle summer ball held at the New Oriental Hotel. Most of the rubber planters attended, along with their wives, and Louisa had enjoyed being out with Elliot on such a romantic occasion. It had always been special to them. This year she would have to go with her father.

She thought back to the previous year and remembered that although they had been getting on well, Elliot had disappeared for nearly an hour during the evening. When he finally returned, he'd made some excuse about chatting to an old friend and she'd felt a little annoyed. It had seemed slightly odd at the time, though not of any real consequence. Now she wondered if Elliot's debts had already begun back then.

The agreement she and Leo needed to sign to allow her to export his cinnamon had finally arrived after a tediously long delay. She hadn't set eyes on Leo since the trip to Colombo, and she couldn't work through the complexity of how she had felt about him then. That she felt something, she couldn't deny, even now, and she wondered if it might be safe to ask him to accompany her to the ball. She didn't want to give him the wrong idea and, although nervous at the thought, she was also aware of a tingling feeling of pleasure. After taking a deep breath, she laughed at how youthful it made her feel and decided she would do it. But because she was still faintly aware of an inchoate desire to get back at Elliot, she knew she had to be clear about her motivation in asking Leo. She walked back and forth, turning it over, but decided anything that made her feel as if she was moving forward couldn't be wrong.

She was just checking her hair in the hall mirror when a knock at the front door broke into her thoughts. She didn't wait for Ashan and, opening the door herself, was surprised to see a stranger standing there, a fair-haired man.

"Can I help you?" she asked, wondering if he might be some kind of salesman and wishing she'd let Ashan answer.

The man looked a little uncertain as he began to speak. "I'm sorry to intrude. But I'm looking for Margo Reeve. I was told in Colombo that she's staying with you."

Louisa frowned. "Is she expecting you?"

He glanced down at his feet and twisted his hat in his hands.

"I'm William Tyler. She may have mentioned me."

Louisa's hand flew to her mouth and she instantly felt protective of Margo. "Oh . . . Well, I suppose you'd better come in. I'm Louisa Reeve, by the way."

"Very pleased to meet you. I hope you'll accept my sincere condolences, Mrs. Reeve."

"Thank you."

She took him through to the sitting room and then went in search of her sister-in-law, who turned bright pink when Louisa told her William had arrived. Her lips parted in astonishment and her eyes, darting about the room before they settled on Louisa's face, betrayed her nerves.

"Oh, my God. What shall I say to him?"

Louisa couldn't help smiling. "That depends on what he wants."

She went ahead of Margo to the sitting room and, at the door, began to move off.

"No, please stay," Margo whispered and put a hand on Louisa's arm to keep her there.

"Are you sure?"

As soon as they were inside the room William got to his feet. "Margo, I . . ."

Margo didn't go up to him but stood still and Louisa could feel the tension between them. Though the room was silent, outside the birds were making a racket and the gardener was mowing the lawn. Louisa listened to one of her dogs barking at the mower and glanced about the room, itching to make her escape.

"Margo, I really think I —"

"Stay. William can't have anything to say to me that he can't say in front of you."

"Actually, Margo," he said. "I do —"

"I want her to stay," Margo interrupted, in a firm tone of voice.

Louisa nodded and gestured toward the sofa and chairs. "If that's what you really want, but shall we sit rather than just all standing here. I'll ring for some refreshment."

William sat on an easy chair and Margo perched on the edge of the farthest chair she could find. Louisa watched intently as Margo stared at the ground, seemingly unable to look at him for even a moment. Then she summoned her courage.

"What do you want, William?" she said, finally meeting his eyes, but with a catch in her voice. "I can't imagine you've come all this way for nothing."

He seemed to hesitate. "I could have written."

"Yes."

"I had your parents' address. When I went there, your father told me you were here. I'm so very sorry about your brother."

She bowed her head and blinked to stop the tears. "Please don't be nice to me."

There was a short silence.

"I wanted to see you." He paused and hesitated again. "Because Deirdre has asked me for a divorce."

Margo got to her feet, the color draining from her face. "Because of me?" she said, struggling to take it in.

He shook his head. "Not directly, but she says she wants to cite you as co-respondent."

After a sharp intake of breath, Margo's eyes widened. "But that's awful."

"It is. But don't you see what this means?"

Margo gazed at Louisa with a pleading expression. Holding her hands palms up, Louisa shrugged and couldn't help feeling bemused.

"It means we can be married eventually. If you'll still have me," he said, now with a purposeful look, all hesitation gone.

Margo sat down again abruptly, her breath ragged. "My mother will have a fit."

"Does that mean you agree?"

"I didn't say that."

He gave her a warm, genuine smile, half in encouragement, half in hope. "Please, Margo. Think about it. This could be our chance."

With a deep sigh Margo gazed at her hands in her lap. She turned them over and then, glancing up, smiled back, but it was a nervous, hesitant smile. "Tell me every-thing."

"What do you want to know?"

"Why did she decide she wanted a di-vorce? Did you tell her about me?"

"Not until after she raised the subject of divorce. What I told you was true. We haven't been happy for years. Now she has inherited some money and wants to move back to her hometown in Devon."

"She didn't ask you to go with her?"

"No. She knows I need to be where my work is. All my clients are in Kent."

"Where would we live?"

"Do you mean you'll consider it? I'm afraid your name will be dragged through the mud."

She blinked rapidly as if thinking. "I don't know."

"Margo, my darling." He paused. "You must know what you mean to me."

She nodded, but to Louisa it looked as if Margo was close to tears. She went over to stand behind her and placed a comforting hand on her sister-in-law's shoulder.

"Have you missed me?" William said. "I've missed you every minute you've been gone."

"Look," Louisa said, and squeezed Margo's shoulder, "I'm going to see what's happened to Ashan. I think you two should discuss this by yourselves. You don't need me playing gooseberry. And Margo, don't let what Irene will say influence you."

"You think I should agree?"

"I think we all have to take our chance of happiness when we can." And with that she left the room. Poor Margo, she thought, as she went to speak to Ashan; it was a tough decision. Being cited as co-respondent would be miserable and everyone would know her business, but if she did indeed love William, as he claimed he did her, maybe it was the right thing to do.

# 29

His smile when he saw her was startling, lighting up the rugged angles of his face. She opened her mouth but ended up swallowing her words.

"Come on in," Leo said.

He stood back to give her room to pass. They went upstairs into the comfortable but slightly shabby room littered with books, several oil lamps and some candles.

As she stood just inside the threshold, she again struggled to keep the past where it belonged. Fed up with Elliot living in her head, she glanced at Leo and, when he smiled at her so generously, Elliot's ghost faded. Relieved, she gazed at Leo's gentle dark eyes, and although he was still smiling she glimpsed a trace of something she hadn't spotted before. Sadness, possibly. She wasn't sure.

"I'm pleased to see you," he said. "It's been a while."

"Yes."

"So?"

She pulled out an envelope. "I have the agreement for you to sign. Sorry it's taken so long."

"You could have posted it."

"Yes."

"But you came."

"Yes."

"And?" He held out a hand to take the contract. Feeling the warmth of his skin as he brushed her fingers with his, she longed to respond but instead drew her hand away, then sat in a chair and nibbled at her nails.

"Louisa," he said. "I'm sorry if I over-stepped the mark."

"You didn't," she said in a low voice, remembering how she had felt when he had touched her cheek in the fisherman's hut. She glanced out of the window as the sun came out briefly from behind the clouds. She could recall the exact moment she had known she would marry Elliot, and the way those early days had always seemed sunny. They'd been sharing an ice cream at the Galle Face Hotel in Colombo and when he wiped a smear of it from her cheek she had felt so certain. Now she had lost the ability to rely on her emotions but, despite being wary, there did seem to be something compelling between her and Leo. As she lifted her head and looked at him, she silently acknowledged how much she wanted to get to know him.

"What are you thinking?" he said. "At times I feel I know so little about you."

"I'm thinking, if you sign it now I'll take it back with me, and then send it to my manager." She lied, of course, couldn't begin to say what had really been on her mind.

He opened the envelope and drew out the agreement, reading it carefully before going across to the coffee table. While he was doing this, she thought about William and Margo. If there was one thing Elliot's death had taught her, it was that life had to be lived and love still mattered. But it was different for her because she still needed answers, and that muddied everything.

He glanced up at her and she felt a sudden burst of happiness. Then he signed.

"All done."

She nodded.

"So, how have you been?"

It was so quiet she could hear the beat of her own heart. "I wish I could be free."

"You'll get there," he said. "There's no rush."

She stared at her feet. "Sometimes I'm so afraid."

"Of?"

"Anything. Everything. The past, the future. The husband I didn't know."

It was true. She had been living with a low level of anxiety almost every day since Elliot died.

"You know you can talk to me."

She nodded again, but not wanting to say more about how she was feeling about Elliot's death, she changed the subject. "How is Zinnia?" she said, and could tell he was disappointed she hadn't confided in him more fully.

"It's also okay not to talk," he said. "As for Zinnia, she's in a bad way again, I'm afraid." She could see the concern in his eyes and realized, despite his focus on the plantation, he was genuinely worried for his cousin.

She hesitated before speaking. "Can I see her?"

"I thought you didn't want to."

"I think perhaps I must."

"If you're sure."

"I hate the thought of it — well, of her, I suppose — but I think I have to see her in the flesh. Apart from one fleeting moment, I've only ever seen her in her paintings."

"If you're sure."

She sighed. "I'm not sure of anything."

There was a short silence during which she couldn't look at him.

"How is she coping with Conor?" she eventually asked.

"Barely at all. He comes up here a lot, but it's not satisfactory. I do my best — but he needs attention I can't give him, and nor can she now."

"He has lost his father."

Leo nodded.

It was terribly sad, and yet she hadn't forgiven Elliot for having a son and she couldn't help how that affected the way she felt about Conor.

"Will Conor be there?"

"He's down at the sheds with the cinnamon peelers."

"Good. In that case let's go now. I'll just put the papers in the car."

Leo pulled on his boots and they first went to her car and then he led her down to Zinnia's house via a shortcut. She listened to animals scratching in the undergrowth and slapped the swarms of flies from her face.

"Not too rough for you? This path?"

"I'm fine," she said, though her stomach was somersaulting. What would it be like to meet her husband's lover? Was it crazy to do this or, as she suspected, was it the only way she might eventually accept what had happened?

"I had the doctor out again, but she refused point blank to see him. I don't know what's wrong, but she seems in dreadfully low spirits as well as physically ill. Maybe seeing another woman might help her."

"Even me? I expect she hates my very existence."

"Zinnia isn't the hating type."

She stood still and hesitated for a moment. "What type is she?"

Leo sighed. "Hard to say. She's talented and a bit bohemian, but also insecure. She's made some mistakes in her life but has paid for them too. To be honest, I don't think she really knows who she is."

"How do you mean?"

"Well, I'd say, although you are feeling rather at sea just now, you do have a pretty strong sense of who you are, where you came from, where you belong."

She snorted. "You think that?"

"Yes."

"It doesn't feel like it right now."

"Well, Zinnia didn't have the best of starts."

"What happened to her parents? Maybe they could help with Conor."

"I'm afraid her father, my uncle, died some years back."

"And her mother?"

"Her mother was a dipsomaniac. Nobody knows what happened to her. Wherever she is, I don't imagine being a grandmother would be part of her life plan."

Louisa inhaled slowly and then let her breath out in a rush. She felt suddenly hot but still had to ask. "And how did Zinnia become involved with Elliot?"

"I don't know much. She kept the truth of it from me when I first suggested she live here. I knew she was pregnant but didn't know by whom. I gradually discovered it was Elliot and that he was married."

"And you didn't approve?"

"It wasn't for me to approve or not. I tried to get her to end it, though."

"But she didn't."

"I think she tried to once or twice."

"Did she believe Elliot would leave me?"

He looked at her quizzically. "Do you think that?"

She swallowed the lump developing in her throat. "I found a pretty damning letter from him to her, though he'd never sent it for some reason. And, from what I read, it seemed Zinnia had tried to end it."

"Maybe she was trying to force his hand?"

"You think so?"

"I don't know. I do know you are a lot stronger than Zinnia. And, if you don't mind me saying, I feel you are stronger than Elliot was too."

"Really?"

"And because Zinnia is weaker than he was, I imagine it made Elliot feel more of a man than he really was."

She sighed. "That's harsh. You think I made him feel less of a man?"

"I didn't mean it like that, but haven't you noticed some men need to surround themselves with weaker people?"

They carried on walking and then, twenty yards from Zinnia's bungalow, Louisa halted. Apart from the sound of crickets there was an unnatural emptiness about the spot. She felt terribly exposed and for a few minutes she longed to turn back, to quietly rewind her footsteps to a place where she felt safe. Wherever that now was. She glanced up at the lemony sky just showing through the tops of the trees; her thoughts collided and she shrank back.

"Can you handle this?" Leo said, clearly sensing her state of mind. "You don't have to do it."

She was tempted to say, *No, I don't want to go on,* but she drew herself up tall instead.

"I don't have to — but somehow I know I must."

Even so, a knot of dread tightened her throat. Just the idea of Elliot with Zinnia was appalling, but if she was ever to get over it she had to face this horrible situation head on, and now was as good a time as any. If she didn't confront the truth, Elliot's other life would remain shrouded in mystery, just out of sight, his deception constantly haunting her. I don't want to know, she thought. I don't want to see. And yet . . .

Leo led the way past the same heavily overgrown scented plants in pots, and after gently tapping on the door they went in. Louisa gazed around at a room in disarray.

"This is a bit of a shambles," she said.

Various pieces of clothing hung haphazardly over the back of two chairs and lay in an untidy pile on the floor, and everything seemed to be coated in a thin layer of dust.

"Can't you get somebody to see to this?"

"It gets dusty quickly here. I come in once or twice a week and Kamu does what he can, but often as not she locks the door and won't let us in. Shall we go in? Are you ready?"

He opened another door and poked his head around it. Louisa heard him say he'd brought someone to see her, but all Zinnia said in reply was, "No more doctors."

"Not a doctor."

He signaled to Louisa to come through with him and, as she went in, the stale air made her breath catch in her throat. The room was hot and gloomy, with heavy curtains blocking the light. Repulsed by a lingering smell of sour wine, Louisa hesitated, but then stared at Zinnia. As Zinnia stared back, Louisa longed to slip into a corner where she could flee from the woman's dark eyes, so like Leo's, but for the fact that these eyes were hollow and circled by purple shadows. Eventually Louisa glanced about the room but she was increasingly assaulted by images of Elliot: Elliot lying naked in bed beside this woman, or standing there by the window smoking a desultory cigarette, his head thrown back, blowing the blue smoke up to the ceiling. She felt herself buckle.

"Cat got your tongue?" the woman said.

Louisa saw she was terribly pale, far too thin, and her red hair hung limply about her face. What was it about this woman that had led Elliot to betray her?

"I'm Louisa Reeve," she managed to say, but her voice sounded strangled, paralyzed by the heat and anger gripping her throat. And in a flash, more than anything she wanted to hurt the woman who had stolen her husband.

Zinnia shivered and her skin seemed to break out in a sweat. "I know who you are. What are you doing here?"

"Leo is worried about you," Louisa replied, her voice still too thin, and she sat down on a chair before her legs gave way.

"I'm fine," Zinnia said.

While Leo spoke to Zinnia, Louisa was vaguely aware of her heart pounding and her palms growing sweaty. In the semidarkness of the room she tried to shake off the anger. She clenched her fists and dug her nails into her palms and thought back to the catastrophic day she had found out about Zinnia and Conor: the day her world tilted and changed forever. Overnight she had become a different person. There was a before, there was an after, but nothing in between. She sat hunched in the chair and heard Elliot's voice. It went on and on. In her mind, she stood up and screamed at the empty space. In her mind, she tore at his face, his hair. *You bastard. You utter bastard.* But there was no triumph in her anger and the unspoken words fell flat. Elliot wasn't there. She ran her shaking fingers through her hair and listened to a bird singing outside the window.

315

Leo twisted around to look at her. "You okay, Louisa?" he said.

She gathered her courage and faced Zinnia. "I need to ask if you really intended to end it with Elliot."

Zinnia rubbed the side of her head around the temple and winced. "I did end it."

"He didn't believe you?"

"I told him it was over. He kept trying to persuade me otherwise. It was wrong. All of it was wrong. Oh God! My head hurts like hell."

"Have you taken anything for it?"

"Of course." Zinnia closed her eyes and Louisa took the chance to leave the room.

In the outer living area Louisa began to collect up the clothes and, although she felt a strange kind of pity for Zinnia, her anger welled up again. After a few minutes, she called to Leo to come out. "These need washing," she said, lifting a few random items. "Do you think your dhobi can do them?"

"I don't really use a dhobi. Kamu does my washing, and Zinnia's when she lets him."

"Why don't you insist?"

"Believe me, I do."

"I'll arrange for a dhobi to collect all of this. He'll take it away and bring it back clean. Do you think your houseboy would bring down some rags and cleaning fluid?"

"Louisa, this really isn't down to you. I'll sort it out."

She turned on him. "You're right. It is not down to me, but I can hardly walk out leaving her like this. So, let's not discuss it. Just get me some help. She's clearly not looking after herself, let alone Conor. Someone should take a better look at her. What did the doctor say last time she let him see her?"

"Pleurisy, maybe. That's what she thinks."

"Worsened by a heavy dose of misery."

He looked at her intently. "I admire you for this, more than you can know, but now I'm afraid I have to get on. The peelers are waiting for me. I'll have more time this evening, so can get some tidying up done then."

"Just go now. And get the houseboy. I don't want to be on my own here. What's his name again?"

"Kamu. He's Tamil. Came with me from my time on a tea plantation in India."

"Very well, I'll make a start in here."

Once Kamu had arrived with the necessary items, Louisa and he began. First, they bundled the clothing into a sack and, while he sorted out the kitchen, she wiped away the dust in the sitting area. Then she checked Conor's room. When that was done, they washed the windows and the floor, leaving the front door open so that everything might dry. Afterward she sat outside on a log feeling rigid, gulping at air, her heart racing, while Kamu squatted on the ground smoking a cigarette. When her chest felt too tight to breathe, she forced herself to take long slow breaths.

While they waited, she thought about Zinnia with Elliot again. Had she been so much more beautiful than Louisa herself? Or had her talent seduced him? She tried to imagine how Zinnia might have once been, but then a memory of Elliot unfurled, and she gasped at the way his smile used to brighten up a room. And her life. That must have been what attracted Zinnia, that and the way he could gaze into your eyes and make you feel you were the only one who mattered in the whole world.

But what had it been about this woman that meant Elliot had lied to his wife for all those years? That Elliot had been spoiled as a child was clear to her; Irene had brought him up to have such a sense of entitlement. Had it carried on into his adult life? Had he believed that if something caught his eye it was his for the taking? She was aware he had used charm to get what he wanted and she had indulged it, not recognizing there could be such a dark side to it. But that he could deceive her for so long, seemingly with no conscience, was what shocked her most. She felt what? Bitterness, she thought, that's what.

Whatever it had been about Zinnia, the woman clearly needed to see a doctor now. Louisa wondered about asking her own Dr. Russell to come out as soon as possible. She couldn't begin to imagine what might happen if Zinnia didn't get the right medical care.

Just as they were getting ready to go back inside, Leo returned.

"Finished?"

"We haven't started on her room or the bathroom. Conor's room is tidy."

"I'll encourage her to lie on the sofa in the living room. Then we'll be better able to sort out her bedroom."

"Where is Conor?"

"He's up at my place now, hoping for a sandwich. Look, maybe this is enough for Zinnia for one day. She tires so easily. While Kamu goes back to see to Conor, let's you and I go down to the beach. I'm not sure Kamu thinks any of this is part of his job but, as I said, I can come back and finish off this evening."

"I can bring one of my lads with me to help get to grips with Zinnia's room tomorrow. But I don't have a swimming costume with me."

"Never mind that. Wait here and I'll get some towels. Won't be long."

As he and Kamu made their way back up the hill, Louisa watched the darkening purple clouds move over the sky. They were in for another downpour this afternoon for sure. She got up and went inside. Thankfully the room smelled better now and she left a window open to keep it fresh. While she was checking everything, she heard Zinnia call out, "Is that you, Leo?"

Louisa opened the bedroom door and saw Zinnia teetering back from what must be the bathroom. The smell was awful.

"How long have you had diarrhea and vomiting?" she asked.

Zinnia didn't look at her as she struggled back into bed. "Are you a nurse now?"

"You need to see a doctor."

"I've had it off and on. Sometimes I'm okay."

"It doesn't sound like pleurisy to me. I can ask my family doctor to take a look at you, but someone must air this room." As she said the words she was shocked at herself and felt choked. Why care when all

she really wanted was to forget Zin.
ever existed?

Zinnia snorted. "What's it to you?"

Louisa paused to think. "Elliot loved
I loved him. I can't leave you in need."

"Very well." Zinnia nodded and sank t
against the pillow.

Louisa left the room to go back outsi
where she saw Leo arriving with a bund
under his right arm.

"Ready?" he said, his eyes resting on her.

She felt a sudden sadness grab at her. It
was all so awful.

"Ready?" he said again.

She tried to shrug off the shock of finally
seeing Zinnia and the dreadful reality of her
illness and descent into melancholy — her
inability to take care of herself proved the
latter.

"Come on," he said, "you'll feel better
after a swim." They began to walk toward
the beach. "Don't dwell on Zinnia. We're
doing what we can."

"I really hope she'll see my doctor."

When they arrived at the wooded shore they
had the place to themselves. Louisa wanted
to think of happier things and her mood
lifted as she thought again about the summer ball.

"Do you have any formal evening wear?" she asked, aiming for a light tone of voice.

"What an odd question."

"Well, do you?"

"It would need dusting off, but yes. Why do you ask?"

"I wondered if you'd consider accompanying me to the Galle summer ball? It'd mean tidying you up a bit."

He laughed. "Women have tried, and women have failed."

"Would you mind?"

He pulled a face. "Another difficult question. Now let me consider . . ."

She laughed and dug him in the ribs. "A simple yes will do."

"Madam, I would be delighted."

"Can you dance?"

"I have a pretty nifty quickstep, as it happens."

She smiled. "In which case, I can't wait."

The beach lay pale and soft with large waves tumbling and foaming on the sand. He peeled off his clothes to reveal swimming trunks beneath, then he ran into the shifting sea. She rolled up her trousers and paddled barefoot, feeling the wet sand between her toes, but after all that had happened, the longing to join him in the water was irresistible.

322

The metallic-gray sea was heaving so he hadn't gone far out. Now he came back. "Why don't you just undress beneath a towel? I'll close my eyes while you slip into the water."

She gazed at him as she considered his suggestion, then went farther up the sand and picked up one of the towels. She kicked at the sand, feeling a little embarrassed, but wanting to go in so much. While he turned his back, she wrapped the towel around her and struggled out of her trousers and shirt. She wondered about wearing just her under-wear, but in the end wriggled out of her pants and removed her bra. To hell with it. She hadn't been swimming naked since the early days of her marriage to Elliot. This was different. She was thirty-two, for a start, and scarred by life. She felt her heart pounding against her ribs as she ran down to the water's edge, slipped off the towel and slid into the water. Though wild, the sea was not cold, and suddenly it turned incandescent the way it could before a storm. She didn't care. It felt like shedding a skin as she swam a little farther out and gradually her spirits began to lift. Leo swam away from her and then looked back directly at her. She ignored him and rolled over to lie on her back, then gazed up at the bruised sky. After a few moments, she turned to glance at him and saw he was still watching her.

She beckoned him over as she found her feet.

"Better not go out any farther today," he said as he swam across.

She was silent for a moment but her body felt on fire. She glanced at the shoreline where the trees were now bending and twisting as the wind blew them about.

When he reached her he put his hands on her shoulders, his eyes shining. She felt the pressure spreading, so intense that she forgot to worry about what they were doing. The sensation flooded her entire body, wiping thought from her mind and replacing it with feeling. Standing there naked and so close to him, she experienced it as energy coursing through her. The moment went on, then she tilted her head back and gazed up at the darkening sky, her emotions too deep to fathom.

"Sometimes I feel haunted," she said.

"By Elliot?"

"Yes."

"It's in your mind. It will fade."

He touched her left cheek then bent his head toward her. "Do you want me to stop?" he said in a low voice.

She shook her head and smelled the warm saltiness of his skin as he kissed her.

A knot of desire tightened in her throat. She pressed her body against his and felt herself trying to hold back tears. Not tears of sadness. Tears of something like relief, or hope, or something inexpressible, but important, really important. Now in this bubble of peace she felt as if her shredded heart was healing. He hugged her and they stayed buffeted by the wind, standing in the water as if there were only the two of them in the world.

The ocean turned wilder, the water swirling around them under the angry sky, and then the rain came down with such force they had no option but to make a run for it.

# 30

As Louisa drove back, she acknowledged it had been just as well the rain had stopped them. Who knew how far it might have gone otherwise and, though she had wanted him, she knew it was probably too soon to be thinking of being with somebody new. And yet she couldn't help feeling she deserved some happiness.

The air, heavy now, felt oppressive and the trees overhanging the road, laden with moisture, were drooping so low they brushed the hood of the car. She almost wanted the rain to stop, but they needed it badly and she didn't mind the pungent smell of salty sea water and fish in the air.

She pulled up at home and went in by the back door. Upstairs she towel-dried her hair, changed into a dress and enjoyed the memory of Leo holding her. It had been such a sweet relief. She had missed the touch of a man, the closeness that made worries disappear, at least temporarily. And at least Elliot wasn't in her every breath any more, though she had plenty of other worries. De Vos and his false contract for a start, and that awful Australian man. She wished Leo wasn't up at Cinnamon Hills but instead here in Galle, because she guessed he might be the one who would help her to truly live again.

She felt slightly shaken but happy too and went down to the sitting room where Margo and William Tyler were sitting side by side, hands intertwined, the lights low and the room full of shadows. She switched on a stronger light and the room sprang to life.

"So," she said, smiling at the way they looked. "It seems you've come to an agreement."

Margo smiled back. "I've agreed to be cited as co-respondent."

Louisa lifted an eyebrow. "Really? Are you sure?"

Margo let go of his hand and rose from the sofa. She came over to Louisa.

"I love him, so what choice do I have?"

Louisa inclined her head and stared into Margo's eyes. "It was you who said we always have a choice. But if this is what you want, you have my full support."

Margo placed a hand on Louisa's arm.

"Thank you. It means a lot. I was wondering if it would be acceptable for William to stay for a few days."

"Of course. But won't you need to provide the court with some kind of proof for the divorce?"

"Maybe not if we both admit what has happened. But perhaps you might take a photograph of us together, just in case."

"Oh goodness. I'd have to do that?"

"If you don't mind."

William stood and came over to the two women. "I'm so sorry for the imposition. And if it makes you uncomfortable, please don't worry, we can find another way."

"No," she said, liking the straightforwardness of the man and the clarity in his blue eyes. "I'll do it. But what will you say to Irene?"

"I'm not planning to say anything to Mum for now. She'd only try and stop me. To her divorce is scandalous."

Louisa snorted. "How do you think she feels about having an illegitimate grandson?"

"I think she feels confused. Part of her will want to see the child, the other part will be wishing it wasn't true."

"Then I finally have something in common with Irene! But look, let's explain what's been going on to William. It must sound a bit odd."

"Do you mind me telling him everything?"

"Not at all. But first, why not show him where to put his case."

While Margo took William up to the next floor Louisa considered the events of her day. She needed to process having finally met Zinnia, as well as having gotten so close to Leo. And remembering her promise to contact her doctor, she glanced outside. The rain had slowed down so, armed with a large umbrella, she headed for Dr. Russell's house. Several other people were also out on the streets, darting around under umbrellas, taking advantage of the lull, and she nodded at acquaintances as she walked rapidly by. When she reached the door, Dr. Russell's wife answered her knock, then invited her into the hall while she explained her husband was away in Colombo but would be back soon.

"Will you ask him to call on me the moment he's back," Louisa said. "I think it is quite urgent."

"Of course."

She opened the door and Louisa saw the rain was worsening again. "I'd better make a dash for it," she said. "Thank you."

■ ■ ■ ■

That evening Jonathan came for supper and was introduced to William. Later Louisa took him to one side and explained about Margo and William.

Her father looked a little troubled by it. "Well, I am surprised at Margo. Perhaps she's a little more like her brother than we thought."

"That's not very fair."

"Look, I'm as open-minded as the next man, but should they be staying under the same roof? What are the man's intentions?"

"Don't be so old-fashioned. He's hoping to get a divorce, and anyway I've put them in separate rooms for now."

He shrugged. "Does Irene know?"

She shook her head.

"I think all hell will break loose there."

Louisa grimaced. He was absolutely right about that.

After dinner she asked him to come into Elliot's old office with her.

As they went across to the hall and down the corridor she sighed deeply. "I had a note to expect a visit from Inspector Roberts this evening. As you know, the contract De Vos gave me is a complete fake. I passed it to

330

the police weeks ago."

Her father nodded. "It may be a case of extortion. I doubt they'll know how to handle it."

"We are usually a sleepy little town, aren't we," Louisa said. "Just the odd row when sailors have too much to drink."

"Exactly. But I think I should deal with him."

"De Vos? Maybe, but I thought I'd wait until he turns up again and then confront him. I'm not paying out that amount of cash for something that didn't even exist."

They seated themselves and he asked her to update him on the emporium. After she'd explained Himal was getting on well, she told him about joining forces with Leo to export his cinnamon.

"You're sure all this is not too much for you to handle? You have the emporium too. I won't say I'm not worried." He tilted his head to one side and scrutinized her face. "But it sounds as if you like this Leo."

She smiled. "I think I do."

He patted her hand. "Well, be careful. I don't want you getting hurt. Remember you are still vulnerable."

"I know."

They heard a knock on the door and Ashan entered. "I am sorry to interrupt.

Chief Inspector Roberts has arrived, Madam."

"Please show him through."

It was the same red-faced officer who had informed her of Elliot's death. Louisa nodded at him. "Won't you take a seat?"

He perched on the edge of an office chair and gazed at them both.

"So," Jonathan said. "Do we have any progress?"

He pulled a negative face.

"What about the falsified contract I showed you?" Louisa said.

"We may be able to charge Mr. De Vos with attempted extortion. And the fact that he tried that could indicate he may also be linked with the break-in. Maybe he thought he'd find valuable gemstones?"

"I haven't heard from Cooper or De Vos for at least two months."

"It's possible they may have given up."

"Do you really think so?"

"I hope so, Mrs. Reeve. I hope so . . ."

Jonathan stood. "Well, if there is nothing else, I'll show you out. Can you at least keep an eye on my daughter's house? I don't want any of these reprobates bothering Louisa again."

# 31

Louisa rose early, planning to take the dogs to the beach. As rain was never far off just now, she grabbed a mac. As long as she wasn't driving she loved the rain and the full earthy scents rising from the land, though it certainly restricted some outdoor activities and she hated that. Being cooped up indoors didn't agree with her.

She called the dogs, but only Tommy and Bouncer came racing through, tails wagging energetically. Her dogs loved a walk, whatever the weather, but oddly little Zip, the runt of the litter, wasn't with them. She felt a touch of anxiety and checked their baskets in the back hall but, as he wasn't there either, she asked Ashan if he'd seen the little chap. A worried-looking Ashan told her he had assumed Zip had been with the other two — earlier he had opened the door for all three to use the garden but hadn't noticed if they had all come back in.

"That's odd," she said. "Where on earth can he be?"

She went out into the garden to check the back gate. As soon as she reached it she saw it had been closed but left unbolted.

She went back to the house and put leads on the other two dogs. William and Margo offered to help, so they went off in one direction to search the ramparts, while she called one of the houseboys to accompany her on a search of the streets. She hoped Tommy and Bouncer would begin to whine if they sensed they were close to Zip. The streets were shiny with dampness and she had to avoid the dripping trees in the narrower alleyways showering her with droplets, but she spent an hour knocking on doors and asking if anyone had seen anything. Nobody had, so then she went to the shops and the covered market. Still nothing.

She arrived back home just as Dr. Russell appeared, his stoop more pronounced than ever and with more gray in his hair. He pushed his metal-framed spectacles farther up his nose as he spoke. "Louisa, my dear, my wife said it was urgent. Is something wrong?"

"Thank you for coming, but it's not me." She glanced up at the clouds. "Let's go inside and I'll explain."

"You look a little strained," he said as they stood in the hall.

"I've just discovered one of my dogs is missing."

He frowned. "That is a shame, but otherwise you are fine?"

"Yes. Look, give me your coat and I'll hang it up."

He passed her his coat and she took off her own mac, hanging them both on a spare peg in the hall cupboard.

They went through to the sitting room where he sat while she paced back and forth.

"So, what's this all about?" he prompted.

She stood still. "A friend — well, more of an acquaintance — of mine is really unwell. She has refused to see a doctor so far, but my worry is that it might be malaria."

"Let me ask you a few questions."

She nodded.

"Firstly, describe to me what you saw."

"Well, she was shaking and seemed too cold, even though it was a warm day."

"Chills can range from moderate to severe. You think she had a high fever?"

Louisa shook her head. "I don't know, but she was sweating and rubbing her head."

"Headache is common with malaria. What about vomiting or diarrhea?"

"Both, I think."

He winced and paused before he replied. "Doesn't sound too good. How long has this been going on?"

"Months, I think. She seems to revive but then she's ill again."

"That can be a pattern with malaria."

"Will you see her? It's a fair distance."

"Will tomorrow do? I'm pretty tied up today."

"I'm sure that'll be fine."

"As you know, there has indeed been a malaria epidemic, though it's largely confined to more northerly parts of the country."

"She thinks she has pleurisy."

"I doubt it."

"And her state of mind is very low, I'm afraid."

"We'll go together tomorrow and I'll take a blood sample and send it off to the laboratory in Colombo."

Ashan brought in a tea tray.

"I'll pour," she said as she finally sat down.

Later on, Louisa went to the beach with Margo and William to look for Zip. The rain had been replaced by an unearthly lull but, aware it wouldn't last long, Louisa glanced repeatedly up at the brooding sky. By the time they had searched the beach, the young couple were walking a little ahead of Louisa. Just where the scrubby grass gave way to sand, Margo suddenly shouted out. Fearing it might be Zip, Louisa's heart missed a beat and she ran across to find an animal lying in a clump of long grass. Tears blurred her vision as she knelt on the sand.

"It's a fox," Margo said. "Poor thing."

"What do you think happened?" Louisa said and glanced up.

"Judging by the foam at its mouth, it could be rabies or, perhaps more likely, poisoning," William said. "I wouldn't touch it. These things are usually deliberate. Foxes attack their chickens."

Margo sighed. "What a waste of a lovely animal."

"Awful." Louisa gazed at the creature.

"Come on," Margo said and held out a hand to Louisa. "There isn't anything we can do. Let's get back. Zip isn't here."

Back home again, Louisa needed to be on her own; seeking distraction, she went upstairs to sew her patchwork bedspread. She thought of little Zip and felt sick with worry. She remembered how tiny he had been when he was born. She'd thought he might not live, had nursed him herself, feeding him from a baby's bottle, and since then

he had been her constant companion. Seeing the fox lying dead on the beach had also
brought back other thoughts she'd rather
forget. She imagined the scene on the road
to Colombo and wondered how it must
have been. Had Elliot known he was going
to die, or had everything just gone dark?
Had he been scared? And if he realized what
was happening, had he regretted what he'd
done? Had he felt guilt, or was he killed too
quickly for remorse to set in? She could see
him as he crashed, his eyes wide open —
and she closed her own in response, squeezing them tight.

The time passed slowly but she couldn't
just sit and wait, so once more she hurried
outside to walk around the ramparts, keeping her eyes peeled for Zip and staring out
at the shifting color of the sea, the bruised
blues and purples mingling with the gray.
She pictured him running on the sand, his
fur dripping, and the way he had been so
scared of the water to begin with, but once
he had plucked up courage, she hadn't been
able to keep him out of the sea. But although she looked everywhere all over
again, there was still no sign of him. Shading her eyes, she stared out to sea, anxious
that he might have climbed the walls and
slipped. When she imagined him at the bot-

tom of the ocean she felt sick. She went back and forth between the Aurora and Point Utrecht bastions several times, where cannons had once prevented the entry of enemy vessels. Then, as storm clouds were still gathering, she wrapped her arms around herself and glanced up at the sky.

Once home she went upstairs to change and was just undressing when she heard a knock at the front door and Ashan opening it. Unable to make out what was being said, she slipped on her dressing gown and went to the top of the stairs. Looking down, she saw Ashan in the hall holding a small box.

"Who was that?" she said.

"A parcel has been delivered for you."

"Do you know who it's from, Ashan?"

"No, Madam. It was just a boy who brought it. He said a man gave him some money to bring it. I can open it for you."

"No. Put it in the dining room on the table. I'll be down in a few minutes."

"Bring some scissors, Madam, to cut the string."

At first she didn't feel anything much about the parcel and went back into her room where she gazed at her face. Her eyes glittered and her cheeks were raw. She went into the bathroom for a towel and rubbed her wet hair before brushing out the tangles.

Once in dry clothes, she sat at her dressing table thinking about Zip again; then she picked up the book she'd been reading but, remembering the parcel, felt a sudden sense of foreboding.

In her sewing room she dug out her household scissors — not the best ones she used for cutting fabric — then she made her way to the dining room, glancing in at the sitting room and seeing Margo and William deep in conversation.

She cut the string and was aware of a feeling of trepidation as she carefully lifted the lid of the box. Her heart lurched as she glanced inside and, gasping in shock, she dropped the lid on the floor. She let out a long moan, then ran to the downstairs toilet and wretched. When she came out again she stood in the hall, shaking and shivering, with her arms hanging limply by her sides. She could see Margo and William now in the dining room, both staring at the contents of the box with horrified expressions. Louisa closed her eyes but couldn't rid herself of the terrible image of poor Zip, his head lying bloody and mangled inside the box. She felt a wave of ferocious anger. Who could have committed such an act of deliberate cruelty? Margo came straight out to Louisa and pulled her away from the sight of the dining room and into the lounge where Louisa began weeping.

"I can't take any more," she said between sobs.

Margo made soothing sounds, though she must have felt the shock too. When Louisa finally stopped crying, she stared at the door to the dining room. "How could anyone do that to a defenseless animal, Margo? My poor, poor little Zip who never did anybody any harm."

Louisa felt heartbroken and tears began to flow again. She thought of Zip lying on her lap while she stroked his ears, or wagging his tail at the sight of food. She thought of him lagging behind the other two as they raced along the beach. Now he would never do any of those things again. It was senseless and heartless and it made her shake with rage to think of him scared and suffering.

"Where's the number for the police?" Margo asked.

"In the book on the hall table," Louisa said in a choked voice.

"I'll call them," Margo said and got up to speak to William who was now in the hall with Ashan.

As Louisa was still trembling, he asked

Ashan to bring her some sweet tea and brandy.

While Margo called the police, Ashan brought in the brandy and poured a glass for Louisa. She drank in silence with Ashan remaining by her side, as if uncertain how to help and waiting for further instructions.

"Who could have done this?" Margo asked.

Louisa shook her head but felt sure someone was trying to scare her. She tried to tell herself her worry about Cooper was in her head, that there had been a misunderstanding, but the thought of him filled her with misgivings. She couldn't help thinking, if it had been this easy to abduct Zip what else might "they" be capable of? Fear threw all her troubles into stark relief: her home once so secure but now under threat; the marriage that was to have lasted into old age but was now a shadowy insubstantial thing. Everything had become fragile. And now Zip was gone too, and in a most terrible way.

# 32

As she awoke to a beautiful coral sky, the mist still hanging over the ocean, the smell of death lingered in her nostrils. At breakfast both dogs stared at her with melancholy eyes, chins resting on their paws, as if they knew what had happened. So she sat on the floor with her arms draped around both of them.

A little later, she veered between fury at Zip's death and a sense of abject loneliness as she once again gathered her courage before seeing Zinnia. As she drove Dr. Russell to the cinnamon plantation, the day remained bright, but she would rather have stayed at home with her two sad dogs, keeping the world at bay. But she had promised to do this — and so she must. The police had taken the horrible parcel and its contents away, but nothing could rid Louisa of the memory.

The air was not much cooler since the last

downpour and the heat would soon be building further. As she drove, wiping the sweat from her brow from time to time, the silence between them weighed heavily and she was certain the doctor could tell something was wrong. When he asked her how she knew Zinnia, she hesitated a moment longer before speaking, but decided he could be trusted not to spread gossip.

"My husband was seeing her." She hated saying it and didn't dare glance at his face.

"I'm sorry. I didn't mean to pry."

She swallowed the lump in her throat. "I didn't know until after he died. The worst thing is they had a son together."

Now she glanced sideways to check the doctor's reaction and saw him shake his head.

"My dear, that must have been hard for you."

She nodded and her heart thumped in her chest. "It still is," she said.

"So why are you going out of your way to help this woman?"

Feeling a bit self-conscious, she felt herself redden. "I'd like to say common humanity, and maybe it is a little bit." She paused, wondering how much of that was true.

"And what else?"

"I think she tried to break it off with El-liot."

"I see."

"And I want to help her cousin, Leo McNairn. She lives on his land and now she's ill, he's having to care for the child. He's seven."

"That can't be easy."

"You're right. The plantation takes up all his time so it's very difficult. Made harder because the child doesn't go to school. Leo has become a friend of mine. I'm doing what I can."

"And the child?"

She sighed deeply. "That's another story. On the one hand, I can't bear to even look at him . . ."

"But on the other hand?"

"I'm curious, I suppose. He's so like El-liot, you see, and of course it makes me think of what my own children might have looked like."

There was a short silence.

"Look," she said. "We turn off just here. We'll go up to the top first and find Leo, then we can all go down to Zinnia's house together."

"Will the child be there? Maybe I should take a look at him too."

"He wasn't there last time I was here. I

should have mentioned this before, but although I've started clearing up Zinnia's place, her bedroom is still in a bad way. I'm going to try and come back with a houseboy to give it a real spring clean."

"I think you must be a saint, Louisa."

She felt her skin prickle with anxiety. "I'm really not. But so much has been revealed about Elliot I feel as if I never really knew him. Who knows, maybe I'm helping Zinnia so that I can understand something of his other life."

"If there's one thing I've learned from my work it's that people's lives are not tidy."

"I hate myself for how angry I sometimes feel. But I don't want to become vengeful."

"We all have things we don't like about ourselves, thoughts we are embarrassed by, past actions we regret."

She raised her brows. "I'm sure you can't have anything to regret."

"You'd be wrong there. I have allowed work to dominate my life far too much, but there it is. Too late to change now."

"What about when you retire?"

"My wife would like me to retire now, but I'm just not ready to put up my feet."

They reached the top and Louisa parked.

As they both got out of the car, a houseboy came out to say Leo was already down at his cousin's house, but he would be happy to take them there via the shortcut.

Louisa thanked him and held out her hand to the doctor.

"Is your bag heavy? It's quite rough terrain."

"I'm a walker, so I'm sure I'll be fine, and the bag isn't heavy."

They followed the boy, keeping watch for tree roots spreading across the path that snaked down the hill. The air was so full of moisture it seemed to sparkle where the sun filtered through the waving trees and, briefly, Louisa enjoyed the moment. But then, as they drew closer to Zinnia's bungalow, she felt worried again. How would she react if Conor was there? Last time she had not been able to look at him. It wasn't the child's fault, but when she thought of her own daughter, her own little Julia, her skin prickled and the spiky resentment made her feel ashamed. Conor was just a little boy but, at the back of her mind, she couldn't help thinking he was the little boy *she* should have had.

When they reached the clearing outside the house Louisa came to a halt. She knocked at the door and after a few moments Leo opened it. "I'm glad you've come," he said and, though she felt momentarily on edge at seeing him for the first time since they had gone swimming, his broad smile put her at her ease.

"This is our family doctor. Doctor Russell, this is Leo McNairn."

They followed Leo into the sitting room, which remained almost as tidy as Louisa had left it. She noticed a window was open and the air was relatively fresh.

"So where is your cousin?" the doctor said, glancing about the room.

"Follow me," Leo said.

Although Leo had opened the bedroom windows and tidied up the evening before, Zinnia had closed the heavy curtains again, saying the light hurt her eyes, and the smell was still sour. The doctor glanced at Louisa. "Someone needs to air this room thoroughly." Then he walked across to the bed where Zinnia lay with her eyes closed.

He passed a hand in front of her impassive face. Nothing. Then he put a palm to her forehead. "Very indicative of a malarial fever. Keep her cool if you can. Damp cloths on the forehead and back of the neck." He paused. "Zinnia, can you hear me?"

Her eyes flew open and widened in alarm.

Louisa backed against the door, horrified by the dull look of despair she saw. In the intense silence of the room one thing was certain: this desperately ill woman was no longer the person Elliot had been captivated by.

"I'm Doctor Russell. Will you allow me to take a blood sample?"

"Why?" Zinnia had spoken in a thin rasping voice.

"I think you may have malaria, my dear. We can treat it if we know for sure."

Zinnia lifted her hands helplessly as if to say, *Do what you will.*

He opened his brown leather bag and took out a syringe from a zippered case. After he had prepared the needle, taking the blood took longer than anticipated. "She's dehydrated," he said. "Her veins are collapsing. Make sure she drinks."

Then, after it was finally done, he carefully wrapped up the blood sample. "I'll get this sent off to the laboratories. They are inundated, so it might be a few days. Now tell me how long you have been feeling ill, my dear."

As the doctor spoke with Zinnia, Leo indicated he wanted to talk to Louisa in the sitting room. "I thought I'd better warn you Conor could arrive at any minute. Will you be okay?"

A sudden memory of Elliot stopped her. She took in a deep breath and let it out slowly. Adulterer, she said under her breath. *Bloody adulterer.* Once again she felt a burst of something she could barely control and, after she had mastered herself, a feeling of unexpected gloom descended.

"Louisa?"

"What?" she snapped.

He didn't react to her tone. "What can I say or do to make you feel better?"

She blinked rapidly. This was not the way she liked to view herself. She was a positive person, a caring person, not this seething, resentful mess.

"I'm cheerful," she lied, "but scared."

"He's only a little boy."

"Don't make me feel worse than I already do." She glanced at the sky. The brightness was gone and now the yellowy light was tinged with purple, a sure sign more rain was on its way.

He smiled a crooked kind of smile. "Would it help if I told you I've thought about the ball?"

"And?"

"And I've got my houseboy cleaning up my dinner suit. I hope I don't let you down."

"You know the ball is soon. Is your van fixed yet or will you come to my place on your motorbike?"

"The bike, but I'll change at yours if that's

acceptable?"

"Perfectly. I can't wait to see you spruced up."

"You don't like me as I am?"

She wanted to say something significant but didn't reply.

A serious look came over his face. "About the other day . . ."

"It isn't that . . . I feel exhausted by so many conflicting emotions I can't trust my own judgment."

"I imagine trusting anyone at the moment must be tricky."

She sighed and then shook her head. "A little more than tricky, to be perfectly honest."

He took a step toward her and put a hand on her arm: a gesture of infinite tenderness. When he gazed into her eyes his look was full of concern. "Well, just remember I'm here and I'm on your side. If —"

It made her feel good to hear it. When he looked at her like that, his eyes so honest and calm and full of whatever this was that hung between them, she felt better, but then the doctor came out suddenly and they sprang apart.

"Well," he said. "I have the sample. So, Louisa, we should be getting back so I can send this off."

"I'll just drop the doctor at his surgery, Leo, but then I'll come back with a houseboy to try to clean Zinnia's bedroom."

"Are you sure?" Leo said, his dark eyes now looking intense. "Kamu and I can do it."

She sighed. Her nerves had already been stretched taut, and as they climbed up the hill again, Louisa kept an eye out for Conor — but they reached the top, got into the car, and were on their way before he appeared. If she was honest with herself, she felt a little ashamed at how relieved she was to have missed him.

As she drove, the doctor was quiet, and so was she. Even if Zinnia had tried to put a stop to their relationship, the cinnamon plantation was where Elliot's heart had been. Louisa had to finally accept he had in reality left her long before the day he died.

"So, what did you make of her?" she eventually said.

"It's hard to tell. She says she has some good days, but things look somewhat severe to me."

Louisa nodded and concentrated on the road.

"If you can manage to sanitize her room it would be a great help, but Louisa . . ."

"Yes?"

"I hope you don't think I'm speaking out of turn, but in my job I tend to hear gossip and I wouldn't want you to be hurt. I wanted to suggest you don't go in too deep with Leo."

"He's a good man."

"I'm sure he is, but don't underestimate what you've been going through."

"He's taking me to the ball. Just as a friend."

He smiled. "Well, that should be fine. You deserve a little fun. Just be careful. You are more vulnerable than you realize."

"That's exactly what my father said."

"Grief can affect people in different ways and last much longer than they understand, especially if it's complicated."

Louisa wasn't sure if she was grieving for Elliot anymore. She felt she was grieving for the loss of her favorite dog and for herself; for the loss of who she had thought she was. Did that make any sense?

After she had dropped off the doctor, the first person she saw was Margo, who was sitting in the back garden while the rain held off. Louisa's two dogs had been lying at her feet but raised themselves to welcome their mistress.

"I miss Zip so much," Louisa said as she

sat and stroked Bouncer's head. "I can't bear what they did to him."

"I know."

They remained in silence for a few minutes, Louisa thinking about Zip, but the hurt was too raw and she tried to focus on something else. And yet, when she did, all that came to mind was Elliot with Zinnia.

"Where have you been?" Margo asked.

"I took my doctor to see Zinnia. He thinks it might be malaria."

"Goodness."

"I'm going back again in a few minutes to help air her bedroom and give it a spring clean. I was going to see if one of the houseboys is free."

Margo seemed to be thinking. "Are you sure you're up to it?"

"I'd rather keep busy. I don't want to sit around just twiddling my thumbs. It'll do me no good. I'll have the emporium to think about soon but right now I feel so angry about Zip."

"Not about Zinnia?"

"Her too, though if you saw how ill she is . . ."

"I'll come with you, if you like. I'd quite like to see what she's like."

"Honestly, it's hard to tell. She's so sick."

"Shall I come with you anyway?"

"Where's William?"

"Indoors, chatting with your father."

"Dad's here?"

"He just popped in. He wanted to know if you had anyone accompanying you to the ball. If not, he says he'll do it."

"That's not necessary." Louisa thought of the trail of events leading to this moment. "Leo's coming with me."

"I'm glad."

"Will William still be here?"

"Yes, but we're going to have to get a suit made up for him chop-chop. He didn't pack for a ball!"

"I don't suppose he did. And we'd better take our compromising photograph soon."

"Yes. Sorry about that."

"Don't be. It might be fun. Will you be half-dressed?"

Margo laughed. "Something like that."

"Oh Lord! And in bed, no doubt."

"That would do it. Though honestly, once two people have decided to call it quits, shouldn't they just be able to do so without all this rigmarole?"

Louisa wondered if Margo was right. Should people be tied together so inextricably? Was that how Elliot had felt? Trapped? Stifled? She shook her head. It hadn't seemed that way.

■ ■ ■ ■

As they pulled up outside Zinnia's house, Margo took a deep breath and Louisa saw the confusion in her sister-in-law's face and that she appeared to be battling with her thoughts and feelings.

"It feels strange knowing Elliot was here so much," Margo said. "In my head, I keep trying to find a way to make things better. I can't forgive him — and I hate feeling like this."

Louisa didn't reply.

"When I think of all the attention he had as a child. Mother rarely showed any interest in me. I remember us sitting together at the kitchen table while he copied his homework from somebody else's exercise book. He laughed when I said it was wrong and Mum just smiled and said there was no harm in it. She just wanted him to get a high mark. Can you imagine? Now the way he's behaved haunts me, but it must be so much worse for you."

"I want to remember what we had, yet at the same time I don't. Knowing Leo has helped."

"How do you mean?"

"I'm not sure. He makes me feel better about myself, I guess."

# 33

Louisa pushed open the front door to the bungalow, Margo trailing behind. Once they were inside, Louisa glanced back to see her sister-in-law gazing around at the paintings of Zinnia with Conor, just as she herself had done.

Though Margo had been the one who had always seen through Elliot, Louisa could sense it was hard for her to discover the true extent to which her "perfect" brother had not been so perfect after all. She felt a flicker of unease and a tight little stab of jealousy in her chest. It couldn't be denied that Zinnia had been very beautiful, talented too, and maybe a little wild.

"This doesn't look too bad," Margo said.

"I've already cleaned this room."

"Where is she?" Margo whispered behind cupped hands.

"Through there." Louisa drew breath and pointed at a door. "We need to encourage her to come out here and lie on the sofa . . . Oh God, can we do this?"

Battling with a mixture of fear and determination, Louisa stared at Margo.

"I can, if you can," Margo said.

"We might have to carry her, or support her on both sides. She's very weak."

She knocked on Zinnia's door, opened it and peered into the room. This time the curtains were open and the air smelled fresher. Perhaps she's improving, Louisa thought. Then she tiptoed over to the bed.

"Remember me?" she asked.

Zinnia nodded and spoke in a low voice. "There's no need for you to be here."

"I promised Doctor Russell I'd get your room shipshape. If you just sit up a bit, my sister-in-law will help me get you up and walk you through to the sitting room."

Zinnia's eyes widened. "Elliot's sister?"

"Yes."

"You both must hate me."

Louisa glanced away and then back at Zinnia. "I tried to," she said in a small voice.

Margo came into the room carrying a box. "I've brought the cleaning stuff."

Louisa nodded. "Come on, Zinnia, please shuffle up if you can, and then swing your legs over the side."

Zinnia managed to raise herself to a sitting position, then Louisa turned to Margo. "Actually, could you run her a bath? The bathroom is through there. Do you have hot water, Zinnia?"

"Leo's houseboy comes to stoke the boiler once a day, so it should still be hot now."

Margo went through and Louisa could hear the water running.

"I can't manage a bath on my own."

"We'll help you."

"Really?"

Louisa nodded, though her heart was hammering in alarm, or maybe it was confusion. All she knew for certain was this wasn't easy. When she heard Leo calling out, she felt a wave of relief. Because he was there, yes, but also he might be able to help them move Zinnia into the bathroom.

He came into the room. "Louisa," he said and his smile lightened her heart. "I've brought clean bedding."

She took a few steps forward and felt more confident. "We want to give Zinnia a bath before she goes to lie on the sofa. Margo's in there running the water."

"That's kind."

"I'm only doing what has to be done."

When Margo called out that the bath was ready, Zinnia's eyes were glued on Leo and Louisa. "You two seem close."

Louisa took a step back and answered briskly. "We're friends, that's all. Now, Leo, could you carry Zinnia through?"

"Leo can't undress me."

"We'll do that."

"Where's Conor?" Zinnia asked, glancing at Louisa with a worried look.

"Don't worry. He's up at my place, drawing snails," Leo said.

He walked over to the bed. "Now?" He asked Zinnia to wrap her arms around his neck. Then he lifted her gently. "You're as light as a bird, Cousin."

"I've lost weight."

While he carried her to the bathroom, Margo came out and exchanged anxious looks with Louisa.

"It's not easy," she said.

"I know, but she needs us to help her," Louisa said. "After that, will you make a start on the room, please."

"I'll strip the bed first."

"We could send the sheets to the dhobi but it might be quicker to do it here." She sighed. "I'd better go in."

Zinnia was sitting on the edge of the bath as Louisa went in. A few awkward moments followed, during which nothing was said, then Leo spoke up, breaking the uneasy silence. "I'll check up on Conor, but I'll be back later. Can you manage, Louisa? I can stay if it would help?"

"No. You go to Conor. Margo and I will be fine."

After he had left, the women stared at each other. There was so much to say that remained unspoken, yet it seemed to Louisa that neither of them had a clue where to begin.

"I loved him, you know," Zinnia eventually said.

Louisa nodded. "Me too."

"He said your marriage wasn't happy, that he would leave you, but after eight years I began to see it wasn't true. He would never have left you . . . That's why I ended it."

Louisa glanced away and then gazed at Zinnia. "He loved the child?"

"Very much. Your lost children broke his heart."

Louisa swallowed rapidly and then tested the temperature of the water. "We need to get you in. Can you take off your nightdress yourself?"

Margo came in to help and Zinnia lifted her arms, but then they fell limply at her sides. "I haven't the strength."

"Hold up your arms and I'll pull it over your head," Margo said in a matter-of-fact way.

"Margo's a nurse," Louisa added.

When Zinnia was finally naked, Louisa was shocked at her appearance. Just skin and bones, with arms and legs like sticks, and the lines of her ribs showing through the transparent bluish skin of her chest.

"Doesn't Leo feed you?" she tried to say lightly.

"He's always bringing food. I'm just not hungry."

Louisa held one of her arms while Zinnia managed to haul herself into the bath, where she lay back exhausted by the effort.

"Margo, can you get a jug, please. We need to wash her hair."

Margo nodded and Louisa followed her out; she saw she had stripped the bed and piled up everything in the corner.

"Are you all right?" Margo said. "You look drawn."

"She's dreadfully thin."

"But it isn't that, is it?"

"Not just that. I feel so weird being with her and can't help thinking of her with Elliot. I want to help her but I'm still getting flashes of anger."

"I'm not surprised."

"But how can I be angry with someone who is so terribly sick? I feel like a monster."

"Darling, you're anything but. It's natural

you should feel that way. Most women wouldn't even consider helping, under the circumstances."

Louisa gazed at the wooden floor.

"Do you want me to take over in there?"

"No. Have you come across a hairbrush anywhere?"

"There's one on her bedside table."

Louisa picked up the brush, while Margo found a jug in the kitchen area and then they went back to the bathroom.

Zinnia's eyes were closed.

"Can you sit up?" Louisa said.

Zinnia's eyes flew open. "I was thinking of what he'd say if he could see us now," she said.

"He'd probably run a mile."

Zinnia managed to smile. "Maybe he manipulated both of us?"

"Maybe. Now sit up. Can you?"

Margo helped Zinnia to sit but the woman began to cough.

"I'll get a glass of water," Margo said.

Louisa began to pour water over the long, tangled hair. She found some shampoo and asked Zinnia to keep her eyes closed while she lathered it. It took a while to wash out all the shampoo, but after it was done Louisa did her best to brush Zinnia's hair.

"He loved my hair, you know."

"I'm not sure I want to know."

"It was how we met," Zinnia continued.

Louisa sat back on her haunches and let Zinnia soak for a while. She closed her eyes but Elliot was still a daunting presence between them.

"So how did you meet?" she eventually said, curious despite herself.

"He came to an exhibition launch in Colombo, looking for a picture for you, I think. Anyway, he was staring at a self-portrait I'd recently painted. I heard him say, 'What marvelous hair.' He hadn't seen me sitting behind the desk so I went up to him."

Louisa inhaled slowly then let out a shuddering breath.

"I introduced myself and he said my hair was even better in the flesh. We both had a glass of wine and I asked him if he'd like to go on to a bar. My stint behind the desk was over so I was free."

"Did you know he was married?"

"I didn't at first. He was so handsome and charming, I just liked him from the start. He made me feel special. He knew how to do that. But we didn't sleep together for a while after that."

"Because you found out he was buying a picture for his wife."

"No, he didn't say that then. He said it was for a friend."

"So, when did you find out about me?"

"Just after your first miscarriage nearly eight years ago. He came to me, heartbroken. That was the first time we actually slept together."

Louisa gulped and there were a few moments of ghastly silence.

Margo came back in with a glass of water. "Sorry I took so long."

"Can you soap yourself," Louisa said, handing Zinnia a bar of soap and willing herself not to cry.

The woman took the soap and managed fairly well, while Louisa averted her eyes; it was just too intimate. Then she got to her feet and asked Margo to help support Zinnia as she climbed out of the bath.

Zinnia held out a hand to Louisa. Her face clouded over and a stricken look crossed it. "I'm sorry for the harm I caused you."

Louisa didn't take her hand but held her gaze and swallowed hard.

Then she and Margo managed to wrap Zinnia in a couple of towels Leo had brought down with the clean bedding.

"We need to get you to the sitting room," Margo said, taking over, and practical as ever. Louisa gave her a wan smile and, somehow, they supported Zinnia as she stumbled through. Once she was safely on the sofa, Margo removed the towels and covered her with one of the fresh blankets. "Have you a dressing gown?" she asked.

Zinnia pointed at a robe hanging on the bedroom door and collapsed back onto the cushions behind her. Louisa bowed her head as tears blurred her vision, then she slipped outside where she gasped at the air in great emotional gulps, her eyes still stinging. "Oh God," she whispered to herself, not able to get rid of the image of Elliot with Zinnia so soon after her first miscarriage. She remembered he'd said he had pressing business in Colombo and she'd felt hurt by it, but had tried to understand. Now she knew the pressing business had been another woman.

Margo came out. "You surviving?"

Louisa shook her head and Margo came straight over to hug her. When they drew apart she sighed. "Tough, isn't it?"

"Yes."

"If you want to go up to see Leo I'll get on with cleaning her room. It's really just the floor that needs mopping."

"Conor will be up there."

"He's just a child. Maybe it would help if you got to know him a little."

"I don't know."

"Well, stay out here for a while and if you do decide to go up, just go. I'll follow when I'm done, though maybe Leo could come back later to carry her back to her bed."

"What about the sheets?"

"I'll put them to soak in the bath."

"Thanks, Margo. There's a short cut up to Leo's through the trees when you're ready, though it's probably better if you follow the road."

After Margo had gone back in, Louisa deliberated for a while but eventually decided to go on up to Leo's place. By the time she reached his house the rain was just beginning and when there was no reply to her knock at the door she opened it and went in. Upstairs Conor was sitting on the sofa playing with a pack of cards.

"Where's Leo?" Louisa asked, feeling unnerved by the child's silence.

He just shrugged.

"I heard you were doing some drawing. Would you like to show me?"

The boy glanced up at her but still said nothing.

"Well, maybe I'll just sit here and if you feel like showing me you can."

Although she tried not to stare, her eyes kept returning to the child. He was so like

Elliot it was uncanny. She sat for a while, feeling uncomfortable and listening to the rain pounding the ground outside, then she got up to open a window and stare out before returning to wait again.

"Have you had lunch?" she asked.

He shook his head.

"Shall I see if we can rustle up a sandwich?"

He glanced up at her again. "Leo will do it."

She sighed. The child seemed terribly withdrawn.

After about half an hour Leo turned up and she saw his surprise as he took in the fact that she was sitting there with Conor.

"I hope you don't mind," she said. "It was getting a bit much. Margo is washing the floors but she'd like you to carry Zinnia back to bed."

"Of course."

"And I think Conor's hungry. I couldn't get much out of him."

"We'll all have a sandwich. What do you say, young man?"

The boy beamed at him and came over for a hug.

"By the way," Louisa said, "Doctor Russell has asked the laboratory to send the result of Zinnia's blood test direct to you. It'll only take a few more days."

"Good. And thank you for all you've done. Are you all set for the ball?"

She nodded. "Are you?"

"I'll get to your place at about seven. Does that give us time? I want to be sure this young man is tucked up in bed before I leave."

As Conor went outside to play Leo gazed at her.

"What?" she said with a smile.

"I'm planning a little fishing trip with Conor tomorrow. I'm wondering if you might come too."

"But why?"

"I think it would do him good to be around other people. Someone different and not just me. He really needs a break from his mother's illness."

"Wouldn't it be better just the two of you?"

He shook his head. "I think it would lighten the atmosphere if you were there, but look, if it doesn't feel right . . ."

"No. I'll come."

"That's great. I think a day out on the boat will be fun. Zinnia's illness annoys him and that makes him feel guilty."

"He's only a child," Louisa said, though she couldn't imagine ever feeling annoyed with the mother she had lost.

"Can you meet me at the beach at nine?"

# 34

Louisa was the first to arrive at the beach. The mist had burned off and the sky was now a pearly blue. She kicked off her sandals and left footprints in the wet sand as she trod down to the milky foam at the edge of the ocean. She took a few steps in and then ran back out to avoid the rolling waves, squealing as she felt the cool water splashing her legs. She looked up at the sound of laughter and spotted Leo and Conor watching her as they made their way down the beach. It filled her with relief to see the boy looking so willing. She laughed too and feeling herself relax, held her hand out to Conor.

"Why not take your shoes off and join me?" she called out.

After just a moment's hesitation, Conor dropped the buckets he was carrying and raced down toward her, chucking his shoes behind him as he went, and then sprinting to the water's edge. She took his hand and they ran in, staggering back as the waves rolled toward them.

"Isn't anyone going to help me with the boat?" Leo said, as he put down two bags of fishing tackle, an outboard motor, and a small hamper.

"We both will. Won't we, Conor?"

The child grinned and they joined Leo, who led them up the beach a little way to where a peeling, clinker-built boat, about twelve foot long, was tied to a palm tree.

"It was once bright blue," Leo said. "It just needs a new coat of paint to be good as new."

She felt a flicker of apprehension, but noticing the look on her face he smiled. "Don't worry, it's perfectly sound. I had it built locally on British lines, so it's something of a hybrid. Goes just fine."

He unknotted the rope and together they pushed the little boat down the sand toward the water's edge, where he attached the outboard motor.

"Can you hold the rope?" he said, and passed it to Louisa. "I'll just get the stuff."

After a moment he returned, carrying the tackle and the hamper, which he then threw on to the boat. Conor went back for the buckets and the net that was curled up inside one of them. Leo took them from him and placed them at the bow end.

"Right, Louisa and Conor, you two jump in and sit on that middle seat. It's just a couple of planks but safe enough."

They climbed in and as soon as they were seated, Leo began pushing the boat into the water. Once it was afloat he climbed in too, then passed the hamper to Louisa to stow under the covered bow panel, before he sat on the fixed seat at the stern end.

"There's not much power in this motor," he said, as he started it up. "But it's enough to get out and pootle about. Now I need to concentrate. It's easy to start but difficult to control."

Louisa watched the shore recede. Seabirds were flapping about above them and she could see a few fishermen farther out in the ocean. There was a salty breeze to freshen the air and the sea sparkled with reflected sunshine. With no sign of rain, it was a perfect day for fishing.

Once they'd reached the point where Leo felt they might catch some fish, he cut the engine and dropped anchor.

"How are you both doing?" he said.

Louisa smiled and Conor bobbed up and down excitedly. "Can we fish now?" he asked.

"You bet. I'll just get out the tackle."

He unwrapped the longer bag and prepared a rod for Conor. Once he was done he passed it over.

"What about you, Louisa? Do you want a rod? Or you can help me throw out a line if you like."

"I'll help with that."

She looked around at all the paraphernalia of fishing. Now Leo was preparing a line strung with floats and hooks and a net in the style of the local fishermen.

When it was ready he and Louisa flung it over the side. "Now what?" she said.

"We wait. Fishing is about waiting. Surely you know that?"

"I used to go out fishing with my father when I was a child, but Elliot found the whole business too slow. He liked sailing competitively so we never went out to fish."

"I enjoy the physical activity of line-and-net fishing, but if it's peace I'm after there's nothing like a line and rod. It's how I relax. And Conor is turning out to be a good little fisherman, aren't you, young man?"

Conor grinned but didn't speak, clearly concentrating on the task at hand. While they waited Louisa and Leo continued to talk.

"What are we likely to catch?" she asked.

"Mackerel, maybe, and anchovy in the net. We might be lucky and get some mullet or red snapper. Whatever we catch, I thought we'd have a barbecue on the beach afterward."

"Lovely. What's in the hamper?"

"Everything we need for a barbecue, of course, oh, and a flask of tea — would you like some now?"

She nodded.

"Can you carefully move across to the bow — in the hamper there you'll find a flask and spare mug. There's a bottle of lemonade for Conor, too."

As she stood the boat rocked and, with her heart thumping, she held out her arms to stabilize herself. He grinned up at her before she made her way to the hamper and brought back their drinks. Leo poured the tea and opened Conor's bottle, but Conor didn't take it right away. With both hands he was clutching the now very bent rod and beginning to reel the line in.

"Need any help there?" Leo asked.

Conor shook his head, clearly determined to manage the catch all on his own. When he had finally reeled it all in, they saw a shining silvery fish flapping on the end of the line.

"What is it?" he asked Leo, his eyes glowing with pleasure.

"A decent-sized mackerel, I think," Leo said as he took it from him and knocked it on the head. "Now we need a few more of those and we'll have lunch."

While the boy drank his lemonade, Leo prepared Conor's line again and then passed the rod back to him.

They sat in silence for a while, Louisa humming a tune under her breath and transfixed by her surroundings: the sun beating down from a turquoise sky, the feel of the warm breeze, the deep blue color of the sea, and the sound of the water as it lapped against the sides of the boat.

"Singing to the fish, are you?" Leo said with a grin and she laughed.

Suddenly a fish flew through the air and landed with a thump in the bow of the boat. Louisa jumped in surprise and Conor almost dropped his rod.

"Now that is something," Leo said. "A flying fish means we're not far from a pod of dolphins. This little fellow would have been attempting to get out of their way."

"And now he's our lunch," Conor added with glee. "Let's watch out for the dolphins."

As the boat rocked they kept their eyes peeled, scanning the sea for telltale splashes and frothy waves. Conor shouted out and they all spotted a gray-blue shape slipping through the water. They watched excitedly as pelicans began diving down from the sky to feed on the disturbed fish. After a few moments, Conor pointed at two or three dolphins leaping like acrobats as they chased each other at the side of the boat, one of them corkscrewing in the air before crossing underneath the bow. Louisa looked on, grinning with delight, as the Indian Ocean became packed with dolphins.

She had rarely seen a pod of them so close up and, falling under their spell, felt transported by these otherworldly creatures, sent to remind them of cheerful good humor and the utter joy of being alive. As she gazed, utterly mesmerized, they swam playfully alongside for a little longer, before leaping the waves and heading farther out to sea, leaving Louisa feeling exhilarated. The immense ocean was enough to produce this kind of wonder on its own, but the dolphins had been a special treat, infecting them all with a feeling of happiness. When it came to her that she hadn't thought of Elliot all morning, she took a slow deep breath and gave silent thanks.

"Well, what a piece of luck," Leo said and the warmth of his smile curled inside her.

A little while later he and Louisa pulled up the line and net.

"So, what do we have here?" Leo said as he examined the haul. "Ah, not bad. Some anchovies, just as I thought, and a mullet — but look, there are a few giant tiger prawns too. I think, along with the mackerel and the flying fish, we have just managed to catch our lunch. Well done, Conor, you can reel in your line now. We're heading back to shore."

The shore lay somnolent in the hazy midday heat, and Leo chose a spot in the shade of one of the strangler fig trees growing among the shrubland lining the beach. Further up the beach, a few turbaned fishermen had hauled in their nets and Louisa could see the buckets of prawns they'd just caught. They kept clear of the fishermen and Leo built a small fire, using some stones on which he balanced a little grill he had stored in the hamper.

Once the fire was ready he placed the fish on the grill and within a few minutes was sharing out the spoils on to Bakelite plates. The three of them sat on the grass licking their salty fingers as they ate the fish, washed down with more lemonade. Louisa yawned and stretched out her arms.

"Tired?" he asked.

"I don't sleep terribly well since . . ."

"You know what I do when I can't sleep?"

"What?"

"I get up at dawn and watch the day arrive. Why not join me tomorrow? I'll meet you here just before it gets light. I'll even cook you breakfast afterward."

"I'd like that." She paused. "Looking forward to the ball?"

He nodded. "Though it's been a while since I last danced."

"When was that?"

"At the Strand Hotel in Rangoon. An amazing place. If you ever get the chance, do stay there. Very grand."

"You were in Burma as well as Malaya?"

"I worked for a teak-logging company for a couple of years."

"But you didn't stay there as long as Malaya?"

"No."

"What made you leave? Was it what happened with Alicia?"

"Pretty much. I needed a change of scene."

After that they slipped into silence with just the sound of the ocean and the seabirds in the background.

Before long Louisa was humming under her breath again.

"What *is* that song?" Leo asked.

"It's an awful Shirley Temple song. 'On the Good Ship Lollipop.' I can't get it out of my mind."

He laughed. "I suppose that's appropriate," he said and began to sing the silly song too. Before long all three of them were singing at the tops of their voices before collapsing back onto the ground, with tears in their eyes and helpless with laughter, as the bemused fishermen stared at them.

# 35

When Leo arrived at the beach the next morning it was still dark, the sea calm behind them, and as they entered the track up through the plantation, Louisa enjoyed the blanket hush, silent but for their feet crunching the earth and the sound of her own breath. A throb of expectation passed through her as she gazed up at the still starlit sky, and it seemed as if the whole of nature lay waiting. After a few minutes, the stars dimmed and the sky turned indigo. She closed her eyes for a moment, enjoying the peace and the fresh morning air, but the silence was instantly broken by the screech and chatter of fruit bats flying from one tree to another.

As she glanced back over the ocean, the sky quickly changed to a different, slightly brighter blue, with a line of turquoise and a strip of red where it met the purple sea. She savored being out with Leo, while the rest of the world still slept, and a dreamlike feeling gripped her. Not quite day. Not quite night. It felt mystical and she liked it. Gradually, as the blue faded and the sky turned a dark red-gold in color, a few birds began celebrating the approach of day.

"It happens so suddenly, doesn't it?" she said. "The light." And as she spoke the sky began to pale and she could now see the shadowy shapes of the trees looming on either side of the track in the smudgy light.

A breeze got up just as the dawn chorus proper began. As it developed the noise was shattering and she couldn't help laughing. It felt as if the entire forest was singing, building to a wild cacophony.

"Does Conor sleep through this?" she asked, struggling to be heard.

"Yes. I often have to drag him out of bed. Poor thing. His mother allows him to stay up far too late."

"Is she a good mother?"

"She's not a conventional one, that's for sure, but she does her best."

"Do I hear a criticism?"

"Maybe."

"What would you do differently?"

"Well, as you know, I'm not a parent, so I'm probably out of order, but I feel he needs to have a few basic rules. He is free to wander, which is fine, but I think he also needs the restrictions and challenges of school."

"I'd have thought you would be more free-spirited."

"My father was right about one thing. Children do need to know where the boundaries are."

"Does he behave badly?"

"No. He's a good kid. I suppose what I'm saying is, I feel he needs more structure. He's too young to cope with so much freedom and it makes him insular. I'd love to see him spending time with other children."

"You care about him."

"Yes. I'm very fond of him. At first I was worried about Zinnia having her son here, but having Conor in my life, getting to know him, seeing him running about the place, well, it's been a privilege."

They walked on. It was too dense and noisy for further talk. Halfway up the hill a flock of green rose-ringed parakeets fluttered from one tree to another amid noisy chatter.

At the top of the plantation, nearer the jungle, she heard an exquisite liquid birdsong.

"Black-headed orioles," he said.

"Ah yes, I've heard them here before, I think," she said and stood to listen.

After a while she added, "Thank you for this. I often used to slip out to the ramparts with Elliot to watch the sunrise. The bird-song there was never like this."

He smiled. "Glad you enjoyed it. Break-fast?"

"Absolutely. I'm starving."

"Scrambled eggs and toast?"

"Divine."

They walked into the house and up the stairs. While he was brewing coffee and see-ing to the food, she sat out on the veranda and gazed down over the now misty tree-tops. The birds were still singing but it seemed quieter out in the open than in the heart of the plantation.

When he came out with the coffee she drank hers scalding hot. "Coffee has never tasted so good," she said and then began to eat.

He laughed and she noticed the fan of wrinkles around his eyes deepen.

"You certainly have an appetite," he said.

"It's the fresh air. I lost my appetite after Elliot died but I feel it coming back."

"More dawn walks for you, then."

She glanced away from him but felt warmth spreading through her.

385

"You mentioned watching the sunrise with Elliot. What was he really like?"

"I don't know any more. It's not a great feeling when you've spent years seeing someone in a certain way, only to find out he was quite a different person."

"There's always more than one way of seeing things. Maybe it's not that what you thought wasn't real. Maybe it was real, but there was also another side you didn't know about. Doesn't everyone have secrets?"

"I'm not sure. Probably not such big ones."

"True."

She shook her head. "I wasn't always honest about the way his absences affected me. I just got used to them."

"I can understand that."

"What about you, Leo? What are your secrets?"

He shrugged. "My whole life."

She gazed at him, wondering what he meant and what really made him tick. "Do you find it hard to talk about yourself?"

"I'm certainly not used to doing it. But what I meant was, if you don't share yourself intimately with anyone, it's as if you as a person and your whole life become quite secretive. I have Zinnia, and Conor of course, but that's not what I mean."

"You become hidden?"

"In a way."

"Do you like being on your own?"

"I'm happy with my own company, if that's what you mean."

"Can I ask you something?"

He laughed. "You already are, aren't you? But fire away."

She smiled. "What do you wish for?"

"To make the plantation a success."

She narrowed her eyes slightly as she scrutinized his face. "I mean personally. Doesn't the isolation ever get too much?"

"I'm not really isolated. As I said, there's Conor and Zinnia and, of course, Kamu."

"I've never really been on my own until now." And thinking of Elliot she paused. "Perhaps we can never really get inside another person."

"We see what we want to see, don't you think?"

"Or what the other person allows you to see."

He nodded. "That too."

There was a prolonged silence while Louisa thought about what he'd said. She believed people needed each other, that life without close contact must feel empty and purposeless, that sharing love was essential to well-being.

"You're really not lonely?" she finally said.

He was gazing at her with intensity. "I didn't say that. Life here can be lonely at times, especially the evenings, but just as you became accustomed to Elliot's absences I have become accustomed to my life as it is."

"Would you ever share your life with anyone?"

"That sounds like a leading question."

"I didn't mean it like that."

"I wouldn't rule it out," he said. "After Alicia, I found it hard to trust anyone, so got into the habit of backing off if anyone came close."

*And now,* she wanted to say. *How do you feel now?* But instead she leaned back in her chair and closed her eyes. There was only so much she felt she could say and another long silence followed.

"The dawn suits you," he eventually said, and she opened her eyes to see him smiling. "More toast?"

She nodded.

After they'd eaten their toast he rose from his chair. "I shall have to check on Conor before I get to work. Will you be all right walking back down on your own?"

"I'll be fine," she said and she too got to her feet. "Thanks for breakfast."

They gazed at each other.

"I really enjoyed it," he said.

On her way back down the hill, Louisa watched the striped squirrels racing up the tree trunks as they heard her passing. The birds were quieter now, though a few lone ones still continued singing. She went over everything Leo had said and even though they had spoken of Elliot, she hadn't felt the heavy-heartedness that usually followed thoughts of her dead husband. The past seemed to be edging further away. Today she felt light as a bird herself, as if a huge weight had been lifted from her. The day no longer stretched before her emptily, and she laughed out loud as she felt a new resolve bubble through her. It was time to concentrate on the emporium. What would happen between her and Leo was uncertain, but it was clear she had made a good friend.

## 36

It was raining on the morning of the ball, the light dull, so Louisa briefly let the remaining two dogs out into the garden — it was too wet to go for a walk — but she grabbed a mac and umbrella and went over to the emporium. The builders were already hard at work by the time she arrived and had completed the first few tasks, clearing up the mess left behind by the printers, and hoisting men onto the roof to clean the huge circular cupola so they'd all be able to see what they were doing. The carpentry was also underway and the shutters were being sanded. As she walked around she noticed some of the floorboards were broken in the room that had been locked.

"Don't you worry," Himal said. "When we begin sanding the floor we'll mend anything that's loose. My carpenter is already assembling the furniture and it won't be too long before we can give the place a first lick of paint."

Back home she went upstairs to check her evening dress had been pressed. She planned to wear an ice-blue gown made of satin. Its slim silhouette, narrow bias-cut skirt with inset panels, and natural waistline suited her tall, lean shape. The bodice was semi-fitted, with a "V" neckline at the back and front, and cap sleeves. She would wear it with a matching blue chiffon scarf and her sapphire earrings.

The hours passed slowly as they often did during the monsoon. Louisa listened to the rain hammering on the road and tried to read, while Margo and William braved it to pick up his suit in the afternoon, and then the three of them set about taking the photo William would need for his divorce. While Margo and William climbed into bed, Margo with her hair loose and shoulders bare, Louisa adjusted her camera. William took off his shirt, but other than that they were both fully dressed. Margo giggled as Louisa glanced up.

"This feels so weird," she said.

Margo pouted and struck a wanton pose, making them all laugh.

"Maybe put your arm around her," Louisa said.

"He'll have to do better than that," Margo

said jokily.

William looked uncomfortable but agreed with Margo. "There's nothing for it but a smacker full on the lips," he said.

Louisa raised her brows. "Oh God. How embarrassing."

"Are you ready?" William asked.

"All set. Ready when you are," Louisa replied.

While William and Margo kissed, Louisa took several photos and they all again collapsed into laughter.

"Perhaps you should get in with us," Margo said. "That would really put the cat among the pigeons."

Later, as the evening shadows lengthened and sunlight painted pink streaks across her bedroom walls, a nostalgic feeling gripped Louisa. It affected her deeply that, despite sensing she was moving on, Elliot could still be so suddenly present. She sat at her dressing table and half expected to look in the mirror and see him standing behind her.

"You look great," he'd say. And she'd smile and tell him he always said that, only now she wouldn't smile. She'd glare at him and call him a liar.

The room emptied just as suddenly and he was gone. It seemed to her that he had heard her. And now she was left sitting at the edge of what felt like an endless silence, her thoughts and emotions suspended. She didn't turn on the light but allowed dusk to slip into the room.

As seven o'clock came and went, Margo tapped at her door. "Why are you sitting in the dark?" she said as she entered and switched on the overhead light.

"No reason," Louisa said. "You look lovely."

Margo was dressed in deep scarlet which intensified the shiny darkness of her hair and made her bright green eyes glitter. "Any sign of Leo?" she asked.

Louisa shook her head. "He's a bit late, but I'm not surprised. He wanted to make sure Conor was in bed before he set off."

"He's cutting it rather fine."

"Why don't you and William go on ahead and we'll catch you up. Take my father with you."

"I think he wanted to meet Leo."

"He'll meet him at the ball."

"How are you feeling?" Margo said.

Louisa took a long breath in and exhaled slowly. "I was thinking of Elliot."

"I miss him too." Margo came across, bent down and put an arm around Louisa. "But people telling you to let him go doesn't help, does it?"

Louisa shook her head.

"Sorry."

Louisa sighed. "Do you realize I'd never have known about Zinnia and Conor until the day he eventually left me."

Margo shook her head. "*If* he ever left you. I hate to say it of my own brother, but he really knew which side his bread was buttered being married to you. I couldn't see him giving all that up — and for what?"

"To be able to live with his son, I suppose."

"He did want children. Partly to make up for the loss of our brother, I think."

"He never said so but I always felt that."

"Though I was just a toddler at the time, I think my mother's airs and graces must have started back then, and her ambitions for the remaining men in her life. She pushed them to be what they weren't."

"Elliot too?"

"The sky was the limit in her eyes. It must have been hard for him to live up to her aspirations."

"That doesn't excuse him."

"No . . ." She paused for a moment. "I just don't see what it was about Zinnia."

Louisa shrugged. "She's a shadow of who she once was. Back then she must have seemed exotic and enigmatic. Very different from me, anyway. I wanted to hate her, you know, but how can you when someone is so frail?"

"He did love you. I'm sure of it. But none of us really knew Elliot, did we?"

Louisa didn't reply.

"I can't help wondering if there was something I could have done."

"Don't blame yourself, Margo."

"By the way, my mother phoned, asking all manner of questions about Conor. I haven't told her Zinnia is ill. I wouldn't put it past her to come and scoop up the child."

"Leo wouldn't let that happen."

"He may not have a choice. She is the child's grandmother."

Margo left the room and Louisa finished doing her hair and then sat in the sitting room to wait for Leo, feeling very alone, and with just one lamp shining light on her polished nails. Deep silver, the varnish was called. Almost an hour had gone by when she got to her feet and started pacing the room. She didn't believe Leo would be the sort of man to let her down, so something must be keeping him. But by nine o'clock she accepted she'd have to face the ballroom on her own. She was just checking her hair again in the hall mirror when there was a knock at the door. She took a few steps back into the sitting room and allowed Ashan to answer it. Thank goodness, she thought when she heard Leo's voice, and then he came into the room carrying a carryall. He looked at her in astonishment. "Wow!" was all he said.

She felt herself redden.

"Louisa, I'm so sorry. I didn't know if you'd still be here."

"I'm just glad you made it. Did something happen?"

"Zinnia wasn't too well and Conor wouldn't settle. I'm having a telephone line installed but they haven't finished the job yet, so at the moment there's no way of contacting you. I'm so pleased you're still here."

"I waited."

"Yes."

They gazed at each other, both smiling.

"You'll need to change. I'll show you to a guest room."

"Thank you."

He didn't move.

"What?"

"Louisa, you have the most beautiful gold flecks in your eyes."

When he came downstairs, the transformation was complete. Instead of the waxed jacket he wore to ride his motorbike he was in an elegant evening suit. He had tamed his wavy red hair a little, but not so much that he didn't look like him. He wore his good looks easily, almost as if he was unconscious of the effect he had. But gazing at his broad shoulders, long legs and dark eyes she couldn't turn away, nor stop her stomach flipping over.

He gave her a crooked smile. "Will I do?"

"You'll more than do."

He cleared his throat. "I didn't say how beautiful you look."

She glanced away, then back at him. "You said you liked my eyes."

He nodded.

There was a silence between them and, feeling a little like a debutante on her first date, she faltered. A car revved in the street, a lone dog barked, and she heard something fall to the floor in the kitchen. She was tempted to check what might have been broken, but then realized it was just a way of momentarily escaping her nerves.

"Well," he finally said. "Ready?"

And then, despite her misgivings, her heart swelled with happiness as she took his arm.

"Shall we walk?" he said. "The rain has

stopped." He held her back a moment. "I just wanted to say something first."

"Go on."

"It's clear there's something still so hurt in you. I want you to know I understand."

Overcome by a wave of emotion, she nodded.

As they entered the ballroom a foxtrot was in full swing. She held on to his arm and looked around at the glittering chandeliers and the vast bouquets of flowers. The walls, lined with floor-to-ceiling mirrors, reflected the lights and the dancing couples. It was packed and, despite the earlier rain, it was hot. She wanted to find her father to introduce Leo to him, and so they threaded their way around the edges of the room. They eventually found Jonathan chatting with Elspeth Markham, a stalwart of the congregation at All Saints' and one of the principal flower arrangers.

"Hello, Mrs. Markham," Louisa said. "Can I introduce you both to Leo McNairn? Leo, meet my father."

While they all shook hands, it was clear Jonathan was assessing Leo. Louisa knew her father was just looking out for her but couldn't help feeling a bit irritated. She gave Leo a quick sideways glance.

"If it's all the same to you, Dad, Leo and I are going to take to the floor."

Taking the hint, Leo put his hand on her elbow.

"Maybe we could have a drink together later?" Jonathan said. "Shall we say in the bar in an hour's time?"

"Of course," Leo replied.

"My father's going to give you the third degree. Sorry," she whispered as they made their way to a space on the dance floor.

He laughed and took her in his arms. As they began a waltz, Louisa's earlier uncertainties dissolved and she allowed herself to fully enjoy being close to him. Once again, she sensed something flowing between them and felt certain he could feel it too. He drew her even closer and they moved effortlessly together until she felt too hot, so then they made their way to the bar. The room was busy, but she found an empty alcove while Leo went to order two glasses of champagne.

She settled back and closed her eyes, but could hear voices coming from the next alcove. Her eyes flew open when she heard her name mentioned.

"There are all kinds of rumors about Louisa Reeve's husband," a woman was saying.

"I heard he had other women."

"Did she know?"

"Nobody knows."

"Did you hear anything about an illegitimate child?"

"No. How awful!" This had been spoken in a shocked voice.

"How many other women did he have?"

"Any number, I heard."

Louisa got to her feet as Leo arrived back with two glasses. "I'm going to let my father know you're in here."

"Are you coming back?"

"In a while."

"Is something wrong?"

She shook her head. "I'll be fine," she said and took a sip of the champagne he offered her. Then she put the glass down and turned on her heels, glaring at the two women who had been gossiping, one of whom was Elspeth Markham.

She soon found her father and told him where Leo was. Next, she searched for Margo and found her sitting out the dancing and holding William's hand.

"Not dancing, you two lovebirds?"

"I'm not much of a dancer," William said. "Can I get you a drink, Louisa?"

"Thank you," she said, and as he strode off she took the seat he had vacated.

"So, where's Leo?"

"With my dad."

"Let's hope that goes well."

"Why shouldn't it?"

"Well, you remember what he thought of Elliot right from the start."

"And it proved to be right . . . Margo, I heard some women gossiping about Elliot. They said he had more than one other woman."

"Don't listen to gossips. That way madness lies."

"I'm sure you're right. But I so wanted to confront them."

"Let it go. Instead, tell me how it felt to be dancing with Leo."

Louisa closed her eyes and smiled. "I feel at home with him. It's just so easy. I know it's probably too soon, but I can't help how I feel." She sighed. "Why does life have to be so complicated?"

"We complicate it, don't you think? If you like him and he likes you, does it matter?"

As William arrived back, Louisa stood and took the glass from him, then made her way back to the bar, where she found Leo and her father roaring with laughter at some shared joke. It gave her a frisson of pleasure to see them getting along so well and in that moment of certainty she made a snap decision.

"Louisa," her father said. "Take my seat."

He got to his feet and held out a hand to Leo. The two men shook hands and to Louisa it felt like the seal of approval. She was glad. It had been hard when Jonathan hadn't liked Elliot.

After her father left she sat and leaned toward Leo. "Shall we go?"

"It's still early."

"I want to go back to Cinnamon Hills with you. We can pick up my car."

"Are you sure?"

"Absolutely."

# 37

After they had picked up her car, Louisa
drove them both to Cinnamon Hills. She
hadn't expected to feel so calm, despite having to navigate the bumpy potholed track
and then finding the plantation house
completely dark. There was something
infinitely gentle about Leo as he reached
across and touched her hand where it rested
on the steering wheel.

"There's still time to change your mind."

Once she had switched off the headlights
she looked out into the thick darkness of
night and, unable to see anything of the
dramatic view, felt conscious only of being
there with Leo, as if held in a bubble of only
him and her. There was a tingling kind of
pleasure in that, and it struck her that was
one of the reasons why intimacy was so
seductive. For however long it lasted, it offered a delightful kind of shield, a warm
protection from the outside world, some-

thing she had been missing since Elliot died.

They both got out of the car and, lit only by the stars, he guided her to the front door. She sniffed the voluptuous nighttime scents of flowers and trees, while the earth and woods surrounding them seemed dense and close. It was far from silent. She could hear the cicadas, the creatures shifting along the pathways, and the wings of night birds as they flew. And in the background the roar of the ocean. When fireflies darted right in front of her eyes, sprinkling the night with light, she grinned. He pushed the door open and they went upstairs where the smells of the room, tobacco and cinnamon, contrasted with the damp scent of night. As he bent to light an oil lamp and then glanced across at her, she could see his eyes were dark and shiny. She held her breath as the light fell on his face and the room emptied of air.

"I didn't expect you to look so good in evening dress," she said.

For a moment, she sensed a battle going on inside her, and felt tempted to draw back. She resisted the urge and remained standing where she was. He left the room for a few moments and while he was gone she gazed around at his belongings. There wasn't much, just some books, an indoor plant or two, his khaki jacket hanging over the back of a chair, an untidy pile of papers, an old newspaper and a large clock on the wall. The only sound was the ticking of the clock. She saw it wasn't even midnight, and went to look at the books. She picked up a copy of Siegfried Sassoon's war poems and flicked through the pages. Then she unhooked her earrings and left them lying on the table. She felt as if she would always remember the details of the room and how being close to everything that was Leo's affected her. The room was so completely him.

When he came back, the air was thick with promise, or intention, or maybe just plain desire, and she smiled at the fact that she was describing it all to herself in her head as it was happening.

"What are you smiling about?" he said.

"I don't know. This? Us? Life?"

He walked toward her.

She felt herself opening as they kissed, gently at first, and enjoyed the taste of champagne on his lips. Her fingers wrapped around the back of his neck and she noticed herself curve into him. Without willing it consciously, her stomach tightened and her hips tilted very slightly upward, and she could feel his firm body against hers. Like an enchantment, she thought, and wondered if this longing to be relieved of her tension was all it took. Expecting him to lead her to the bedroom, her breath came short and fast and, as she breathed into his neck, she felt a lick of pleasure run through her.

She began to undo the buttons on his shirt, carefully at first but then tugging more urgently until it was open. He pulled down the zip at the back of her dress and slipped it over her shoulders. She placed a hand on his bare chest and felt his heart thumping against her palm. He stroked her shoulders and then, just as he lowered his head to kiss the curve of her neck, there was an almighty crash outside. They leaped apart when they heard a scream. He quickly did up a couple of buttons on his shirt before heading for the door.

"Stay here," he said, as he left the room.

She steadied her breathing, waiting, and then, after a few minutes, saw the door open and Leo return.

"Monkeys," he said. "Just monkeys."

She was intensely aware of standing there partly dressed, but instead of leading her to the bedroom, he came to her and pulled up her dress.

"Louisa, we can't."

"Why not?"

She wanted to be bolder, to insist it was

right, that this was the moment to choose to go ahead, but felt herself deflate.

He looked tormented when he replied. "What if it's too soon? What if you wake up in the morning and feel you've made a terrible mistake?"

She frowned, unwilling to let this go. "I won't. I wouldn't."

"I know you're still in conflict about this."

She took a step back, shook her head and, feeling like crying, was angry that Elliot's ghost still hung between them. She had thought she was sure, had thought it was the right time, but if Leo didn't feel it too, then what was the point? And now she wasn't sure either.

"You can take my bed," he said, his eyes lingering on her face. "I'll sleep on the sofa."

"I can't deprive you of your bed."

"You can and you will."

She spent a restless night and then slept on late into the morning, only being woken by a knock on the door before he came in. She had a flashback to his body pressing into hers and felt a surge of recollected desire, though he looked perfectly normal, wearing work clothes and carrying a tray of toast and coffee. She noticed he also had an envelope in one hand.

She glanced at the rugged angles of his face, exaggerated by the morning light slanting through the shutters, then she shuffled up in the bed and ran a hand through her disheveled hair.

"You look especially beautiful," he said, and touched her cheek.

She smiled, conscious of his gaze, but felt a sense of loss as her cheek burned. He removed his hand, rolled up his shirtsleeves, and then poured her coffee. She wanted to reach out and touch his lower arm where the hairs now shone like gold.

Instead, she asked what was in the envelope.

He sighed and now she noticed the look in his eyes. "It's the result from the laboratory. Zinnia does indeed have malaria."

She drank her coffee quickly as the truth sank in. "In that case, I'll head off to the dispensary with the result and pick up some quinine."

"I'll come with you."

"No, you stay with Zinnia. She needs to be told. It might be best if she isn't left alone."

"I haven't looked in on her yet, but she wasn't too good yesterday evening, so that's not a bad idea. Come to think of it, I haven't seen Conor yet either."

"I'll come back as soon as I have the quinine, and then take you back to pick up your motorbike."

Just then the rain began again and they listened to it pounding the roof. Louisa loved the romantic sound of rain if she was safely indoors: either the gentle rhythmic tapping that would send you to sleep, or the powerful squalls that kept you awake as you snuggled down under the covers.

"Wish I could stay in bed," she said and shivered, but didn't add *with you*. "It's just the thought of going out in the rain."

A silence fell and his eyes narrowed as he gazed at her.

"And are you all right about last night?" he eventually said, leaning toward her.

She looked back at him and, while holding her breath for a second, she nodded.

He was quiet, as if deciding what to say next. "You know I wanted to, right?"

She exhaled slowly. "I know."

At the dispensary in Galle, Louisa discovered they were awaiting new supplies that might take several days to arrive. She felt a dark mood descending. There had already been too many deaths in her life, and Zinnia's illness cruelly reminded her of Julia and Elliot. Not that she had ever forgotten them, but this brought them to the forefront of her mind and, now she felt the grief edging toward her again, she feared it would never be over. She fought against it and decided she would travel to Colombo to try to get the quinine sooner, and she would ask Margo to accompany her.

Back at the house, she spotted a small case in the hall and a minute later Margo and William came in; Margo's eyes looked red and a little puffy.

"William's catching the bus," she said. "It's time."

Louisa looked from one to the other. "Zinnia's definitely got malaria, and there's no quinine to be had here. I want to pick some up in Colombo, so I can take you."

"That is kind," William said. "And preferable to the bus."

"You'd be doing me a favor. And Margo, why don't you come too? It will give you a little longer together."

"I've booked a room at the Galle Face Hotel," William said.

"Well, book a double room too and I'll take your single. I can't drive back in the dark in this rain anyway. Margo can come back with me tomorrow."

"And I'll come to Cinnamon Hills with you too. Zinnia will need nursing."

"You'd do that for Zinnia?"

"I'd do it for you."

The journey was slow, but eventually they reached Colombo and Louisa drove them all to the Galle Face. A cluster of thin palms stood waving wildly outside but luckily, as they got out of the car, the rain held off. William carried their bags into the large reception hall and on into the Palm Lounge, past the two imposing curved staircases. After they were seated, Louisa glanced over at the other tables and chairs dotted around the polished teak floor, then she stood up saying she'd check that their rooms were properly booked.

At the front desk the receptionist confirmed their reservation was in order, so she went back over to Margo and William to ask if they'd look after her overnight bag until she returned from the dispensary.

"I'd like to get the quinine now. Just to be on the safe side."

"We'll take your bag to our room and meet you down here in an hour."

Louisa didn't like the idea of driving again, but it was too wet to walk. It had proved to be the briefest of lulls and now rain was ricocheting off the bushes and pavements.

After queuing for half an hour at the dispensary, she managed to pick up what she needed. She half regretted not driving straight back to Cinnamon Hills, but the weather was atrocious and it would mean driving in the dark. Zinnia had waited this long for treatment; surely another few hours wouldn't make much difference.

# 38

The air smelled of damp leaves and earth as Louisa pulled up near Zinnia's bungalow the next day. The first person she saw was Conor bursting out of the front door and then heading for the dripping woods at a run.

"What do you think that was about?" Margo said.

Louisa shook her head. "Probably in trouble for something."

"I wish I could meet him properly. After all, he is my nephew." She glanced at Louisa and reddened slightly. "Sorry, I didn't mean —"

"It's fine. You'll definitely meet him," Louisa interrupted, "but the child is a bit on the feral side." She got out of the car and Margo followed.

"Have you got the quinine?" Margo asked.

"It's in my bag." She fished her bag out from the backseat and then began to make her way toward the house.

"It seems very quiet," Margo said.

Louisa glanced around her but didn't look at anything with any great interest. The woods were especially quiet, apart from the dripping of the rain and the breeze making the treetops dance, just how she liked them, but her mind was on the fact she was about to see Zinnia again. She went to the front door and pushed it open. She saw right away that it was unnaturally still in the room and Leo was sitting on the sofa gazing into the distance with a blank look on his face.

"I've got the quinine," she said, talking too fast. "We had to go to Colombo for it after all. I got here as quickly as I could. We just saw Conor —"

Leo held up a hand to stop her.

"What?"

He shook his head but the look on his face was awful.

She walked toward him. "Leo, you're scaring me."

He got to his feet and held out a hand to her. "We're too late."

She took his hand but her heart sank.

"Zinnia died this morning."

He let go of her hand and sat down again. He stared at the floor, looking terrible. Wanting to find a way to comfort him, she gazed at his worn face and then his slumped shoulders, where Zinnia's death now weighed so heavily. She wanted to pull him toward her and smooth out his unkempt hair, but feeling her heart thud, she sat down next to him and waited for him to speak. The finality of Zinnia's death shocked her almost as much as Elliot's had. Having already experienced death didn't help. There was always the feeling you should have done more. Could have done more. If only you'd tried. And it was always too late.

"She led such a strange lonely life here," he said and raised his eyes to look at her. "I never felt it really suited her. She should have stayed in Colombo with the bohemian crowd who were her friends."

Louisa, holding his gaze, flinched at the sight of his eyes, now so deeply shadowed by pain. "Why did she come here?"

He drew breath before speaking. "She had no home for Conor. But it never was ideal."

Margo spoke up. "We saw Conor running out. Should we try and find him?"

"Not yet," Leo said. "He's only just found out. Let it sink in a little first. He's probably best left to go to one of his special hiding places."

"But he's so little to lose his mother," Margo said.

Louisa looked up at her. "I blame myself. I should have driven back last night."

Leo shook his head. "It wouldn't have made any difference. It was already too late for Zinnia. If anyone is to blame, it's me. I should have insisted she see a doctor earlier. I just didn't realize . . ."

"Don't blame yourself," Louisa said, but as her blood pounded in her ears she knew he would anyway. It was what people did, always looking for ways to shoulder the blame, seeking out some little detail that might have meant things would have worked out all right. Wondering about how they could have made a difference. She had done it with Julia and Elliot too.

"What happens next?" Margo asked.

Nobody spoke for a few minutes, then Leo stood as a shaft of brilliant sunlight lightened the gloomy room. "Louisa, could you ask your doctor to come out to issue the death certificate, please. He can arrange for her to be taken to the morgue in Galle."

Margo got to her feet. "Why don't I go? I know where his house is and Louisa can stay and help you here." She turned to Louisa. "Do you trust me with your car?"

Louisa nodded.

"Can I come with you to pick up my bike? It shouldn't take long and I'm going to need

416

it. My van is still at the mechanic's. You can wait up at my house, Louisa. I'm sure I'll be back before Conor turns up there. Once he goes off to one of his special places he's always away for hours and I can never find him."

"But shouldn't you be here?"

"I'll be as quick as I can. But I need my bike to deal with everything that must be done."

"Very well," she said, though she was concerned about how she would cope with the grieving boy and worried too that Leo had misjudged the child's reaction.

Leo locked the front door of the bungalow so Conor couldn't come in again to be with his mother on his own. After he and Margo had gone off, Louisa sat on a log outside, feeling terribly sad for Zinnia. The woman hadn't stood a chance, and now not only was Elliot dead but she was too, leaving Conor an orphan. Louisa remembered, even now, how she had felt the day her own mother died. Her father had tried to spare her the pain but she had run into her parents' bedroom and seen her mother laid out on the bed. The room had seemed very hot and there had been an overwhelming smell of lilies. Afterward she had never liked lilies and had become a fresh-air fiend. She had screamed until the ayah had led her away struggling and weeping. For ages everything had scared her until she learned how to put on a brave face. Now she worried about Conor out there somewhere all on his own. Maybe Leo was right and he needed time to let his mother's death sink in, but he was so young and she couldn't help thinking he shouldn't be alone.

It wasn't cold but she shivered. She took several long slow breaths and then made a move. When she got to the top of the hill, she was surprised to see the little boy sitting on the bench in front of Leo's house. He didn't look up at first so she went to sit beside him.

"I'm sorry about your mother," she said.

No reply, just a desperately solemn look.

"Shall I tell you a story? It's about a little girl who was the same age as you when her mother died."

He glanced across at her and she could see his eyes were red from crying.

"She thought it was the end of the world. Is that how you feel?"

He nodded.

"She felt as if nothing would ever feel right again."

He nodded again.

"And she felt she would never smile again."

There was a long silence and Louisa listened to the birds and the wind shifting the branches of the trees. She looked up at the sky and saw there were patches of blue between the darker clouds, allowing weak sunlight to filter through.

"What happened to her?" he suddenly said, a look of panic in his eyes. "What happened to the little girl?"

"She was fine in the end but she was sad for a time."

"I'm sad," he said.

Leo's houseboy came out and told them there was lemonade and tea inside, but it didn't seem to even register with Conor.

"Come on," Louisa said. "Come and have some lemonade. Maybe Kamu can find some biscuits too."

The child got onto his feet but didn't speak again.

They went inside and he sat hunched in on himself, his lemonade remaining untouched on the coffee table in front of him. Louisa sipped her tea and thought about Zinnia. She had so wanted not to care but had ended up feeling sorry for her, and now here was Zinnia and Elliot's child sitting before her, with his heart breaking. How cruel life could be. She suddenly remembered what Margo had said about Irene wanting to scoop up the child, surely all the more so now that Zinnia had died.

When they heard the motorbike pulling up some time later, Conor leaped up and ran outside. She followed to see him hurl himself at Leo, whose eyes were creased with worry. She felt her own eyes water as Leo picked the boy up and wrapped him in a warm embrace. Only then did she hear the little boy sobbing.

Leo carried him in and the child remained on his lap with his arms firmly around his neck.

"It hurts," the child said. "It hurts."

Louisa could see how affected Leo was too when he answered in a gruff voice, "I know. It hurts me too."

Louisa poured Leo a cup of tea and passed it to him. When Conor seemed to have fallen asleep, he carried the child to the bedroom and only then did he drink the tea, while sitting staring morosely at his feet. There was a long, painful silence during which Louisa could hear her own breathing.

"I saw the doctor with Margo," he said eventually. "He's coming over so I'll have to go down to Zinnia's soon."

"I'll stay here in case Conor wakes up."

He glanced up at her. "Do you think he needs to see her again?"

"He saw her already? I mean after . . ."

"Yes."

She put a hand on his arm and shook her head. "Then once is enough. Look, Leo, whatever I can do to help I will. I just want you to know. Just don't think you have to do it alone."

He smiled at her through what she could now see were tears. "By the way, the phone line is now installed — they came to finish the job yesterday. I'll jot down my number in case you might need it."

## 39

Zinnia's tiny funeral had passed uneventfully and Leo had done his best to help Conor through it, holding his hand and hugging him from time to time. There were, no doubt, those who thought Conor too young to attend the funeral, but Louisa and Leo had talked it through and he had made up his mind. It was important Conor be there. She hadn't allowed memories of Elliot's funeral to get in the way of supporting Leo and the boy. Leo's grief at Zinnia's death was mainly silent, but she could tell from the way he looked so tense and sorrowful at times that it hurt him deeply. It was hard to know how close the two cousins had been, and clearly they were very different people, but that he felt her loss powerfully she had no doubt.

And so, life went on in the way it did.

Work was going well on the emporium and though Louisa was aware of a policeman outside her house from time to time, there had been no further sign of Cooper or De Vos, for which she was grateful. The weather trapped her indoors for much of the time, although, while it was still the monsoon season, they had bright days too. Despite that the air remained uncomfortably thick and humid.

She called in at the emporium and saw that it looked wonderful. Everything was clean and two carpenters were busy assembling the cabinets. The grilles for the back windows had been installed and she could now really picture how the whole place would look once freshly painted white. She couldn't wait to see it packed with jewelry and silks, and buzzing with life.

She was just on her way home with the dogs when Leo roared up on his motorcycle. She hadn't seen him for a week and had been missing him, and wondering how he was getting on with Conor. Now he parked outside her house and they went in together.

"Well," she said as she hung up her hat and then took his jacket. "How are things?" She pointed at the sitting-room door. "Shall we go in?"

Camille came to ask if they'd like coffee and Louisa nodded.

"So?"

He seated himself on an easy chair. "To be honest, it's not going well. We're so busy and I haven't the time to take care of Conor properly. Not in the way he needs. He spends far too long moping in the woods. Kamu's looking after him while I'm here — but it's not ideal."

"You must be worried."

He glanced at her and sighed. "Look, I know you offered to help . . ."

"And I meant it."

"Would it be too much to ask if Conor could come here?"

She took a quick breath. "Oh!"

"Just during the week. Kamu and I can manage the weekends, but it's a woman's presence he needs."

Louisa thought about it. Perhaps it was a good idea but . . . She inhaled, feeling deeply uncertain. "Well, I suppose," she said. "And Margo is here now. I'm sure she'd help; after all, she is his aunt."

"So?"

"He needs to go to school."

"And that's maybe how we can sell it to him," he said. "He'll be coming here to spend time with his aunt while she's here and to go to school."

"Will that work?"

"I know he'll hate leaving his beloved

woods and his home."

She looked at him, horrified. "He's surely not living in Zinnia's house?"

He shook his head. "No, I meant the plantation is his home. I have a boxroom we've made into a bedroom for him. I feel dreadful sending him away but I can't think of another way."

While Camille brought the coffee, they remained silent, Louisa thinking about what Leo had asked of her. She was full of contradictory feelings. On the one hand she wanted to help Leo but, on the other, even though she and Conor had gotten along well during the fishing trip, how would it feel to be faced with Elliot's child every single day? She sat and gazed out of the window while Camille poured and then she sipped her coffee.

"What if," she said, "we give it a trial, but if he's unhappy we might have to think again."

Margo came into the room at that point. "Gosh, you two look grim. Has something else happened?"

In a halting voice, Louisa explained her decision.

"Are you sure? I'll do what I can, of course," Margo said and then paused. "To be honest, I've been itching to see my young nephew again."

Louisa felt a little strange. She was the one who was not a blood relative and yet she would have so much responsibility, and she suspected it wouldn't be easy.

"When will you bring him?" she asked.

"Sooner the better. Will the day after tomorrow give you time to prepare?"

After he'd gone Louisa and Margo walked to Jonathan's house to see if they could dig out any of her old childhood toys. Dolls had never appealed to her and mostly she had ridden her bike, but there would be board games, she thought, and books too. It might be worth a visit to the big toyshop in Colombo to buy tin soldiers, though she had no idea what the little boy liked.

The back door was usually left unlocked so they were able to make their way inside and then up to an unused room where Jonathan stored tea chests. Louisa shifted a few of them and found one marked with her own name. Inside was a faded box, for an old board game.

"It's Pirate and Traveler," she said. "I remember playing it with my dad. You had to draw a travel card which identified the journeys you had to make. You spun a wheel to determine how far you could move, and the person who arrived first won. The routes were based on real railroad and steamship lines. Gosh, it's ages since I've seen this!"

"Do you think Conor might like it?"

"I have no idea. Let's see what else there is."

"He'd probably like toy soldiers."

"I didn't have any of those."

"My mother has probably kept all of Elliot's."

Louisa stared at her. "Please don't tell Irene Conor will be here. I can't have her interfering at this stage. Things will be delicate enough without Irene wading in."

"Understood," Margo said.

"I'm sure I had a Meccano set. It'll be here somewhere."

"Isn't that for boys?"

"Because Dad bought all my presents I was given a lot of stuff intended for boys. I loved it."

"Why shouldn't girls have the chance to make things too?"

"Absolutely. Anyway, if we can find it, it should come in handy."

After that they came across another tea chest marked *Louisa* and inside, among other things, they found a one-eyed teddy bear with worn fur.

"My goodness. It's Albert the bear. He slept with me every night until I was twelve.

Look at his arms. They're all wonky." She smelled his fur then hugged him to her. "You never know, Conor might like Albert."

The little bear had awoken the past and she stood surrounded by mementoes of her childhood, feeling a little frayed. Albert had been her comfort after her mother died and she used to confide her deepest secrets to him. The memory was special, but reminded her that firm ground was never quite as firm as you thought it was.

"What else is there?" Margo asked.

She sighed and stopped replaying the past.

"I had jigsaw puzzles, but I never had a train set or any model cars. Let's see if there are any other boxes."

Margo pulled out a small box marked *Noah.* "I wonder what's in here?" she said.

"It may be my wooden Noah's ark. I played with it all the time."

Margo undid the string and opened the box. She pulled out a figure of a zebra. "Gosh, this is beautiful." She took out more animals and finally the figures of Noah and his wife, and then the ark itself. "It's so well made."

"I'd forgotten about these," Louisa said.

Though it was lovely to rediscover these toys, much of her childhood had been tinged with sadness following her mother's death; she could still feel the isolation and an awful sense of not being like other girls. It wasn't hard to imagine how Conor must be feeling following the loss of both father and mother, and now he would feel as if he was being rejected by Leo. She ran her fingers through her hair and hoped they were making the right decision.

Suddenly she remembered a butterfly collection a friend of her father had given her. Maybe Conor would like that?

They found the display case of butterflies, then gathered together the toys they'd unearthed and bagged them up to carry back to Louisa's. On the way out, Louisa spotted her father in his study and asked Margo to wait while she went in to have a word.

"I thought you'd be at the cutting house?" she said.

He smiled at her. "No, I've paperwork here to see to."

"I've just been collecting some of my old toys," she said. "Conor is going to be staying with me during the week."

Her father looked startled and rose from his chair. "Goodness, that seems rather unwise. Are you sure?"

She gazed at his kind face and sighed. "As sure as I can be which, to be honest, isn't very, but I have to help Leo."

"But Elliot's illegitimate child?"

She frowned. "Conor can't help who he is, can he?"

"Won't it be terribly hard for you?"

"It might be."

Jonathan looked worried. "Think of how we'll explain it to people. Can you imagine the outcry? Everyone will be asking about this child who has suddenly come to stay with you."

"I'll just say he's . . . well, I'm not sure actually."

"Think about it. People are already gossiping. You wouldn't want them turning up their noses at Conor, especially if he's going to be going to school. People can be so cruel, especially the Elspeth Markhams of this world."

"I had thought he would go to school, but you're right, people already know Elliot had a son. I heard them talking at the ball."

"Won't you have a rethink? If you do go ahead you'll have to be prepared to really tough it out."

She nodded.

"Well, it has to be your decision, but take note of what I've said. On another matter," he added, now with an edge to his voice, "I saw De Vos yesterday hanging around outside your house. He moved off when he saw me."

"I imagine he still wants the money."

"Hasn't he come back to you yet?"

She shook her head.

"Make sure you keep your doors locked back and front."

The day Leo brought Conor to Louisa's the rain had stopped and the sky looked washed-out and pale. They had arrived in his now fixed van, an old Crossley army ambulance; the back of a motorbike wasn't suitable for a young child, and he needed to bring a carryall of Conor's clothes and other belongings.

Louisa and Margo watched as the child climbed out of the van, hanging his head and staring at the ground, his face expressionless.

"Come on, Conor," Leo said. "Say hello to Louisa."

The child did not speak.

"And look, here's your aunt Margo."

"Hello Aunt," the little boy said, glancing up at Margo shyly.

"Hello," she said. "I hope we are going to become great friends."

He didn't reply. At least he'd acknowledged Margo, Louisa thought. It might take

431

a little longer before he would communicate with her. It made her feel uncomfortable but it was to be expected from a traumatized child.

"Have you time for some refreshment, Leo?"

He shook his head. "Sorry. I'm very behind."

Suddenly the child wrapped his arms around Leo and held on tightly.

Leo bent down. "Now, Conor, I promise I'll take you back to the plantation at the end of the week, but you need to go to school now here in Galle and Louisa has agreed to look after you."

"I want you and Kamu."

Leo stroked the child's hair. "Come now. You know that won't work. You're a big boy and I am sure you're going to be brave."

Conor let go of Leo and kicked the wheels of the van.

As Leo sighed, Louisa thought how small and lost the child looked.

Leo reached for Conor again and then crouched beside him. "I've explained how it must be. But it's just for now, and you'll have lots of new things to do here, won't he, Louisa?"

"Lots."

Conor burst into tears and Margo stepped

forward. She leaned down and took his hand. "Would you like to come inside with me? Louisa has toys to show you."

He perked up a little.

"Do you like toys?"

He nodded.

"Come on then. You'll see Leo again on the day you start school, and then again at the weekend. The time will whizz by. You'll see." The two of them walked into the house, leaving Louisa and Leo outside.

"Thank God Margo is here," Louisa said. "He hates me."

Leo shook his head. "He doesn't hate you. He doesn't trust you yet."

"Maybe he's picking up on my mixed feelings."

"If you'd rather not . . ."

She bit her lip. "He seems so terribly sad."

"You'll rub along together fine. It's all very new for him. He just needs time."

"Hope you're right."

He reached out a hand and held hers. "Thank you for everything."

She looked into his eyes and saw how much the situation weighed on him. "Any evening you have time to pop over, please do. And I have plenty of room if you want to stay."

"I'd love to, though I think for now it's

best if I don't stay."

She nodded but couldn't help feeling a little shiver of disappointment.

He smiled. "I'll see you when I take Conor to school on his first day."

# 40

That night, once Conor was asleep, Louisa sat up late reading a book in the downstairs living room, wishing Margo hadn't gone to bed. She felt anxious — after all, what did she know about children — especially as Conor had lived such an unusual life and was now in the depths of grief. She resolved to do everything she could to make him feel at home but couldn't help feeling nervous. The boy's clear resemblance to Elliot didn't help.

She was just about to go upstairs to bed when she heard a light tapping on the French windows. She got up to look out and had a shock when she saw it was Leo standing outside in the garden. She hurried across and opened the window.

"What is it?" she whispered. "Has something happened?"

"The only thing that's happened is that I wanted to see you. Do you mind me coming so late?" He smiled. "I didn't want to ring the doorbell and wake everyone, but you did invite me to pop in."

She couldn't stop herself laughing. "I didn't mean quite this late."

"It's only eleven thirty."

"Come in. But let's not alert the servants. I don't want to set tongues wagging if I can help it."

"We could sit in the garden and watch the fireflies."

"Great idea. I'll fetch my wrap."

He went to sit on a bench farthest from the house where they wouldn't be overheard and, after she had found her cashmere wrap, she joined him.

"I love this time of night," he said, as she made herself comfortable, near to him but not quite touching.

She listened to all the nighttime sounds. The buzzings and croakings and the night birds in the trees.

"There," he said, spotting the tiny flashes of light.

"Wonderful."

It felt illicit to be sitting in the garden with him while everyone else slept and she enjoyed the thrill it gave her. It was night. They were alone. She drew in her breath.

"Do you read much?" he said. "When you

have time."

"I do, but I prefer to draw."

"Paint as well?"

"No, I just mainly draw buildings. What about you?"

"I don't have time for hobbies but I like to read in the evenings." He paused and took hold of her hand. "Louisa, you must know how I feel about you."

There. He'd said her name again in the way she liked. Low-voiced. Warm. She didn't speak for a few moments, just enjoyed feeling her palm tingling as he stroked it.

Finally he said, "I just want you to know that I understand you've been going through an awful lot and I don't want to add to that in any way."

"You don't. You aren't."

"Well, I'm just saying . . ." he persisted.

"I know. It's all right."

"Are you sure? There's so much I'd like to say to you . . ." He turned her palm over and kissed it.

She swallowed rapidly, longing for him to do it again. "Well, say it," she whispered.

"You've brought something good into my life. I just wanted you to know. There's so much I'd love to do with you, new places I'd like to go, that sort of thing, but I don't want to move too fast."

"Spending time with you is lovely . . . it isn't that that worries me."

He put an arm around her and she leaned against him as he twisted a lock of her hair around his fingers. The garden's nighttime scents mixed with the musky trace of his aftershave, and she ached for the moment to stretch out forever.

"Conor?" he said and she felt his breath, warm on her cheek.

"A little bit. I'm worried I can't do it."

"Don't worry. I have confidence in you. I wouldn't leave him with you if I didn't, believe me."

They sat in silence for a while. Aware of an undercurrent of tension between them, she lifted a hand and with her fingertips caressed the side of his cheek. She wanted to be even closer, so close she could reach inside him and, when he drew her to him, she felt herself letting go.

He bent his head and with a hand on the nape of her neck pulled her gently around to face him; she gasped. Then he kissed her very softly on the lips. Her body was on fire, more alive than she could remember. She kissed him back and felt herself dissolving. They held each other after that, his heart pounding against her chest. She wanted to ask him to stay, but with Conor in the house it didn't feel quite right.

"So," she finally said and pulled away a little.

"I don't want to but I'd better go," he said and lifted the hair from where it hid her face.

"Yes."

After breakfast the next day, Louisa led Conor into the sitting room where she had arranged the old toys she'd found at her father's house. The dust motes in the air shimmered in the early sunshine, so much so that the room glowed with light, and she felt as if the radiance signaled a brave new day. If she could find a way to reach Conor it would work out fine. Leo had confidence in her and that inspired her to find some confidence in herself. *Leo.* Whenever she thought of him her heart skipped a beat.

Now she took a deep breath and began showing Conor the toys, but it soon became apparent that although he picked up a few things, he had no real interest in playing. She'd bought some crayons and a pad of paper and gave those to him too. He didn't respond. Her heart went out to him as he stared listlessly at the floor. Poor little mite. It was just too overwhelming and it seemed as if nothing was going to work, but as she stood listening to the birds in the garden an idea popped into her head.

"I know," she said. "I'll get the butterflies."

She went upstairs and then came back down with a flat wooden box, fully expecting this would interest the child.

At first he looked at it with a puzzled expression, hastily disguised as disinterest but, when she opened the lid, curiosity seemed to get the better of him and he leaned forward. She smiled at him, happy to have hit on something he liked. But as soon as he saw the lifeless insects pinned to a velvet base he stepped back in shock.

"They're dead! The butterflies are dead!"

She tried another smile. "It's a collection. I thought you might like to see them."

He stared at her, the horror distorting his features. "I hate them."

Then he ran from the room and she heard him thundering up the stairs, followed by the slam of his bedroom door.

Well, that went well, she thought.

For the rest of the morning Louisa got on with sewing her bedspread, but felt like a failure. She wanted to go to his room, but sensing he might need to be alone, decided to wait until she heard his footsteps again. Margo came into the room and tried to cheer her up.

"I don't know what to do," Louisa said.

"The trouble is, neither of us has any experience of children. Is there somebody you could ask for advice?"

"Maybe. There's Gwen Hooper. She has two."

"Why not give her a call? If you trust her."

"Absolutely. She lost a child and I feel she understands so much."

Then, at about eleven, the phone rang. Unfortunately, it was Irene insisting Margo return home. The morning dragged on and by lunchtime Conor still hadn't come back down, so Louisa asked Margo to fetch him.

But lunch was a strained affair. Conor stared at his meal and barely lifted his fork.

"What do you like to eat, Conor?" Margo asked.

"Hoppers," he said, "and biscuits with cinnamon."

"Well, if you tell Louisa what you'd like, she'll make sure you get it."

"What else do you like?" Louisa added.

No reply.

"I have to go to Colombo tomorrow," Margo said.

The little boy gave her a sad look. "Are you coming back?"

She smiled. "Very soon."

"Can I come too?"

Margo shook her head. "No, you'll stay here with Louisa."

He pulled a face. "But she's not my auntie. Why must I? Who will look after me?"

"Louisa will."

He carefully placed his fork on the plate and, with a stubborn look, stared at her. "I want you."

"I know, sweetheart, but we can't always have what we want, now can we? You'll be right as rain once you get used to Louisa."

"I have a lovely new school uniform for you," Louisa said, trying a different tactic.

He shook his head.

"The school term starts tomorrow. Shall we go to your room and try your uniform on?"

No reply.

Louisa exchanged glances with Margo. Was it always going to be like this?

But they went upstairs and with Margo's help she managed to persuade Conor to try on his school clothes. After he'd changed back, she decided to let him play in the garden, all the while keeping an eye out that he didn't run off through the back gate. He seemed happier playing with the dogs than doing anything else, so she let it go on. When the rain forced him inside again, she listened to it pounding on the paving outside and, although it felt as if it was beating in her head, she tried once more with the toys.

"Would you like to play a game?" she asked.

He frowned and stuck out his bottom lip.

"Maybe you haven't heard of this one? It's called Pirate and Traveler. What do you think? Do you like pirates?"

"I don't like games."

Heartened that he was at least speaking, it gave her a kernel of hope. If she could just get him talking, this might stand a chance of working.

That evening she phoned Gwen, who told her that as she and Laurence would be in Colombo for two days, she would take the car and drive on down to Galle from there, bringing the baby.

In the morning, Margo encouraged Conor to dress in his new uniform before she caught the early bus. Louisa then waited at the front door for Leo to arrive, as they had agreed they would both walk Conor to the school building. As she glanced up the road, she felt excited at the thought of seeing him again, although she knew she'd have to conceal her feelings for the sake of the child. But when Leo arrived he gave her a broad smile and, seeing the warmth in his eyes, she relaxed.

"Conor's in the garden," she said.

He squeezed her arm and then went to find the boy.

Although Conor held Leo's hand as they left the house, he refused to hold Louisa's and shuffled along, sullen and silent, hanging back all the time. Leo squatted down to give him a few words of encouragement, saying he'd make lots of new friends and would spend a wonderful weekend back at the plantation. Conor gave him a half-smile and once again Louisa's heart went out to him. It must feel so strange for a child who had never been to school, but she believed it was for the best — at the very least it would be a distraction — and she didn't think moping around on your own was healthy. They walked into the playground together and then went to the office, where Leo introduced Conor to the school secretary. He'd already been in contact with the head to arrange a place for the boy.

Leo left shortly after, saying he wished he could stay longer but there was too much he had to get on with. Back at home, Louisa felt suddenly alone. She went into Conor's room and found a well-thumbed book of insects and another about wild animals and birds. He was clearly interested in nature, so maybe that might be a way to reach him. She passed the time over trivial household matters and arranged for a lunch she hoped he would like.

After that she went to collect Conor, but as she arrived the secretary was waiting to speak to her, and ushered her away from the other parents.

"Could you come this way, Mrs. Reeve."

Louisa followed her to the school office, where the head teacher was waiting with Conor. She glanced at the boy and saw immediately his lip was red and swollen. She frowned. "What happened?"

"If you wouldn't mind coming with me. My secretary will look after the child."

She followed him into an inner office, where he seated himself behind a large wooden desk and indicated she should sit opposite. It was a forbidding sort of a room and she felt as if she were a child herself, hauled up in front of a master for some wrongdoing.

The head twisted his hands together and smiled before he began. "I'm sure you'll understand we are a small private school and we have a reputation to uphold."

"But what happened?"

"Conor got involved in a fight."

"Why?"

He glanced at a spot above her head before meeting her eyes. "Mrs. Reeve, I'd like you to be honest with me."

"Of course."

"Is the child illegitimate?"

She drew breath before speaking. "What does that have to do with anything?"

"I'm afraid he was called a name, rather an unpleasant one, as it happens."

"By whom?"

She noticed the lines between his eyebrows deepen before he spoke. "Elspeth Markham's little boy, Colin, was one, but the others joined in. They were calling him a bastard, I'm afraid."

Her jaw stiffened. "But that's hardly his fault."

"Mrs. Reeve, you cannot be so naive as to think I believe it is the poor child's fault. That isn't the problem."

"So, what is?"

"The other parents, I'm afraid. I can't afford to upset them. Mrs. Markham came to see me earlier, having been tipped off that Conor would be starting today. She insists that we cannot have an illegitimate child attending here and believes that Conor's presence will undermine the morality of the other children. And now, especially in the

light of what has happened, I'm afraid
Conor won't be able to remain at the
school."

As Louisa took this news in, she felt upset
to think how much this must have hurt the
little boy.

"Surely we should be standing up to bul-
lying?"

"I'm sorry."

She rose as anger surged through her. "So,
you're just going to give in?"

"I have no choice."

"Then how will we ever change people's
attitudes?"

He shook his head. "Changing parental
attitudes is not my job, educating their
children is. I'm very sorry, Mrs. Reeve.
Perhaps the Sinhalese school will be more
suitable?"

Louisa turned her back on him and went
to collect Conor. She took hold of his hand
and practically ran out of the office. The
headmaster must have known the Sinhalese
school was not an option, as Conor would
be perceived as even more different there,
so now she was faced with having to educate
him at home. She felt angry and sad about
what had happened to him at school, but
anxious too. Now she would be in charge of
Conor full time. Thank goodness Gwen

would be arriving soon.

Fortified by a good lunch, she spent the early afternoon trying to encourage Conor to talk, but with no success. He wasn't accustomed to being with children his own age, she knew that, but it was hardly good for him to only be with adults, especially one he wouldn't talk to. He'd been fine with her on the fishing trip when Leo was there, but he wasn't at all happy about her looking after him now. She asked him what he liked about the plantation. Was it the woods? Or the scent of cinnamon? Or the way you could smell the sea? Nothing seemed to work. If only she could find out what he missed, then she might be able to find a way to make up for it. Leo had told her about his secret places, so maybe if they played hide and seek he might find new secret places inside the house. Unfortunately, he refused to take part, and then when she laid out the Noah's ark with all the animals around it, he got up from the floor and stamped on the wooden boat.

"That's not acceptable," she said, fighting to stay calm. "I'm only trying to help you."

He glared at her.

"Pick up the pieces and put them in the box."

He didn't move.

"Conor, I'm asking you nicely to put the animals of the ark away."

Silence.

She sighed. "Very well. Maybe it's best if you go to your room and think about why you deliberately broke a toy. I, meanwhile, will put everything away."

She listened as he left the room and felt defeated. The only thing that made her feel better was thinking about Leo. She closed her eyes and imagined him sitting close to her. I have confidence in you, he'd said. She had to make things work with Conor, for the little boy's sake, yes, but also for Leo's sake too. She could not let him down.

The following morning, she went into Conor's room and found he had emptied his chest of drawers. The window was open and when she glanced out, it became clear he'd thrown all his clothes out into the garden. Feeling annoyed and not knowing how to handle the situation, she felt a flicker of panic.

"Come with me," she said, standing with her hands on her hips. "We need to retrieve your clothing."

He stayed where he was with his arms folded. This was awful. Instead of things improving they seemed to be getting worse hour by hour. She looked out of the window again when she heard the lilting notes of a single flute playing Sinhalese music. The clouds were darkening and it looked like rain, so she needed to quickly get his clothes back indoors.

"What's the matter, Conor?" she said, squatting down in front of him. "Won't you tell me?"

"I want Leo," he said and seemed to look straight through her.

She tried to shrug it off and gave a little laugh to lighten the mood. "You know Leo is busy. But he'll come and get you on Saturday. You'll spend all weekend together, and maybe the three of us could go out on the boat again soon. Would you like that?"

"I just want to go with Leo."

"Well, I'm sure you could do that. Come now, why not help me gather up your clothes."

He followed her down to the garden and although she did most of the picking up, at least he had accompanied her. It was only a very small victory but better than nothing.

The rest of the day passed in a similar vein. Louisa attempted to read to him but he yawned loudly to show his contempt. When she asked if he knew his alphabet, he took a crayon and wrote it out immaculately. At least Zinnia had managed to teach him something before her illness made things impossible. She tried to find out what he knew of geography but his disinterest was obvious. The same thing happened with history, but when she began to write down some sums, he immediately perked up. She passed them to him, then glancing across at him surreptitiously, she pretended not to notice his interest. Within moments he had completed all the sums she'd given him and, when he had finished, he picked up a book and curled up on the sofa to read. At least she now knew he could read and he liked arithmetic. It was a shaky start.

# 41

On Friday Gwen arrived in the afternoon while Conor was outside playing with the dogs.

"I'm so glad you made it," Louisa said and gave her a hug.

"I set off very early. So, are things any better?" She glanced around and then put the baby down to sleep on the sofa with cushions around her. "She's not so portable now she's bigger, but luckily she still likes her naps. I'll have to keep an eye on her while she's on the sofa. I've brought a Moses basket for the night."

Louisa shook her head. "We'll keep watch, but isn't she gorgeous with all that lovely dark hair. Curly like yours."

Gwen smiled. "So? Are things any better?"

Louisa looked directly at her friend. There was no point pretending. "To be honest, I'm not sure what to do. And . . ." She paused. "I'm afraid there's something I didn't tell you. The thing is, the child I'm looking after didn't just lose his mother."

"Oh?"

"He's Elliot's son."

Gwen stared at her, with enormous eyes and paling cheeks.

"He lives on a cinnamon plantation but he's here during the week as his current guardian, Leo McNairn who owns the plantation, is tied up with work. Leo is Conor's late mother's cousin. I will tell you all about it but I'd rather not go into the whole story just now."

Gwen nodded. "Don't worry. You can tell me when you're good and ready."

"Thank you."

"Shall we talk about Conor instead?"

Louisa nodded.

"I kept a close eye on Hugh after Liyoni died, mainly because he was so unnaturally quiet. But I soon guessed it was his way of coping and I had to wait for him to talk when he was ready."

"Conor's suffering in silence, I know that."

"Perhaps we can find a way to get through to him."

"I don't know."

"He must be feeling terribly overwhelmed by everything that's happened. School may have been the last straw."

"Do you think there's anything I can do?"

Gwen seemed to be thinking and didn't reply right away.

"Maybe not," she eventually said. "He'll need time to get used to what are terrible losses. Does he say anything?"

"He's mainly communicating that he doesn't like me."

"Be honest now. Do *you* like him?"

"Because of his resemblance to Elliot it's not always easy. I see Elliot reflected in Conor's eyes, or in the shape of his head, or in a certain quizzical look on his face. The similarity takes my breath away and then I feel shaken by thoughts of what might have been."

"Hard for both of you."

"Yes."

"He's feeling sad, of course, but probably also very angry. I know Hugh was. Conor might well be taking it out on you."

Louisa pointed at the garden. "Look, he's outside now. If we go up to the window we can see what he's doing."

They went across to the French windows and watched Conor enthusiastically throwing a ball for the dogs. They were barking and racing after it frantically, then returning for more. It lifted Louisa's spirits to see the little boy playing so happily.

"I think patience is the key," Gwen said.

Conor suddenly stood still as if listening. After a moment, he went up to a bush and squatted down. He picked something up and cradled it in his hands. Then he glanced up at the house and spotted them. Louisa waved, then opened the door and she and Gwen went out.

In the garden a wet breeze was caressing the shrubs and plants. Louisa ran a hand over her hair. "Plays havoc with my hair, this humidity."

Gwen nodded in agreement.

"Conor, this is my friend Gwen," Louisa said. "She has her baby here. Would you like to see her?"

He shook his head.

"What have you got there?" Gwen said.

His voice quivered. "It's a bird, but there's something wrong with it."

"Can I have a look?"

He nodded and Gwen went up close.

"It doesn't fly. Just shivers."

"Let me see." She observed the bird. "A sunbird, I think, but it's stunned. Let's just watch it for five minutes and if it doesn't recover, shall we take it indoors and make a bed for it in your room? Stunned birds often recover quickly."

When the bird was still unresponsive after

about five minutes, they went indoors.

"Louisa, have you got a cardboard box we can use?" Gwen asked.

Louisa found a box, positioned a folded piece of soft cloth inside it and then poked holes in the top for air. "Will this do?" she asked Conor, and he nodded.

"We need to leave the bird to recover for an hour and then come back and see how he's getting on."

They left the box in Conor's room and went to wait downstairs.

"How will it eat?" he asked.

"Later we could try sugar water from an eye dropper I have. Would you like to do that?" Louisa suggested.

After an hour, they went to the kitchen where Louisa found the dropper. She heated some water and asked Conor to mix in the sugar. This he did very solemnly. Once the sugar water had cooled to room temperature she asked him to fetch the box and when he came back she passed the dropper to him.

"Squeeze it to draw up the water and then just be very careful when you open the lid."

He opened the box and offered the eye dropper to the bird. It took just the slightest amount from the end of the glass tube, opening and closing its beak very fast.

"Let's take it outside and see if it's feeling

ready to fly again," Louisa said.

They went out to the garden and Conor lifted the lid again. The bird glanced about and then, with a brief flutter, it was off.

Louisa smiled. "Well done, Conor. You helped the little bird get better."

Saturday was a bright shiny day, and Louisa found herself looking forward to seeing Leo again. After the incident with the bird, things had improved but overall it had been a hard week. She took extra care over dressing and brushed her hair until it shone, all the while convincing herself it wasn't for Leo, and trying to ignore her longing to feel him close again.

Conor was even more excited than she was, and, for the first time, was as animated as you'd expect a seven-year-old to be. It warmed Louisa's heart to see him looking happier, though she felt relieved that for two days she would have time for herself. Since Elliot's death, she'd become accustomed to her own company, had even become accustomed to sleeping alone, something she had thought might never happen.

She was surprised when the first person to arrive was her father, and he'd brought with him a present for Conor, but had left

457

it outside for the time being.

"Well, let's see it," she said. "Shall we, Conor?"

The child didn't reply.

But with Louisa he followed Jonathan out and his eyes shone when he saw a new bicycle right beside the front door.

"Is it really for me?" he asked, looking up at Jonathan with enormous eyes.

Clearly thrilled when Jonathan nodded, he ran his hands over the saddle, but then his face fell.

"I can't ride a bicycle," he said.

"We all have to start somewhere," Jonathan said. "Why don't you get up on to it and I'll hold on to the handlebars while you pedal."

Conor looked dubious but did as Jonathan suggested, and the two of them sailed up the road and were soon out of sight. While they were gone, Leo turned up in his van and Louisa was glad to have a few minutes alone with him. It wasn't much, but better than nothing. The street was completely still and they stood for a moment in silence, then chatted inconsequentially while watching a cat with orange eyes slink along a wall. She felt very aware of the space between them and, knowing they needed to talk properly, wanted to say more.

He reached out a hand as if to reassure her.

"I've missed you," he said.

"Me too."

Then he asked how things had been with Conor. She sighed, not wanting to disappoint him, but knowing he deserved to hear the truth. "I can't get much out of him and nothing I do seems to be right."

"Give him time. He'll come around."

"That's what my friend Gwen says too. She's come to stay for a couple of days to give me some advice. I hope you're right. To be honest, it's been exhausting trying to think up things he might want to do. The worst thing is the school won't have him."

He stiffened. "Why on earth not?"

"Some of the other children were calling him a bastard, and then he got into a fight. The head says the other parents complained about his illegitimacy."

He frowned. "You should have phoned me."

"Sorry. I knew you were busy."

"Poor kid. So where is he now?"

"Out on a bicycle my father bought for him. Dad's teaching him how to ride it."

"Well, that sounds positive."

"It's surprising, but a master stroke on Dad's part. Conor had never met my father before, yet off he went, happy as Larry."

"It's a good sign."

She frowned. "He doesn't mind Margo either. It's me he suddenly doesn't like."

"He probably thinks you're trying to take his mother's place."

She didn't speak.

He put a hand on her arm and she felt the heat of it on her bare skin. "We both know you're not. We need to make sure he knows it too."

Suddenly there was a shout. "Leo! Look!"

It was Conor, now cycling on his own with no fear at all. Jonathan came up behind him, laughing as he attempted to catch up.

"Well, that didn't take long," Louisa said while the child dismounted, leaned the bike against the house, and then ran to Leo.

Her father grinned with pleasure and shook hands with Leo. "He's a natural. Got the hang of it in five minutes. The hardest part was getting him to slow down."

"Can we take it home?" Conor asked, cheeks flushed and eyes shiny with excitement. "Please, Leo?"

Leo nodded. "I'll put it in the back of the van."

"You'll have to be careful on the track at home," Louisa said. "It's a lot bumpier than here."

Conor ignored her but Leo said Louisa

460

was right and he'd have to slow down a bit or risk falling off.

"I'll be careful," Conor said and gave Leo a hug.

Leo loaded the bike into the back of the van, gave Louisa a wide smile, and within minutes they were gone.

"Thanks for that, Pa," Louisa said. "Hopefully, when he comes back, it might make things easier. You know the school won't have him?"

"I heard about it from Elspeth Markham. Everyone seems to know he's Elliot's son."

"Does it bother you?"

He shrugged. "I have to admit it does. But more because I feel angry at Elliot than anything else. Conor's a good little kid and he's been through such a lot. To hell with the gossips, I say."

She smiled at him proudly. Her father never let her down. "The thing is, I can't educate him alone. I was wondering about a tutor."

"Don't you have a French kitchen maid?"

"Yes. Camille."

"Ask her to teach him some basic French. I'll happily lend a hand with history and geography when I have time. If you can cope with maths, English and natural history."

"Sounds like a plan. I don't want to overload him, but he needs to be kept busy or he'll brood. Would you have time to spend an hour with him on Monday? I think he'll take it from you and that might get the day off to a better start. Or maybe I'll take him for a bike ride first — see what creatures we can find — and you can have him later."

"Monday it is." He scrutinized her face. "Now let's take a walk around the ramparts. You look as if you could do with the wind in your hair."

"Gwen's here, feeding the baby. I'll see if she'd like to come."

She went indoors but came out shaking her head. "No, she's trying to put Alice down for her nap."

Just before they set off the postman arrived and handed Louisa a single envelope. She tore it open then sighed deeply.

"What is it?"

"A note from De Vos asking me to meet him on Monday at midday in the court square."

"Is it signed?"

"Yes. He must be after his money again."

She pocketed the note and they began to move off.

"A legal debt would have to come out of Elliot's estate," Jonathan said.

462

She snorted. "What estate! Anyway, it isn't a legal debt, is it? The contract was a forgery."

"Then you can just walk away. That's all there is to it."

"Couldn't we just find the money? Make the man go away once and for all?"

"It's an awful lot, and you still don't know what happened to all the cash Elliot took out from his bank account. It must be somewhere."

"Some of it went to Zinnia, I think, but he did talk about putting money aside for them in a letter I found. Trouble is, I don't know where else to look."

"Will you meet De Vos?"

"I think so."

"I'll come with you."

"No, I'd rather do it alone."

"Why?"

"Because I feel I must be the one to stand up to him. If I don't, I'll never be rid of him."

There was a short silence as they walked on.

"Well," her father eventually said, "let me know if you change your mind. Now, tell me how things are proceeding with the emporium."

Louisa told him the builders were doing

well and that they thought they might complete the job within a few weeks, but she could do with encouraging another jeweler to get on board.

"I have a contact for you on that count," Jonathan said. "A silversmith, who makes all manner of brushes, combs, ornaments and jewelry."

"That's just what I need."

Louisa and Gwen set off to have lunch at the New Oriental Hotel, carrying the baby between them in her basket, although now she was bigger it wasn't so easy. Luckily, she still slept regularly and so their lunch was planned to fit around her nap.

"Gosh," Gwen said when they arrived. "It was Christmas when I was last here. Hasn't the time flown by?"

They walked through the imposing but smoky entrance hall into the elegant dining room.

Once settled at a table in the window, where they could watch people passing by, they talked in a desultory kind of a way. Then, after they had ordered, Gwen told her more about her life at the tea plantation and about how she had met Laurence in London.

"I knew the moment I saw him."

"Love at first sight?"

Gwen nodded. "I think so. It was at a musical evening in London. I was lost the moment he charged over, held out his hand and grinned at me."

"Romantic."

"We saw each other every day after that. My parents weren't happy that a thirty-seven-year-old widower wanted to marry me, but they came around when Laurence offered to leave a manager in charge of the plantation and return to live in England. I wouldn't hear of it. I told him if Ceylon was where his heart belonged, it was where my heart would belong too."

"And it has."

"Yes."

Louisa took a deep breath. "I wanted to explain more about Conor."

Gwen smiled warmly. "Only if you're ready."

Louisa nodded and told her the whole story about Elliot's debts and about Zinnia and their son.

"I still don't understand why he did it," she said. "The affair had been going on for about eight years. Can you believe it? For two thirds of the time we were married."

Gwen reached across the table for Louisa's hand. "It's not your fault, you know that?"

"It's what I tell myself."

"Believe it."

"I think it might have been different if we'd had a child. I feel like a mother, you know."

"That must be so hard. I am sorry."

Louisa gazed out of the window and spotted Janesha the shopkeeper passing. She raised a hand to wave.

"He was so caring when we lost Julia. I used to think I couldn't have asked for a better husband. Now I just feel like a fool."

"He was the fool for not realizing what he had."

"That's the thing. I think in many ways he did realize but he just couldn't help himself. He couldn't resist the temptation and went to her straight after my first miscarriage. I suppose our fate was sealed then."

"Not if he had stopped."

"Maybe."

"At first it seemed that everything was falling apart. I felt utterly duped, as if I had suddenly become nothing. That I didn't matter. That he couldn't have done it if I'd mattered. I felt so small, as if I wasn't even real."

"And now?"

"Now the deception still hurts, but maintaining the anger is just too exhausting." She sighed. "Anyway, I feel as if I've got myself back now. Or at least the parts I need most."

"I felt as if I'd lost myself after Liyoni."

"I'm so sorry. It's a horrible feeling, isn't it? I'm stronger now. If I wasn't, I couldn't look after Conor."

"You may feel stronger but things have a habit of catching up with us."

It was then that the food arrived and they busied themselves with eating. Alice murmured in her sleep and Gwen bent down to check on her.

"She's dreaming," she said and stroked her daughter's cheek. "Now tell me more about Leo."

"We're friends."

She grinned at Louisa. "And?"

"Well, as I said, he runs a cinnamon plantation not far from Galle. It's where Zinnia lived too. They were cousins. It's a pity you were busy when he collected Conor this morning." She paused.

"So?" Gwen prompted.

"So, the truth is, I really like being with him."

"Aha! Sounds exactly what you need."

"Not too soon?"

"Does he make you happy?"

Louisa thought about it. "He makes me feel alive again and seems so solid after Elliot. We've spent quite a bit of time together and I find it so easy to talk to him. I wish you could meet him."

"Maybe I will when he brings Conor back tomorrow. Has he ever been married?"

Louisa shook her head.

"A bit of a bachelor."

"A bit but there's more to him."

"I think if anything makes you feel good about yourself it's a good idea. What Elliot did must have knocked your confidence terribly."

Louisa nodded.

"Whatever the outcome, don't look a gift horse in the mouth."

"You really think so? I'm nervous about making a mistake. How can you tell if someone genuinely cares for you?"

"We have to trust our instincts."

"But that's exactly it. I want so much to trust Leo and sometimes I think I really do, but after Elliot . . ."

"Don't let Elliot ruin your future. If Leo is what you want, turn your back on what happened. You must." Gwen sighed. "I don't know, but whatever life flings at us we have to find a way to get through it, don't we?"

"But you've been happy with Laurence?"

"Yes, but we've had our trials."

"Of course. Losing your daughter must have been so terribly sad for you both."

Gwen glanced down and Louisa wondered if there was something more her friend wasn't saying.

The rest of the day passed uneventfully but, contrary to her expectation, Louisa found she was missing having Conor around the house. And when Gwen took a late afternoon nap with Alice, apart from the usual creaks and groans of old floorboards and new plumbing, the house was too quiet. Feeling like a stranger in her own home, she read part of a novel, caught up with sewing her patchwork quilt, and took the dogs for a walk. And, in the silence, she found herself daydreaming about Leo, her mind returning to him again and again. The way he talked, the way he moved, and the way his dark eyes shone when he smiled at her. She could picture him so clearly it was as if he were in the room. What she had told Gwen was true; Leo had helped her to recover her confidence and she eagerly looked forward to seeing him again.

The next day, hearing a baby's cry, Louisa

woke suddenly. But with her eyes wide open she knew it had been a dream. No baby. Then as if to mock her, she heard baby Alice crying. She thought of Conor. She had a child to look after now, didn't she, and a child was a child, so Conor might be her only chance.

That afternoon Irene and Margo turned up unexpectedly. Louisa felt apprehensive and gave Margo a look as she ushered them into the sitting room. Margo raised her brows and shrugged.

"It's a shame you missed tea," Louisa said. "Instead of our usual Sunday cake we had a French one made by Camille. A tarte Tatin. She's actually very good."

Margo nodded.

"Dinner won't be long but I'll get Cook to rustle up a sandwich. Will that do?"

"It will have to," Irene said and puckered her lips.

"You should have let me know you were coming."

"Sorry. We got the early bus," Margo said. "It was all rather a rush."

"I won't beat around the bush," Irene said. "I've come to see my grandson. Margo says he's here. Not that she wanted to tell me, mind."

Margo mouthed an apology at Louisa.

Louisa sighed. "I'm afraid he's not here."

Irene shot her a piercing look. "Where is he then?"

"The plan is for him to spend weekdays here and weekends with Leo until he's old enough to go to boarding school."

"That sounds most unsatisfactory. Children need continuity, stability, things to remain the same. All this chopping and changing won't do at all."

"We think we can make it work."

"I plan to stay for a week at least. Though Harold is not for it, I want to get to know the boy."

Louisa's heart sank. "That's not such a great idea, Irene. Let him settle down with me first."

"I'm afraid I'm going to have to insist."

"He needs time, Irene, before he meets anyone new. It's been a huge change."

"I am not anyone! I am the child's grandmother. I warn you, I have instructed my solicitor to take out an application for custody."

Louisa sighed. That was all they needed.

Irene was the last person she wanted judging her attempts at communication with Conor, especially as she seemed serious about custody. She glanced across at her sister-in-law, but Margo appeared subdued and that made Louisa wonder if it was because of something to do with William and his divorce.

There was a knock at the door and Camille, the French maid, brought in a plate of sandwiches.

"Excuse me," she said. "Ashan has had to go out. Is there anything else you need?"

"Gin and tonic," Irene piped up.

"Just water for me, please," Margo said.

"Actually, Camille, while you're here, I wanted to ask if you'd be prepared to help the little boy staying with us to learn some basic French."

"It would be my pleasure, Madame."

Once the girl had left the room Irene glared at Louisa. "You're asking a kitchen maid to tutor my grandson?"

"It's a good idea. He has never been to school and has a lot of catching up to do."

"Why can't he go to school here?"

"They won't have him because he's illegitimate. Only a nastier word was used by the children."

Irene's eyes widened. "I won't say it isn't an obstacle, but were we to adopt Conor that would give him legitimacy, wouldn't it? And if he were at school in Colombo —"

Louisa interrupted. "I don't think Leo would allow it, Irene. His home is the

472

cinnamon plantation. It's all he has ever known."

"Who is this Leo to the child? From what I hear from a friend of Elspeth Markham's, he's just a second cousin of some sort, or a first cousin once removed. I forget which it is. Either way, a grandparent takes precedence."

Camille came back with the drinks and the room went quiet. Louisa wished Irene hadn't arrived. It was going to complicate everything. As for Conor, she didn't know what to expect but hoped for better behavior, or she'd have to suffer Irene's gloating comments.

# 42

When Leo brought Conor back, the late afternoon sky was still a gentle pearly lilac with little wind and showing no sign of imminent rain. Gwen and Louisa went outside together and Louisa introduced her friend to Leo.

"It's a pleasure to meet you," Gwen said, smiling broadly and holding out her hand.

Leo shook it. "Likewise."

"How has Conor been?" Gwen asked.

Leo tilted his head. "Very good."

And indeed, Conor seemed like a changed boy. Instead of his habitual glower he smiled at Louisa and she noticed there was color in his cheeks. It was a welcome sight and she hoped it might signal an easier week ahead.

"Conor has been on his bicycle almost the whole weekend," Leo added. "I told him he could cycle around Galle too if somebody goes with him."

"I love to cycle," Louisa said and bent down to talk to Conor. "When I was a child I spent all my time on my bike. First thing tomorrow morning we'll go for a ride. If you like, that is. And later, my dad will help with your history lesson."

Margo came out and, as she and Gwen chatted with Conor, Louisa drew Leo aside. "I'm afraid Conor's grandmother, Irene, has turned up with all sorts of plans."

"Such as?"

"Taking him to live in Colombo, for starters. Honestly, Leo, she's the last person who should take care of him. She'll ruin him."

"Well, she'll have me to deal with first. Don't worry. It may come to nothing."

She sighed. "I hope you're right."

While Conor was absorbed with Gwen and Margo, Louisa suddenly turned and gazed at Leo and felt the full weight of this, whatever this was. She hardly dared think of what the future might bring but wanted to hold on tight to the feeling of being so close she could hear him breathe.

"Are you okay?" he said softly.

She nodded.

"If you need me, just call. And not just for Conor. Do you understand what I'm saying?"

She nodded again. Her eyes misted up

and she blinked rapidly.

"Anyway, before I leave, perhaps you could introduce me to Irene?"

Just then Irene came out and glanced at Louisa and Leo with a puzzled face.

Louisa felt paralyzed but Leo held out a hand to Irene. "Leo McNairn, Conor's guardian."

Irene sniffed but took his hand. "Irene Reeve." She turned to Conor and without the slightest hesitation clapped her hands and started cooing over him. "And this must be my darling little grandson. But my, how like your father you look. How lovely is that? Uncanny, isn't it, Louisa?"

"Yes. Just like Elliot," she said, but even without looking at Conor's face she knew the child was perplexed by the sudden acquisition of a grandmother. It hadn't been the subtlest meeting and she worried about how Conor was taking the news.

"Well," Leo said. "It's nice to meet you, Irene, and you too, Gwen, but I must be making tracks. Be good, Conor."

Conor gave him a hug and then stepped back and looked as if he was struggling with something. "Is she really my grandmother?" he eventually blurted out.

Leo nodded. "But Louisa is looking after you. Remember that."

Louisa would have preferred to introduce Conor to Irene indoors, once Leo had gone, but now the woman had seen the way Leo had been gazing at Louisa and how close she'd been to tears. Louisa knew it might lead to pointed comments and goodness knows what other opposition. As Leo and Louisa walked over to his van he spoke in a quiet voice out of Irene's hearing. "Would you be able to get away one evening? I'd love to see you properly."

She felt a frisson of pleasure. "Yes."

He broke into a broad smile.

"I had thought to pop over here again, but with your mother-in-law around it might not be too comfortable for either of us."

"How about Tuesday? That should give Conor time to settle back in."

"Excellent. And don't let Irene get under your skin."

"I have to tell you, she really is after getting custody of Conor."

He narrowed his eyes. "Seriously. Not a chance!" He paused for a moment. "Look, while Conor is with Irene can you slip away?"

"Now?"

"Yes."

She nodded. "Just for a little while."

"Come on. Let's go to the ramparts."

Walking close to each other but not quite touching, they made their way, smelling the fish hanging out to dry as they passed that shop. Everyone greeted Louisa as they went by and she smiled back at one and all.

"You know the whole town," he said.

"Pretty much."

"Would you like an ice cream?" he asked and stopped outside an ice-cream vendor's tiny shop.

"Mango sorbet, please," she said.

He bought the ices and handed one to her.

They passed the softly scented frangipani tree and reached the old walls, where they looked out across the shimmering silvery ocean in the dusk.

"It seems to go on forever, doesn't it."

She nodded as they sat themselves on the wall and she carried on licking her ice. "I love the salty smell of the sea and the way it always changes."

"What does it mean to you? Living here, that is." He waved an arm across the view.

"I feel rooted here."

He glanced at her and reached across to touch her chin where a drop of her ice had dripped. He wiped it away with his finger-tips and then licked them.

"Thanks," she said.

"Would you ever live anywhere else?" he asked.

"That depends on the reason for moving. What about you?"

"I suppose the plantation is the first place I've called my own. I'm enjoying having control over my life."

She tilted her head and frowned. "You didn't before?"

"In a way I always have, but a lot of my decisions resulted from chance. This is something I've actually chosen and committed years of my life to."

"And you have Conor to think of now."

He nodded. "Which changes everything."

She paused. "Leo, do you think trust is more important than love?"

"Maybe you can't have one without the other."

"I trusted Elliot."

"We've all given our trust where it wasn't deserved."

"But you can't let one betrayal dominate your life, can you, otherwise you'll never really live."

He turned and tipped up her chin as he gazed at her. "And now? How are you feeling now?"

"I feel as if I'm coming alive again."

■ ■ ■ ■

That evening things passed relatively peace-
fully and when Conor was safely tucked up
in bed, Gwen smiled at Louisa and told her
how much she had liked Leo. Even on such
a short acquaintance she could tell he was a
genuine person. "Very real," she said.

Louisa was happy to hear it and also felt
relieved Conor seemed more settled; he had
willingly cleaned his teeth and put on his
pajamas without a fuss. He'd even allowed
her to read him a bedtime story. Once she'd
finished he asked about the little girl she'd
told him about.

"The one whose mummy died too."

"She grew up."

"And was she happy?"

She smiled at him. "Conor, that little girl
was me and, yes, I have been very happy. It
doesn't mean I haven't missed my mum."

"Can you still see her?"

"Can you see your mum?"

"All the time. I imagine she's sitting on
my bed in the morning. And I imagine her
coming for a walk with me in the cinnamon
plantation. I tell her about all the creatures."

"Well, that's good. We keep the people we
love in our hearts."

"Even when they are gone?"

"Even then. Yes."

She touched his cheek, then got up and turned out the light. For a few moments, she stood outside his room and felt her heart lift. The conversation had reminded her of how she used to picture her mother in the kitchen stirring a cake mixture in an earthenware bowl, her fair hair falling over her face. And how she would see her hanging on to her hat when the blustery sea breezes blew too wildly. Or how she would curl up on the sofa, concentrating on a magazine, the pages rustling as she turned them, while the monsoon raged outside. These were not memories. They were invented images she used to console herself with as she grew up. The actual memories were hazy, incomplete moments: a hint of a smile and the lingering warmth of an embrace. No more than that.

Later, when the adults were comfortably seated in the sitting room after dinner, they heard Alice crying, so Gwen went upstairs to see to her. It was then that Irene spoke up.

"I should be the one to put the boy to bed. Don't you think the sooner he gets used to me the better? When I have custody —"

"Maybe when he knows you better," Louisa interrupted, aiming for a conciliatory tone.

Irene puffed out her cheeks. "Your husband hardly more than six months in his grave and . . ."

Louisa felt her jaw stiffen but continued to keep her voice calm. "Is it any of your business, Irene?"

"But in front of the child . . ."

She wanted to hit back at Irene, but couldn't bear to give her the satisfaction, so went on speaking in a level tone. "Look, Irene, Leo and I are good friends and that's all. He has been very supportive during what has been a most trying and upsetting time for me while I've been dealing with your son's betrayal of me and of our marriage."

Irene sniffed. "When a husband strays, I blame the wife."

"And by that you mean?"

"If you'd only had children . . ."

Louisa felt stunned. "So you blame me for his extramarital affair. And what about his debts? Were they my doing too?"

Irene shrugged.

Louisa fumed as she listened to the sounds from the kitchen, the staff's footsteps, the hum of a radio. It was the time of night when everyone was busy finishing off the chores of the day but soon the house would go to sleep and she could nurse her anger alone.

Her mother-in-law had always been a challenge, but this was the last straw and the trouble was, other than throwing the woman out, there was no way to encourage her to leave.

Margo had been looking at her feet while all of this was going on but then she glanced up at her mother.

"That was grossly unfair. I think you should apologize to Louisa."

"I knew you'd defend her. You prefer being with her than coming home to stay with me. Don't think I haven't cottoned on. And while you've given me no clue as to why you threw up your job in London, I have no doubt you've told Louisa the whole story."

As Irene rose from her seat, Margo replied, "Have you even thought why that might be?"

"You are my daughter."

"And you my mother."

"So?"

"I fell in love with a married man."

With a sharp intake of breath, Irene promptly sat down again. "You should have told me. Is it over?"

"No. He's getting a divorce."

Irene looked pale and shocked. "Oh Margo! I don't understand you."

"Exactly my point."

"Well, this is such a disappointment. I think I've heard enough for one night." And with that she rose to her feet again and, this time, swept out of the room.

"I feel disloyal, but sometimes I wonder what I did to deserve her as a mother," Margo said, while Louisa shook her head.

"I think an early night, don't you? Thank God tomorrow's another day. Maybe it'll be better."

"And at least Mum doesn't get up early," Margo said. "Gives you a chance to slip out with Conor."

Louisa grinned at her.

A little later Leo phoned. Louisa picked up and when she heard his voice her heart skipped a beat. "Is everything all right?" she said.

"I just wanted to know if Conor's okay."

"He's fine. He talked about Zinnia."

"I'm glad. That's progress." She heard him cough and then when he spoke his voice sounded gruff. "Well, that's not actually the whole truth. I do want to know about Conor, but I also wanted to hear your voice."

She smiled, happy. "It's lovely to hear you, too."

"I . . . Well, what I mean is, I'm looking forward to seeing you. That's all."

She felt the warmth curling inside her chest, and sensed that something that might change everything was on the verge of happening.

# 43

Louisa Rose at dawn with Gwen, who was driving back to Colombo and had decided not to wait for breakfast, as she wanted to make an early start. In the silence of the kitchen Louisa brewed her a pot of tea, made up the baby's bottle, and tucked some bananas into a brown paper bag. After the two had hugged and promised to write, Louisa helped her carry Alice to the car.

"Thank you for coming. And thanks so much for your support," Louisa said, and then kissed her friend on the cheek.

"It was absolutely my pleasure. We must meet up in Colombo again."

"That sounds terrific. Drive carefully."

Then Louisa slipped back upstairs and threw open her shutters to gaze out at the pale sky. Maybe the rain would hold off? She quickly washed and dressed and made her way back to the kitchen, where Cook was now brewing the first coffee of the day.

After a cup or two Louisa ran upstairs to wake Conor, itching to get out of the house before Irene had a chance to ruin things. She touched him gently on the shoulder and he awoke instantly, gazing up at her in surprise.

"It's a game," she said and smiled, feeling hopeful things would go well. "I want to see if we can get out on our bikes before anyone else wakes up."

She was delighted when he nodded and then dressed silently. That augured well. Maybe her feelings of hopefulness were justified.

They ate a breakfast of mangoes followed by buffalo-milk curd and honey, after which they went out to the garden to retrieve their bikes, now kept in a small shed. He seemed shy in her presence and she worried he might not really want to cycle with her, but within moments they were out of the garden and on their way.

"Shall we cycle around the ramparts?" she said, tilting her head upward to look at the sky. Blue now with just a few wispy clouds and a welcome breeze.

He still wasn't saying much but they made their way out of Church Street and cycled along Rampart Street toward the wall, where they ended up at the Clock Tower.

"Can you tell the time?" she asked him.

He checked the clock and grinned. "It's half past seven."

"Well done!"

They cycled on, then paused to look out across the cricket field just beyond the Main Gate. "Do you like cricket?"

He glanced across at her. "I've never played."

"Well, we must see if my father and Leo will teach you. It's good fun. Your father often used to play."

His face darkened.

"Sorry. I didn't mean to upset you."

He shook his head but didn't reply, and Louisa hoped she hadn't put her foot in it, but she couldn't help feeling it was better to mention Elliot than to avoid speaking of him.

They cycled past the Main Gate and then out of the Old Gate and on to the Sun Bastion with its gorgeous view of the harbor.

"I know you like boats."

He nodded.

"We can go down and look at them properly sometime."

"Can Leo come too?" he said.

"Of course." They turned, passing the point where they could look up at the New Oriental Hotel, and went on. When they reached Court Square, where the court and various offices surrounded huge banyan trees, they dismounted and wheeled their bikes around it.

"Look," he squealed and she glanced at where he was pointing at a green garden lizard. "It's a big one."

"It is. You like lizards?"

"And birds and insects. I've got an insect book. I wish I had it now."

"Where is it?"

"At your house."

"Tell you what. I'll get you a saddlebag so you can take your book with you whenever you're out on your bike and check out everything you see."

He gave her a smile but didn't speak. She sensed that maybe he felt he'd said too much and was now withdrawing into his shell.

She spotted a man selling fresh papaya, with or without chili, from his cart.

"Would you like some?" she said. "Without chili?"

He nodded and after she'd bought two slices they went to sit on a bench to watch the vast square coming to life. A few people had arrived and were now standing and looking rather troubled under the shady hanging branches of the banyan trees.

"I think they're waiting to go to court," she said. "That's why they look so nervous."

He carried on eating his papaya.

Louisa was beginning to feel hot and was wondering about cutting short the bike ride.

"Can we go to the beach?" Conor said. "Leo says there's a beach."

"It's just a strip of sand really, not very big, but we could paddle. It's not far."

"And swim?"

"We haven't got our bathing suits. We can swim another time. Will that do?"

"I want to watch the seabirds."

Louisa was amazed at the change in Conor. He was still quiet and she worried about how he was coping with his mother's death, but despite everything, she had a sense they were making progress. And, as it became easier, she felt less conflicted about him. It seemed the bicycle was doing the trick. They weren't there yet, but at least they were finding their feet and she was surprised by how much she was enjoying his company.

As they left the court square they heard a screaming monkey and it made Conor laugh. It filled her with pleasure and provided much-needed hope. She'd give anything to take the child's pain away.

Once at Lighthouse Beach they left their

bikes leaning against a tree. He was wearing shorts so he only needed to remove his socks and shoes while she rolled up her trousers. They trod carefully to the water's edge and smelling the salty sea breezes, she pointed at the birds racing up and down the beach between the waves.

"Sanderlings," he said. "They're catching crabs and shrimp."

He looked at his feet for a moment and she could tell something was wrong.

"What is it?" she said.

He hesitated before speaking. "My mother took me to the beach."

"Oh Conor. I am so sorry. Do you want to go back?"

He shook his head.

"You must miss your mother."

He looked so achingly vulnerable as he bit his lip that she felt like scooping him up into her arms. Those spiky feelings of resentment had vanished and she longed to know how to comfort him.

"I like watching the sanderlings," he said. "They're so fat."

"They are, aren't they? Must catch a lot of crabs."

While they paddled in the water, Louisa could see Elliot with startling vividness, almost as if his ghost were walking by her side. Everything about him seemed so solid she felt momentarily ambushed. She could smell his cedar cologne, feel the touch of his hand on the back of her neck. *Go away,* she whispered, and felt relieved when he faded. The child pocketed a few shells and then they put their shoes back on and continued cycling, only stopping when they reached the lighthouse that topped the Point Utrecht Bastion. "It's very tall, isn't it?" she said.

He gazed up at it. "It has to be tall so people can see the light far out at sea."

"That's right. Shall we go on along Rampart Street to Flag Rock?"

They climbed back on their bikes and cycled the short distance. When they came to a halt he stood gazing out to sea before turning to ask her why it was called Flag Rock.

"This is where ships used to be warned of dangerous rocks by signals from the bastion. Sometimes muskets were fired from Pigeon Island to warn ships too."

"Are there a lot of rocks?"

"There are, but many of them are submerged so the ships couldn't see them. Many ships were wrecked around here."

"Real shipwrecks," he said in open admiration.

She nodded. "Lots."

"Leo told me about shipwrecks. Pirates too."

They remained gazing out at the water and listening to the sound of the waves. Despite the blue sky the ocean was now choppy.

Then they went a little farther to the Triton Bastion; the best place to see sunsets, she told him.

"We're looking at the Indian Ocean," she said.

He seemed impressed. "Have you been to India?"

"No, but I'd like to go. What about you?"

He shook his head and when he spoke it was in a small voice. "My mother said we would go."

"Well, maybe Leo will take you when you're a bit older."

He gazed at his feet. "I was angry with my mother."

"Oh?"

"Because she was ill. I was angry."

"I'm sure she knew you loved her."

He nodded very slowly. "Do you think that?"

"Absolutely."

There was a short silence during which Louisa thought about what he'd said. Poor child. Plagued not only by grief but also guilt. No wonder he didn't talk much.

"What's going to happen about school?" he eventually said.

"Leo hasn't decided yet so, for now, we don't need to worry."

After that they made their way back via Pedlar Street and then Lighthouse Street to Church Street. Louisa increasingly felt that Conor needed to talk about Zinnia, and though, so far, she had primarily been attempting to keep him occupied, she hoped he would soon feel safe enough to open up. The fact that he had mentioned his mother without being prompted made her feel happier.

By the time they reached home, it was getting on for midday; the time De Vos wanted to meet with her. Unfortunately, the moment they were through the front door, Irene came sweeping into the hall.

"Where have you been? I've been waiting all morning! It really was most inconsiderate, Louisa."

"We went out for a bike ride, didn't we, Conor?"

"Well, I have got some especially delicious sweets you might like, young man. You do like sweets?"

He nodded but didn't speak.

"Goodness, Louisa, you've tired him out. You really know nothing about caring for children, do you?" And with that she scooped Conor up and with an arm around his waist shepherded him into the sitting room.

Louisa watched them from the hallway and saw Irene crouch down beside Conor where he now sat on the floor. She opened a large picture book and pointed to one of the pages.

"You like animals?"

"Yes."

"Well, these are dinosaurs."

"I like dinosaurs. My mother bought me a book. Not as big as this one."

"Shall we look at the pictures together and you can tell me what they all are?"

As Conor nodded, Louisa, still watching, felt the child was bringing out a softer side to Irene.

"I just have to nip out," she called to her mother-in-law, who waved a hand as if to say, *Feel free.*

She glanced at her watch. She'd have to be quick if she was to make it by twelve so she left the house and briskly made her way to the court square again. The air was now strongly scented with spices and salty wind, just the kind of day she savored, but she couldn't linger. She soon saw De Vos leaning against one of the banyan trees and walked across to him.

"Mr. De Vos."

"You know why we're having this little meeting," he said, softly spoken as ever, and smiling.

"I'm not altogether sure. You know very well the contract you gave me has no validity."

"I'm sorry about that. I wanted to spare you."

She frowned. "From what?"

"The truth. Your husband owed me a great deal of money, Mrs. Reeve."

"For what, exactly?"

"Huge gambling debts." He shook his head. "Believe me, I would like to forget them, but I have colleagues who are less amenable."

"You mean Cooper, the Australian man?"

He shrugged. "Now, I would really advise you to pay up quickly. This situation has gone on far too long."

"Or?"

He didn't speak.

She glanced around the square. There were plenty of people around. She swallowed rapidly. "I don't give in to threats, Mr. De Vos, even veiled ones. And, in any case, how can you guarantee these are genuine debts? Without any formal proof, you could be telling me anything. Elliot's not here to confirm or deny them."

He inclined his head. "There is something you should know. On the day of his death, your husband was on his way to meet me to agree arrangements for the payment. As you know, his first check bounced."

She stared at him.

"I will give you one week. But I must insist on the whole sum, Mrs. Reeve. The whole sum."

He turned his back on her and, whistling, walked away. She wished she knew what to think and, if De Vos was at last telling the truth, couldn't help feeling furious with Elliot. What had possessed him to gamble away so much?

On her way back home she went to see her father at the cutting and polishing house.

She found him with his head bent over some ledgers, but when he spotted her he smiled and pushed the hair back from his forehead. "To what do I owe the pleasure?"

"I saw De Vos," she said, but then she noticed how tired her father looked and how much grayer his hair seemed to have become.

Brows knitted together, he frowned and stared into her eyes.

"I'm worried he's getting desperate," she explained.

"All the more reason not to pay. If we call his bluff he'll eventually give up."

"Unless he in turn owes money, to Cooper perhaps, or someone else."

"The police advised us not to pay."

She took a breath and exhaled slowly. "De Vos maintains it was for gambling debts."

"Which may or may not be genuine."

"That's what I said."

Jonathan shook his head. "To be honest with you, Louisa, I sometimes feel I shall never forgive Elliot. To deceive us all in the way he did."

"He didn't take you in at first though, did he?"

Her father shook his head again. "I wish I'd stuck to my guns."

"It wouldn't have made any difference. I'd only have gone off to live with him in Colombo."

"You always did know your own mind, just like your mother."

She smiled at him. "Thank you for being kind to Conor. That bicycle has made all the difference."

"The child is innocent. He deserves none

of this, though I can't imagine what will happen in the long run. He will need to go to school."

"I think Leo's trying to raise funds to send him to boarding school."

# 44

The next day passed relatively happily. Louisa took Conor to the beach, once again before Irene was up, and then they played ball games in the garden with Margo. In the afternoon, they played Pirate and Traveler and I Spy. Meanwhile, Irene claimed her application was being processed, and soon she'd be ready to go to court to petition for custody of Conor. In the fading light of dusk Louisa was wondering about the wisdom of going to see Leo. She told herself she wanted him to know about the progress she'd made and how she was beginning to really care for the little boy, but it meant leaving straight after Conor had gone to bed and then Irene would be very much in charge. But as soon as she had finished reading Conor a bedtime story, he reached out his arms for a hug, and she felt so thrilled she knew she just had to share it with Leo. Now that she was less tense around the child, he was relaxing too and that filled her with pleasure.

Once she felt certain Conor had fallen asleep, she listened to the repetitive melancholic Islamic call to prayer, then made her way out of Galle, and before long arrived at Cinnamon Hills. It was already getting dark, and as she climbed out of her car she glanced up to where a scattering of stars peppered the indigo sky. She felt an unexpected rush of happiness as she spotted a group of noisy fruit bats swooping past.

Leo opened the door and came out to her. She noted all the things she liked about him. His deep brown eyes. The warmth of his touch. His rugged good looks. His dark wavy hair. The way he moved with ease, seemingly happy in his own skin. The way he cared about Conor. And the way his eyes lit up when he smiled at her. He was smiling now.

"It's lovely to see you. Before we go up I want to show you something."

"Oh?"

"It's a surprise."

Holding her hand he led her into the woods by a narrow track lit only by his flashlight. The vegetation seemed to have grown thicker in the darkness, with creepers laced around the large trees, and tangled roots winding beneath her feet, but eventually she spotted lights dancing through the undergrowth. She heard the howl of a wild dog and froze for a moment, but he squeezed her hand and soon they reached a small clearing, where she saw half a dozen men sitting cross-legged on mats around a central fire. One of the men was gently drumming while another seemed to be chanting.

"Come," Leo said and patted the ground. "Sit beside me."

As they joined the circle one of the men looked across and smiled at Louisa.

The air was smoky and she began to cough but it quickly passed and then she was able to concentrate.

"It's a kind of rhythmic poetry," Leo whispered. "A way of storytelling."

"Do you often come?"

"Whenever I can. I like to keep my relationship with the men close. They need to know I understand what hard work is and that I value their culture."

The atmosphere was strangely seductive and, closing her eyes, Louisa listened to the hypnotic sounds.

"They believe the poems protect them from marauding animals. It is not uncommon to hear that sometimes these events run on all night."

They stayed for maybe half an hour and then Leo nodded at the man who had smiled and they got up to leave. Louisa glanced at the smoke drifting into the sky and was glad he'd brought her to see this.

Back at his house he pointed upstairs. "Shall we sit on the veranda? I have mosquito repellent."

She nodded so they went in and then up the stairs to the veranda. She seated herself on one of the rattan chairs and smelled the heady sweet fragrance of night flowers.

"The plantation runs on trust," he said, once they were settled. "I try to be loyal to them and protective of their interests. I mentioned to you before that they work on a profit-share basis. What I didn't explain then is that they work for nothing until their share is distributed."

"Isn't that hard on them?"

"It works best this way. It means they have a real stake in the outcome. In the meantime, I provide them with food."

"I see."

"And talking of food," he said after handing her the mosquito-repellent oil. "If you're hungry. Just rice and curry."

"Lovely," she said, though she wasn't really hungry. She rubbed the oil into her arms and lower legs.

As they waited for the houseboy, Kamu, to bring out the food they talked about Irene.

"I think she's serious about wanting custody. Might she stand a chance? As Conor's grandparent, I mean?"

"Possibly, but it would be awful for him to lose all this." He waved at the plantation surrounding the house. "And I'd miss him terribly. But why does she want him anyway? She doesn't seem the kind of person to welcome an illegitimate child."

"She's not. Under normal circumstances she'd be horrified. But this is Elliot's son. She has lost Elliot and I think she sees Conor as a way of bringing Elliot back. She wants to adopt him."

He appeared to be thinking. "I've known Conor since he was born and I'm very fond of him. In the normal run of things there's no chance I'd let him go to Irene . . . but at the back of my mind I wonder if I'm being selfish. What if she could provide a more traditional home and the money for a good boarding school? Things I can't give him. At least not now."

"No. She spoiled Elliot terribly, brought him up to think everything was his God-given right."

"Then maybe I should get on and initiate a formal adoption process myself? Until now, I've just assumed he would stay with me."

Once the food came a silence fell, but while thinking about Irene, she toyed with her curry.

"Not hungry?" he said.

"Not very. De Vos has given me a final demand for the money he says Elliot owed him. I have to pay him in less than a week."

"Or what?"

"He didn't say."

"It's probably a bluff."

"Could we go in when you've finished? I'm getting bitten."

After they went indoors Louisa felt an awkward kind of expectancy and didn't know how to behave, so she just sat on the edge of a chair.

"You don't look very comfortable there," he said and reached out a hand to her.

She had been holding her breath but when he smiled everything felt better. She took his hand and he pulled her up. They stood close together staring into each other's eyes but not touching. After only a momentary pause, Louisa felt a burst of confidence and, taking a step toward him, she kissed him on the lips, then drew back to gauge his reaction. His eyes were dark and shiny.

She smiled. "I'm ready. How about you?"

He took her in his arms and held her so close she could feel his heartbeat against her chest.

Then he led her to the bedroom where she sat on the bed and took off her shoes while he lit a candle. The light of it flickered on his face and, as he came over to her, he removed his shirt. She felt a strong sense of connection as he sat beside her and, unable to take her eyes from his face, she kept very still. It felt extraordinary to be so close to somebody who wasn't Elliot, and who was so completely different from Elliot. Leo was not so full of easy charm but there was a depth to him she really liked. He was not the withdrawn man she had once thought, but instead was kind and sensitive.

"I'm out of practice," she said.

"Believe me, so am I."

She laughed. "They say it's like riding a bike. But it's been seven months."

He tipped up her chin and, as she gazed at the ceiling, he kissed her neck, then behind her ears. She felt her body tingle as she lowered her head to look at him. There was something so touching about his handsome, serious face. She took it in her hands and kissed him on the cheeks and forehead.

Then she leaned back and allowed him to undo the buttons of her shirt. She unhooked her bra and then wriggled out of it. He cupped both breasts with his hands and then kissed the curve of them, before moving slowly to the nipples. She gasped with pleasure. It was wonderful, but also frightening, to let go like this. Out of the blue she felt a moment's hesitancy. He picked up on it instantly and paused.

"Louisa?" he said.

She murmured that she was fine and then he helped her out of her trousers and remaining underwear. Now she was completely naked, she lay back on the bed. A sensation of being wonderfully at ease with herself took over and she felt herself sinking into stillness as she met his eyes. The moment went on, but then he pulled off his trousers and came to lie naked beside her. She looked around the room, watching the candlelight flickering shadows onto the walls and ceiling, with peace spreading through her: a warm generous feeling she had been so in need of. He put a hand behind her head and twisted her hair away from her neck, then he gently traced his fingertip from behind her ear and on down to her stomach. Her breath came thickly now and soon he was kissing her again, their tongues exploring each other. She began to tilt her hips toward him. He seemed to take this as a sign and after he had kissed her throat, the whole world seemed to have faded away. There was only this moment. Only him. Only her.

When it was over she lay on her stomach and he stroked her back.

She felt a protectiveness in him so very different from Elliot. She didn't like that she had compared him to Elliot again and gave herself a shake. Instead she focused on the wonder of the moment and how it was possible she could feel so happy.

"Conor wants you to teach him cricket," she said.

"When?"

"What about Saturday when you come to pick him up? I'll ask my dad to join in too."

He nestled close to her. "You smell delicious," he said.

"You smell of cinnamon and tobacco."

"Oh." He sounded disappointed.

"It's nice. I love it."

"Can you stay?"

"Just until dawn. I need to be sure to get back before Conor or Irene is up."

"That gives us plenty of time."

"For sleep?"

"Maybe."

She laughed and rolled over on to her back. "By the way," she said. "Conor gave me a hug when I put him to bed. It made me feel so happy."

At dawn she tiptoed into her house and then, carrying her shoes, went to the kitchen for a glass of water. She swallowed it rapidly then made her way into the hall intending to run up to her bedroom without being seen. She was shocked to find Irene standing with arms crossed at the bottom of the stairs. Her face said it all. A mixture of triumph and disbelief played across her features and her eyes were shining. Louisa couldn't think of what to say and just stared at her mother-in-law.

"So, this is the kind of example you set the child! Creeping in like an alley cat."

"I didn't want to wake anyone."

"Clearly!"

"I . . ."

"That poor child has been having nightmares. You weren't here and it was left to me to comfort him. The sooner he comes under my sole care, the better." And with that she turned her back on Louisa and made her way upstairs.

Louisa sat on the bottom step feeling a mixture of fury that Irene could make her feel so small, but also dismay at the thought that Conor had been scared in the night and she hadn't been there. As it sank in how much Conor mattered to her, she gazed around her. She cared for Elliot's son, really cared, and a new feeling of vulnerability took her breath away. Whatever the consequences she had to protect him from Irene.

# 45

That night Louisa woke to the sound of sobbing coming from Conor's room. She opened his door and tiptoed in without turning on the light. She could see him sitting upright in the moonlight, his face glistening with tears. She thought about Gwen's advice; patience was key. She would take this very slowly.

"Conor," she said.

He made a soft gulping sound and she saw his shoulders heave.

"I know you're very sad." He nodded.

She reached out a hand and was pleased when he took it.

"I'm frightened," he said.

"Do you know what you're frightened of?"

"I'm scared on my own."

They remained in silence for a few moments while she sat on the bed close to him.

"Would you like to sleep in my room?"

He nodded so she scooped him up and

carried him to her bed. "You just curl up in there. I'm going to make some hot chocolate. Would you like that?"

"Please," he said in a small voice.

She went down to the kitchen and came back with two mugs of chocolate, but when she turned on the bedside lamp she saw he was already fast asleep.

As the rest of the week progressed Leo phoned in the evenings to ask about Conor, though she knew it wasn't just that, and every time he rang she felt her heart ease. The weather remained patchy and the seas rough. She sent out invitations to the grand opening of Sapphire, the new and exclusive Galle emporium, which was to be in three weeks' time. By then the rains should be over, plus she wanted there to be enough time for the emporium to properly establish itself and be ready to capture some of the Christmas rush. The sooner it became profitable, the better.

At night Conor came into her bed. She held his hand when he felt sad and he cuddled up close to her, like a puppy seeking maternal comfort. She didn't tell Irene and ensured they were both up early before her mother-in-law rose. When Irene eventually left on the Friday morning, this time insisting Margo go with her, and maintaining she would be talking with her solicitor the moment she reached Colombo, Louisa felt relieved the woman had gone. She thought of Leo. At least when he came to pick up Conor, Irene wouldn't be breathing down their necks.

By Saturday the rain was holding off and Louisa had high hopes it would be dry enough at the cricket ground to attempt to teach Conor how to play. They waited in the garden. Conor was immediately drawn to a little overgrown patch at the back bursting with wild flowers, butterflies and humming birds. Then he rolled on the grass with Tommy and Bouncer, and Louisa couldn't help thinking of poor Zip. The police had been no use at all. They hadn't even been able to trace the child who had been paid to deliver the box.

When Leo came straight through to the garden, he grinned at Louisa and she felt her skin tingle at the memory of the night they'd spent together. Conor leaped onto Leo and he carried the child to the sitting room where they were to wait for Jonathan.

"So," Leo said, as he held the child on his lap. "How have you been getting on?"

"We have been cycling, and swimming, and I painted a picture of you. And I can say *Bonjour.*"

"That's great. Who has been teaching you?"

"Camille. She's French."

As if on cue, the French kitchen maid came into the room and smiled at Louisa. "Do you wish a packed lunch for the cricket?"

"No, I think we'll be back for lunch."

"Very well, Madame."

"How did you like Irene?" Leo asked Conor.

"She's all right."

"Good."

Soon after that Jonathan turned up, dressed in white flannels, and they all set off for the cricket ground. Louisa had dug out Elliot's old cricket bats and two tennis balls and Jonathan had unearthed some stumps for the wicket.

"By rights we should all be wearing white," Leo said, as they arrived, "and have pads up to our knees."

"The first thing he needs to understand is the point of the game," Jonathan said.

Leo shook his head. "I'll show him how to hold the bat first. Listen, Conor, the important thing is to keep a straight bat and play a forward defense."

"That's too complicated for him," Jonathan said. "Just let him try and hit a few balls." He turned to Conor. "Here, take hold of the bat and Leo will bowl."

"I still think if he starts off with a straight bat he'll do better," Leo said, but he went several yards away and bowled underarm as gently as he could. Conor, struggling a bit with the too-big bat, missed the first two attempts, but at the third bowl he hit the ball. Louisa cheered while Conor jumped up and down in triumph.

"Well done," said Jonathan. "Now, there are usually two batsmen, one standing at either end of the wicket. After the one facing the bowler hits the ball they both begin to run, swapping places with each other. That's called a run."

"Me and Louisa can be the batsmen," Conor said. "You have to run fast, Louisa."

She nodded but was finding it hard to keep her eyes off Leo. "Aye aye, Captain."

"We should explain the game a bit more," persisted Jonathan.

"Before he knows how to hold the bat?" Leo said and snorted.

Jonathan put on a serious face. "There are usually two teams with eleven players each, and the whole idea is to score as many runs as possible without losing players."

"How can you lose the players?" Conor asked.

"See where I've put the stumps just behind you?" Jonathan said.

"Yes."

"There would be another set of stumps not far from the bowler and that's where the second batsman stands. Louisa in this case. The other side can get you out either by catching the ball when you hit it, or touching the ball to one set of the stumps before you finish your run."

"So, I hit the ball and then Louisa and me run between the stumps and we score runs?"

"Excellent. You've got it. And from one set of stumps to the other is called the wicket."

"What happens if you are out?"

"You go off and another batsman from your side takes your place."

"Now I really do want to show you how to keep a straight bat," Leo said. "It's best if you learn from the start."

Jonathan frowned. "I still think we should just let him have a go."

"But he'll stand a better chance if he's not cross-batting."

Louisa laughed. "Come on, you two. This is a friendly game."

And so the morning went on with Jonathan and Leo arguing about the best way to teach Conor to play cricket. Louisa watched with a wry smile and performed her duty as second batsman, getting caught out at every attempt.

At lunchtime Jonathan walked ahead to the house with Conor, but Leo held back and then he and Louisa followed slowly, well behind the other two.

"Thank you for the other night," he said, and touched her cheek.

She smiled and felt energy coursing through her body.

"It's wonderful to see you. And to see Conor so happy. But I wanted a quick word while we're alone."

"Oh?"

"I've been driving myself crazy thinking about Conor and Irene."

"And?"

"And wondering if it might be best if Irene does have custody of Conor, after all."

She stopped walking and stared at him. "You have no idea what she's like."

"So you said."

She frowned. "So I said?"

"I'm sorry, that came out all wrong." He shook his head. "Conor could always visit me from time to time. Holidays and the like."

"How can you even consider such a thing?"

"Well, he may not be able to stay with you forever. You know that."

"Why not? I've grown very fond of him."

He swallowed before he spoke. "I can see how he might become a substitute child for you, Louisa. But —"

She frowned. "But *what*? He needs a mother."

He took a step away and then turned back to look at her. "If anything were to change, I wouldn't want you to be hurt."

"Nothing has to change."

He shook his head sadly. "I've looked at it from every angle and no matter how much I want to, I just can't give him everything he needs. It breaks my heart — but Irene has the time, the money, can give him a stable home, and she and Harold are his closest blood relatives."

"I can't believe what I'm hearing! Didn't you listen when I told you how she ruined Elliot's character?"

"Does it occur that you might be . . . how can I say it? A little biased?"

*"What?"*

"Come on, Louisa. We have to think of

what's best for Conor. Irene can pay for a good education. You know the plantation is still expanding, but I'm not there yet."

"But you love him!"

"I do and I'm sure Irene will too."

"Conor loves you, not Irene. I thought you believed he was best off with you."

"I did."

"But now you just want him off your hands. That's it, isn't it? Well, I must say I'm terribly disappointed."

"Louisa, come on. Be rational."

"No. There's nothing rational about this."

"Look, when can I see you again? We can talk about it then."

He put a hand on her shoulder but she shook him off. "No. I don't think so. You don't want the responsibility of Conor. I'm glad I've seen the truth before anything more could happen between us. Bring Conor back tomorrow evening. I'm going home."

She marched off, overtaking her father and Conor, and then she went into the house and up to her room. Upstairs she lay on her bed and felt the disappointment in the pit of her stomach. She had thought Leo was different, that he cared for Conor and that between them they would find a way to look after the little boy. To hand Conor over to Irene seemed like the worst possible outcome.

The next morning her father turned up again, unexpectedly, saying he had something for her, but that it was outside in the garden. They went through the French windows and there, trembling in Ashan's arms, was a small brown-and-white spaniel puppy.

She ran across and Ashan grinned as she took the little one in her arms. Its pink tongue leaped out and licked her on the cheek. "Oh, you adorable thing. What shall I call you?"

"I got him from a man called Oliver," her father said.

"Oliver is a lovely name."

She buried her nose in his fur and then burst into tears.

"Oh darling, I'm sorry. Have I been insensitive? I know nothing can replace Zip."

She shook her head. "He's perfect. It was a lovely thing to do and Conor will adore him."

In fact, she couldn't wait for the evening when Conor would be back and for the rest of the day introduced Oliver to Tommy and Bouncer, who sniffed the newcomer and smelled all his parts before apparently accepting him as one of the family. Much of the afternoon the puppy slept on Louisa's lap as she flicked through magazines, with her only rising now and again to take him outside to do his business. If Tommy and Bouncer were jealous they didn't show it. And if she felt anxious about seeing Leo again she didn't admit it.

That evening she went to the door when she heard them arrive in the van. Leo looked stiff and serious and she barely glanced at him before welcoming Conor back and telling him there was a lovely surprise waiting for him.

"Can Leo see the surprise too?" he asked.

"Maybe another time. I'm sure Leo must have plenty of work to do."

Conor gave Leo a hug.

Then she put an arm around the child and told him to wait in the sitting room.

"Right," she said to Leo. "I shall expect you back next Saturday morning. Goodbye."

Then she shut the door on him while trying to ignore her pounding heart. She knew she might be overreacting; maybe Leo really did have Conor's best interests at heart. But she wanted him to fight for Conor, not take the easy way out.

Afterward she and Conor went outside to

where all the dogs had curled up together. At first it was hard to make out the puppy among all the various paws, but then he wriggled to his feet and raced across, wagging his tail.

"He's called Oliver. Do you like him?"

"Is he for me?"

"Well, he's for both of us. We can share him. How does that sound?"

The look of adoration on the child's face as he fondled the puppy gave Louisa a rush of joy. She felt hugely protective not just of the new puppy, but of Conor himself. They had come such a long way since those difficult early days and, she had to admit, she really was beginning to think of the child as hers.

# 46

On Monday Louisa received a call from Margo saying the solicitors had agreed that she wouldn't have to appear in the divorce court, as just the photos would be used in evidence. After that Himal, the builder, turned up at the door carrying something. As it was blustery they didn't talk on the doorstep and Louisa showed him into the hall where he handed her a package.

"What is this?" she said.

He grinned. "Open it. We found it under those loose floorboards."

She opened it up and found a thick wad of banknotes. She immediately suspected this had to be the missing money Elliot had withdrawn from his account, but why he'd taken it out she still didn't know, unless he'd been planning to use it to pay off his debt to De Vos. As she thought of De Vos she wondered if he might turn up later. The week he had given her was now up, but she had heard nothing from him yet. Perhaps he'd given up hope?

"That was very good of you, Himal," she said. "Thank you."

"I thought you'd be pleased."

She glanced up at him. "I am. Of course, I am. And I'm pretty sure I know where it came from." She paused, thinking she couldn't reveal too much in front of the man. "Thank you for your honesty."

"That isn't all. There is a problem, I'm afraid."

"Oh?"

He nodded and looked apologetic. "The shop fittings are installed but one of my decorators has broken his leg. I only have one working at the moment, so it will take twice as long. I know you wanted to open in two weeks' time."

"Can't you find a replacement?"

"None of my regular casuals are free. There's a big painting job on at the New Oriental, and everyone's working there."

Louisa thought about it. "I can do some of the painting myself. I'm pretty good up a ladder."

"But, Madam, that would be somewhat unusual."

"I painted my sitting room here myself.

Let me get changed and I'll be along directly."

The builder looked uncertain. "If you are sure, Madam?"

She smiled, but then remembered Conor. "Oh," she said. "I'll have to bring the child with me. But I'll think of something to keep him out of harm's way."

"Maybe he could read while you work?"

"Or better still, if I give him a paintbrush he might enjoy painting too. And if he gets bored I'll give him some sheets of paper to draw on."

"We're fitting the roll-down metal shutters at the front this week."

"That's wonderful. Thank you."

Once he'd gone she counted the banknotes and found almost fifteen thousand rupees.

A little later Louisa was dressed in overalls, while she had given Conor one of her shirts to wear. She rolled up his sleeves and surveyed his appearance.

"There. What do you think?"

"I like painting. My mother taught me."

"But you know we're just painting the walls, don't you?"

"Yes. And we can tell Leo all about it."

She nodded but the mention of Leo only

made her feel sad.

After the builder had covered the floor with cheesecloth to protect the parquet tiles, and the ebony counters too, Louisa decanted some white paint from the bigger pot and passed a smaller one to Conor. Then she gave him a paintbrush and told him to paint the lower section of a wall, and she climbed a ladder and began painting the upper section.

For about an hour all you could hear was the sound of brushes and the birds singing outside the open windows. Conor seemed happy to be working with her and when she began to sing, he joined in. Later he drew on the paper she had provided too and when it was time for lunch, she climbed down the ladder and told him they'd eat outside in the courtyard. She wiped his hands and her own and then pushed open the door. The wind had died down and sunlight flooded the overgrown courtyard. She cleared the leaves from a step and patted it.

"Come and sit with me."

She placed the hamper on the ground and Conor opened it.

"Lemonade," he said enthusiastically.

"And fruit, and egg sandwiches. Camille prepared them for us so they should be good. There's even a little pot of lentil salad."

With the sun warming her skin Louisa reflected on how good it felt to be sitting with Conor like this, especially now he had rediscovered his appetite and was eating normally. There had been no further nightmares either, so on the whole he was much more settled.

"Yummy sandwiches," he said. "Please may I have another."

She gave him a squeeze. "You can have as many as you want."

Himal came out to find them and said he had managed to find a decorator to finish the painting after all. Louisa felt relieved. She had hoped the emporium would be finished by the end of the week as the following week the various exhibitors would be delivering their goods. The week after that, Louisa had a grand opening with canapés and drinks planned. Now it looked as if everything might be on time after all. It was all set to be wonderful, if only things hadn't gone wrong with Leo. She wouldn't be experiencing the awful hurt of losing something that had barely begun and that she had needed so much. She shook her head. There was no point dwelling on what might have been. There wasn't any way she could agree with his suggestion that Conor should live with Irene.

When they had finished eating, she gazed at Conor. "Perhaps we've done enough painting. How do you like the sound of a swim? After you've digested your lunch, of course."

He jumped up. "Yes!"

But the problems at the emporium weren't over, as Louisa found out when Himal knocked on the door the next day, following a stormy night that had kept them all awake. His face as he explained what had happened was grave.

"A coconut palm has fallen on the roof, Madam. It must have blown over last night. We found it this morning. It's damaged the cupola very badly."

"Oh no! What can you do about it?"

"We have placed a temporary awning over the cupola as the glass is all gone. We probably need a structural engineer to come to give us a report on the state of the roof, in case there is any further damage."

"How soon can that happen?"

"A few days. And the glass has made a terrible mess. It'll all need to be cleared up before the cabinets can be used."

"What about my opening party?" Louisa

said forlornly.

"You will need to delay it."

"But all the invitations have been sent out, and all the suppliers are keyed up to deliver their goods."

"I'm very sorry, Madam."

On Wednesday the sun was bright, but with a heavy heart she spent the morning sending out cancellation notices to all her invitees and letting the suppliers know the opening of Sapphire would be delayed. By the afternoon there had been no sign of rain and children would be playing ball all over the town after school, getting in the way of bullock carts and generally causing mayhem. When at three o'clock Conor begged to be allowed to cycle in the nearby streets on his own, Louisa agreed, but told him he must be back in time for tea at four. She gave him her old watch so he could keep an eye on the time and checked that he really knew how to use it. There were only a few vehicles around so it wasn't a worry and everyone knew to watch out for children.

Her sadness over Leo remained; she had felt so full of hope. Unable to steer her mind to happier thoughts, she gazed out of the window for a while, but eventually managed to pass an hour or so reading *Hangman's*

*Holiday,* a book of short stories by Dorothy L. Sayers, which William had brought over for Margo. Louisa liked short stories. You could read in short bursts and then get on with other things, whereas a novel could eat up entire days, and with Conor and a puppy around that wasn't possible.

She glanced at her watch. Ten past four already. Ashan came in to say tea was served in the dining room. They always had high tea, with sandwiches, biscuits and cake, and she usually enjoyed it with Conor. She took the dogs out to the garden and left them there to run around while she kept an eye out for Conor in the street. He must have gone further than she had expected because there was no sign of him. She wasn't unduly worried. As a child, she'd spent hours outside on her bike alone. She went back inside and, giving it another fifteen minutes before checking again, she decided to start tea without him. She poured and then drank a cup of already lukewarm tea and ate a cucumber sandwich. After tea she called the dogs indoors, put a lead on Tommy and took him out with her while she went to look for Conor again. It was now four thirty-five.

She walked down her street, turning off at intervals into the various alleys. To begin with there was no sign of him, but eventually she spotted a child's bicycle poking out from behind some crates outside the vegetable shop. She pulled the bike out and recognized it as Conor's. Had he gone into the shop for some reason? She went inside and asked the Sinhalese owner whether he'd seen a small boy with dark curly hair. The owner thought for a moment.

"I saw him cycling down the street when I went out to bring in a crate of bananas."

"You didn't speak to him?"

"No."

She felt a flicker of anxiety. She was probably being silly. He must have left the bike and decided to walk, maybe to the beach. She went to check the beach, but he wasn't there either, and gazing at the limitless ocean she felt the numb well of anxiety slowly deepen. Surely Conor wouldn't have gone into the water on his own? She went back to the maze of streets and walked around for more than an hour, but there was still no sign of him. She returned for the bike and decided to speak to the shopkeeper again.

"I remembered something," the man said. "When I went out to get a second box, that one was packed with rambutans, I saw the child again."

"What was he doing? Still cycling?"

"No. He was standing astride his bike talking to a man in an old green car. The car caught my eye, because I usually know all the ones from around here."

"And that one wasn't?"

"No."

"Then what happened?"

He shook his head. "I was busy taking the fruit in. Maybe the man was asking for directions?"

"Thank you," Louisa said.

She asked in a few other shops but without learning anything further, and then wheeled the bike home with one hand while hanging on to Tommy's lead with the other. Where could the child have got to?

She accepted there was nothing for it. She would have to phone Leo. She'd written his new number in her address book and flicked through to find it, trying to tell herself it would all be fine. Conor would turn up soon, looking shamefaced and full of apologies.

She dialed the number hoping Leo was in. It was a quarter to six, so with nightfall not far off and a bit of luck, he might already be home. It was Kamu who answered but he told her Leo was there. She waited and when Leo came on the line her breath faltered.

"Leo," she said, and, swallowing hard, fought to keep the telltale catch out of her voice. "I . . . I can't find Conor."

"What do you mean?"

"Exactly what I said. He's been missing for nearly two hours and I've been out looking for him. I've found his bike but not him."

"Stay put in case he turns up. I'll come straight over on the motorbike."

"I'll be here."

Louisa hadn't seen Leo since her curt dismissal of him on Sunday evening, and when he arrived she noticed the stubble on his jawline and a tired look around his eyes. She wanted to be frosty with him but knew she had to put her feelings aside if they were to work together to find Conor.

"I'll never forgive myself if . . ." she said, and paused, still struggling to suppress her anxiety.

"Let's not allow our imaginations to run away with us," he said. "Let's just get on with finding him. Have you thought he might be at your father's house?"

She gave a huge sigh of relief. "Of course, I didn't think! We'll go straight there now."

They walked in silence to Jonathan's house and while she rang the bell he looked at his feet before glancing up at her. "Look, Louisa, I wanted to —"

But he was interrupted by her father's butler answering the door. While they waited for her father in the hall she spoke. "What did you want to say?"

She looked into his dark, intelligent eyes.

He shook his head. "It can wait."

A moment later Jonathan came in, wiping his hands on a towel. "Just finishing off a spot of gardening while the light held," he said.

"Dad, is Conor with you?"

He frowned. "I haven't seen him at all today. Why?"

"We can't find him. I've looked everywhere I can think of."

"What about Flag Rock?"

"He wouldn't jump into the sea from there. He's far too small."

"I doubt he'd jump, but he might have gone to watch those who do."

Leo was already heading for the door. "I'll go. Louisa, it's best if you wait at home in case he turns up."

"I'll wait with you, sweetheart. Don't worry, we'll find him, won't we, Leo?"

"Absolutely." And with that Leo opened the door and left.

As they walked back, she told her father

what the shopkeeper had mentioned about seeing Conor talking to a man in a car.

"I don't like the sound of that," he said.

"He could have just been giving the man directions."

"Maybe."

When they arrived at the house Louisa asked Ashan to pour her father a whisky.

"What about you?" Jonathan asked as he sat down on the sofa.

She shook her head. "What do we do now?"

"I'll call the police. Let them know he's missing." He got up and went into the hall to use the phone.

Louisa couldn't settle. She walked back and forth and then went to gaze out of the window.

Her father came back in. "They'll keep an eye out for him. They have a man looking now."

"Could he have climbed the ramparts and fallen off? Maybe he's lying somewhere with a broken ankle? It'll be too dark soon to see anything, won't it?"

"Try not to think too much."

After a few moments they heard the front door open and close.

"Leo's back," she said, but it was Ashan who came into the room with a solemn expression on his face.

"A child just delivered this envelope."

She tore it open and then read the note inside. Her hand flew to her mouth.

"What is it?"

She passed the note to her father who read it and then gazed at her. "Dear God!"

"Yes," she said, and almost choked on her words.

"They want thirty thousand rupees. Twice what you told me Himal found under the floorboards. That's a fortune: it would buy a few decent houses."

"Read the rest, Dad."

*"Don't involve the police. Wait for us to get in touch."*

She sat down with her head in her hands and rocked back and forth.

"Madam," Ashan said. "How can I help?"

Unable to speak, Louisa just shook her head and Ashan left the room.

When Leo arrived back to tell them he had seen no sign of Conor, Louisa glanced up at her father. "Show him the note."

Leo read it and a look of horror passed over his face. "Sweet Jesus. Just let me get my hands on them!"

"We need to think," Jonathan said.

"There's nothing to think about," Leo

snapped. "We have to get out and find them."

Louisa looked at them both as heat began to spread through her. She felt her heart thumping, her eyes burning. "But we don't know where to look. What if they hurt him? I can't bear . . ."

Jonathan was striding up and down the sitting room. "They won't hurt him while he's worth money. I think we should speak to Chief Inspector Roberts."

"They say no police," Leo said.

Louisa's tears began to fall. "I should never have let him out on his own. It's my fault."

"You can't think like that," Leo said and he looked as if he was about to come over to her.

Instead, Jonathan came across to Louisa and opened his arms to her. She got to her feet and he held her close.

"I think you're right, Dad," Louisa said, pulling away, "we have to involve the police, but they must understand it has to be on the quiet."

After Jonathan had called Roberts, they sat drinking whisky and waiting for the policeman to arrive. They'd told him to slip in by the garden gate just in case anyone was watching the main street entrance.

When Roberts arrived, it was getting late.

First of all, he called Ashan to the room to ask him about who had delivered the note.

"It was a child, just a boy," Ashan said, his eyes darkening in alarm. "I asked who it was from, but he said a man had given him a rupee to deliver it."

"Did he know who the man was?"

Ashan shook his head. "I did not get that impression. I'm sorry I can't tell you more."

"Thank you, Ashan," Roberts said, running his hand through his thatch of wiry hair. "You can go."

"So, what now?" Leo asked.

"Well, we have no clues as to the child's whereabouts, but we know who must be behind this."

"De Vos or Cooper. Or both," Louisa said, and her heart sank.

"It does seem likely. They didn't believe they'd get their hands on the money any other way, so now one of them has resorted to this."

Roberts had been holding his hat in his hands; now he put it on. "I'd better be off. Call my private number at home if you hear anything more tonight. Otherwise we'll talk tomorrow, but I won't come around in daylight hours. We don't want them to know

I'm involved."

"So, what do we do?"

"Try to get some sleep. That's all I can suggest."

Jonathan made a move too. "You go out the back, Inspector. I'll go out through the front door. He's right, Louisa, try to get some sleep."

After Roberts and Jonathan had left, Louisa stared at Leo. There was an awkward silence between them.

"Louisa," he said. "I'm so sorry. I was wrong about Irene."

"Really?"

"I don't know what I was thinking. I was worried I wouldn't be able to give Conor what he needed, and it just seemed like a solution. But now with all this . . ." He spread his hands out wide. "Well, we have to get him back and I promise, when we do, I will never let him go."

She swallowed rapidly. "Will we get him back?"

He came across to her. "Of course." Then he wrapped his arms around her.

When they parted, he told her he'd sleep in one of the guest rooms.

"No," she said. "I need you near me."

They went upstairs together and lay on the bed fully dressed. "Please just hold me," she said as the night stilled around them. "I'm not going to be able to sleep."

After that she stared into the airless darkness, listening to the sounds of the ocean and the waves breaking on the shore, with fear swallowing her every breath. Even with Leo beside her and feeling the warmth of his body, it was an empty, lonely night.

realize it was so serious. I didn't tell him anything. Just said Conor might be allowed to play outside sometimes, and I didn't know for sure."

"Didn't you think what that might mean?"

Camille shook her head.

Louisa felt like throttling her. "Dear God. So *you* are the one who has been revealing my movements to them. Has this been going on for months? Since the break-in?"

The girl shrank back from her. "What are you going to do?

She shook her head. "One thing is certain: the police will want to talk to you. You stupid, stupid girl. If anything happens to the child it will be your fault."

After that Louisa and Leo went around to every house and every shop in the town, asking if anyone had seen what had happened when Conor was taken. They left the ramparts to the police, who had a man surreptitiously checking the child hadn't been hidden somewhere near the sea. Only one shopkeeper told them he had seen a green car with two men and a child in it heading for the Old Gate.

"So, if that was them, they have him concealed somewhere out of town," Leo said.

"But that could be anywhere! We don't even know if they've headed west to Colombo or east."

He sighed deeply. "Let's go home. There's nothing more we can do here."

They had been home for about an hour, circling each other in shocked silence, picking up magazines but not knowing what they read, putting them down, asking for tea but not drinking it when it came, and then the piercing sound of the telephone broke into their thoughts. They heard Ashan answer the call. When Louisa glanced at Leo, he gave her a half-smile and they exchanged a look of hope. She cherished the moment of connection, the blessed preciousness of it. But then Ashan called Louisa to come into the hall.

He was pale as she took the phone and listened.

"I will only say this once." It was a heavily disguised voice. "At midday tomorrow come to the Sun Bastion with the thirty thousand rupees. Put them in a shoebox, and wrap it up in brown paper, like an ordinary parcel. There is a warehouse nearby, and the door will be open. Leave the package in there. Do you understand?"

She murmured that she did.

"If you do as I say the child will be

returned to you. Do not involve the police."

With a click the line went dead.

As Leo came out she stood in the hall, holding the receiver and shaking from head to foot. She felt a wave of heat followed by the kind of nausea you feel just before you faint. He took the phone from her, replaced it in the cradle and gently led her back into the sitting room.

"Come on," he said. "You need to sit down."

She told him what the man on the end of the line had said. "I need to tell my father too."

"Just sit for a minute until you've stopped shaking."

She took a few deep breaths while he stroked her back and then she got to her feet.

"I'll come with you," he said.

"No, you stay here in case there are any more calls."

"I could go to Jonathan for you."

"I'd rather go myself."

She glanced out of the window at the darkening sky. The weather had changed so she grabbed an umbrella and headed out of the front door to walk to her father's house.

Though it wasn't far, every step felt like a hundred miles, and by the time she reached the house her breath was coming in short gasps.

Jonathan took her into his study and gave her a glass of water. "Take your time," he said. "Drink slowly."

She drank the water and then she told him about the phone call.

"We have to give them the money," she said. "What if they hurt him, Dad? He's such a little boy."

Her father patted her hand. "And you care about him, I know."

"I never thought I would feel this way about Conor, but I'd do anything to have him back."

"It's an awful lot of money, but I agree. You've still got what Himal found and I'll try to raise the rest. It'll be a stretch, but I can call in some favors. It's a child's life, after all."

Soon after that, Leo turned up, saying he couldn't just sit and wait.

"I'll get in touch with Roberts," Jonathan said, "let him know about the call."

"We will get him back, won't we?" she said.

"I hope so. But you must prepare yourself. Even if we hand over the money, things might not turn out the way we want them to," Jonathan said. "Conor will be the only one who can give evidence about who abducted him."

"Let's take Chief Inspector Roberts' advice about what to do," Leo said.

They waited while Jonathan spoke to Roberts, who said he'd have plainclothes officers from Colombo watching the streets in the morning. They'd be less likely to be recognized. The policeman also said he felt the best person to deliver the package of money would be Leo.

"I should be the one to go," Louisa said.

Jonathan shook his head. "Roberts says not. The culprits will be lying in wait somewhere in the town, he thinks, and he believes the police have a good chance of apprehending them. But they'll want to hurry out of town as soon as they have the cash. It could be dangerous."

The rest of that day passed anxiously. Louisa still couldn't eat, though Leo persuaded her to at least drink some milk. Mostly she just stared out of the window, praying Conor was, and would remain, unharmed.

"As soon as we get him back I'll start the adoption process," Leo said.

"I don't know how far Irene has got with applying for custody."

"I'm sure the courts would prefer the

child to stay in his own home and with a younger guardian."

"What about school?"

"I'm saving up to put him through boarding school."

"I could help with that." A lump came into her throat. "But Leo, what if they hurt him —"

"Don't go thinking like that, Louisa. We must believe it will work out. We have to."

He talked a little more about the future, but Louisa knew he was just trying to distract her from the horror of what might happen if it all went wrong. It was only a very few years since the kidnapping of the Lindbergh baby and its tragic outcome had appalled the world. What if they never saw Conor alive again?

# 48

Louisa had slept a little but woke very early on Friday morning and immediately worried about what the day would bring. She tried to push the fear back, but beneath the surface her thoughts jammed up, keeping her trapped in gut-wrenching anxiety. As Leo lay asleep beside her she listened to his breathing and wished they could always be together. But not like this, not with this horrible dread gnawing at her. When he opened his eyes he smiled at her.

"It's going to be all right," he said. "We must believe that."

As she shook her head, it sank home just how much Conor meant to her. "I have this sick feeling in my stomach."

"That's the nerves. It's natural. I feel pretty sick myself."

They dressed quickly and went out for a walk along the ramparts where she gazed out at the sea, so gray and still and full of secret wrecks. She glanced up at the heavy sky. Rain was on its way again. The wind got up and everything seemed so fragile, as if one large wave could sweep her world away.

She turned toward him and he held her against his chest. There were no words for this, just animal fear and animal comfort. He brushed the hair from her eyes and she nodded in answer to his silent question. But she wasn't coping and he knew it. He took her hand and they walked back home.

By ten o'clock she was so tense she could hardly draw breath. She felt tears pricking her eyelids but forced herself not to cry. They waited in the sitting room, circling the furniture, sitting for a while and then pacing again, every few minutes checking their watches. She held on to Leo's hand from time to time, squeezing tightly.

Roberts had said plainclothesmen would be watching all the likely areas but still Louisa worried it might all go wrong. As the minutes ticked by, her heart slammed against her ribs and she could see Leo growing more tense. Jonathan arrived with the other half of the money, and by half past eleven Leo was preparing to set off with the package.

Once he'd gone, Louisa was beside herself

as she waited, thinking about Conor and now Leo too. Memories of the child flashed in her head and she recalled the day she had first seen him, and how horrified she'd been by his resemblance to Elliot. Gradually a delicate bond had developed between them, although she knew how achingly vulnerable he was, and that he was still suffering at the terrible loss of both his parents. Would go on doing so. Would go on remembering. Hurting. He had been through too much, and it would be unthinkable if anything awful happened to him now.

Now that he was out of her reach, out of the reach of any of them, she went up to his bedroom and picked up Albert the bear, then breathed in the smell of Conor's tousled hair still lingering on his pillow. She held the old bear to her nose and, as pain ripped through her, she cradled it like a baby. *Please God. Keep him safe. Please.* She stood in silence for a little longer, yearning to bring him back at any cost, and then she began tidying up his things. He'd like a tidy room, wouldn't he? Be pleased that she'd made it nice for him when he came home? A sharp intake of breath. *When, not if. When, not if.*

She bent down to look under his bed and came across some drawings he'd hidden there. She gazed at the childish images of the people in his life. There was Zinnia, with her long red hair, and a man with green eyes and dark curly hair, clearly Elliot. There was a picture of Conor himself in a fishing boat with a red-headed man who was obviously Leo. But he'd also drawn a picture of the new puppy, Oliver, and finally one of Louisa herself riding her bicycle beside Conor riding his. It meant a lot to her, and tears moistened her eyes as she saw she had been included in his world.

She opened his half-full laundry basket, fished out a few items, then carried them down to the laundry room. It wasn't her job to wash their clothing but she had to keep busy or the anxiety would swallow her up. She dropped a pair of pajamas, some shorts and two shirts into their new Wringer Washer, their first electric-powered washer. She still sent their larger items to the dhobi, but nowadays more and more people were having these new machines installed and theirs was particularly useful with Conor around. Once the machine was running she left the laundry room and went out to the garden, where Jonathan was sitting on a bench staring into the distance.

"Mind if I join you?" she said.

He patted the bench beside him.

"Oh God. I don't think I can bear this."

"I know."

Oliver lay on his back at her feet and she bent down to tickle his tummy. "Conor loves Oliver," she said with a catch in her voice.

"Keep strong," her father said.

She watched her father and saw his brows knit closely together, the worry clearly visible. Then she bent down and, picking the puppy up for comfort, began fondling his soft ears. The waiting had become unbearable, her mind taking her into dark corners where she cowered in fear. She felt as if her life had unraveled and was now as loosely woven as a piece of worn household linen. She gazed at her watch every few minutes and, when an hour had passed, took a deep breath before speaking. "Surely we'd have heard by now?"

"Not necessarily."

"I should have gone myself. Do you think Leo is safe?"

"He's a man who can handle himself. Don't worry."

"I can't help it."

They shared a long silence as Louisa closed her eyes to pray. Jonathan took hold of her hand and squeezed it, and she knew he was as worried as she was, but doing his best to hide it.

At a sound in the street, Oliver jumped down and rushed to the garden gate. Louisa stood to see what was happening and watched as the gate swung open. Her mouth went dry as Conor ran into the garden followed by Leo. Everything went still as Conor froze, even the wind seemed to drop, but with her heart in her throat, Louisa held her nerve and reached out her trembling hands to the child. They gazed at each other momentarily, and she wasn't sure what he would do. She wanted to hold him, protect him from harm, never let him go, but the first move had to come from him. The wait seemed to go on, but then he took a step forward and within moments he was running to her with tears in his eyes and then flinging himself into her arms. Her heart somersaulted with relief as she carried him to the bench where she sat, hugging him to her, wrapping him in all the love she could summon. Jonathan stood and went across to Leo to shake his hand.

"Well done, young man," he said.

Meanwhile Louisa was whispering in Conor's ear. "You're safe now, sweetheart. Nothing bad is going to happen again."

She wiped away his tears with her fingers. "It's all over. And look, here's Oliver come to kiss you all better."

The dog jumped up on to the bench and licked Conor's face.

"There, you see, Oliver will look after you."

"And Leo," he said, glancing up at her, his green eyes still swimming with tears.

"And Leo," she said.

"And you?"

"Of course."

# 49

*Cinnamon Hills, two months later*

The rains were now completely over and on a gorgeous early December day Louisa and Conor were walking deep in the cinnamon plantation. Conor was excited to be taking her to one of his special places and, when they reached a small clearing surrounded by rhododendron bushes, he spread his arms and twirled around.

"This is my place," he said.

Louisa listened to birds ruffling their feathers and shifting in the trees, then sniffed the cinnamon and could almost taste the salty ocean.

"Do you like my place?" he said.

"I love it. Thank you for showing me."

"Now we have to throw a pebble as far as we can and then walk around in a circle. I'll show you."

He selected a pebble and, with a furrowed brow, concentrated, then threw it to see how far it would go. After that he walked around the enclosed clearing, scuffing his sandals in the twigs and leaves crackling beneath his feet.

"Your turn now."

Louisa copied Conor and they both laughed at how seriously she did it. She reached out her hand to him and he took it. "Ready for your birthday tea?"

He nodded and grinned at her.

They made their way through the trees along paths that had now become familiar to Louisa. While she still maintained her household in Galle, and Sapphire was about to start trading, after a longer delay than she'd expected, she had spent much of the last two months with Conor and Leo at the plantation.

Leo had explained that after·he'd left the money for the kidnappers at the warehouse, the police had trailed them in the green car, and had managed to apprehend De Vos and Cooper at an empty house near the beach a few miles outside Galle, where they had held Conor.

The only dark cloud on the horizon now was the custody battle that lay ahead. As the date for the hearing drew closer, Leo's brow had become more furrowed.

It was too early to predict what would

happen, but they were both worried about the outcome. In the meantime, Leo had given Louisa more than enough proof that he loved her, and she envisaged spending the rest of her life with him. They'd discussed marriage as a way of strengthening his case for adopting Conor, but had decided that rushing ahead wasn't the right way to start married life. It should be special and not tied to anything else. He had, however, given her a diamond engagement ring that had once been his grandmother's.

They reached the top of the hill and Conor clapped his hands when he saw a table set out in front of the house, laid with plates and glasses. And with eight balloons, two tied to each corner.

"Where's the jelly?" he said, as Leo came out to join them.

"We can't bring out the food until everyone's here."

"When *are* they coming? When?"

Louisa gazed at Leo. He'd tidied himself up: the stubble was gone and he wore a crisp white shirt that showed off his glorious tan. She felt a prickle of pleasure.

They listened to the sound of a car coming up the track.

"They're here. They're here!" shouted Conor.

The car pulled up and Jonathan, Margo and Irene climbed out. Louisa and Leo exchanged looks, both clearly surprised to see Irene.

Margo walked to the back of the car and opened the trunk, then brought out an armload of presents.

"Presents first, I think, and then birthday cake," Leo said.

"Yes. Yes." Conor clapped his hands again.

"Happy birthday," Jonathan said and handed him a big square box.

Conor tore at the wrapping paper. "It's a train," he yelled. "A real train!"

"It's the Lionel Blue Comet train set," Jonathan said. "It's a copy of a real American train called the Blue Comet that ran in New Jersey. It was painted blue to match the Jersey seashore. Take the roof off and look inside."

Conor took the roof off and they all peered in, exclaiming at the intricacy of the detail. Everything from the seats to the electric lights looked so real.

"That must have cost a fortune, Pa," Louisa said quietly.

"It did, but look at the child's face! And, after all, we got our money back."

After that there were more presents, of jigsaws, books and a painting set. Finally,

Irene held out a small parcel and he unwrapped a beautiful, leather-bound sketchbook. "For you to draw all your insects," she said, all smiles. "And I have more presents for later."

Louisa was worried about why Irene had come, but after they'd had their fill of jelly and cake, while Margo and Jonathan helped Conor set up the train set, Irene asked for a quiet word with Leo and Louisa. They went upstairs to the sitting room, and once they were seated, she began.

"It's only fair to tell you I have been thinking things over."

Louisa glanced at Leo, wondering what this might mean.

"After a long talk with Harold . . . by the way, he sends his apologies for not being here, pressure of work, you know. He's due to retire any day now but they keep him at it. Anyway, I talked with Margo too, and came to a realization."

"Oh?" Louisa said.

"I now see that by fighting for custody of Conor I was trying to bring Elliot back. Margo made me realize it was unfair to the child to expect him to take Elliot's place."

Louisa nodded.

"Margo also made it clear that because of Conor's illegitimacy none of my friends would be able to accept him, and that would be hard to bear."

"Go on," Louisa said.

"I can't bring back my dead son and using the child to try to do so would be a terrible burden for him. I can't bring back either of my dead sons, just as you, Louisa, can't bring back your stillborn baby girl."

"No," Louisa said.

"It wasn't an easy decision. I had my heart set on rearing the child. It was hard to let him go. I felt as if I was letting Elliot go all over again and it hurt. But Conor isn't Elliot — and he belongs with you, Leo. I'm too old to take on a child now."

"It's a brave decision," Leo said. "And I'm truly grateful."

"Well, since I have withdrawn my application, I suspect you will be granted full legal custody, and you will soon after that be able to adopt him."

Louisa felt overjoyed. Nothing had prepared them for this turnaround.

"My only condition is that you will bring him to see me from time to time."

"Goes without saying," Leo said in a gruff voice. "We will make sure he sees his grandmother regularly. You have my word: you will be important in his life. Thank you, Irene."

Irene dabbed her eyes with a hanky. "I made many mistakes with Elliot. I realize that now. And although I may live to regret it, I see this as the only way ahead. We have to do what's right for the child, don't we?"

Louisa glanced at Leo, who was smiling broadly. He stood and came across to Irene. Then he held out his hand to her. "Thank you. Thank you so much."

A little later Louisa and Margo were discussing what had happened.

"I'm glad it worked," Margo said. "It was terribly hard for Mum to climb down. You know what she's like. But in the end, she saw the truth."

"Thank you so much for bringing her around."

"Now, tell me what's happening with De Vos and that awful man, Cooper."

"They're still in police custody and their trial comes up soon. There's little doubt they'll be going away for a very long time. Abducting a child is a very serious charge."

"Thank God for Leo. I'm so glad you and he are now together properly, after everything you've been through. I really like him."

"What happened brought us closer. The agony we felt knowing we might lose Conor made us realize we had no time to waste."

"I have news too. The divorce won't come through for quite a while yet, but William is arriving back here next month."

"Have you told Irene?"

"No. While I was working on her to change her mind about Conor, I didn't want anything else to get in the way."

"I suppose that means you'll be going back to England?"

Margo nodded. "His work is there and I'll easily get a job nursing again."

"But you'll marry here?"

Margo grinned. "Only if the divorce comes through in time."

That evening, after everyone had gone, and Conor was tucked up in bed, Louisa and Leo were sitting side by side, covered in mosquito repellent, out on the veranda.

"Happy?" he said.

"More than I ever thought was possible."

They gazed up at the indigo sky. The night was clear and warm, the heavens were lit by stars, and the air smelled of damp earth and woodsmoke.

"Listen to the ocean," she said, wishing she could see its silvery surface in the darkness. "It's endless, isn't it?"

"But we are not."

"No."

He leaned over and though he gave her the lightest of kisses on the lips, she felt it throughout her entire body.

"We have to make the most of every moment," she whispered as he touched the hollow of her neck.

"No more looking back," he said. "But you never need to pretend with me. And I will understand if it isn't always easy."

She glanced up at the stars. A picture of Elliot entered her mind, but she shook her head and the image faded. She would no longer fear his silent haunting.

"No more Elliot," she said. "No more anguish. No more dreams. Just here. Just now. Just you and me."

"And Conor."

"And Conor."

Then they held hands and looked out over the sultry plantation night, with fireflies sparking among the bushes and the insistent sound of cicadas.

"This is so beautiful," she said.

"As are you."

Louisa knew there might be bumpy times ahead as they adjusted to their new life as a family, but she was happy, happier than she'd thought she would ever be, and together they would find their way through. The emporium would take up much of her time but she was strong now, stronger than she'd ever been before.

The sun was shining two days later as Louisa surveyed the emporium. The central area sparkled with sapphires in their glass cabinets, and the ebony counters shone: a wonderful contrast to the brilliance of the white walls, just as she had imagined it would be. Upstairs, in the gallery, Savi Ravasinghe's paintings were hanging in pride of place, and in the first of the ground-floor rooms gorgeous silks shone with light reflected from the chandelier. The merchants were ready, just putting the final touches to their displays, and a table had been heaped with bottles of champagne and plates of canapés.

As the early guests arrived Louisa welcomed them warmly. She had decided on wearing a gold evening dress with a wrap of silver silk. After all, this was the culmination of months of work and she wanted to make a splash. From the very first she'd had a vision of how the emporium would be, and now that it had come to fruition she beamed with pleasure. Leo grinned at her from the other side of the main hall, while Conor offered plates of canapés to the delighted guests and her father shook hands with his friends.

All her friends and acquaintances had arrived too, and she was pleased to see several rubber planters and their wives. The rooms filled quickly, and as Louisa rang a bell a hush descended.

"Thank you all for coming," she said. "I now declare the emporium well and truly open. I hope you all enjoy yourselves."

The assembled crowd clapped warmly, and after that she stood back to watch.

Gwen walked over, carrying Alice in her arms.

"I can't get over how big she is now," Louisa said.

"She's over a year old now."

"Is she crawling yet?"

"Gosh yes. Much more than that. She's trying to walk and does a very fast bottom-shuffle. I can't let her out of my sight!" She tickled the little girl and was rewarded by an enthusiastic chuckle. "She's full of fun."

"And Hugh?"

Gwen glanced around. "I think he's helping Conor with the canapés."

Louisa smiled. "Wouldn't it be lovely if they became friends?"

Gwen nodded, then kissed Louisa on the cheek before going off to find Laurence.

As Louisa heard the tills beginning to ring, she felt relieved that despite all the trials of the previous few months, she had made the right decision to go ahead with the project. Sapphire was going to be a success. She also felt immensely grateful for all the support she'd had from her father, Margo, Gwen and Leo. Without them it might have been a different story; good friends were everything, the very foundations of her life. Leo continued smiling at her from his vantage point, then he came across to her and, as she held his hand in hers, her heart was full.

What a year it had been. Had she forgiven Elliot? If she was honest, not quite. Her eyes misted over at the thought. Those old easy careless days with him were long gone and, given what had followed, it was impossible to treasure what they had once had. She wanted to think back fondly, uncontaminated by anger, and knew that forgiving him was the only way she would ever be completely at peace. She would do it. She was sure of that, and while she still remembered how deeply she had once loved him, he could no longer hurt her in the way he had, because she was choosing to let him go. She had strength and she had courage but, most of all, she had everything to live for now.

The unraveling of her self had given birth to an older, wiser, Louisa, and having experienced the darkest pain, the sunshine of life was all the brighter. And in the end, despite the tragedies that had happened, despite the loss of Julia, of Elliot and of Zinnia, life had given her a precious child to care for. She tilted her head to look up at the cupola and made a promise: whatever life might fling at them, she would never let Conor down.

# ACKNOWLEDGMENTS

I'm grateful to my agent, Caroline Hardman of Hardman & Swainson, for her support, hard work and all-round brilliance. She has been a rock since day one and I'm very lucky to have her in my corner. I'd also particularly like to thank my editor and publishing director at Viking/Penguin, Venetia Butterfield, who has the ability to read my early drafts and "see" where I need to go with the manuscript. The first feedback is so valuable, and both Caroline and Venetia are wonderful, clear-thinking collaborators who I trust completely.

I'd like to thank the entire Penguin team: Isabel Wall, who read an early draft, my publicist Anna Ridley, who is just the loveliest person, and of course the marketing trio — Rose Poole, Elke Desanghere and Josie Murdoch. Also, thanks must go to my copy editor, Elisabeth Merriman, to the art department, the rights team, production, sales and distribution. I'm very aware that everyone has played a part in bringing this book, and my other four, to publication.

Huge thanks too to the bloggers who kindly read and reviewed the book. They are the unsung heroes. In addition, Janine Vanigasooriya in Sri Lanka was extremely helpful in sending me information about the birds of the south. And, finally, I want to thank Richard Jefferies for his immaculate research while also keeping me fed.

This writing journey was not something I ever expected to happen but I am so grateful that it has and I hope to continue writing for as long as people want to read my books. So perhaps the biggest acknowledgement of all has to go to you, my readers. Thank you.

# ABOUT THE AUTHOR

**Dinah Jefferies** was born in Malaysia and moved to England at the age of nine. Her idyllic childhood always held a special place in her imagination, and when she began writing novels in her sixties she was able to return there — first in her fiction and then on annual research trips for each new novel. Dinah Jefferies is the author of five novels, *The Separation, The Tea Planter's Wife* (a number one *Sunday Times* bestseller), *The Silk Merchant's Daughter, Before the Rains,* and *The Sapphire Widow.* She lives in Gloucestershire.

The employees of Thorndike Press hope you have enjoyed this Large Print book. All our Thorndike, Wheeler, and Kennebec Large Print titles are designed for easy reading, and all our books are made to last. Other Thorndike Press Large Print books are available at your library, through selected bookstores, or directly from us.

For information about titles, please call:
(800) 223-1244

or visit our website at:
gale.com/thorndike

To share your comments, please write:
Publisher
Thorndike Press
10 Water St., Suite 310
Waterville, ME 04901